Phelan Kell struggled impotently against the two men forcing him down into the chair. *Where the hell did they get these guys?* Though he'd never considered himself especially large or strong, he'd not been manhandled so easily since his childhood. Try as he might to twist his wrists free of his captors' grasp, he could not. *They almost seem happy that I'm struggling. I'm giving them something against which to measure themselves.*

His captors shoved him roughly down into the high-backed metal chair. They snapped cuffs over his forearms to hold his hands in place, then strapped his upper arms down and bound his legs. Both men moved with the efficiency of medtechs securing a patient, then stood and withdrew behind him, shutting the door as they left.

Phelan decided against testing his bonds. *These synthetic straps will give but won't break, and I can't do anything about the metal wrist-cuffs anyway. No sense in wasting the energy.*

He glanced down at his right wrist. A bracelet woven from synthetic white cord encircled his wrist. The soft material did not irritate his skin, nor was it tight enough to cause him any physical discomfort, but he disliked it nonetheless. *An ID tag or electronic locator I could understand, but a piece of rope? There's something unusual going on here, and I definitely don't like it.*

A harsh white spotlight flashed on and stabbed its beam down from over Phelan's head. A male voice clipped numbers and words off like an automaton. "150949L, state your name."

LETHAL HERITAGE

Other BattleTech Novels:

The Gray Death Legion Saga
by William H. Keith, Jr.
Decision at Thunder Rift
Mercenary's Star
The Price of Glory

The Sword and the Dagger
by Ardath Mayhar

The Warrior Saga
by Michael A. Stackpole
Warrior: En Garde
Warrior: Riposte
Warrior: Coupe

Wolves on the Border
by Robert Charrette

Heir to the Dragon
by Robert Charrette

LETHAL HERITAGE

by

Michael A. Stackpole

FASA CORPORATION

From the Author and Publisher

Thank you for selecting *Lethal Heritage* to read. If you enjoyed the book and happened to borrow it from a friend or library, please do us a favor. The next time you see a collection jar for a worthy cause that you would like to support, drop in a quarter.

FASA Corporation
P.O. Box 6930
Chicago, IL 60680

Cover Art: Les Dorscheid
Cover Design: Jim Nelson

Dedication
For Charles James
Thanks for letting me know there's a big, wide world out there
and that happiness in what you're doing is the greatest measure
of success.

The author would like to thank the following people for their help in this book: Liz Danforth for listening to the whole thing in bits and pieces; Ricia Mainhardt for making it feasible; Ross Babcock, Donna Ippolito, and Jordan Weisman for forcing me to write well and in English; and lastly, Brian Fargo for his understanding as yet another of his projects waited for this book to be finished.

Prologue

Outreach
Tikonov Free Republic
16 August 3030

The fiery-haired mercenary Natasha Kerensky walked into Colonel Jaime Wolf's office without knocking or hesitation. She held the yellow sheet of paper out for his inspection, but he looked straight through it and her. Seated behind a cluttered desk, he leaned back in his chair and pressed his hands together, fingertip to fingertip. Only the rise and fall of his chest told her he was alive.

She kept her voice soft and friendly—both of a volume and tone her troops would have sworn she could never manage—and placed the paper on his desk. "I thought you'd want to see this immediately, Jaime. It came in over Field Marshal Ardan Sortek's signature. The Tikonov Republic has, at Prince Hanse Davion's suggestion, given us free and clear title to Outreach."

The news brought animation back to Wolf's face. Though a small man, he gave off an aura of strength and his presence was commanding. Still, long years of almost constant warfare had taken their toll. His once-black hair was shot through with white, while the lines around his eyes and creasing his forehead showed how heavy had been the weight of some burdens. The slump in his shoulders told that he knew more difficulties were in the offing, but the glint in his gray eyes left no doubt he would face what he must.

He gave the Black Widow a smile. "Yes, Natasha. Thank you. This is welcome news indeed."

Kerensky glanced out through the arched window near Wolf's desk. "I thought we'd have had more trouble getting this world for our home. I assumed Hanse Davion would be determined to keep it once he heard we wanted it."

Wolf shrugged. "Davion is well aware that Outreach was once the Warrior World. He knows that the Star League's Army used to hold their martial Olympics here and that not quite all of the useful equipment has been stripped from it in the three centuries since General Kerensky and his Star League troops left the Inner Sphere forever."

The dying sun burned highlights into Kerensky's hair as she turned to face him. "Do you think Davion knows exactly how much equipment is left? He'd surely have asked Quintus Allard to send some of his damnable operatives here to see what we would be getting."

The leader of Wolf's Dragoons smiled like a man with a secret. "Hanse has lived up to his nickname of 'the Fox' rather admirably on this one. Quintus Allard asked us to complete a technological survey because he claimed he couldn't spare an agent for Outreach at this time. Hanse must certainly expect that we've withheld some information, but I don't think it matters to him. He's happy to have us here because it prevents local rebellions or a strike from the Free Worlds League. The report we sent back to Allard should be enough to quiet any complaints we were handed a treasure trove of lostech."

The use of the idiom for valuable technology lost after the fall of the Star League era brought a brief smile to Kerensky's full lips, but her tone was worried. "Is our own survey complete yet? Is there enough equipment here for our needs?"

Wolf shook his head and steepled his fingers again. "It looks as though things like computers and obvious manufacturing resources were carried off long ago, but I don't think anyone out there even guesses at the vast complex of stuff under the surface here. We've got the facilities we need to repair and manufacture BattleMechs. But whether it's enough to complete our mission is hard to say."

She fairly trembled with irritation. "You can't still be clinging to the idea that we have a mission, can you? We've done what they required of us. I say we should get ourselves healthy, get our machines at a hundred and ten percent, and then go kick some tail!"

The Widow's outburst made Wolf smile in spite of himself. "Natasha," he said quietly, "I'd like nothing better, but you know I can't agree to that. You also know that the others won't be able to stop them. We've been entrusted with a duty that we cannot abandon."

Natasha leaned forward over his desk. "It's impossible, Jaime. *That's* what I know. For the last twenty-five years, we've fought for every Great House in the Inner Sphere, and we've fought *against* every House, too. We know their strengths and weaknesses. We know it's hopeless…"

Wolf stood abruptly and paced the length of the room. "It's not hopeless, Natasha. Some of them show promise. We have a place to start."

Her sharp laugh brought him up short. "Did you just miss the last two years, Jaime? Two years of a war that's left everything changed, including us! The Capellan Confederation has all but fallen to the Federated Suns. The Draconis Combine has been hit hard and lost dozens of worlds and crack units. The Lyran Commonwealth was almost split apart by the war, not to mention the death of Frederick Steiner and the loss of his Tenth Lyran Guards in the suicidal attack on Dromini VI. As for the Free Worlds League, ha! Their government is so bound by red tape that they couldn't even mount a defense against the Tikonov Free Republic's troops, and we both know that the province of Andurien is going to secede before year's end with no trouble at all. Hanse Davion may have planned this war well, and his Federated Suns come out the big winner, but he's razed his economy and his people are afraid of another ComStar Interdiction.

"In short, my friend, the Successor States have clubbed themselves senseless."

Wolf's eyes flashed at her badgering tone. "That's all well and good, Natasha, but haven't you left out some of the more important factors that concern us? The Successor States might be in sad shape, but not so all of the military. The Kell Hounds survived the war in good shape, as have the Eridani Light Horse and the Northwind Highlanders. I'll admit they're not enough to do everything, but it's a place to start."

Natasha seated herself on the edge of Wolf's desk, watching him pace. "You're not thinking of bringing them here to train, are you? You wouldn't compromise our security that way!" Suddenly she slapped the open palm of her right hand against her forehead. "You *are* planning to do that, aren't you? That's why Morgan Kell and his wife Salome are already heading here from their JumpShip. Are you mad? How much does Kell know?"

Wolf drew himself up to his full height. "Morgan Kell knows what I have trusted him with—and trust him I do. He and Salome are coming here so we can run some tests and help them with an infertility problem."

The Black Widow's mouth gaped open. "You told them about…"

The small man shook his head. "No, I've not told Morgan everything, though I imagine he has figured out what I didn't. The man is a friend and I've decided to help him. He is also a MechWarrior of great skill and courage. While I do not plan to bring his Kell Hounds here to train, I believe Morgan might be persuaded to prepare his forces to help us when the time comes. Furthermore, I think he would be willing to let us train certain of his people so that what we know can be passed on to others without jeopardizing our security."

A shudder passed through her body. "The next thing I expect to hear you say is that you're going to invite ComStar to set up a communications center here on Outreach."

That suggestion won a chuckle from Wolf. "Not a chance. Com-Star may well control communications between stars in the Inner Sphere, but their benign pacifism died with Primus Julian Tiepolo. The new Primus, this Myndo Waterly, is aggressive and dangerous. She's already forced Davion to allow her to post BattleMechs in Com-Star compounds as a condition for lifting the communications ban ComStar imposed over his Federated Suns. I'll not put us in that position."

Natasha smiled. "Ah, thank God you are sane after all." She sighed wearily. "Look at us. We've been fighting here for twenty-five years. We should be retiring, not worrying about preparing others for a war that may not come. That task should fall to the whelps up and coming."

Jaime laid a hand on Natasha's shoulder. "I agree with you, but we have a problem. The youngsters have been raised here in the Successor States of the Inner Sphere. We lost a good number of them fifteen years ago in the Free Worlds League, and then even more escaping from the Draconis Combine two years ago. The survivors weren't raised with the same traditions as we. They barely understand that we're different. And now we have outsiders among us. They, too, must be trained and inculcated with our ways. The only people who can do the training are those of us who have survived all these years."

The Black Widow shook her head ruefully. "You're right, of course. And they were right to put you and not me in charge of this fool's mission." She brought her head up and thrust her chin forward defiantly. "If they're going to come, I only hope they come soon, before I'm too old to pilot a 'Mech. They've got a lot to answer for, and I mean to make them pay."

Wolf stood back and folded his hands across his chest. "They're coming, all right, and it may be sooner than we think. As much as I understand your wish, I hope you don't get it." He looked her straight in the eye. "Because if we're still around and in fighting shape, you know the others won't have had time to prepare. And that means the Fourth Succession War that's just ended will seem like the overture to the end of Mankind."

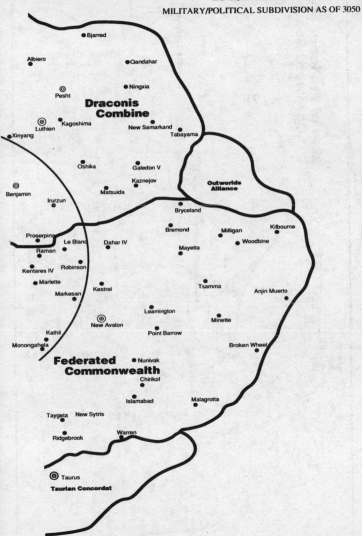

MAP OF THE INNER SPHERE

AND MAJOR PERIPHERY STATES

MILITARY/POLITICAL SUBDIVISION AS OF 3050

● Bjarred

Albiero

● Qandahar

◎ Pesht

● Ningxia

Draconis Combine

◎ Luthien ● Kagoshima

● New Samarkand

Xinyang ● Tabayama

● Oshika

● Galedon V

● Kaznejov

Outworlds Alliance

◎ Benjamin ● Irurzun

● Matsuida

● Bryceland

● Bremond

● Milligan ● Kilbourne

Proserpina ● Le Blanc ● Dahar IV

● Woodbine

Raman ● ● Mayetta

Kentares IV ● Robinson

● Marlette

● Kestrel

● Tsamma ● Anjin Muerto

● Markesan

● Leamington

● Minette

Kathil ● ◎ New Avalon ● Point Barrow

Monongahela ● ● Broken Wheel

Federated Commonwealth

● Nunivak

● Chirikof

● Islamabad ● Malagrotta

Taygeta ● New Sytris

● Warren

Ridgebrook ●

◎ Taurus

Taurian Concordat

.١٧.

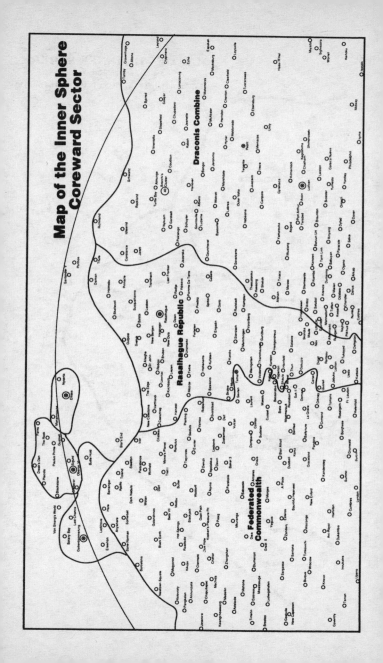

BOOK I

Shadow
of the Beast

Stortalar City, Gunzburg
Radstadt Province, Free Rasalhague Republic
19 May 3049

Feeling like a spy trapped light years behind enemy lines, Phelan Kell forced himself to walk nonchalantly into the smoky beerhaus. *For the first time this evening, I wish I'd listened to Jack Tang when he forbade me to head out on this search. Someday I'll learn he's not giving orders just to hear himself talk.* The young mercenary squinted to pierce the gloom, but made no effort to remove his mirrored sunglasses. *I might have been stupid enough to wander off the reservation, but I'm not removing my disguise, especially not in here. C'mon, Tyra. Be here.*

When someone touched his arm, Phelan swung around instantly and nearly jumped out of his skin at the sight of the Gunzburg Eagles uniform. At that moment, he thought he would have to fight his way out of the Allt Ingar, but then he recognized the uniformed woman. Phelan's grimace changed to a smile, but died almost as quickly at the fury on her face.

"Are you crazy?" she hissed, her tone as wintry as the nightwinds howling in the streets of Stortalar City. She jerked Phelan away from the door and back into a darkened booth. "What the hell are you doing off the reservation?"

Phelan wedged his long, lean body into the shadowy corner. "Where is she, Anika? I have to talk with her."

"I don't know, and right now I don't care," Anika Janssen said wearily. "But you've got to get back to the reservation, Phelan. You're

3

only asking for trouble being out here."

Phelan removed his glasses and hung them by an earpiece at the throat of the thick sweater he wore under the black parka. "I'm going to find her. If you think it means trouble for me to be found outside the mercenary's quarter, wait and see what happens if *I* don't find Tyra tonight!"

Anika grabbed Phelan's balled right fist in both her hands. "Dammit, Phelan. Don't fight me on this. If you recall, I backed Tyra's play concerning you to the hilt. Don't act stupid and make me regret it." She snorted with exasperation. "I should have seen it wouldn't work…"

Phelan relaxed his fist, but the tension in his body remained. "Not you too, Nik." A sour expression drew his black eyebrows together. "I thought you were free of the anti-mercenary feeling that runs through the Republic."

"So did I." She matched Phelan's green-eyed stare with one of arctic blue and forced him to yield. "You Kell Hounds, during this unplanned stay in Stortalar City, have done a great deal to explode the myth we Rasalhagians hold so dearly."

Phelan laughed angrily. "A myth you cling to like a drowning man."

Anika tightened her right hand, letting the nails dig into his wrist. "There you go, making me wonder if I'm right to give you a chance at all. Just when I'm about to agree with you, you take a cheap shot that gets my back up. I don't deserve that and you know it."

Phelan looked down and picked at a set of initials carved into the lacquered table-top. "You're right, Nik." His eyes came back up. "Sentiment among the Hounds has gotten nastier now that we're leaving. You know that the merchants in the restricted zone have gouged the hell out of us, and that there are citizen groups patrolling the area, just waiting for some excuse to bust mercenary skulls."

Anika winced as she nodded in agreement. "And I don't like it any better than you do. But can't you see that even though Rasalhague is a young nation, we fought for centuries to win back our independence from the Draconis Combine. Then just when we thought we had it— with the Combine's blessings to boot—we had to fight renegade Combine soldiers in the Ronin Wars. A lot of mercenaries deserted our cause because of technicalities in their contracts, and that left a bad taste. People here resented the mercs even more when we had to turn around almost immediately and hire more to supplement our armed forces to hang on to our freedom. Is it any wonder so many of us hate mercenaries?"

4

"No, I don't wonder about that," Phelan said, a twinkle in his eyes. "In fact, with so much of the resentment coming from the Royal Rasalhague Army, I'm proud to count you and Tyra as friends. Even if you *are* aerojocks…"

Anika grinned. "Someone has to teach you dirt-stompers some manners."

Phelan raked a hand back through his thick black hair. "So, where is she?"

Anika stiffened. "I told you before that I don't know."

The young mercenary's eyes narrowed. "But what about the other half of what you said? You do care where she is, Nik." Phelan chewed his lower lip for a moment. "I bet you're out looking for her yourself, aren't you?"

Anika stared hard at Phelan. "Yes, I do care where she is. She's my wingmate and my flight leader and my friend. Your deduction about why I'm out tonight, however, is grossly off the mark. In point of fact, I was out looking for you." She pointed at his parka and the mirrored sunglasses. "Did you really think that borrowing a Home Guard's jacket and wearing those glasses would disguise you? You're brighter than that."

Her remark struck home, kindling both anger and frustration. *This is getting to be a majority opinion, Phelan.* "Perhaps I'm not that intelligent, Löjtnant Janssen."

Anika pounded her fist into the table, then cast a quick glance around to see if anyone had noticed. "There you go again," she said in an angry whisper. "Most of the time I forget you're just an eighteen-year-old kid because you act so much more mature."

Phelan's eyes focused distantly. "Growing up in a mercenary company doesn't give you much of an opportunity to be a kid." *Especially if your father is a living legend and your cousin is heir to the thrones of the Federated Suns and Lyran Commonwealth. Everyone treats you as though you're different.* "Not much of a chance to be a kid at all."

"*This* is not the place to be making up for lost time," Anika told him. "You go from being intelligent and understanding to pig-headed and pouty in an instant. No wonder the Nagelring bounced you out when it had the chance."

Phelan's head came up sharply, but he said nothing. *How could you? I thought you were a friend.* He stared at Anika, unbelieving, then slid from the booth and pulled his glasses onto his face like a mask.

Anika grabbed his left wrist to turn him back to face her. "Listen, Phelan…"

The outrage in Phelan's voice cut her off. "No, you listen, Nik. I don't know what Tyra said about my leaving the Academy or what she told you about the Honor Board's findings. I had my reasons for what I did and those Academy morons chose to ignore them and the *positive* consequences of my actions. Well, I didn't need them and I don't need you patronizing me and trying to direct my life!"

He loomed over her, but never lost control of his fury. "One thing I do know is this: no matter why Tyra told you about all that, I know she wouldn't have done it if she knew how you'd use that information. You've betrayed her trust." He straightened to his full height and zipped up the black parka to his throat. "Tell her I was looking for her, or don't—as you wish."

By the time Phelan's anger cooled off enough to let him see straight, he was a block down from the Allt Ingar, his course unconsciously taking him further from the mercenary quarter. *Dammit, Phelan, you totally and utterly blew it. Nik's been the only Rasalhagian who's not told Tyra she's crazy for continuing to see you after finding out who and what you are. She was probably just trying to keep you from getting into trouble. Her remark might have been out of line, but it was the only way she could get through to you.*

He hunched his shoulders against the cold, then fished mittens from his pockets and pulled them on. Looking up at the orange and gold striations of Gunzburg's nearest planetary neighbor, Phelan shook his head. "Yeah," he said to the deaf world floating above him in the dark void, "wandering off the reservation was stupid. If I get chucked into the local jail, I'll not be out before the *Lugh* leaves this dirtball to rendezvous with the *Cucamulus*. The idea of being stuck here until our transport returns from the Periphery thrills me not at all."

Phelan snorted out twin plumes of steam. *And it would be just one more instance of how insubordinate you are. Jack Tang is going to have your head for this little outing. Why do you have to be such a loner? Just like Tyra, the people in your lance would be your friends if you gave them time.*

Time, that's the key, isn't it? You're always in a hurry to do what you think needs to be done. That means Phelan answers only to Phelan, and that's what lands you in so much trouble. And your familiarity with trouble is what keeps most people back. No one in his right mind wants to play toss with live munitions.

As Phelan crossed the snow-dusted, cobblestone street and

6

started back toward the outskirts of Stortalar City, the holographic display on the wall of a building flashed to life with a new advertisement. The image of a silver-maned, gray-bearded man burned onto the screen. Dressed in a military uniform, the man gave off great power and vitality. He greeted the nearly deserted street with a confident smile, but the jagged scar that ran from over the man's left eye down into his beard robbed the smile of its warmth.

The expression faded to a more serious one as the man began to speak and the translation scrolled across the bottom of the screen. Though Phelan could not read the text written in Swedenese—the bastardized Swedish and Japanese dialect used by most people on the planet—he knew it to be an admonishment by the planet's military governor that the people of Rasalhague pull together to help create an even stronger union.

Is it so easy as that? Phelan thought bitterly as the message droned on. *Is it so easy for people to abandon themselves to some greater cause? Don't they ever question the motivations of their leaders? Don't they ever look out for themselves? What does one do when his loyalty to a great cause comes in conflict with his own best interest?*

During the ad, the camera panned back just enough to make it plain to all viewers that the man was seated in a wheelchair. Phelan shook his head as the image faded slowly to black. "Trust Tor Miraborg never to miss a chance to remind people that he lost the use of his legs fighting for their freedom." Phelan frowned as the steam from his breath covered his face with a translucent veil. "Trust Tor Miraborg never to let people forget that mercenaries betrayed him and caused his injury."

The echoes of Miraborg's voice recalled to Phelan his first meeting with Gunzburg's Varldherre, when he'd traveled down to Gunzburg with Captain Gwyneth Wilson in a shuttle to ask Miraborg for the liquid helium needed to repair the *Cu. I guess the Captain must have thought it would help to have the son of a legendary MechWarrior along when visiting the high and mighty. Such a good icebreaker: "Oh, Morgan Kell is your* father?" All Wilson wanted was enough liquid helium to refill one of the tanks surrounding the Kearny-Fuchida jump drive, but she hadn't counted on tangling with the Iron Jarl.

Phelan spat at a snowbank. *The way Tor reacted, you'd have thought we were the Periphery raiders the Kell Hounds had been hired to fight. He took special offense with me, as if my father's accomplishments somehow diminished his own bravery. Of course, I didn't help things by bristling as he insulted my parents.*

Phelan stared at the Varldherre's stern visage as it appeared on another holodisplay set further down the street. "Why didn't you just give us the freeze-juice and be done with it? If you had, none of this would have happened." His chest tightened as he crossed the snowy street to a row of brick buildings. *I'd not have met Tyra and the Kell Hounds would have been off fighting Periphery pirates instead of being stuck here for three months.*

Stepping into the mouth of an alley shortcut he'd discovered, Phelan hunched against the cold and thrust his mittened hands deeper in his pockets as he walked. "Couldn't do it the easy way, could you?"

Stars exploded into shimmering blue and gold balls as the round-house right slammed into the left side of Phelan's face. The punch snapped his head around to the right and sent him flying back out into the street. Staggered by the blow, Phelan clawed ineffectually at the air as he fell. His feet slipped on the icy layer beneath the powdered snow on the ground and he crashed heavily to the roadway.

Snowflakes burned on the bare flesh of his face. Scrambling to gather his limbs beneath himself, Phelan shook his head to clear it. *Jesus, I've not been hit that hard since...since....Blake's Blood! I've never been hit that hard. Gotta focus.*

His attempt to concentrate on his martial arts training was interrupted by a booted kick to the stomach that flipped Phelan over on his back. A wave of nausea washed through him as he continued to roll onto one side and then vomited. His attacker's derisive laughter mocked Phelan's agonized moan.

Snow crunched beneath the attacker's booted feet as he closed for another kick. Phelan, lying on his right side, scythed his legs backward through his foe's shins, dumping the man onto his face. Striking before his enemy had time to react, Phelan rolled to his back and snapped his left heel down onto the base of the man's spine. He didn't hear the crisp sound of bones breaking, but a harsh cry of anger and pain told him he'd hurt his foe.

Unsteadily gaining his feet, Phelan spat at the ground and wiped vomitus from his lips with the back of his right hand. "Now I can see you, you bastard. Come on." The pain in his stomach made his words come in short, clipped bursts. He bent his knees slightly, lowering his center of gravity, and balled his fists.

Beyond his downed assailant, from every tiny snatch of shadow that defined the buildings on the darkened street, human forms moved forward. Phelan's heart sank. *Four, five, no...six. You've really screwed up this time. If they don't kill you, Captain Wilson and Lieutenant Tang will. Focus, focus, Phelan, or you're worm food.*

8

"Mercenary scum," someone cursed. "Take our money, take our women. We don't need your kind here."

Phelan pulled off his glasses and tossed them backward. *They know about Tyra. This is going to be nasty.*

The Kell Hound forced himself to relax for the second or two it took the mob to gather its courage and attack. He let his head bob for a moment and his hands hang limp, as though the effects of the initial punch had not worn off yet. As they moved toward him, Phelan's years of training allowed him to spot which of the approaching men could hurt him most. *There, that trio of them. If I take them first, then the others might scatter.*

The mercenary slid a half-step to the right and jabbed straight out at his nearest attacker. His punch crushed the man's nose, whipping his head back to the right. The man spun away, careening into a second attacker and knocking him aside. Phelan pivoted on his right foot, turning his back to this opening in the circle of enemies and expanded it by lashing out with his left fist to catch another man in the throat.

Spitting and coughing, that man went down, but his defeat did not daunt the trio still standing. The centermost man, a burly, bull-necked individual, burrowed in low and fast. Phelan straightened him up with a knee to the face, but his bulk just carried him forward. He locked his arms around Phelan's waist, pinning the MechWarrior in place as the other vigilantes closed in for the kill.

Phelan desperately rained blow after blow on the head and shoulders of the man holding him. The Kell Hound ducked and dodged his head as much as possible, but his lack of mobility meant body blows found him an easy target. The thick padding of his parka and the sweater underneath prevented the punches from breaking any bones, but the pounding sent shockwaves through his stomach, kidneys, and lungs.

A forearm smash to the side of the wrestler's head finally broke the man's grip and sent him off to the side. The Kell Hound immediately moved so that the stumbling wrestler blocked another man's approach. Phelan used the chance to turn around and face the man coming in on his right. He landed two quick blows on the man's chest, then rocked him back on his heels with a choppy uppercut.

When the man dropped into a crumpled heap, Phelan's hopes that he might actually escape soared for a nanosecond. Then, as he scanned the battlefield, his hopes crashed and burned. *Damn, the guy who hit me first is up. Where?*

Silhouetted against the street lights, the first attacker eclipsed Phelan's view of the street. His right fist again arced in toward the left side of Phelan's face, but Phelan saw the blow coming and ducked. As he pivoted to drive a short right jab into the man's ribs, his left foot slipped on some ice, dumping him down hard on his tailbone.

A bolt of pain shot up Phelan's spine and exploded in his brain. His pelvis felt as if it had been shattered in the fall, and the pain in his midsection numbed all sensation from his legs. Time slowed as his foe's left hand slammed down over Phelan's right eye and blasted him back against the street.

Sprawled out like a dead man, Phelan's view of the world went black for a second or two, but snapped back into stark and painful detail as fingers tangled themselves in his hair to pull him to a sitting position. With his free hand, the mob's leader donned Phelan's sunglasses slowly and deliberately.

Something sparked in the back of the MechWarrior's mind. *I know you….That scar on your face and your pug nose…you're, you're* …Tantalizingly elusive, the man's identity could not penetrate Phelan's storm of pain.

The man let a slow chuckle roll from his throat. "Should've stayed where you're wanted, *outcast*. And you should *never* have presumed to be worthy of Tyra."

At the sound of police sirens keening in the distance, Phelan smiled. His assailant glanced over in the direction of the sounds and shared the mercenary's smile.

Then his fist fell again and again…

10

The Nagelring, Tharkad
District of Donegal, Lyran Commonwealth
19 May 3049

Victor Ian Steiner-Davion pressed his back to the smooth wall of the Kommandant's living quarters, letting the crowd's commotion roil around him. A faint smile touched his lips as he watched other members of the graduating class, wearing the same smart, dress-gray uniforms with sky-blue trim, guiding their parents, siblings, and guests through introductions with other people's proud kith and kin. *It's funny to see how we change when family and friends from outside the Academy come to visit. The Nagelring's little world and its social order dissolve as the real world comes pouring in.*

Victor's blond head came up and his smile broadened as his roommate stepped into and nearly filled the doorway leading from the Kommandant's garden. Victor raised his hand and waved. "Over here, Renny."

Tall and broad-shouldered, Renard Sanderlin acknowledged Victor's greeting with a smile and a nod. He turned back and led three more people into the room, then ate up the distance between himself and Victor with long-legged strides. Engulfing Victor's hand with his own massive paw, he pumped Victor's arm warmly. "Hey, Vic, glad to see you still here. There was a line at the restaurant…"

Victor waved off the excuse and grabbed Renny's left sleeve, pulling the larger man around just enough to see the unit insignia newly sewn onto the uniform's shoulder. Embroidered on a gold background in black thread, the head and mane of a roaring lion stared

11

out at him. Victor's smile mirrored that of his friend. "You made it into the Uhlans! That's great, Renny. Congratulations!"

The embarrassed flush that began with Victor's enthusiastic response deepened as Renny looked back over his shoulder at the trio he'd led across the room. Swallowing hard, he broke his grip on Victor's hand, then turned further to the left and the group moved forward. "God, where are my manners? Vic, these are my parents, Albert and Nadine Sanderlin…"

Victor released their son and extended his hand to each in turn. "I am most pleased to meet you." Albert Sanderlin wore a dark business suit, which Davion knew was brand new, both from the stylish cut and the uneasy way Renny's father wore it. Nadine Sanderlin wore a formal gown of dark blue satin that complemented her slender figure. *I think Renny had it right. His mother forced his father to buy a new suit, then she made her own gown. She probably also sewed the Uhlans' patch on Renny's uniform.*

Victor then smiled at the beautiful young woman who completed the group. "And you are Rebecca Waldeck. I recognize you from the holograph Renny has on his desk, though I must say that it doesn't do you justice." Victor took Rebecca's extended hand and bowed slightly as he kissed it. Her dress, a gown of purple silk, might have been a year out of date, but on her it looked fresh and stylish.

Renny's mother smiled politely. "Victor?" she said hesitantly, waiting for Renny to supply his roommate's family name.

Renny shot his mother a horrified glance, then relaxed at the amused expression on his friend's face. "Mother, this is my roommate, Victor Davion." He hesitated for a moment, then added more softly, "Duke Victor Ian Steiner-Davion."

Victor saw Nadine Sanderlin stiffen, then begin to drop into a curtsey. He leaned forward, gently catching her by the shoulders. "Please don't," he said, color rising to his cheeks. He pointed to a gold cord looped around Renny's left shoulder and then to the similar braid around his own. "This reception is for those of us fortunate enough to be in the top 5 percent of our class. Here, thank God, I am among equals and wish to be treated no differently than my friends."

Nadine Sanderlin pressed a hand to her mouth. "Forgive me, Highness. I should have recognized you from the news holovids…It's just that you seem so much, I mean, in the holovids, you're…" She stopped, embarrassed again.

Victor reassured her with a smile. "I know. I think the holovids make me look taller, too." He laughed easily. "I feel sorry for the camera operators, most of whom are your son's size. Their directors have them shoot from impossibly low angles to make me seem taller. At 1.6 meters, that means the angles are *very* low, indeed."

Victor glanced at Renny and slapped the back of his right hand against his roommate's flat stomach. "Of course, finding uniforms to fit me is easier than it is for pituitary giants like your son."

A grin brought life to Albert Sanderlin's angular face. "You have to understand, Highness…"

Davion held up his hand. "Victor…please."

Sanderlin nodded briefly. "Victor, we weren't quite sure if Renard was stretching the truth a bit when he sent us a holodisc saying he'd become your roommate his last year at the Nagelring." He held up his calloused hands as though to ward off a protest. "Not that we'd expect Renny to lie, but we wondered whether he might be exaggerating somewhat. Even when his messages talked about 'his roommate, Victor,' well, it all sounded so…"

"I understand, Mr. Sanderlin." Victor smiled warmly. "As I hear it, if someone in the cadet corps hasn't reported himself to be my roommate, he's at least claiming to be in the same company." He turned to Renny. "No, Renny and I became friends when he took pity on me and helped me through cryophysics and astronavigation back in our trey year. In fact, if not for your son, I'd not be here at this reception."

Renny licked his lips nervously. "You'd have gotten all that stuff anyway, Vic. But if you hadn't spoken to your cousin, I'd not have been admitted to the First Kathil Uhlans."

Victor shrugged. "I just told Morgan he'd be missing the hottest graduate of the Nagelring since Katrina Steiner herself. If you hadn't measured up, you'd not have been made a Lion." The Prince of the Federated Suns and the Lyran Commonwealth turned his attention back to Renny's guests. "Enough of this mutual admiration society. Renny was very happy when he got the message that you'd be able to attend our graduation. And he went sailing down the corridors of Kell Hall whooping like a grazerang when he learned you'd be coming along, Rebecca."

The girl, her long blond hair just a shade darker than Victor's, nodded shyly. "When Mr. Sanderlin offered to bring me to Tharkad to see Renard graduate, I couldn't say no." She twisted a simple silver band on the ring finger of her left hand. "We haven't seen each other since Ren left for the Academy."

Albert smiled proudly. "The quillar crop was very good the past two years. Nadine and I promised ourselves a trip off Rijeka before we died, so we decided to do it now and see Renny graduate…"

Albert Sanderlin's voice trailed off as another cadet and his family expanded the intimate group. "Mother, Father, I wish to present to you Duke Victor Ian Steiner-Davion. Victor, these are my parents, Don Fernando Oquendo y Ramirez and his wife, Lenore."

Victor formed his face into a very public smile and kept it frozen in place. His voice, deadened from the enthusiastic friendliness of moments before, was nonetheless cordial. "I am most pleased to meet you." He lifted his head, stiffening his spine and giving the cadet's parents an appraising glance.

Don Fernando bowed from the waist before extending his hand to Victor. Victor shook his hand courteously, then waited for Lenore to curtsey before taking her hand and brushing his lips against her knuckles. "Our son, Ciro, has told us much about you, Highness."

Victor acknowledged Lenore's comment with a slight nod. "I'm sure he has, Donna Lenore. It was a pleasure meeting you. I hope you enjoy the reception." Victor's plastic smile remained in place long enough for the nobles to realize they had been dismissed, then it melted into a more genuine expression as he turned back to the Sanderlins.

Renny let a low chuckle rumble from his chest as Ciro and his parents withdrew. "I wonder what Ciro the Hero told his folks, Vic. Do you think he mentioned how you took his forces apart in the tactical simulations we did last year?"

Victor composed his face into a fair imitation of the recently departed cadet and let his voice rise up to match Ciro's. "Si, Mummy, the Duke and I engaged our forces against each other in class last fall. I wouldn't say I embarrassed Victor, but the outcome was most unexpected." Letting his voice return to normal, Victor added. "It's true. He didn't embarrass me and I never expected to win that quickly."

Rebecca looked back over her shoulder at Ciro, then frowned. "He sounds dangerous. What unit will he be assigned to?"

Victor and Renny shared a private smile. "We're negotiating on his behalf to get him a position with Romano Liao's personal bodyguard unit or a Periphery pirate gang," Victor laughed.

Renny elbowed his roommate. "Spooks, 1130 and closing."

Victor looked over toward the room's main entrance. Several men and women, moving singly and in pairs, entered the room. They smiled cordially and drifted through the crowd with seeming purposelessness, but their wary eyes continuously scanned the room. *Renny tagged it perfectly. That's the advance team.*

Victor saw the puzzled looks on the faces of Renny's guests. "Not to worry, Mrs. Sanderlin. Renny and I have spent a certain amount of time eluding the CID agents assigned to safeguard me. He's even better

14

at spotting them than I am." He glanced back at the doorway. "This many infesting the party means my parents cannot be too far behind."

Some of the color drained from Albert Sanderlin's face. "Well, it was nice meeting you, Victor." He turned to his son. "Come on, Renard, we should, ah, circulate some more."

Victor held up his hand. "No. Please don't go."

Nadine shook her head slightly. "Highness, we are simple quillar farmers from Rijeka…" She looked over at Ciro Oquendo and his parents huddled nearby. "We're no one special…"

A heartbeat's worth of anger shot through Victor's eyes. "You're wrong in that, Mrs. Sanderlin. *You* are the parents of someone I am very proud to call a friend, and that makes you special, indeed. Between friends, and by extension, between their families, there are no ranks.

"You've come all this way to see your son graduate and to see something of the rest of the Inner Sphere. You've endured a long trip, and I know well the physical strain caused by jumping from star system to star system. You called this a once-in-a-lifetime trip, so let's make it even more memorable." Victor dropped his eyes and his voice. "Please do me the honor of letting me introduce you to my parents."

Albert Sanderlin gave his wife's hand a reassuring squeeze, then nodded at Victor in silent assent. As Davion turned his attention back to the doorway, a buzzing whisper filled the room. He felt his own heart beating faster and the ache of a lump in his throat.

His mother appeared first, on the arm of the Nagelring's Kommandant. Tall and girlishly slender, Melissa Steiner Davion showed her age only in the mature grace of her movements. The blue gown she wore, a shade darker than the blue trim on the Cadets' uniforms, was cut in a stylishly youthful fashion. The silken material had been slashed diagonally to her left knee, exposing a shapely calf, and again at the right shoulder, baring her right arm. The diamond and sapphire necklace and drop earrings matched the gown's hue. Her blond hair, worn up, was encircled by a simple platinum coronet.

Behind her, escorting the Kommandant's wife, came Prince Hanse Davion. Wearing the navy-blue dress uniform of the Davion Heavy Guards, Hanse Davion stood tall and proud. Age had leeched some of the ruddy color from his hair, especially at the sides and back, and had given his face a few seams, but no one would ever mistake that for a sign of weakness. The Prince, his blue eyes bright, exuded a confidence and power that crackled through the gathering like static electricity.

Victor felt the ache in his throat drain and his smile broaden. *It's been far too long since I last saw you.* He tugged at the hem of his dress jacket. *I hope I've made you proud.*

Melissa freed herself from the Kommandant's arm and made her way across the room to her son. As she came toward him, Victor was reminded of his late grandmother, Katrina Steiner. *The way my mother carries herself, and those gray eyes, she is so much like her mother.* The memory of his grandmother faded as Melissa came nearer, and he smiled with the pleasure of seeing her again. *Then again, my mother is like no one else.*

Victor opened his arms and took her into a warm embrace. "Hello, Mother," he said, planting a kiss on her cheek, and giving her another squeeze. Still with one arm around her, he turned to greet his father. Their hands met in a firm grip, then Melissa stepped aside as father and son pulled each other into a backslapping hug.

Victor turned to Renny and his family. "Father, Mother, it is my great pleasure to introduce Cadet Renard Sanderlin, his parents Albert and Nadine, and his special friend, Rebecca Waldeck." Victor smiled as he avoided Renny's earlier mistake. "These are my parents, Prince Hanse Davion and Archon Melissa Steiner Davion."

Hanse immediately kissed Nadine Sanderlin's hand. "I understand we have your son to thank for Victor's successes in the more difficult mathematical subjects taught here." Hanse smiled warmly. "Would that Renard had been at Albion when I was there. Then I might have graduated at the top of my class."

Nadine, mute with terror, nodded and smiled, but no one noticed her silence in the round of exchanged greetings. Renny snapped a smart salute to the Prince, which Hanse returned equally crisply before shaking Renny's hand. Melissa immediately won over Rebecca and Nadine by complimenting them on their dresses, and that unfroze Nadine's tongue enough that she could return the compliment.

The informal curtain of bodyguards that drifted between the royal family and the rest of the party held Ciro Oquendo and his kin at bay, but did not prevent three other people from joining Victor and his parents. The first was a tall, broad-shouldered man, whose coppery hair was worn long enough to hide the golden Marshal's epaulets on his black uniform and to half-obscure the dozens of campaign ribbons on his left breast. The woman on his arm wore a black and gold gown that contrasted dramatically with her fair hair.

Victor greeted both with a smile, then turned to introduce them to the others. "Renny, this is your new commanding officer, Marshal of the Armies Morgan Hasek-Davion, and his wife, Duchess Kym Hasek-Davion." Victor left it to Renny to introduce his parents as he

16

turned toward the third newcomer.

Standing closer to what Victor considered a reasonable height, the slender man smiled warmly at the Prince. The laugh lines at the corners of his almond-shaped eyes and the occasional snowy strand showing through his coal-black hair were the only hints of the man's true age. He extended his right hand to Victor, allowing his glove-sheathed left hand to remain hidden at his side. "Congratulations, Highness, on your graduation with honors."

Victor shook the visitor's hand firmly. "Thank you, Secretary Allard."

Justin Allard narrowed his brown eyes. "You are aware, I believe, that no one has ever beat the La Mancha simulator scenario before."

Victor raised an eyebrow. "But I've heard rumors that your son salvaged a victory from it in his final New Avalon Military Academy tests. In fact, news of Kai's success prompted me to try my solution."

A mild look of surprise spread over Justin's face before he brought his expression under control. "Your intelligence-gathering network is good, Victor. I'll have to look into the leaks in NAMA security."

The younger man shook his head. "No crisis, I assure you. Just don't let my brother Peter near a diplomatic Hermes bundle again." Victor hesitated for a moment. "Isn't Kai graduating this week as well? I mean, the ceremonies run concurrently, don't they?"

Justin nodded, unable to totally mask his feelings. "Yes, they do. I wanted to be there, but duty called and so I am here."

Victor heard no animosity in Justin's voice, only the matter-of-fact reporting of a situation. "Will Kai's mother be able to attend?"

Pain shot through the Intelligence Secretary's dark eyes. "I'm afraid affairs of state delayed her departure from the St. Ives Compact. But after he gets settled in his new posting, we will see him. I probably won't head back to New Avalon until next fall, but the detour will be easy to arrange."

Victor raised an eyebrow. "What detour? I thought Kai was joining the Heavy Guards, and they're stationed on New Avalon. Anyway, those were his plans during the year I spent as a transfer at NAMA. I know he had good enough grades to make it."

Hanse Davion's spymaster smiled with fatherly pride at Victor's last comment. "His grades were good enough, but he changed his mind. He told me of his decision two weeks ago when I met with him just before leaving to come here. He's been assigned to the Tenth Lyran Guards. Kai asked me to congratulate you on his behalf and to express his gratitude for your half of the work you did together during your time at NAMA."

Victor nodded, smiling as he remembered Kai Allard. "Before this week is over, I'll record a holodisc message and we can arrange to have it waiting for Kai when he arrives at his unit." Victor turned and brought Justin into the circle, introducing him to everyone. Then, along with the others, he accepted a glass of champagne from a waiter's silver tray.

Conversation in the room died as Prince Hanse Davion turned to the crowd and lifted his glass high. "I would like to offer a toast to our assembled sons and daughters, brothers and sisters, friends and companions." With pride in his eyes, he glanced at Victor and Renny, then faced the crowd again. "They are the future of the Successor States and we are blessed that so able a group is ready to fulfill such a mighty responsibility."

Victor sipped the champagne, but tasted none of it. *Deep down inside, Father, I know you're right. I am ready for the burdens an accident of birth will thrust upon me.* He swallowed hard. *Still, I must dread the coming of that day, for it will mean billions of lives depend on my judgment—and a mistake made then will be irreversible.*

Starglass Beach, Emerald Ocean, New Avalon
Crucis March, Federated Suns
19 May 3049

Kai Allard felt his heart sink as he spit out the hydrolizer pack's regulator. He swayed with the minor swells of the warm ocean water, but resisted its urging long enough to remove his swimfins and set his diving mask back on his head. *No sense in delaying it, Kai. It's obvious she knows.* He licked the tangy brine from his lips. *You can't run now.*

Wading in toward the black sandy shore where she waited, he shrugged off the hydrolizer, yet still felt weighed down by an oppressive heaviness. The waves pushing him into shore warred with the undertow trying to drag him back out to the depths, but neither force could gain sufficient purchase on his lithe form to win the battle. As Kai drew close enough to see the redness rimming her eyes, he toyed momentarily with the idea of surrendering to the undertow, of letting it drag him out and down to where he would have no more troubles.

No, he told himself resolutely. *Suicide's not an option for you, Kai Allard-Liao. It would dishonor your parents and that you* must *never do.*

Sunlight sparkled off the grains of ebon sand, making them blaze like stars. Kai tossed the hydrolizer into the sand next to the towel he'd laid out earlier, then sent the swim mask and fins flying after it. Chasing the water from his closely cropped black hair with one hand, he turned to face her. Her uniform, the dress blues all NAMA cadets wore for graduation, looked far too warm for the beach, and the incoming tide had already soaked the bottoms of her trousers.

"How long have you been here, Wendy?" Kai tried to keep his voice neutral, but the woman stared up at him, then looked down as tears dropped to the sand. "Not long enough, I guess." The mournfulness of her tone tore at him, but Kai knew that nothing he could say would help her. Feeling impotent and awkward, he just waited and watched as Wendy Sylvester fought to transform her emotions into words.

Finally, her head came up again and she pushed back tear-dampened strands of straw-blond hair from her cheeks. "I've been trying to figure out why you did it, but whenever I get that squared away, trying to fathom why you didn't tell me about it keeps crossing me up." She opened her hands, then tightened them back into fists again. "I don't understand it. Everything was going to be perfect."

She looked at him and took his silence as a negation of her words. "I've told you again and again that I don't care that you're a couple of years younger than I am. It doesn't matter. Not at all. I thought you understood that." She paused and looked out toward the water, bringing Kai's awareness back to the sound of waves crashing against the shore. "I thought I meant something to you," she said, looking up at him again.

Kai breathed in slowly, filling his lungs with the salt air, but he was unable to meet her eyes. "You do mean something to me. You mean a great deal to me—more than anyone else ever." He sighed deeply. *Why can't you see it, Wendy? If not now, I would only have screwed it up later.* "I *do* love you."

"Do you? You have a curious way of showing it. I told you of my family's tradition. My father and mother, my grandparents on both sides, and for as far back as I have heard, all belonged to the Davion Heavy Guards. I grew up steeped in the lore of the Heavy Guards and joining the Guards is all I've ever wanted to do."

Kai finally met her stare. "I know that and I respect your family's tradition more than you know."

Wendy shook her head. A breeze coming from the sea blew her hair back from her face and rustled through the sea grasses behind her. "I hear your words, Kai, but I see something different in your actions. Don't you understand I wanted the same thing for you?"

She hesitated, waiting for some reaction, then continued on when he didn't give her one. "Perhaps you thought I wanted you to join the Heavy Guards because *I* was going to, because it's a family tradition for us Sylvesters to serve with our spouses in the Guards. Well, that's true. I won't deny it, but I wanted you to join the regiment for other reasons as well."

20

Kai started to speak, but she held up her hand to stop him. "Kai, I've seen you grow so much in the last year. You were, and are, as smart as a whip, but until someone like Victor backed your plans, you were your own worst critic."

Wendy squatted down on her haunches and picked up a piece of driftwood. "You've never said much about your family life, but I know it can't have been easy. Your father was at the beck and call of Prince Hanse. I've met him—your father, I mean—and I know he's not a cold man, but he seems so private and so suspicious. That's good for a man heading up the Intelligence Secretariat, but it has to be hell on his children."

Kai stiffened. *You've got that wrong, Wendy. My father, a man who lived a lie for the good of his nation, and a man later trained to separate truth from deception, has kept nothing hidden from us. Because he knew at any moment that he could be killed—and likely as not by my mother's sister, Romano Liao—he made a special effort to let us know his feelings and hopes for each of us. He might not always have been right there because of official duties, but he made certain we never felt abandoned or unwanted.*

Wendy stood again, grasping the small gray stick in both hands. "Your mother is the leader of a sovereign nation that she mostly rules from New Avalon so she can be with your father, but no matter how many summers you all spent together on St. Ives, it must have been hard sometimes."

Something in her eyes pleaded with him to speak, but he couldn't. *There's no denying I had anything but a normal family life, but who's to say what's normal? I grew up knowing both my parents loved me and wanted to give me every opportunity to make the best of myself.* Kai swallowed past the lump rising in his throat. *They always taught me that nothing was beyond my reach.*

"My God, Kai, say something." With a sharp crack, Wendy angrily broke the piece of driftwood in two. "Romano Liao spends her time trying to kill your parents or your aunts and uncles. Dan Allard is off running the Kell Hounds and your aunt Riva won a Nobel prize for her work with neurocybernetics! All these people have so much power, but none of them could take off a little time to be here for your graduation! How could they do that to you?"

Wendy sank to her knees as tears of frustration welled in her eyes. She flung the broken pieces of wood away from her. "No, dammit! I told myself I won't let this happen." She looked up at him. "All I wanted was for you to join the Heavy Guards, to become part of *my* family. I wanted to make a place where you could feel confident and secure. I was so happy that day we filled out our assignment requests and both listed the Heavy Guards as our first choices."

She hung her head, letting her hair fall forward to hide her face. "Then, today, I saw the assignment lists. I'm in the Heavy Guards and you've been assigned to the Tenth Lyran Guards." She spat out the name of the Commonwealth regiment as though it were some bitter poison. "You'll be stationed on Skondia in the Isle of Skye. What did I do to drive you so far away?"

Kai shook his head. "You did not drive me away."

She snapped her head up sharply. "Then why did you change assignments?"

Kai hesitated, heart pounding. "If I had taken my first choice, we would not have served together."

Anger pulsed through the vein in her forehead. "What are you talking about? You're fifth in the class. Your grades *guarantee* your choice of assignment and I saw you list the Guards—the Heavy Guards—as your first choice!"

Her rage slammed into him like the waves against the beach. "If I had taken my first choice, we would not have served together," he repeated in a whisper. Even as realization of what he was saying dawned on Wendy's face, Kai droned on like a machine. "My father met me to congratulate me on my posting before he left with Prince Davion to attend Victor's graduation. When I saw the listing for the Heavy Guards, your name was first on the alternates list."

He turned away as she covered her face with her hands. *Just for a moment, Kai. Let her regain her composure,* he told himself. But it was a lie and he knew it. He was the one who needed the time to rein in his own racing emotions, but he forced himself to believe that everything would work out right.

Wendy's voice was barely audible over the screams of the sea birds hovering over the shore. "You did that for me? You threw away the best assignment in the Armed Forces of the Federated Commonwealth for me?"

"The regiment is your home, Wendy." *It was my performance in the La Mancha scenario that skewed the grade curve. If not for that, you would have had the grades to get into the Guards free and clear.* Kai reinforced his voice with a confidence he could never feel about himself. "There have been Sylvesters in the Heavy Guards since before the fall of the Star League. I could never usurp your place in the regiment."

"But, if I couldn't get in on my own…"

Kai whirled, making his anger at himself burn in his dark eyes and

22

fill his voice. "Don't talk nonsense. Openings in the regiment fluctuate from year to year—we both know that. We also know your grades and test scores were better than half the people who entered that unit from NAMA last year. You've lived and breathed the Heavy Guards for as long as you can remember. To deny you the chance would have been a crime."

"But why did you get posted to a unit so far away?" Wendy said. "Why didn't you get an assignment here on New Avalon?"

Kai looked away. "There were no other openings," he lied.

She reached out and laid a hand on his arm. "I won't believe you unless you look me in the eye when you say that."

He refused to meet her stare. "Believe it, Wendy. It's true." *It's for the best. It's your family's tradition to marry someone from within the Heavy Guards. You grew up dreaming of just that. It might not be a problem at first, but sooner or later, it would. And if not that, then you'd begin to resent the fact that you owed your position in the Guards to me. I don't see how we could withstand those strains. Better for us to be apart but keep our happy memories.*

Her hand withdrew. "I see." She straightened up and brushed the sand from her trousers. "That's it, then, isn't it?"

Kai nodded.

Wendy mimicked his nod. "Well, let me leave you with this, Kai Allard. Somewhere inside of you, you're terribly afraid. I don't know what you have to fear because you're brilliant and hard-working. I'd hoped that together we could conquer your demons, but that's impossible now—by your choice."

She moved closer and kissed him on the cheek. "No matter what, I wish you the best of luck, but mostly I hope you discover what you're afraid of and how to deal with it. Until then, how will you ever be truly happy? Good bye, Kai. I'll always love you."

Kai stared at the spray from green waves crashing against the wet black beach. He desperately wanted to turn and run after her, to bring her back and explain everything, but he didn't. *She would only try to solve the problem, and she cannot. That would not stop her from working at it, forever if need be, and the effort would destroy her. Better she leave now and recover from it while she can. It is best.*

Kai dropped to one knee and picked up the two halves of the driftwood stick that Wendy had tossed down toward the shoreline. He tried to fit them back together, but the broken ends, swollen from the brief soaking, no longer fit with one another. Angry, he jammed them together, then one cracked and slipped, driving a jagged wooden splinter into his left hand.

"Dammit!" Kai plucked the wood from his palm and sucked at the wound. The blood tasted bitter in his mouth. *Idiot! How can you be so stupid?*

He sagged down onto the sand and lay back. "Why couldn't you see that what you wanted for me would have destroyed me? You wanted me to become one with the Heavy Guards. You wanted to welcome me into that family and have me take pride in their traditions and to uphold their honor." He shook his head. "Why couldn't you see how that would have made the house of cards called Kai Allard-Liao collapse?"

Kai lay his left hand on the beach where advancing waves could wash over it and the wound in his palm. Speaking to no one but the gulls who mocked him, Kai let his pain infuse his words. "You said you hoped I'd discover what it is I'm afraid of. Well, I know. I've known ever since it dawned on me what the name Allard-Liao actually means. You were afraid I had no family, no anchor for my life. The fact is that I have two anchors, and their combined weight is what drags me under."

The brine pouring over his hand burned like fire, but Kai consciously overrode his body's reflex to pull his hand back from the sea. He savored the pain and the minor victory over himself it represented. "I already have so much to live up to that I don't know if I can stand it. My mother was a successful MechWarrior and military commander before she took on duties within the government of the Capellan Confederation. She managed to survive within the lunatic asylum that was the Chancellor's Palace on Sian, then left when things became unbearable. Her people, the people of St. Ives, chose to follow her when she left the Confederation—billions upon billions of them willing to endure the hardships of a possible civil war out of love for and belief in her."

Kai swallowed hard. "And my father. Already a decorated war hero, he agreed to undertake an incredibly dangerous spy mission that put him body and soul into the Capellan court. Before he could get there, though, he wandered off to Solaris, the Game World, and proved himself the best MechWarrior in the Successor States, despite having been maimed in a previous battle. Once at the court of Maximilian Liao, my father became his trusted advisor and managed to thwart all of Liao's counterstrikes against the Federated Suns while the Suns ate up half the Confederation. Then my father returned to New Avalon and was proclaimed a hero by Prince Hanse Davion."

Kai chewed on his lower lip to stop it from trembling. "That's why I couldn't join you in the Heavy Guards. I already have so much to live up to. My parents, God love them, take pride in everything I do, and I struggle never to fail them. But that's the problem. I know I *will* fail them." He glanced down at his punctured hand. "In some way, some day, I will fail. I just don't want you to go down with me."

Kai rolled onto his side and looked back, hoping perhaps that Wendy had returned and had overheard him. Instead of her smiling face, understanding and accepting, he only saw the long line of her footsteps angling back along the shore. The waves had already stolen those footprints nearest him and threatened to blot out all evidence of her presence.

Kai nodded grimly. *It's for the best, Kai. In the Lyran Commonwealth, you will be alone. You can be yourself, and that way, when you stumble and fall, no one will be hurt but you.*

Tyra's mouth soured with fear as the Jarlwards opened the door
and pushed Phelan Kell—half-naked and barefoot—into Varldherre
Tor Miraborg's waiting room. The mercenary stumbled forward a few
steps, his normal, long-legged gait hobbled by the chains. He grunted
and tried to straighten up, but the cruelly short length of chain binding
the leg irons to his handcuffs snapped taut and kept him hunched over.

Tyra shuddered at the sight of the man who had been her lover.
My God, Phelan, what have they done to you? Dozens of purplish
bruises mottled the smooth flesh of his muscular chest. Both his eyes
had been blackened, with the left one nearly swollen shut. Phelan, still
fighting the chains, moved slowly and stiffly, his face a defiant mask
to keep his captors from knowing how much he really hurt.

Then he saw her and the mask shattered to reveal the agony and
fear in his eyes. He started to tip off-balance, but managed to catch
himself quickly enough to slump undecorously onto the red leather
bench next to the wall.

One of the Jarlwards raised a hand to cuff him, but Tyra barked
an order before he could strike. "No!" The man stopped, hand
quivering, and looked at her. "Free him."

The Jarlward straightened up and shot a grin at his partner. "I am
not obliged to obey you, *Kapten.*" The man sneered officiously. "I
serve the Corrections Ministry, which puts me outside your command."

26

Tyra stared at him furiously. "Do you *really* want to see how fast I can arrange for a transfer?" She shifted her gaze to the other Jarlward, whose sneer died at birth. "The same goes for you. Now free him." She smiled humorlessly. "And give him your jacket."

The second Jarlward stiffened, but broke beneath her cold gaze and unfastened the clasps on his scarlet-trimmed, gray wool jacket. As one man knelt to free Phelan of the chains, the other settled his jacket over the mercenary's shoulders. Staring into space, the Kell Hound pulled it tight but did not slip his arms through the sleeves.

Tyra dismissed the Jarlwards with a wave of her hand. Both hesitated and looked at the door leading into the Varldherre's office. The anteroom's recessed lighting burned reddish highlights into her long, bronze hair. "There will be no trouble. Leave us."

As the door clicked shut behind them, she crossed to the bench and sat next to Phelan. She started to reach out to him, then hesitated. "I want to hold you but I'm afraid it will hurt."

Phelan's mouth smiled, but any reflection of that smile in his eyes was lost within the bloated, discolored flesh surrounding them. "You can't hurt me, Tyra. Just go easy on the ribs. I could definitely use a hug. Your basic Jarlward is not a well of human kindness."

"Jarlwards are not born," she quipped, pulling him close. "They're grown in vats of dung with mushrooms and other semi-intelligent fungi." Tyra held him as tightly as seemed safe, stroking his hair with her free hand. After several moments, she leaned back and tipped his face up so she could look into his good eye. "How did this happen?"

He shrugged. "I was off the reservation and got jumped by a bunch of folks. They knew about us and that I'd asked you to join the Kell Hounds. They took exception to that. A big guy with a Radstadt Academy scar on his left cheek organized the little party."

Tyra saw something flash through the malachite depths of Phelan's right eye. *You call it a Radstadt Academy scar, but you know what most people call it. It's a Miraborg scar, just like the one the Varldherre has. Many of our warriors wear it as a symbol of their willingness to make the same sort of sacrifice as he did in the name of nationalism.* Tyra stroked the right side of Phelan's face with her left hand. "Tall and blond, I'll bet. It must have been Hanson Kuusik. He was out last night and seemed very pleased with himself this morning."

Phelan nodded wearily. "I thought I recognized him from that first Liaison meeting I attended on your base."

"You should have told me."

The Kell Hound sighed. "What good would it have done? My word against his and no jury of his peers would believe a mercenary against a loyal aerojock." Phelan's characteristic smile struggled to return. "Besides, I figured that I'd look him up and settle our account after we returned from the Periphery."

Tyra flinched at Phelan's use of the word "we." His good eye shut and he turned away from her. "I guess I was wrong when I said you couldn't hurt me." He hung his head. "You're not coming, are you?"

Tyra looked down at her hands. *How do I tell you this?* "I am honored and flattered that you managed to make room for me in the Kell Hounds…"

"Hey, don't imagine it was my word that got you the offer," Phelan cut in. "I suggested Captain Wilson take a look at you, and she liked what she saw. I'm not an officer and being my father's son makes things lots harder for me—just as her knowledge of our relationship made things tougher for you. Despite that, she made you an offer."

Tyra nodded and rubbed her right hand up and down Phelan's hunched back. "I know, love. I know." She paused, choked up with emotion. "All that we discussed is true: my skills are not being fully realized here in the Gunzburg Eagles. And it's not that I can't stand the idea of being a mercenary…"

"Could you, Tyra? Could you really accept being a mercenary?"

It was a question she'd pondered deeply so many times since knowing Phelan, but it was still a hard one to answer. "I think I could," she said, continuing to stroke his back, "despite the prejudice I've grown up with. Even here, all the stories about Wolf's Dragoons, the Kell Hounds, and the Eridani Light Horse work their magic. No matter how suspicious many people are of mercenaries, some units still have that aura of the noble outlaw about them."

Phelan scratched gingerly at his left eye. "That makes me feel better. I'd hate to see what folks here do to mercs they *don't* like."

Tyra ignored Phelan's comment. "It's not that I couldn't handle the idea of being a mercenary. It's the idea of becoming a person without a nation that I couldn't live with."

Phelan frowned. "What are you talking about? I was born on Arc-Royal. I'm a citizen of the Lyran Commonwealth. I have my loyalties…"

Tyra's blue eyes narrowed. "Do you? Phelan, I've come to know you intimately in the three months the Kell Hounds have been marooned on Gunzburg. I think you have loyalties, but not to any nation. You've told me yourself how much traveling you've done in your life. The Hounds have seen service in the Federated Suns, the

Lyran Commonwealth, and then the St. Ives Compact since your birth. You've spent more time on the Dragoons' baseworld of Outreach than you have on Arc-Royal. You have loyalties, but they are more to your family and your friends than to any place."

"Is that bad?" Phelan said quietly.

Tyra took his left hand in hers and gave it a squeeze. "No, not in itself. But it can get you into trouble. It got you bounced from the Nagelring…"

Phelan's face closed. "And it made me lose you."

Tyra took Phelan by the shoulders and twisted him around to face her again. "Yes, but not in the way you mean. I can no more give up being Rasalhagian than you can give up being a Kell Hound. Both of us are tied strongly to our backgrounds because it's shaped us and given us our sense of justice, our sense of right and wrong."

She reached into the pocket of her silver flight jacket and removed a paper-wrapped object. Placing it in Phelan's left palm, she folded his fingers over it. "You've made me think about many things, Phelan, and for that I am far more grateful than you could ever know." She swallowed hard again. "The reason you couldn't find me last night was because I'd gone to my father's house to finish making this for you."

Phelan slowly unfolded the paper, then stiffened as the treasure within it fell into his open palm. Cast in silver, the belt-buckle took the form of the hound's-head crest of the Kell Hounds Regiments. Inlaid onyx filled the face of it and malachite colored the Hound's eyes a fierce, cold green.

Phelan's mouth hung open. "God, Tyra, this is beautiful. How can I ever…"

She pressed a finger to his lips, then quickly kissed him. "I know the hound's eyes are supposed to be red to match the unit crest, but I used malachite to match your eyes. I made it to fit your gunbelt because you like to wear a sidearm while piloting your 'Mech. I want it to keep you safe."

Phelan swept Tyra into a bearhug, hanging on tightly until she actually felt the tremors of strain in his body. She rubbed both hands on his back, then eased herself out of his grasp. "We'd best head into the office for our joint audience."

Clutching the belt buckle in his right hand as if drawing strength from it, Phelan rose stiffly. "Whatever happens in there—and I'm making no promises—I want you to know that my loyalties include you as well." He shook his head. "I guess we should have believed it when everyone said it couldn't work—that nothing but trouble could come if a mercenary and a daughter of Free Rasalhague tried to get together."

Tyra smiled gently. "But it did work, Phelan…for three months. Can't we be thankful for that?"

Phelan was smiling again. "We did defy the odds, didn't we?"

Tyra winked, took his left hand and led the way into the Varldherre's office.

Seated behind a massive mahogany desk, Tor Miraborg did not look up as they entered. Trimmed with gold piping, his gray jacket matched the color of his hair and beard except for the black whiskers running down either side of his mouth. Miraborg's dark eyes glittered as he closed the folder he was reading and set it atop the data monitor on the corner of his desk. As he looked up to see Phelan and Tyra holding hands, his scarred face openly displayed his anger.

"I trust you found our accommodations to your liking, Herr Kell." Sarcasm laced Miraborg's deep, rich voice.

Phelan straightened up as though his body didn't hurt at all. "Room service is less than stellar, but the complimentary massages were great fun. And I also enjoyed teaching the cockroaches to do tricks."

Miraborg's head came up. "Indeed? And how is that done?"

Phelan laughed. "It's not hard. First off, though, you have to be *smarter* than the cockroach."

As the mercenary's cut hit home, Miraborg's eyes glowed with anger. "Be careful, Herr Kell, that someone doesn't mistake *you* for a cockroach. And here, cockroaches often get stepped on and crushed!"

Miraborg rolled himself back from the desk, bringing his wheelchair into view. The sight of it killed Phelan's cruel riposte before he could vocalize it, but Tyra and the Varldherre read it in his eyes. *No, Phelan, don't…*

Miraborg's eyes narrowed to black slits in a pinched face. "That's right, Kell. I cannot do the stepping and crushing, but it's the fault of your kind that I cannot! I did not hire you mercenaries to protect us from the Periphery pirates, nor did I welcome your presence on *my* world!"

"Ha!" Phelan's explosive laugh echoed off the glass wall behind Miraborg. "You wanted us here, all right. You wanted us right here on your world so you could torment us. You could have given us the liquid helium we needed to repair the *Cucamulus* the second we showed up in your system and blew that seal. I stood here in this office when

30

Captain Wilson made her request, but you said that you couldn't give us the helium because it was a strategic stockpile—even though we offered to pay for it and replace it!"

Miraborg's chest swelled with outrage. "Who are you to question me? Your history of disrespect for authority and lack of responsibility is disgraceful. You were thrown out of the Nagelring for dereliction of duty and you have logged more violations of the curfew and quarantine restrictions on this planet than everyone else in your unit combined."

Miraborg leaned back, steepling his fingers. "I'm glad you liked teaching cockroaches tricks, Kell, because you'll have plenty of time to do it."

Phelan scoffed at the older man. "We're leaving today."

The Varldherre shook his head. "The Kell Hounds are leaving today, but you'll not be with them. You'll be bound over for trial."

"No!" Tyra's voice filled the room and shocked both men to silence. "No, you will not bind Phelan over for trial."

Betrayal threaded through Miraborg's voice. "How dare you speak to me in that tone?"

Tyra took a deep breath and approached the man in the wheelchair. "I dare, Father, to prevent you from doing something that would disgrace you and Gunzburg."

Muscles bunched at Miraborg's jaws. "How could I be more disgraced than to have my daughter sleeping with the same scum that crippled me?"

Tyra's slap rocked Tor Miraborg's head back, and she stood staring down at her father. *How could you? How could you imagine that I would intentionally do anything to hurt you?* She turned and walked away from him, immediately aware that Phelan had taken several steps in her direction. Though she desperately wanted to feel his arms around her, she held out a hand to keep him back.

Her father's voice, softer and uncertain, reached out to her. "I'm sorry, truly sorry, Tyra. I didn't think."

Inside her, it was as if a dam broke, but somehow she held back the torrent of emotions. "Phelan, please leave us." She did nothing to keep the strain from her voice.

Her father's tone had regained its edge, too. "Yes, Kell, leave us. The charges against you will be dropped," he said, reaching into a desk drawer. "Oh, and I believe these are yours." The clatter of plastic and metal bouncing across the desktop brought Tyra around to see Phelan's sunglasses roll to a stop beside the monitor.

Phelan's hands convulsed into fists. "You bastard! The people

31

who attacked me took those from me last night. You know who they are."

Miraborg shook his head nonchalantly in a sham denial of the charge. "I know nothing about that. These were turned in to me by a good citizen wanting to make sure you left nothing behind here on Gunzburg." He gave the glasses a push in Phelan's direction.

Phelan glanced at Tyra, then shook his head. "No, Miraborg. You keep them. To the victor go the spoils. You've won this round, but someday I'll come back for them."

Miraborg laughed harshly. "You do that."

The mercenary turned, then rested his hands on Tyra's shoulders. "I'm sorry the way things turned out, but I'll never regret what we had." He kissed her on the forehead and then was gone.

As the door shut behind Phelan, her father smiled coldly. "Good. Now things can return to normal around here."

Despite her pain and hurt, Tyra kept her voice even. "I don't think so, Father." She felt a great sense of relief, knowing she was doing this for herself, not to hurt him. "I will be leaving Gunzburg."

"What!" He shot a horrified glance at the door. "I thought...You cannot go with them, Tyra. I will not allow it! How could you do this to me?"

With each word, she saw her father growing smaller and smaller. *You've been living with hatred for so long, Father, that it's become part of you, like something in your blood that rules you.* "Not to worry, Father, the great Tor Miraborg did not lose a contest of wills with a mere mercenary. I am not joining the Kell Hounds, though their offer did sorely tempt me. I am too much your daughter to do that."

Miraborg's eyes narrowed. "If that were true, my daughter, you'd not have taken up with him in the first place."

She stared at him in disbelief. "You still don't understand, do you? I met Phelan at the Allt Ingar the night Lars Pehkonin played there. Neither of us knew anything about the other. And if we had, our prejudices would have made us bitter enemies from the start. How could a mercenary let himself be attracted to the daughter of Gunzburg's Iron Jarl? Especially someone like Phelan? He and Lars talked about music and about building synthesizers and whole universes of things that being here on Gunzburg denies me. I only learned his first name that night, but I thought of him often until we met again.

"It wasn't until two weeks later, when the Kell Hounds were formally introduced to the Eagles, that I learned Phelan's real identity. Neither one of us expected things to develop the way they did, but neither did we try to prevent it. When Captain Wilson offered me a place in the Kell Hounds, I knew that I couldn't accept it. What surprised me, though, was the intensity of my desire to leave Gunzburg."

Her father's face had gone ashen. "Why? I've always tried to make things good for you."

Tyra looked at her father sympathetically. "Yes, Father, you have, especially after mother died. You've been loving and considerate, but you've also changed."

Miraborg caressed the steel chair that served as his legs. "I had to adapt after the *incident*."

Tyra nodded. "I know, but that was only the beginning of the change. You became stronger, accepted more authority and responsibility."

"Someone had to do it." He turned to look out the glass wall behind him. "Chaos came with independence. With the Kurita administrators gone, every half-wit with a vision of utopia staked out a new nation and declared himself emperor for life." He took in all of Stortalar City with a wave of his left hand. "There were constant food shortages and riots. I had to do something."

"I remember, Father. I remember being proud of you when you went out one morning saying you would restore order. People rallied around you, as well they should have, and you reestablished order…"

Miraborg cringed and said the next word for her: "But…"

"Yes, *but*," Tyra repeated. "You became a symbol. People looked to you to lead them and they adopted your cares and concerns. Because they thought you hated mercenaries, they hate mercenaries. No, don't look away. I remember, Father. I remember that you didn't blame *all* mercenaries for your wounding, and once you even told me that Colonel Vinson had been right to pull his Vigilantes out when the terms of his contract had been met. There was once a time when you recognized that fact."

Tyra shook his head. "You're smart enough to know that a leader must be attuned to his people, but you let their feelings and impressions affect you. Because of their hatred of mercenaries, your own hate seemed to become even greater. You championed the necessity of sacrifice in the name of our fledgling nation and you became a model anyone would be proud to follow. Unfortunately, you also revel in perversions of that symbol."

She pointed to the scar on the left side of his face. "Young men and women maim themselves to look like you and proclaim their willingness to sacrifice themselves for Gunzburg as you did." Her right hand brushed a tear from her unblemished left cheek. "I have never done it because I hoped you already knew how much our world and our nation mean to me without any melodramatic display."

An air of defeat hung over Tor Miraborg as he nodded slowly. "I *did* think that before all of *this*." He turned his chair and faced her. "Now you say you are leaving. How will it look to the people that my daughter has deserted me?"

"Fear not, Father. I will make you proud." She straightened up. "I have requested and been granted a transfer to the First Rasalhague Drakøns."

The hint of a smile graced her father's lips. "The Prince's Honor Guard…"

Tyra nodded solemnly. "Yes, a promotion that should make you proud. Again you sacrifice part of your life for the greater good of Free Rasalhague. Anika Janssen is going with me." She glanced at the mirrored sunglasses on his desk. "I imagine you will promote Hanson Kuusik to replace me."

Tor Miraborg looked at the glasses, then lowered his eyes in shame. "Will you ever come home?"

Home is where the heart is, Tyra thought and winced to realize she no longer considered Gunzburg her home. "I don't know. I have much to think about, much to see. Perhaps someday you'll understand."

Tyra waited for her father to speak, but the emotions playing across his face seemed too much. He stared up at her, then closed his eyes and turned his chair away so she could not see him weep.

Having burned her last bridge on Gunzburg, the Iron Jarl's daughter left the world of her birth.

Edo, Turtle Bay
Pesht Military District, Draconis Combine
1 June 3049

Tai-i Shin Yodama heaved his duffelbag from his shoulder and tossed it onto the rickety, iron-framed cot, whose springs squealed and creaked in protest. *Kashira* Kenji Yamashima looked up in dismay.

"Sumimasen, Yodama-*san,"* he said. *"Tai-i* Buford preferred the cot…" He shrugged, indicating distaste for the previous occupant of the cinderblock-walled room. "If you desire, I will obtain proper bedding for you."

Shin smiled to himself and bowed slightly. "Yes, tatami, please, Yamashima-*san.* When the rest of my things are off-loaded from the DropShip, you will see that they are brought up here?"

Yamashima bowed his graying head. *"Hai.* Shall this unworthy servant have your things unpacked for you?"

Shin smiled. *Your mouthing the old courtesies is music to my ears after the weeks spent traveling here in that independent freighter.* Shin noticed the absence of several joints on the man's little fingers and the multi-colored head of a snake against the yellow flesh of his neck. *But I should not have expected anything less of you, should I?*

"That will not be necessary," Shin said, "but I am honored by your concern. I will see to the unpacking later." Glancing at the full-length mirror on the back of the door, he straightened up, trying to shake off the slump of weariness left from a week traveling to Turtle Bay from the system jump point. There were slight discolorations beneath his eyes, too, but no one else would notice them. He combed

35

his short black hair with his fingers, then smiled at Yamashima. "I think I should pay my respects."

Yamashima smiled like a tutor pleased with a pupil who has learned his lessons well. "*Tai-sa* Tarukito Niiro asked that you join him for *cha* once you were settled. While you are meeting with him, I shall arrange your visit with the Old Man."

Shin cocked his head inquiringly. "Old Man?"

Yamashima began to speak, then caught himself. His dark eyes darted from Shin's unblemished hands to the lapel of his black service tunic. "*Excuse me, Tai-i.* I presumed knowledge where I had only rumors. I meant no offense."

Shin returned the sergeant's deep bow. "You were not rude, Yamashima-*san*. You were not in error. I was not aware that the yakuza in Edo used that title for their lord." Yamashima straightened up, relief clearly visible on his seamed face. "So, after you take me to the *Tai-sa*," Shin said, smiling, "please do arrange my visit to the Old Man."

Shin Yodama entered *Tai-sa* Tarukito Niiro's office and knelt on the *tatami* mats before sliding the *shoji*-paneled door closed. The translucent panels of lacquered paper, especially those forming the southern wall opposite the door, let in enough light to brighten the entire room. *He keeps his sanctuary uncluttered and simple. He draws his strength from this room. I can feel it.*

Shin bowed first to Tarukito Niiro. Easily twenty-five years Shin's senior, the *Tai-sa* had not let vanity get the better of him. Instead of dyeing his salt-and-pepper hair black, as another might have, he wore it short and shaved back away from his temples for better contact with the neuroreceptors in his BattleMech's neurohelmet. His dark eyes met Shin's directly and without judgment, then he lowered his gaze so that his subordinate would not think him ill-mannered. Though the *Tai-sa* did not smile, Shin felt instinctively that he appreciated the depth of his bow and the respect it implied. Tarukito returned the bow fully and gracefully.

Shin then bowed to the other man in the room. It was slightly disturbing to Shin that this man, who was obviously his junior, should hold the rank of *Sho-sa*, making him a superior. *The only reason he would be here is because he is my commanding officer. I thought the reforms had done away with commissions being awarded on the basis of social rank alone. All I need is this kid giving me orders inspired by flower arrangements or using plans concocted as a result of consultation with the entrails of a teyexta.* Despite his misgivings, Shin took

36

comfort in the grace and respect in the younger man's return bow.

Tarukito spoke in a low voice, but one resonant with power and self-control. "I trust your journey in-system was not too difficult."

"*No, Tai-sa.* The pilot was most skilled and successfully threaded the needle between two bad storm systems."

"Good." Tarukito turned and drew Shin's attention to the other man with a casual gesture. "Forgive my poor manners at delaying the introductions. This is your immediate superior, *Sho-sa* Hohiro Kurita."

Shin's heart leaped to his throat, and he failed utterly to keep the surprise from his face. *Theodore Kurita's eldest son! He looks so different from holographs I've seen.* Shin bowed again, this time deepening the gesture and holding it longer. "*Excuse me,* Kurita-*sama.* I should have recognized you."

Hohiro returned the bow, a smile beginning on his face. "There is no reason you should have known me, Yodama-*san.* Most of the official holographs were taken years ago and not been updated for security purposes."

Though the smile remained, the look in Hohiro's eyes and his tone of voice shifted the conversation to a more serious level. "I should also tell you that, even as your superior officer, I would appreciate all advice and help you can give me. In addition to your skill with a BattleMech, I hope you will avail me of your vast combat experience as well."

Shin bowed his head. "You honor me, *Sho-sa,* but I am not worthy of such praise. I am, after all, only two years your senior, and I have not had the benefit of a Sun Zhang Academy education."

Tarukito Niiro smiled and opened a folder lying on the low, black-lacquered desk. "Your lack of a formal education would be considered a plus in many categories, Yodama. As Hohiro has aptly pointed out to me, your career as a warrior already spans twenty years. That means you possess a considerable storehouse of martial knowledge."

Shin shook his head. "Again I am honored, but I think you read too much into the accounts of my early life. Yes, I was orphaned during the fighting on Marfik in 3028, but I was only seven years old at the time. I was among those who fled the advancing Steiner troops, but it was only by purest luck that a group of guerrillas found and kept me with them as an omen of luck. I will admit to planting the satchel charge that destroyed the bridge at Pawluk's Ford, but that was because I was the only person small enough to crawl through the drainage pipe."

Hohiro shook his head slightly. "Neither of us placed much

37

weight on the accomplishments on Marfik, because we realized that, while they required courage and cunning, they merely attested to your ability to follow orders. No, we were more impressed by the raid you organized against the stronghold of renegade units on Najha during the Ronin Wars. It was an extremely well-organized and executed 'Mech action for a leader who was only eighteen years of age."

"Again you credit me for what was my good fortune." Shin felt the hot flush of embarrassment over his cheeks. "When the renegades tried to destroy our unit's training center because they hated us for being yakuza, it came down to *giri*. It was my *duty* to my compatriots and to those who had given us the honor of becoming MechWarriors to lead my cadet company's defense. Had the renegades known the base area as we did, or if their 'Mechs had not suffered equipment failures during the fight, I would not be here talking to you." The memory of a *Centurion* pointing its autocannon at the cockpit of his *Panther* suddenly hit Shin. *If that cannon hadn't jammed, I would have been killed.*

Tarukito watched Shin for a moment, then bowed his head slowly. "After so many years of soldiering with arrogant warriors who seek nothing but personal glory, your humility is as refreshing as it is undeserved. Your career since Najha has been exemplary. I look forward to your taking command of Hyo company."

Hohiro nodded in agreement with Tarukito's assessment. "We will have it your way, then, Yodama-*san*. I hope, in addition to your skill and experience, you will grant me some of your good luck as well."

Shin bowed. "I pledge all that I have and am to your service."

Tarukito smiled broadly. "Excellent! Now we need fear no one." He clapped his hands twice. "You were summoned here for tea, and that is what we shall have. After that, *Tai-i* Shin Yodama, you will have the run of Edo and a chance to become acquainted with your new home."

The rings around the world of Turtle Bay were etched across the night sky from horizon to horizon. The world's shadow slowly blackened the rings as evening wore on, but the furthest reaches still caught enough sunlight to burn brilliantly in crimson, purple, and gold. Though Shin had witnessed the effect during the the DropShip trip coming insystem, it was entirely different looking up at the colors from the ground than from in space.

Shin stopped where he was, gawking like a tourist. *This world is certainly more beautiful than any other where I have lived. I hope never to lose my sense of wonder for a sight so magnificent.*

After some moments, Shin shifted the unopened bottle of *sake* from his left hand to his right and set off again, carefully reading the street signs directing him through the hilly Edo landscape. With all the planet's heavy industry in space, mining the asteroids in the rings and refining the ore into the raw materials, the city of Edo was lovely and serene and free of large industrial complexes. He caught himself remembering the words of his *oyabun* back on Marfik. "We are civilized, Shin," his chief used to say, "and therefore should live in a civilized way." *My* oyabun *would have loved this place.*

Shin's path took him down a hill and through a darkened gate. He heard the hum of electronic equipment in the shadows, but nothing and no one kept him from passing through. The roadway wound off to the left and up the hill. As he turned the corner, his destination came into view.

The building had been styled after castles raised in Japan fifteen hundred years before. Massive stoneblock walls formed the foundation of the seven-story-high tower. Each level covered slightly less area than the one below it, tapering the structure gracefully to bring the hill's natural lines to fulfillment. The eaves of each level curled up at the corners into ferocious dragons'-heads that stared down at the approaching MechWarrior. Beneath the eaves, the gentle flickering of candles showed through the *shoji* panels to silhouette the intricate patterns of the wooden guard-rails around each level's balcony.

Shin let himself smile with true pleasure at the building. *The way the rings hovered overhead and the two stands of pine on each side balanced the castle is perfection. The architect was a genius and the landscaper an artist.* He mounted the steps up to the broad, flat courtyard before the towering building, then soundlessly crossed the wooden bridge over a white-stone river to the entrance.

Two men bowed to him as he entered the foyer. As Shin returned their bows and slipped his boots off, one man carried the bottle of *sake* away. Shin frowned, but a reassuring look from the remaining man told him the rice wine would be decanted and presented at the appropriate time. *Just so long as they satisfy themselves it is not poisoned.*

Shin pulled a pair of black slippers from an alcove above where he had placed his boots and donned them. Wordlessly, he followed the remaining servant through the house, marveling at the beauty of the place. *Someday, somehow, I will live in a palace like this.*

The beautifully painted *shoji* divided rooms from the wood-floor hallways. In some rooms, the furnishings were quite modern and contained everything from tables and couches to holovid viewers and even holographic gaming tables. With one exception, the young men lounging in the room laughed and drank raucously.

The one dour individual wore no shirt, but Shin had to look twice to be absolutely certain of the fact. Though the man was attempting to be stoic, his expression suggested that he wanted to scream aloud, and that he probably would have if his peers were not in the room. On the left side of his chest, a black line-drawing of a dragon coiled from shoulder to waist and around—Shin surmised—to his spine in the back. The dragon's tail ran down the man's arm to just below his elbow.

That is the first stage in getting a tattoo in the old way, with paint and a bamboo needle. If that fellow thinks it hurts now, wait until they go back in to give the dragon color and life. Shin grinned and nodded a salute to the man, which seemed to briefly relieve his pained expression. *He must have done something special for his* oyabun *to authorize a tattooing.*

Shin's guide led him up a cedar stairway, then paused next to a *shoji* panel. He drew it aside and waited for Shin to pass into the chamber before closing it and departing silently.

Shin knelt and bowed to the room's only other occupant. "I apologize for intruding on your valuable time. My gratitude knows no bounds that you have made this visit possible." Shin brought his body up, but did not make eye contact with the other man. "I am Shin Yodama, born on Marfik in the seventeenth year of Takashi Kurita's reign."

The skeletally thin old man across from him bowed respectfully, but remained aloof. "In the name of the *Ryugawa-gumi*, I, Ryoichi Toyama, welcome you to Turtle Bay and Edo." He slipped his left arm from the gray silk kimono he wore and bared the left side of his body. "This I got when admitted to the Dragon River Gang in the first year of Takashi Kurita's reign."

Though similar in design to the infant tattoo Shin had seen downstairs, the *oyabun*'s tattoo showed an artistry from another era entirely. Even the bullet-wound scar on the older man's stomach could not rob the forty-five-year-old design of its exquisite power. The dragon, as it rose and fell with the old man's breathing, seemed to come alive. Shin could have sworn he heard the rustle of scales and the scraping of the beast's talons across the man's ribs.

Shin forced himself to look away. "Excuse me, Toyama-*sama*. I am a lout who knows only gutter-etiquette. It is beautiful, but its power comes from you."

Toyama said nothing as he pulled his kimono back into place. He tightened the *obi* sash once again, then looked at Shin expectantly. "I see you have lost no fingers."

Shin bowed his head. "My masters have turned a blind eye to my failures."

"You do not wear a lapel pin to mark your affiliation."

"Forgive me, Toyama-*sama*, but the commander at my last station forbade us to wear tokens of our families."

Toyama smiled and bowed his head. "*Tai-sa* Niiro and I have reached an understanding about that. Here, however, you must wear a device that identifies you with us in Edo. I will grant you such if you do, indeed, prove to be Shin Yodama."

Shin sat up straight and removed his uniform jacket. He folded it carefully and set it down on the *tatami* to his right before unfastening the buttons on his shirt. As the Chief of the *Ryugawa-gumi* had done before him, Shin bared the left side of his chest. "I am Shin Yodama and I belong to the *Kuroi Kiri* of Marfik."

"The Black Mist!" the old man hissed in awe. "I have heard, but could scarcely believe…"

Shin's tattoo entirely covered his left torso and arm to just above his wrist. Stylistically traditional, the design consisted of a boiling black cloud. Gold flecks and lines curling in and out of the design defined the cloud's different parts and levels. Yet, even as the gold was very much part of the cloud, it was also something on its own. Its curving, sometimes jagged, lines followed the smooth muscles of Shin's chest, stomach, and arm, mechanically marking him as a man, yet clearly transforming him into something else, something more.

Toyama bowed deeply. "Then it is true. You *are* Shin Yodama and you are a *buso-senshi*." A proud smile spread across the old man's face. "It is I who am honored by this visit."

Shin returned the bow, relishing the respectful tones in Toyama's voice. *Buso-senshi—a MechWarrior. I am part of the bargain struck between the yakuza and Theodore Kurita in his drive to save the Draconis Combine. Because of the services of the* Kuroi Kiri *in the war, we were given the honor of supplying the first of the new yakuza MechWarriors. I am one of those—one who fights for more than honor.*

The sharp clap of Toyama's hands snapped Shin from his musings. "Come, Yodama-*san*, we will drink your *sake* properly and then I will show the wastrels working for me what a real yakuza is like. You are one of us now, one of the *Ryugawa-gumi*. Whatever you need, ask, for you embody the hope of the Dragon—and we will not let that hope die."

41

Triad, Tharkad City, Tharkad
District of Donegal, Lyran Commonwealth
20 June 3049

"Trellwan!" Victor Steiner-Davion locked his face in a feral snarl. "I don't care if Kanrei Theodore Kurita stations his eldest son on Atreus to drool over Isis Marik. I don't see why his posting means I get exiled to some backwater!" That the others in the room watched him with amused smiles only darkened and deepened his mood. "I want to be on the Combine border, or even down near the Capellan Confederation. I want to be stationed where I can see some action!"

Morgan Hasek-Davion raised an eyebrow. "You'll see plenty of action out there, Victor."

Victor snorted derisively. "Sure, Periphery pirates and the occasional raid by some looney Rasalhague unit wanting to prove they're tough. There's been no trouble on Trell since the birthing of the Gray Death Legion..." He looked over at Justin Allard. "Hell, the Kell Hounds have dispatched one company from their Second Regiment to take care of the pirates up there. That'll leave me nothing to do but cool my heels."

Justin Allard glanced at Prince Hanse Davion, then allowed himself to smile. "I see you've been studying the troop assessment reports."

"Damned right, Justin." Victor pointed to the map of the Successor States tacked up on the wall of his room. "I know where we've got what, and I've a fair idea of what the Draconis Combine has going up against us. You don't need troops up here in the hinterlands. Hell, a

42

troop of Youth Scouts could defend that area against anything coming in from the Periphery."

Victor stabbed his finger at the border between the Commonwealth's Isle of Skye and the Combine's Dieron Military District. "This is where you need me. We all know that when trouble erupts between the Combine and our forces, it will be here. You've got the Tenth Lyran Guards stationed on Skondia, Justin. I saw the reports listing Kai as being assigned there. And Morgan, I know you're rotating the First Kathil Uhlans to Skye in the next six months. Why am I being left out?

"Dammit, I trained to be a MechWarrior. I want to go where that's what I can do. Posting me out in the middle of nowhere because Theodore Kurita did the same with his son offends me."

Hanse Davion shook his head. "Ah, the impetuosity of youth."

At that, Victor gave both his father and Justin Allard a withering stare, then turned to his cousin to plead his case. "I don't expect those two fossils to understand, Morgan, but surely you can. You remember what it's like to be ready to take what you've learned and turn it into action."

Morgan nodded slowly, and clasped his hands at the small of his back. "I do recall what it's like to be young and eager, cousin." Morgan glanced at Hanse. "I also recall that your father held me back until the time was right."

Victor winced. *So much of your history is wrapped up in the exploits of the First Kathil Uhlans—the Lions of Davion—that I keep forgetting how long you waited for your chance. I can see in your face that you sympathize with me, but that you also feel my father's plan is a good one.*

Resignation written all over his face, Victor pulled his dress jacket from the rack and shrugged it on. "Why is it so important for me to be stationed on Trell I?" He held up his hand to forestall an immediate answer. "And you can spare me the explanation about the Twelfth Donegal Guards being an excellent unit. I've read the files and I agree that they're good. On the off-chance we do see some action, the enemy will have to be plenty tough to drive us off."

Hanse Davion's blue eyes narrowed. "I believe you are well aware, my son, that dealing with the Draconis Combine has never been easy. In the past, all we needed was to understand how their culture measures honor and embarrassment, or balances duty and compassion, and we could predict what they might do and how they would react. In the past—up to fifteen years ago—we could count on retaliation for every raid and a countermove for every one we made.

Their troops would mount suicidal and foolish attacks just for the sake of winning honor for their families. More than once, a leader betrayed by his superiors committed suicide because he could not live with the shame of failure, even though that failure was not his own doing. It was madness, and we benefited from the predictability it gave their actions."

The Prince rose from his seat at the foot of Victor's bed and stared at the map. "Over twenty years ago, before the war, Takashi Kurita ordered the creation of two new 'Mech units: the Genyosha and the Ryuken. The Genyosha was an elite unit about the size of a reinforced battalion. Its MechWarriors were the cream of the crop and were trained to see honor as something on a grand scale, not a personal one. Their glories were the unit's glories, and the unit's glories were the Combine's glories. Under the leadership of Yorinaga Kurita, a brilliant MechWarrior, the members of the Genyosha fought as a unit rather than as individuals seeking personal glory. And that made them deadly."

Hanse's eyes focused beyond the map. "The Ryuken was a unit several regiments in size. It was built up to parallel Wolf's Dragoons and its training style matched that of the Dragoons. As such, Mech-Warriors in that unit also worked well together. They learned how to support one another and mastered tactics that made them formidable. When they faced their mentors in 3028—on a world appropriately named Misery—both sides were savaged. The Ryuken were not fit enough as a unit to take part in the Fourth Succession War when it broke out, but the Genyosha were. At the war's end, remnants of the Genyosha pledged themselves to Theodore Kurita."

The Prince turned back to his son. "The Genyosha felt that Theodore's father, Takashi, had mistreated and dishonored their dead commander. A few Genyosha warriors even defected to the Kell Hounds. It was also at this time that Theodore drew to himself the remnants of the Ryuken, who had also lost their commander. He quickly organized training battalions around the Genyosha and Ryuken survivors, and also recruited heavily from among the yakuza. Even though his father ordered the dissolution and division of the Ryuken and Genyosha, Theodore had put together an excellent military force."

Justin cleared his throat. "In fact, the break-up of the two elite units seems only to have spread Theodore's new military philosophy further instead of destroying it, as Takashi had hoped. While old-liners did mount some revolts—and were largely responsible for what they call the Ronin Wars when Rasalhague went independent—Theodore's new and more efficient military doctrine won out."

Victor chewed his lower lip. "It was this new military doctrine that let Theodore pound us back in 3039?"

Hanse hesitated, a bit stung by the question. "That did, indeed, contribute to the military reversal we suffered. More important than that, however, was the number of 'Mechs the Combine had available for use. Theodore obtained reinforcements at an incredible rate, despite the fact his father saw him as a threat and did things like trying to hold up delivery of spare parts and munitions."

Victor frowned. "That was stupid. He was cutting off his nose to spite his face."

Morgan glanced at his chronometer and then straightened the line of his black and gold dress jacket. "That, Victor, is what we thought, which is why we moved when we did. Theodore has proved his worth, and since that time, we've been watching each other closely."

Hanse walked over and straightened the sunburst epaulet on Victor's left shoulder. "When Theodore posted his son to Turtle Bay and the Fourteenth Legion of Vega six months ago, I felt he was sending us a signal. At first, we feared that a buildup in the area would oblige us to reinforce the Rasalhague border, and that would be politically bothersome…"

Victor saw a look of distaste wash over his father's face. *Ryan Steiner's meddling again, I would guess. He's only my mother's second cousin—and the same relation to me as Phelan Kell—but he causes enough trouble to be in a direct line for the Archon's throne.*

An odd thought struck Victor and made him smile. *I wonder if it's the province of second cousins one generation removed to cause trouble? Phelan got himself kicked out of the Nagelring, and Ryan married Morasha Kelswa to strengthen his power base with her claim to the throne of the Tamar Pact. As half the Pact became a chunk of the Free Rasalhague Republic, it would be difficult for my father to build up troops in that area while still denying Ryan's requests to go to war to regain his wife's holdings.*

Victor looked up. "I take it Theodore did not increase troop or munitions shipments to his son's unit?"

Justin nodded carefully. "As nearly as the Ministry of Intelligence can determine, he has not. It looks as though shipments to that garrison are sufficient to replace materiel lost fighting pirates and nothing more."

Victor stepped back from his father and tugged at the wrists of his coat. "So you will send me up there to suggest to Theodore that you will answer him in kind?"

Hanse shook his head. "Both you and Hohiro Kurita are very good at what you do. Hohiro's scores from the Sun Zhang were leaked to us as a courtesy, and they were excellent. We have given Theodore a similar look at your file. If he wishes our differences settled by the two of us, he will strike at the Isle of Skye. If he wants to leave our conflict to future generations…"

"His son will strike at me." Victor's blue eyes narrowed, unconsciously mimicking the face his father made when concentrating. *The analysis is flawless, as I have come to expect from these three. The challenge is there, as I have been trained to expect from Theodore Kurita.* "What of you, Father? Do you wish the fight to fall to your next generation?"

Hanse threw back his head and laughed while his two advisors exchanged amused glances. "Yes, gentlemen, you were right. He did ask." Hanse's smile faded as he rested both his hands on Victor's shoulders. "I fought a war before you were born, and recovering from the war was long and hard. Deciding to attack the Draconis Combine ten years later was probably a mistake and I should be thankful to Theodore for making that so evident."

The Prince looked down onto his son's face. "In my day, some considered me a military genius, but it seems the title is generational in nature. My tactics in the Fourth Succession War worked because they hit at weaknesses my enemies had not recognized in their defenses. Just ten years later, in the War of 3039, Theodore Kurita saw the flaws in my tactics, and pointed them out to me in a most dramatic manner. It's true that we soft-soaped the whole story for public consumption, and given the nearly even exchange of worlds, the war looked like another stalemate. But those of us gathered here know how shocked we all were that Kurita could so successfully turn back the combined armies of the Federated Suns and the Lyran Commonwealth."

Hanse sighed heavily. "The time for me to plan and execute a war is passing—passing to Morgan and to you."

A small smile tugged at the corners of the Prince's mouth. "Let the wars pass to your generation, and when you take the throne, you can decide when or where or even *if* to strike. If you become a great warrior, if you reunite the Successor States to form a new Star League, you will make me very proud. If you never fight a war, I will be just as proud."

Again Morgan looked at his chronometer. "It's past time, my friends. I will agree with you that this discussion is more interesting than the Archon's Liberty Medals Banquet is likely to be, but I also

46

think it would be better held in a properly secure briefing room."

Hanse stood up and began to straighten his own jacket. "The only real problem with shuttling court back and forth between New Avalon and Tharkad is that every night is taken up with awards banquets and other 'cultural events' of questionable merit. He winked at Victor. "But if we miss them, your mother will have our heads."

Victor pointed toward the door. "Then let's go." He turned to his father. "Do you think I'll have to preside over similar occasions on Trell I?"

Hanse shook his head. "Out there? I doubt it."

Victor laughed and closed the door behind them. "There is a silver lining to this cloud after all…"

Gearadeus Base, Skondia
Isle of Skye, Lyran Commonwealth
30 July 3049

Kai Allard covered his mouth with one fist as he yawned. "I'm here, Sergeant. What's the big problem?"

The small, blocky man looked terribly apologetic. "Jeez, Leftenant, I didn't expect you to show up right now. I mean, I just wanted you to appear sometime today. I know you wanted to get some shuteye after that trip in on the *Argus.*"

Kai shook his head. "Not a problem. With all my traveling, I've mastered the trick of sleeping on DropShips even as they enter atmosphere." DropShips, incapable of interstellar travel by themselves, moved passengers and cargo from planets to JumpShips. With its Kearny-Fuchida jump drive, a JumpShip was able to warp space around itself and its DropShips, traveling instantaneously to another star system up to thirty light years distant. Transit time between planet and jump point varied according to the type of star, but no one counted such journeys as pleasant or restful.

The Sergeant glanced down at his noteputer. "The end of the month is coming up and I need to get you checked out on your 'Mech. I mean, we need to make sure nothing shook loose. Besides, your 'Mech is hardly stock…" He half-turned toward the 'Mech bay, then waited for Kai to follow him into the cavernous home of the most fearsome weapons ever developed by mankind.

A thrill ran up Kai's spine as he stepped into the bay's shadowy interior. BattleMechs ranging in height from nine to almost twelve

48

meters towered above him. The white and blue camouflage designed to hide 'Mechs in Skondia's icier reaches softened some of the machines' harder edges, yet Kai thought it also made the 'Mechs seem colder and more forbidding. Some were of humanoid design, with the look of men encased in giant, powered armor. Others resembled fierce animals or monstrous insects.

A third category of 'Mechs looked equally daunting. Most of them stood on birdlike legs, but the resemblance to living creatures ended there. Their squat, compact bodies sprouted stubby wings that bristled with laser ports or missile pods in most cases. The most fearsome of these, the *Marauder*, stood hunched over, with its twin arms ending in blocky weapon pods that contained lasers and terrifying particle projection cannons. Augmented by a cannon mounted atop the jutting torso, that weaponry made the *Marauder* one of the most deadly BattleMechs ever produced.

The noncom led Kai back through row upon row of 'Mechs. At one point, he plucked a thick vest from a basket and tossed it back to the MechWarrior. Gray ballistic cloth formed the garment's outer layer, and Kai found its weight reassuring. Unsnapping the four clasps, Kai opened the jacket to reveal the interior layer of black goretex that lined the vest. Sandwiched between the goretex and body armor ran tubes of coolant fluid. The garment, when plugged into a 'Mech's command couch, helped the pilot's body deal with the incredible heat build-up in the BattleMech's cockpit.

Kai had stripped off his shirt and donned the cooling vest by the time he and the Sergeant reached their destination. The smaller man stopped abruptly, but Kai neatly avoided running into him. "This is it, isn't it, Leftenant? I mean, this is the real *Yen-lo-wang*."

Kai nodded solemnly. "The real thing. This is *Yen-lo-wang*."

The *Centurion* standing before them lacked the bulkiness of some other humanoid 'Mechs. Though its slender lines made it seem more alive, the autocannon muzzle that replaced its right hand would never let anyone mistake it for a living creature. The head had been designed with a crest reminiscent of an ancient Roman helmet, but both Kai and the Sergeant knew it was more than decoration. The crest had been fitted with thousands of sensors that, in fact, made it the giant war machine's eyes and ears.

Yen-lo-wang did not share the other 'Mech's ice and snow camouflage. Until recently, it had been kept on the planet Kestrel, the Allard ancestral holding. It had been painted in a mottled brown and black pattern, with some blue near the faceplate, mimicking the coloration of a falcon. Over the left breast, the falcon rampant crest of the Kestrel Militia had been stenciled in black.

The smaller man shuddered. "I saw it in its first fight, you know."

"You were on Solaris twenty years ago?" Kai smiled solicitously.

The man shook his head. "Well, I wasn't actually there. I saw the 'Mech go against Peter Armstrong's when the fight was first broadcast. Let's see, I was stationed on Cor Caroli at the time. I remember watching Armstrong's *Griffin*—I think he called it *Mars...*"

"*Ares*," Kai corrected him gently.

"Yeah, *Ares*." The Sergeant shrugged sheepishly. "Hey, all them old god names get confusing, you know? Isn't *Yen-lo-wang* a god, too?"

"The Chinese god of the dead," Kai whispered, "The King of the Nine Hells."

The Sergeant smiled broadly. "Yeah, that's it. That's why the holovids of that fight were billed as 'The Battle of the Gods.' Well, I saw it all. On a whim, I bet on your father—mainly 'cause the other guys gave me great odds. When your pop blew the hell out of Armstrong, I cleaned up. Got doubled odds because he killed Armstrong."

The man's ebullience made Kai's mouth run sour. *I remember the time I sneaked a viewing of a holovid of that fight and started bragging about the fact my father had killed a man. I must have been, what, six years old at the time, and was using the holovid to win one of those 'my father can beat up your father' fights with a kid from school. It upset the other kid so much, they had to send him home from school. That night my father sat me down for a long talk. He held me close as we both watched the fight again, and I could feel him tremble. He told me what he'd been thinking as the faceplate on Armstrong's 'Mech exploded out. He wanted Armstrong to punch out, to escape the death of his 'Mech, but when fire filled the cockpit and shot out in twenty-meter long gouts of flame, my father's heart sank.*

"Killing a man is not easy, and never should be," he told me. I was too young to fully understand, but I've learned since then, and have never forgotten. Killing is, ultimately, a failure of all other methods to influence and change someone. That it is sometimes the only way to protect yourself does not give to it any more sanctity or merit.

The Sergeant patted *Yen-lo-wang* on the foot with an affection another man might lavish on a pet dog or horse. "I never thought I'd ever see this baby up close." He grinned sheepishly as he turned back to Kai. "If you have no objections, sir, I'd like to take care of your 'Mech personally. You know, sort of become your personal Tech—in addition to my other duties, of course."

Kai returned the Sergeant's smile, his thoughts and feelings deflected from their somber course. "It would be my pleasure, Sergeant, to have you work on my 'Mech." Kai glanced up at the *Centurion*. "And I'm sure he won't mind at all."

The Tech nodded and patted the 'Mech's foot again. "Don't you worry, sir, old Marty Rumble and *Yen-lo-wang* are going to become the best of friends. I'll have him running tip-top." He moved to steady the rope ladder running from the *Centurion's* cockpit to the ground. "First, let's get you up there and see what he can do. I'll be in the targeting-course control tower. Call me on TacCom 27 when you're ready to roll."

Kai mounted and quickly scaled the ladder. Once inside the 'Mech's cockpit, he waved Rumble away from the ladder and hit the retraction switch. With the ladder reeled into the storage space in the 'Mech's chin, the polarized faceplate slid down and clicked into place. Sealed tightly, the cockpit pressurized itself, making Kai's ears pop.

Kai dropped into the Mech's command couch and removed his long woolen trousers, leaving on his standard-issue shorts. The chill air raised goosebumps on his legs, but as he flipped the switch that started the fusion reactor burning in the 'Mech's chest, he felt warm air currents eddy up into the cockpit. Well he knew that the cockpit could become so stiflingly hot that his shorts would be all he could stand to have on.

After fastening the crisscrossing safety belts, Kai pulled the cooling vest's powercord from the small pocket on its left side and snapped it into the coupling on the left side of the command couch. It took a half-second for his flesh to get used to the sensation of a million worms crawling over it as the sluggish cooling fluid started to flow within the vest. Then he smiled, recalling one instructor's comment: "Better caressed by worms than parboiled."

Kai opened a panel on the right side of the command couch and pulled out four short cables and a strip of shiny paper. He peeled the medical-sensor adhesive pads from the paper and pressed one each to his thighs and upper arms. He then snapped the rounded ends of the cables to the four sensor pads and threaded the plug ends up through the loops on his cooling vest. The plugs clinked against one another as they flopped loosely near his throat.

Reaching up and behind his head, Kai pulled his neurohelmet from the shelf above the command couch. He settled it down over his head, letting the bulk of its weight rest on the cooling vest's padded shoulders. He worked it around, adjusting it so the ring of neurosensors built into the helmet fitted snugly against his skull. It gave him a bit of trouble, but he finally got it seated correctly. *I guess I need to get my hair cut again…*

He inserted the medsensor plugs into the four sockets at the helmet's throat. Moving his head around for a test, he satisfied himself that the helmet's hexagonal faceplate was indeed centered. He pressed down on the velcro tabs that kept the helmet in place. Ready for the next step, he reached out and touched a glowing yellow button on his command console.

The computer's synthesized voice filled his neurohelmet. "I am *Yen-lo-wang*. Who presents himself to the King of the Nine Hells?"

"I am Kai Allard-Liao."

White noise played through the speakers for a moment before the computer replied. "Voiceprint pattern match obtained. What is the one immutable law?"

Kai swallowed hard. "Honor thy mother and thy father."

"Authorization confirmed. Know well, Kai Allard-Liao, you have made your parents proud."

Kai rocked back in his couch, barely noticing as the war machine's monitors blinked to life and the computer brought all the weapon systems on line. *The computer's not programmed to say that!* Then he remembered his father wanting to climb back into the cockpit "one more time" when they met before the senior Allard departed for Victor's graduation ceremony. *I should have known he was up to something when he insisted on marching* Yen-lo-wang *into the belly of the DropShip that brought me here. I've not been in it since then.*

A lump rose in his throat. *His allowing me to take* Yen-lo-wang *and use it for my tour of duty was one hell of a graduation gift, but that …that was something else.* The words only barely choking out, Kai made a whispered vow. "I will do nothing to betray your faith in me… Nothing!"

He keyed the radio. "*Centurion* to Course Control. Can you read me?"

Rumble sounded a bit breathless. "Just got here, Leftenant. Cor-Con ready. Are you all set?"

"All systems go."

"Good. Turn to heading one-eighty and proceed south. Just walk it for the first klick, then you can take it up to cruising speed. The gunnery course isn't very sophisticated. Mostly scrap steel structures with sensor pods that will make your 'Mech put targets up on the display."

"Roger." Kai hit two buttons on the command console to the

right. "I'm sending you diagnostic feeds on TacCom 30 and 31. That's mechanicals and gunnery, respectively."

Rumble sounded impressed. "You can do that?"

"Yeah. It's a special option used on Solaris so the bookies can monitor a Mech's performance during a fight. It lets them lay off bets when a 'Mech takes internal damage that isn't clearly visible to the spectators. Feed starts now."

Streams of data poured across Kai's secondary monitor. He watched it long enough to assure himself he was sending the right information out on the correct frequency, then called up another program that presented a computer diagnostic view of *Yen-lo-wang* on the monitor. The computer reported the 'Mech's trio of active weapon systems were primed and ready. Because of the 'Mech's special modifications, especially the Pontiac 1000 heavy autocannon replacing the lighter Luxor AC in the 'Mech's right arm, and the added weight, the *Centurion* no longer carried a long-range missile launcher and ammo bays for the same in its chest. Ammo for the autocannon was stored in the *Centurion's* right breast. *Yen-lo-wang* also sported twin medium lasers forward and aft in its center torso.

The neurohelmet fed Kai's sense of balance directly into the computer, enabling the fifty-ton metallic giant to lumber forward and execute the turn to the south with amazing agility. At the pilot's direction, the computer instantly translated micro-electric pulses into gross motor movements by sending out jolts of electricity to contract and expand the 'Mech's myomer muscles. With his many years of training, Kai made the death machine carry him along almost effortlessly.

The *Centurion* strode from the 'Mech bay boldly and smoothly, but Kai detected and berated himself for tiny errors. He wouldn't allow himself the excuses of a two-month layoff because of his transit to Skondia or his general level of fatigue, but pushed himself to do better.

Concentrate, Kai! Your father handled Yen-lo-wang *as though he'd practiced with it every day for the past twenty years. He marched into the* Argus *as smartly as any elite drill team member. You're sloppy and slow. You have to do better.*

Kai punched another button on the command console with his right hand. A meter from his face, running from the cockpit's low ceiling down about a meter and a half and measuring two full meters from side to side, a computer-generated data display burned to life. Though the curved display took up only a 160-degree arc, it provided a full 360-degree view of the area surrounding the *Centurion*. Faint lines broke the display into forward, left, right, and rear arcs of fire, and

53

two gold targeting crosshairs hovered in the center area.

The translucent display allowed Kai a clear view of his command console, its data monitors, and the all-important heat-level displays. By focusing beyond it, he could see out through the *Centurion's* faceplate, but the view from ten meters up tended to be a bit distorted. The initial display showed the terrain outside in a magnified form using visible light, making it the rough equivalent of looking through a pair of weak binoculars. The program used by the computer to digitize the external visual feeds exaggerated crucial detail and included labels for items identified. In this case, it meant an increase of resolution for the gunnery-range warning signs and the identification of a passing aerofighter as a friendly, sixty-five-ton *Lucifer* on maneuvers from the base.

Kai keyed the radio. "I'm a klick out. I'm going to take *Yen-lo-wang* up to top speed." Without waiting for confirmation from CorCon, Kai leaned the 'Mech forward and started its legs pumping. Huge metal feet pounded into the snowy ground, crunching through the icy crust of early winter snow and actually digging up dirt from below. As the speed crept up to the 'Mech's maximum ground speed of 64.8 kph, Kai felt his heart begin to race. *After two months of doing nothing, this feels great.*

Rumble's voice crackled as it came out of the speakers. "All systems reporting fine, *Centurion*. Fifteen seconds to range on my mark. You'll get no artificial visuals on vislight scan, only magres or infrared. Labels on all three. Mark. Good luck."

Kai dropped his hands onto the joystick controllers on the arms of the command couch. The control in his right hand directed the crosshairs that targeted for the autocannon and the forward laser, while the other joystick handled the aft-arc laser. The button under his right thumb triggered the autocannon, while the index finger triggers on both controls fired the lasers.

Warning klaxons heralded his entry onto the gunnery range with hideous shrieks. Snowshoe hares sprinted away from the small wooden shack the computer labeled a Goblin medium tank. Kai dropped the forward crosshairs onto its projected image, let them pulse bright gold for a second, then stabbed his thumb down on the firing button.

With a thunderous roar, the *Centurion's* autocannon sprayed out a stream of depleted-uranium projectiles. They traced a line up the hill and into the shack. The door exploded in a cloud of splinters, then the roof disintegrated, spreading shingles all over the snowy hilltop. For the barest of moments, the unsteady structure remained standing, despite looking as though an invisible buzz-saw had split it right down the middle. Then, as Kai fought the autocannon's tendency to rise, the metal storm blew the rest of the building to pieces.

Almost instantly, off to the left, the computer painted the rusting skeleton of a bent and broken oil derrick with a label marking it as a *Valkyrie*. Kai swept the gold cross over to cover it, and snapped off a shot with the chest-mounted medium laser. The ruby beam shot low, vaporizing snow into great gouts of live steam. They rose up to form a thick white cloud that hung over the derelict tower, obscuring Kai's line of sight.

With his left hand, Kai shifted the display from vislight to magnetic resonance. The display went from normal visual analogs to a vector graphic picture of the landscape. For a half-second, the derrick appeared as it truly was, then the computer scrambled its lines and reformed them into the silhouette of the light 'Mech the derrick was supposed to represent.

Kai brought up the crosshairs and triggered the autocannon again. Through the display, he saw steel crossbraces spark and snap as the heavy weapon's shells slammed through them. The computer's projection, taking into account the nature of the damage that would have been done to the *Valkyrie*, sent shards of armor flying from the 'Mech's chest. Kai saw the *Valkyrie* stagger as reports of the incredible damage done to it scrolled by on his primary data monitor.

The *Valkyrie* collapsed as its real-world analog sagged slowly to the ground. Beyond it, the computer identified another imaginary threat and another one after that. Kai, acting without thinking, sped through the targeting range. When the heat build-up in his 'Mech caused the heat monitors to rise from blue to green and then to yellow, he temporarily abandoned use of the autocannon and concentrated on using the lasers. Though they could do less damage—and the forward laser had a tendency to shoot low—they produced less heat for the 'Mech to dissipate.

At the end of the run, sweat pouring off him like rain, Kai laughed aloud. "I feel like I've been resurrected from the grave. That felt great!"

Rumble's reply fed back the enthusiasm in Kai's voice. "Jesus, Mary, and Joseph, that was bloody incredible. Your time/score ratio is only twenty points behind the base record—and that was with you compensating for a misaligned forward laser!"

Kai smiled broadly. "Thank you, Mr. Rumble." He wanted to make another comment, but hearing the pleasure in his own voice sent a haunting echo through his mind. *That was easy, Kai, because those targets weren't shooting back. You've excelled at a game, but nothing more. One mistake, one misstep in battle, and you'll be very, very dead.*

Kai sobered up. "We'll have to realign and recalibrate the forward laser. And I can't bypass a target, then take it out with the rear laser..."

Rumble sounded confused. "But you did that after you executed the standard maneuver to evade fire from a Savannah Master hover-craft. That's the toughest target we have on this course and you snagged it with a clean shot."

"It was sloppy and stupid. That's the sort of thing you might expect to see in an 'Immortal Warrior' holovid." Kai caught himself and filtered the anger out of his voice. *It's not his fault, Kai. You got carried away and got lucky. He's just commenting on your perform- ance.*

Kai forced some levity into his voice, though he no longer felt pleased with himself. "Have to remember the basics, Sergeant, and that's what these training runs are for. Let's leave the flashy moves for fighters on Solaris and the holovids."

"Yes, sir."

"And let's downplay the fact that this is *Yen-lo-wang* and how well I did on this run. In fact, if we could downplay who my father is, I'd appreciate it. I don't want some idiot who thinks he's a hero to be challenging me to timed runs through this course just to prove how tough he is."

"Got it. See you down in the 'Mech bay, Stall 1F00."

"Roger." Kai switched off the radio as he turned the *Centurion* and headed back into base. *Be careful, Kai, and stay in control at all times. Your father programmed this 'Mech to remind you that he and your mother are proud of you. Don't do anything to change that.*

"Hound Deuce to Hound Leader. I have positive contact." Phelan punched an increase in magnification into the computer of his *Wolf-hound*. "Kenny Ryan might think he's a chip off the old block, but we'll put an end to that lie right now."

Lieutenant Jackson Tang answered immediately. "Copy that, Deuce. Is this confirmed?"

"Affirmative, Leader." *Dammit, Jack, I know the amount of iron in this rock has been playing hob with our sensors.* "I have a vislight image at one thousand mag. I mark one *Locust* and one *Griffin* at a klick. Their gold paint scheme and red insignia stand out against the rocks. Want me to count pores on the pilots for you?"

The tone of Tang's reply was apologetic. "Negative, Deuce. Good work. I've got your position. We'll be working our way up."

Phelan glanced at his auxiliary monitor, where the computer displayed a diagram of the star system for a myriameter in radius around his position. Up near the top of the display, Phelan saw the icon representing the JumpShip *Cucamulus*, but it was only shown at half-intensity green. That meant the asteroids between Sisyphus's Lament and the ship prevented communications between it and Tang's lance of four 'Mechs. Likewise, the half-intensity red icon used to mark the last-known position of Captain Wilson and the company's other two lances meant those other 'Mechs were incommunicado.

"Hound Leader, do I sit put until we establish a commlink with the base, or do I move in? I have cover out another five hundred meters." Phelan punched up a data feed and had the computer relay it to Jack Tang's *Blackjack*.

"Hold on, Deuce. The data feed is coming across fuzzy. Let's try to stick together on this. Don't want you jumped like you were back on Gunzburg. I'm one ridge behind you. Trey and Kat are coming up to your left."

The young mercenary frowned. *I guess I deserved that*. "Roger, Leader."

Phelan wiped his sweaty palms against the ballistic cloth covering of his cooling vest. His right hand brushed the cool metal of the belt-buckle Tyra had given him. He smiled and adjusted the Mauser and Gray M-43 needler pistol on his right thigh. He knew that if his cockpit module were breached, this cold rock had just enough of an oxygen atmosphere to rust the rocks and let him freeze to death if no help came. *Even if I could draw the pistol with frozen fingers, it wouldn't do me any good. Somehow, though, it is comforting to wear it. It must be the superstition of routine that makes me feel that way. Strapping the thing on is the only normal piece of this whole operation.*

The *Cucamulus* had arrived in The Rock system at a pirate jump point. Because of the massive gravitational forces and subsequent warping of space around stars, JumpShips were limited to entering star systems at a "safe" distance—"safe" being dependent on the size and energy level of the star. Most JumpShips appeared at the apex or nadir jump points located directly above or below the stellar poles because those were the most efficient places to unfurl the ship's solar collectors to recharge the Kearny-Fuchida jump drive. While the Jump Ship recharged, the DropShips made the long journey insystem from the jump point.

Pirate points were jump points a safe distance from the sun, but calculated to be on or near the star's orbital plane. This placed the JumpShip much closer to a system's planets, but also put the ship at much greater risk during jump. Pirate points had to be calculated exactly because of the increased amount of matter located in and around the planets. In a system consisting mostly of asteroids, like The Rock System, a JumpShip captain had to be a genius or crazy to bring his vessel in at a pirate jump point.

Janos Vandermeer, Captain of the *Cucamulus*, could qualify as either. He brought the *Cu* in close to the largest asteroid. Known as The Rock, it had given its name to the whole system. It had an atmosphere that made it habitable, and aside from the need to harvest water from the iceballs floating in the asteroid belt, it was supposed to be a pleasant place. Kenny Ryan's pirates had just begun to use it as a base, and the Kell Hounds hoped to catch them by surprise by bringing the *Cu* in close.

When the ship appeared insystem, the initial scans picked up no communications at all from The Rock. Vandermeer had ordered an immediate scan of the surrounding area and got snippets of radio contacts from several sites in the asteroid belt. Captain Wilson deployed her forces and slowly began a sweep of the asteroids best suited to supporting a pirate band's secret haven.

And we got Sisyphus's Lament. After five hours of humping up and down these iron mountains, thank God we got something. Phelan glanced sourly at his display, then punched up another increase in magnification. "Holy Mother of God, Jack, I mean Hound Leader. Ryan's folks are running from something. I have definite visuals on lasers going in and out and something I mark as long-range missile fire incoming."

Over across the valley, Phelan saw a small, birdlike *Locust* ducking and dodging between reddish mounds of rock. The awkwardness of its gait was accentuated by the large hops the asteroid's lighter gravity allowed it. Missiles arced up and over the hills behind it, peppering the whole area around the fleeing 'Mech with explosions. Staggered barrages herded the *Locust* diagonally across the hillside, then another 'Mech appeared in a narrow pass between two bluffs.

Phelan frowned heavily as the computer sharpened and tried to label the image of the new 'Mech. Confused, the computer identified the 'Mech first as a *Catapult*, then almost immediately reclassified it as a *Marauder*. *It's got that hunched-over torso with the bird legs common to both designs, all right. And it's got the* Catapult's *wing-mounted LRM launchers, but it also has the* Marauder's *weapon pods. And I've never seen that flat gray color scheme before, either. Who and what the hell is it?*

The unidentified 'Mech jabbed both blocky pods at the *Locust*, sending out twin ruby lasers to skewer the *Locust's* right flank. The first beam melted the armor from the *Locust's* torso, making it drip steaming to the asteroid's surface while exposing the 'Mech's skeleton and internal structures.

The second beam stabbed through the hole the first had made. Its fiery touch ignited the machine gun ammo stored in the 'Mech's chest, then destroyed the *Locust's* gyrostabilizers. As the light 'Mech's right side sagged in on itself, the 'Mech stumbled and rolled down the hillside. Its headlong spill ended with a jarring collision against a huge iron boulder the color of dried blood.

Three more of Ryan's bandit 'Mechs broke from cover and tried to rush across the valley toward Phelan's hidden-watch position. Two of them, the humanoid *Griffin* he'd seen earlier and another humanoid 'Mech, a *Panther*, darted from cover to cover. Both pilots used their 'Mechs' jump jets to quickly cross areas strewn with rocks too small for cover, but large enough to slow their sprint speed. Bringing up the rear came another humanoid 'Mech. Instead of arms, it sprouted twin-barrelled weapon pods. Larger than either the *Griffin* or *Panther*, and without jump jets, it moved more slowly than either of its compatriots. Phelan sensed the pilot's panic as he guided the *Rifleman* down the hillside and discovered he'd boxed himself in.

"Hound Leader, continue your present heading to make the plain. We've got help trapping the rats."

Confusion rang through Jack's voice. "Who...what?"

Phelan shrugged and moved from cover. "I can't identify our help, but they're on the ridge a kilometer off, driving Ryan toward us."

Tang laughed lightly. "Enemy of my enemy is my friend?"

Phelan saw Tang's black and red *Blackjack* appear down on the edge of the plain. Tang's barrel-chested, humanoid 'Mech had arms that ended in the autocannon muzzles, with the muzzle of a medium laser riding piggyback on the outside of the forearm. The scout lance leader wove his 'Mech through the dolmen at the nearest edge of the plain, closing on Ryan's 'Mechs without being seen.

Opposite Tang's position, two more strange-looking 'Mechs entered the battlefield. Phelan's computer again vacillated in assigning a label to the new machines. *It's calling them* Warhammer*s because of the chassis type, but the addition of* Marauder-*type arms instead of the particle projection cannons is giving it fits.* Both 'Mechs moved in on the trapped *Rifleman*.

Ryan's *Griffin* turned its attention to Tang's approaching *Black-jack*. Phelan tightbeamed a warning to his Lieutenant, then brought his 'Mech around from behind the outcropping he'd been using for cover. Opening a widebeam broadcast, he snapped a challenge at the pirate captain. "Over here, you excuse for retroactive birth control. We're the ones you said would never get you. Move it. Let's prove natural selection was correct."

The *Griffin* reoriented itself toward him, then Phelan saw it freeze for a moment. The *Wolfhound* Phelan piloted had a humanoid form and walked upright, but its unusual silhouette gave most enemy pilots reason to pause. Its right wrist ended in the muzzle of a large laser, and three medium laser ports dotted its scarlet chest in a triangular pattern. Most startling, however, was the 'Mech's head and cockpit assembly whose design accented and heightened the implied threat of the *Wolfhound*'s lean deadliness.

The head had been crafted for both image and function. Its jutting muzzle and twin viewports combined with the upthrust triangular sensor panels on either side to give the *Wolfhound* a canine appearance. Phelan had taken the image one step further and painted the 'Mech's muzzle to appear that the war machine was baring white fangs in a fierce snarl. Aluminum strips inlaid beneath the paint job outlined the teeth so that the 'Mech's wolfish grin appeared even on magscan and infrared sensor modes.

Phelan started his 'Mech down the hillside as Tang's *Blackjack* broke from cover and raised both its arms. The 'Mech's twin autocannons fired salvos at the pirate *Panther*. Phelan's computer marked the distance between the *Blackjack* and the *Panther* as 800 meters, putting the shot at the extreme edge of Tang's effective range. Despite the difficulty, Tang hit with one of his two shots, pulverizing armor plates over the *Panther*'s heart.

Picking up speed, Phelan worked his way through the debris scattered over the plain's near side. As he saw it, Ryan seemed more intent on running from the 'Mechs pursuing him than evading the Kell Hounds. *It's his funeral...* With each jump, the *Griffin* came closer and closer to Phelan.

As the range dropped to 600 meters, Phelan brought his 'Mech to a stop and crouched behind the last house-sized boulder between him and the smooth valley floor. *One more jump and you're mine. Five hundred meters may top out my range on this large laser, but if Jack can hit at max, so can I. Come on, Kenny Ryan, let's get it over with.*

Phelan's right hand moved the joystick that dropped the golden crosshairs onto the *Griffin*'s broad chest. A dot in the center of the cross flashed red. Phelan hit the firing stud beneath his right thumb and felt a wave of heat wash through the cockpit as the large laser unleashed its beam of coherent light.

The coruscating beam stabbed into the *Griffin*'s left shoulder, blasting away steaming shards of half-melted ceramic armor. As though unsatisfied with the armor it had destroyed, the beam's terrible energy cut through the myomer muscles on the 'Mech's upper arm, which split like hunks of meat being torn to pieces by some beast. Lastly, the beam heated the ferro-titanium humerus to the point where it glowed white, further melting myomer muscles.

Ryan hit his jump jets at the last second, but it did nothing to mitigate the damage. The abrupt take-off wrenched the damaged arm badly, snapping the metal bone and sending the severed limb flying.

Suddenly unbalanced, the *Griffin* reeled like a drunken acrobat and slammed into the ground on its right shoulder. The jump jets pushed the one-armed 'Mech across the plain, leaving sparks and armor plates in its wake until Ryan finally shut them down.

Phelan stared at the *Griffin's* wreckage. *My large laser shouldn't have done that much damage! Those other guys must really have softened them up.* Phelan shifted his vision to the *Panther* Tang was sparring with. *Yeah, it's been hit all over, but most of the damage has been done to the legs and arms.*

A cold chill ran down his spine as Phelan realized the *Griffin* and the *Rifleman* had been similarly savaged. *Either those other guys are very unlucky, or they're placing shots with greater care than almost any MechWarrior this side of Jaime Wolf or my father.*

As if they had read his thoughts, the three unknown 'Mechs moved in. The one that had brought the *Locust* down came to a stop just over nine hundred meters from the *Panther* and brought both pods up. Twin large-laser beams flashed out and caught the *Panther* in the back of its thighs. What little armor still remained on the pirate 'Mech's legs vanished in a cloud of ceramic steam. Myomer muscles ran like water and boiled away where they touched the titano-magnesium femurs that held the *Panther* upright. The lasers amputated the *Panther's* legs with surgical precision. Its legs cut out from under it, the *Panther* smashed flat on its back and did not move as the dust stirred up by its fall quickly drifted down to coat it with a red blanket.

"Blake's Blood! Did you see that, Phelan?" A tremble in Jack Tang's normally calm voice betrayed his unease.

Phelan stared at the computer projection of the range and damage done to the *Panther. Seven hundred meters for a large laser! That's impossible! They can only hit at 450 max.* He hit a button that opened a tight channel between him and Hound Leader. "I don't like this, Jack. Keep Trey and Kat out of this. Jesus Christ Almighty, look at what they've done to the *Rifleman!*"

The twin 'Mechs moving in on the last operational pirate machine simultaneously let fly with short-range missile barrages and bursts from their dual autocannons. The missiles covered the trapped *Rifleman* with explosions. The blasts staggered the machine and opened cratered wounds in its armor, which oozed melted metal. The pilot, fighting for control, somehow managed to keep the *Rifleman* on its broad, flat feet.

Phelan suddenly found himself hoping for the impossible, that the *Rifleman* could win out.

The gray 'Mechs it faced did not give the pirate a chance. Sparks lanced from the barrels of his guns as one of the pilots walked his autocannon fire along them and into the *Rifleman's* right shoulder. Armor flew in a blizzard from the damaged limb, then an explosion flipped the arm up and out. It cartwheeled through the air, bouncing off several rocks before it crashed to the ground.

The second mystery 'Mech raked one stream of autocannon shells across the *Rifleman's* belly. The projectiles ripped jagged scars in the 'Mech's armored flesh while the other autocannon's destructive fire gnawed away at the *Rifleman's* already-mauled left shoulder. It sliced through the remaining armor and drive mechanisms with the ease of a razor carving flesh. The 'Mech's left arm lurched, then dropped toward the ground, only to be jerked to a halt by useless drive chains and belted links of autocannon ammo. Swinging slowly back and forth, the arm dangled like an ornament, mocking the *Rifleman's* once-formidable destructive capabilities.

"Hound Deuce, I'm going to hail these guys. I'll offer them the salvage on these 'Mechs. Maybe they'll give us Kenny to take back and collect our pay."

Fear boiled up from Phelan's gut. "Jack, don't. Get the hell out of here." He started running the *Wolfhound* forward. *Move it, Jack! They're up to something!*

"Get back here, Phelan! That's an order!" Anger rippled through Tang's voice. "Dammit, follow my orders just for once!"

"And let you die? No way. Move it, Jack! Jump out of there!"

The two 'Mechs that had dusted the *Rifleman* locked their weapons down on the *Blackjack* in the plain below them. As they triggered their bursts, the *Rifleman* shot at both of them with its torso-mounted medium lasers. At the same time, Tang hit his jump jets, sending his 'Mech into the thin atmosphere on silvery ion jets.

The *Rifleman's* attacks caught the mystery 'Mechs by surprise, spoiling their aim somewhat. Still, despite the distraction, the range, and Tang's jump, one of the pilots managed to hit with both autocannon shots. The depleted-uranium slugs zipped up the back of the *Blackjack's* left leg. Its armor peeled off and fell away as if it were diaphanous silk instead of tons of ceramic armor. A silver spray of ions shot out at the back of the *Blackjack's* thigh, starting the 'Mech into a slow spin.

"Feather the right jet, Jack! This rock's light gravity and thin air mean you can go further. Get clear!" *He'll make it if that other 'Mech doesn't take a shot at him!* Bursting into the open, Phelan turned toward the first gray 'Mech he had seen. He brought the *Wolfhound's* large laser up and triggered a shot, but being beyond his maximum effective range, the shot did nothing.

The first gray 'Mech launched two flights of LRMs at the slowly spinning *Blackjack*. Moving at ten times the damaged 'Mech's speed, the lethal rockets slammed into it mercilessly. Explosions wreathed both legs in golden-red flame, then a silver corona ripped the fireball in half. As the brilliant light of uncontrolled jump jets vanished, taking the *Blackjack's* legs with it, the airborne 'Mech's arms flailed helplessly to counter the backward somersault the missiles had given it.

Phelan tried to turn away as Jack's 'Mech tumbled to the ground, but he could not tear his eyes from the display. The 'Mech's leg stumps slammed into the ground first, scoring deep furrows in the planet's surface. The sudden stop reversed the 'Mech's rotation and smashed it face-first against a rusty hillock. Armor flew whirling in uneven clumps, then the *Blackjack's* domed head sheared off. It bounced halfway up the hill as the torso flipped and twisted awkwardly. The *Blackjack's* body ripped itself apart as the autocannon ammo nestled in its breast detonated.

Hot, salty tears poured down Phelan's cheeks as he cut his 'Mech to the right. The first 'Mech's twin lasers burned parallel tracks through where he had just been, reducing iron ore to glowing slag. *There, dammit, you missed! You're not invincible*.

Something inside his head screamed at him that what he was doing was suicidal, but another part of him didn't care. Yet his awareness of the hideous threat posed by these unidentifiable 'Mechs made him key a dump of his battle recorder's data and create a simultaneous battle-feed to a widebeam broadcast. He pumped extra power into the broadcast, draining it away from the *Wolfhound's* rear-arc medium laser. "Trey, Kat, anybody. I hope like hell this makes it out. Get clear. This data is more important than getting killed to avenge either one of us."

Phelan dipped the *Wolfhound's* left shoulder as if preparing to cut back that way, then broke even more sharply to the right. The 'Mech he faced again sent two laser blasts sizzling through the space he should have occupied.

"Your average is falling, friend, and your heat has to be building up." Phelan glanced at his own heat levels and found them hovering on the edge of the yellow cautionary zone. "You can dish it out with all those weapons, but that means you can't be carrying much armor. Now let's see if you can take as good as you give!"

The computer's range indicator put Phelan at 350 meters and closing fast. Phelan planted the *Wolfhound's* right foot and cut to the left, then only two steps later, planted the left and dashed straight in at his target. The other pilot, determined not to miss a third time, had spread his 'Mech's arms apart to have one weapon available no matter where Phelan moved—as long as it wasn't straight up the middle.

Laughing triumphantly as the enemy's large lasers flashed past on either side, Phelan dropped his targeting sight straight on the 'Mech's jutting beak. He stabbed his thumb down on the large laser's firing stud and tightened his fingers on the buttons for the medium lasers. *Got you!*

The large laser hammered into the enemy 'Mech's left side. It peeled back armor, and for a moment, Phelan hoped against hope it had pierced the 'Mech's armored hide. As his medium lasers stitched the 'Mech's left arm and leg with stinging ruby bolts, his heart began to sink. *All I'm getting is armor! But that's impossible...Any 'Mech hauling that much of an arsenal should have paper-thin armor. It's crazy.*

The gray 'Mech's two gunnery-pods converged and focused on the *Wolfhound*. The dual large lasers vaporized all the armor on the *Wolfhound*'s broad chest the second they touched it. Phelan's computer barely had time to update the diagnostic display on the secondary monitor when four medium lasers, two mounted beneath the larger lasers on the arms and one each on the sides of the 'Mech's chest, impaled the Kell Hound 'Mech.

Searing waves of heat swirled up through the *Wolfhound*'s cockpit as the lasers destroyed the magnetic shields controlling the 'Mech's fusion-reaction power plant. A rainbow of warning lights ignited the command console and a warning siren began to wail. "Reactor detonation inescapable," shouted the computer. "Eject, eject!"

Phelan slapped his right hand on a large square button. He heard two explosions beneath him and felt them jolt up through his command couch and pound his insides into aching jelly. An invisible hand jammed him down into the couch and snapped his helmeted head back against the padded headrest. A roar filled the cockpit, drowning out the warning siren's screams, and the *Wolfhound*'s escape module lifted free of the 'Mech's doomed torso.

Phelan jammed his right foot down against the pedals at the foot of his command couch. That boosted thrust through the control jet on the right side of the *Wolfhound*'s head, hurling the escape pod up and to the left. He pushed the burn for three seconds, then poured on the left thrust to get as much altitude as he could.

Below, on the asteroid's surface, the headless *Wolfhound* lumbered forward. The fires burning in its chest silhouetted the 'Mech's skeleton. Then a roiling ball of argent plasma freed itself from the engine casings and engulfed the *Wolfhound*'s torso. In a flash of blinding silver fire, it consumed the 'Mech from the knees up and let the lower legs trip and pinwheel across the ochre plain.

Phelan fought against the shockwave of the fusion engine's explosion, but it shook the *Wolfhound*'s head furiously and upended the muzzle. It also caused the escape pod to prematurely deploy its parafoil, which failed to expand properly in the thin atmosphere and became fouled as the pod slowly flipped up and over in a lazy imitation of the dying *Blackjack*.

Phelan pulled his feet off the thrusters and snapped the gyrostabilizers on line with the press of a button. The asteroid's inhospitable surface filled his viewports as a massive spark arced across the command console. Controls flickered and monitors died in a puff of acrid white smoke. As thick as it was, the smoke could not obscure the vision of the asteroid as it grew larger and larger.

Stabbing both feet down on the thrusters, Phelan threw his head back and braced for a collision. *Hope it's just the monitors that shorted out, not the jets themselves. This better work!*

Phelan Kell never found out if his effort did succeed, for the escape pod's third bounce across the surface tossed him against his restraining belts and one of them parted. Slewed half out of the command couch, he could do nothing to help himself as the fourth bounce smashed his neurohelmet against the command console and blackness stole his sight.

Book II

Claws of
the Beast

ComStar First Circuit Compound, Hilton Head Island
North America, Terra
15 September 3049

Myndo Waterly, Primus of ComStar, extended a hand to her visitor. "The Peace of Blake be with you, Precentor Martial."

The tall man genuflected with the same crisp motion he might have used to salute another warrior. Then he took her hand, allowing her fingers to curl over his index finger, and raised her hand to his lips. "Thank you, Primus," he said, staightening up. "And with you as well."

The ramrod-straightness of his stance made her marvel at his body's power despite age and the traumas inflicted in a long career. The black thong of his eye patch circled his head, holding his flowing white hair in check and covering the empty socket of his right eye. The crow's feet radiating from his left eye might have hinted at his age, but the sense of inner peace Myndo read in his stance contradicted it.

I fear my time as Primus has not allowed me to age as well as you. A soul-sucking weariness seemed to fill her bones with lead and make her feel as though each breath were drawn from a vacuum. *Your calm is your power. Is this something the years in that Combine monastery granted you, or did you pick it up during your training in the ways of ComStar?*

Myndo forced herself to smile as she slipped her right hand into her left sleeve. "Before we begin, I wish to congratulate you."

The Precentor Martial looked confused. "Congratulate me?"

"Today you are 78 years old. That is quite an achievement,

69

Anastasius Focht."

Focht folded his arms across his chest as though warding off a chill. "I suppose it is. My birthday, that is. That is so much a part of my old life, though, that I hardly consider it. Really, I mark my life as starting with my conversion." A smile caught at the corners of his mouth. "That makes me less than a quarter of my chronological age."

Hiding her envy behind a mask of friendly pleasure, the Primus said, "Then you are truly blessed with the Peace of Blake."

The Precentor Martial acknowledged her kind words with a courteous bow, but his grin faded. "I came as soon as my staff and I had completed our preliminary study of the material you sent. The suborbital plane had to change its reentry vector to get around some bad weather in the gulf or I would have been here sooner."

"Did you find the material as disturbing as I did?"

"Yes, Primus. Perhaps even more so. I found the reports of fighting in the Periphery curious."

Myndo arched a brow. "Obviously. If I had not found the messages entrusted to our center at Verthandi unusual, I would not have sent copies down to you and then summoned you away from the training exercises in Azania. My concern was due to the Kell Hounds spending so much of their own money to transmit a message to their home base."

Focht opened his hands. "Battling in the Periphery, especially in the area of the Oberon Confederation, is not at all remarkable. The warring bands of pirates out there generally let people know when they've stomped on a rival or sent a mercenary unit home with a bloodied nose. Granted, their reports seldom check out in terms of casualties or 'Mechs lost for either side, but the outcome of the battle is seldom in error because the losers cannot afford to advertise their weakness."

The Precentor Martial began to pace, his white robe gathering and clutching at his long legs as he moved back and forth. "In this case, we've not heard from Kenny Ryan, which means he did not win this contest with the Kell Hounds. Nothing short of his death would prevent him from bragging about a victory. The Kell Hounds themselves have acknowledged defeat, but deny it came at the hands of Ryan's band. That rings true, despite the fact that the Hounds only sent out a company to chase the pirates. Even without Morgan Kell, his nephew Christian, Dan Allard, or Akira Brahe leading them, the Hounds would have been more than a match for that lot of bandits."

Myndo found herself becoming irritated. "Your analysis eliminates some of the more obvious answers to the mystery, Precentor.

Could it be that Captain Wilson lied in her report to cover Phelan Kell's death? Certainly, the death of his son would make Morgan Kell very angry."

Focht's left eye narrowed as if summoning up an ancient memory. "That is true, and an angry Morgan Kell is not someone I would want to deal with, no matter what the circumstances. I would accept your explanation had the battle-recorder data not been appended to the message they asked us to send."

Myndo shook her head, then hooked a lock of hair back behind her left ear. "Not being a MechWarrior, perhaps I don't understand the significance you attach to that information."

Focht smiled indulgently. "Aside from the data being unique, the fact that it was broadcast is remarkable. Each 'Mech has a battle recorder that keeps track of everything from sensor inputs to a complete diagnostics record for the 'Mech. After a battle, providing the recorder remains intact, the action may be reviewed. When plugged into a simulator, for example, pilots can see exactly what happened in the battle, including all their monitors and instruments."

The Precentor Martial pressed his hands together. "Kell's broadcast was a desperate move, because sending the data out on such a widebeam meant his enemies as well as his friends could get it. Granted the transmission quality was bad, but that is more due to the electromagnetic properties of Sisyphus's Lament than any problem with the equipment at that point."

Something dreadful tugged at the corners of her consciousness, but the Primus could not identify it. "So, Morgan Kell's whelp does not have his father's nerves of steel and panicked..."

Focht raised a hand to stop her. "Phelan may not be his father, but that battle tape shows no lack of nerve. He identified the forces he faced as unusual in the extreme, and realized he would not escape that encounter. His broadcast was a message from the dead—a warning to those who survived."

The Precentor Martial clapped his hands once. "Computer, project the holographic reconstruction of the primary BattleMech from the Kell tape, clarified and at one-tenth scale."

In silent compliance, the computer materialized a holographic image of the *Catapult/Marauder* bastard that had broken the *Locust* and destroyed Phelan Kell's *Wolfhound*. Even at only a meter in height, the machine's image retained all its menace. *It feels so malevolent.* A shiver ran down Myndo's spine and she fought to keep revulsion from her face.

The Precentor Martial, however, was not looking in her direction.

He slowly circled the projection like a wolf stalking prey, his gaze flicking from point to point seeking out flaws in the design. When he found none, a smile crept onto his lips and he nodded with admiration and respect.

"Primus, I have taken to calling this model the Mad Cat. As with the *Catapult* 'Mech, the machine boasts two long-range missile pods, one on each side of the forward-thrust torso. It walks on bird's legs, which gives it a hopping-bobbing gait, though this pilot seems to have been able to conquer that tendency. Quite an achievement, with the low gravity on the asteroid. In addition to the standard *Catapult* features, two *Marauder*-type weapons pods have been added. They have large lasers over medium lasers. Two more medium lasers, one on each side of the torso and two machine guns mounted in the center torso, round out the weapons selection. Yes, a most impressive machine."

Indeed. With an army of such 'Mechs, we could make Blake's dream of a united humanity a reality in short order. Myndo stared through the image at Focht. "I shall order our armorers to modify our existing *Catapult*s to this configuration."

Anger creased the Precentor Martial's brow for an instant, then disappeared as if banished by the force of his will. "I am afraid that is not possible, Primus. As you saw in the battletape, Phelan Kell attacked the machine but failed to damage it. Were we to create a 'Mech with such an array of weapons, we would be unable to armor it sufficiently. On the other hand, if we gave it the armor it needed, the 'Mech would be unable to move because of the current power-to-weight ratios available in our fusion engines. In short, either this 'Mech has incredibly light but durable armor, or it has a power plant of a design surpassing anything we have to offer."

Myndo's mouth went sour. *New technology in the hands of someone other than ComStar!* "That's terrible!"

Focht's grim nod echoed her concern. "It gets worse. The ranges at which these new 'Mechs were able to hit their targets is 300 to 400 percent better than what our current targeting and delivery system allows. It also appears that their heat compensators are much better or else their pilots can tolerate higher levels of heat because the rate of fire shown would have virtually fried any 'Mech known in the Successor States."

Myndo chewed her lower lip to stop it from trembling. "Explanation?"

The Precentor Martial shrugged. "Their 'Mechs show evidence of technology beyond what we know. My advisors and I wrestled with the question of where these 'Mechs might originate and who piloted them right up until the time I left to join you here."

The Primus's dark eyes half-closed. "Are they Kerensky's army come back to haunt us?"

The Precentor Martial took a deep breath before answering. "That was one of the more popular theories we came up with, but some of the surface evidence seems against it. These 'Mech designs are alien to those the Star League army had when it abandoned the Inner Sphere three hundred years ago. When Kerensky's people left, they took with them support personnel, but no research scientists and no manufacturing facilities."

"As nearly as we know, Precentor Martial. With the slaughter of the intelligentsia that preceded the First Succession War, we cannot be certain who died that way and who had vanished beforehand."

Focht bowed his head to his Mistress. "Your point is valid, Primus. There are other reasons, however, and they also cast doubt on the Kerensky solution. For example, the paint scheme on the mystery machines is unlike that of any known Star League unit. More important, the most thorough scouting missions carried out on Kerensky's trail lost track of him over 130 light years beyond the Periphery borders. General Kerensky and his people are long gone from here."

Myndo's head came up. "Surely you cannot dismiss the return of Kerensky's people that easily."

Focht shook his head. "If I gave you the impression that we had easily ruled out the return of the Star League Defense Forces, I apologize. No, we considered it long and hard before setting it aside. Still, Primus, you should understand that 'the Return' is a bogeyman used to explain every unusual group that shows up in the Successor States. Wolf's Dragoons, for example, are the latest in a long line of groups tagged as having come from Kerensky—the Black Widow's surname adding much fuel to that fire. Even so, even if it were true, the Dragoons—and all the other groups before them—have only had 'Mechs with designs and features that date from the time of the Star League. Again, we have no evidence that Kerensky's people had the information or means to produce these new 'Mechs."

"I see." Myndo clasped her hands together, holding them at her waist in a pose of forced calm. "What, then, is the explanation you favor?"

The Precentor Martial hesitated for a moment. "Most of the explanations were mundane and ranged from a Periphery pirate band running across a hidden, Star League-vintage research station to a variation on any of a hundred 'lost colony' tales. Still, none of them possessed technology beyond that of the Star-League era. We need more evidence before verifying any conclusion, but I believe we must not rule out the possibility that these are non-humans."

That's impossible! Myndo's mind reeled at the thought of another sentient race because it pounded away at the foundation of her reality. She had been taught that mankind was the pinnacle of evolution, and was meant to rule the stars. ComStar, of course, would lead mankind to the fulfillment of its destiny. Her thoughts insisted that there could be no other sentients in the universe—but if there were, they would have to be destroyed.

Myndo glared at Focht. "Why would another species use 'Mechs so similar to ours?"

The Precentor Martial's quick smile unsettled her. "It is as simple as it is horrifying, Primus. This is a race that has mastered the ultimate evolutionary tool: conscious genetic manipulation. They adapt quickly and efficiently. They mold themselves to their environment and then, like any sentient species, they manipulate the environment to broaden the niche they have chosen."

Before she could voice an objection, Focht continued his explanation. "Recall, if you will, the protonaria from the Davion world of Gambier. Those multicelled creatures ingest and co-opt genetic material from their meals. In this way, when food is scarce, they eat plants and develop chloroplasts so they can produce their own food. When Gambier's orbit places that dust cloud between it and the sun, the protonaria live off the scavenger bacteria that live off the dying plants.

"If you remember, protonaria were in great demand as a novelty item forty years ago. People would raise them in an aquarium and feed them virus-laden solutions. The different viruses would contain the genes for coloration, including lucifrase, so a tank of protonaria would be a multicolored, swirling mass that could even glow in the dark."

Myndo's anxiety locked a frown onto her features. "Those are simple creatures, Precentor. Protonaria could hardly pilot 'Mechs."

Focht's quick nod marked his agreement with her. "Imagine a higher creature, Primus, one capable of more complex genetic assimilation. It would only need to obtain human genetic material to be able to assume our form. If it could consciously manipulate its development, it could even begin to maximize its new potential."

Myndo shuddered. "How would it get....Blake's Blood—Kerensky!"

The Precentor Martial nodded sadly, mourning the demise of a superior military mind. "As wild as it seems, we cannot discount the possibility that somewhere out there Kerensky and his people settled on a world that harbored these things and that it spelled the end for them. As we've not heard from Kerensky or his people, this could easily explain what happened to them."

His expression grew pained and his good eye focused distantly. "The assault could have come in any of a million different ways. To my mind, the most gruesome comes as a perversion of everything we hold dear. Imagine one of these creatures digging down into a grave and consuming just a piece of a dead body. Within a week or a month or a year—however long it took—the creature would become the person whose DNA it ingested."

Myndo's hands fell to her sides and clenched into fists. "The creatures would have been welcomed by the kin that had been left behind. Even if they remembered nothing of their former lives, their appearance would have been marked as a miracle."

"Worse yet," the Precentor Martial told her. "They appear as children and are adopted into families. Just like humans, they are educated and acculturated. Because of their ability to adapt, they have an enhanced survival rate. Because they can adapt to the heat of 'Mechs, and can manipulate their genetic code to make them better pilots, they quickly move into the armed forces, and at some point, they go to war with humanity."

He pointed to the Mad Cat 'Mech image. "They make technological breakthroughs that increase engine power while decreasing its size. They modify weapons systems to make their machines superior, and they destroy Kerensky's people in a world-by-world campaign that borders on genocide."

"Why would they come here?" Myndo demanded. "Why would they backtrack Kerensky here?"

Focht shrugged. "Many reasons are possible, but two suggest themselves right off. In doing what they have done, they have become human. They are coming here because we have the planets best suited to human life and we have everything that makes up human culture."

Myndo's expression eased as she realized a portion of the Precentor's argument. "You're saying that while they are likely to be bigger, faster, and stronger than us, they will be socially immature?"

Focht winced. "That's too broad a generalization, I think. Coming from a society of warriors, they are likely to be aggressive and militaristic, which is reason enough to respect and fear them. Though discipline bordering on the Draconis Combine's code of bushido is very likely, I would also guess that braggadocio, carousing, and gambling will also be seen as nearly sacred. Honor will be everything, which means they will be unprepared for guile and subterfuge."

Myndo exhaled slowly, trying in vain to release the tension in her body. "We must determine what they want and assess their ability to attain it."

Focht looked up. "I am prepared to head out at any time, Primus."

"No. You are too valuable to ComStar."

"I beg to differ, Primus." The Precentor Martial smiled warily. "My junior officers are more than capable of handling the training and drilling of our forces. I would also suggest, if this wildest of explanations is correct, that sending ComStar's highest military official as your representative to them would be seen as an overwhelming sign of respect. It could open them up to allow us to influence them. If the truth is more plain, I would assume a liaison with ComStar still would not be unwelcome."

Myndo hesitated, then nodded. "Very well. You will leave for the Periphery immediately." The Precentor Martial turned to depart, but Myndo stopped him. "Precentor, you said there were two possible reasons why the aliens would be coming to the Successor States, but you only stated one. What is the second?"

She saw the ripple of revulsion shoot through Focht's body as he faced around again. "It's the same reason the Kell Hounds never found the bodies of Phelan Kell or the Ryan pirates." He swallowed hard. "To maximize their potential, the aliens need more raw material. They are coming here to harvest mankind."

DropShip Devil's Island
Location unknown
Date unknown

Phelan Kell struggled impotently against the two men forcing him down into the chair. *Where the hell did they get these guys?* Though he'd never considered himself especially large or strong, he'd not been manhandled so easily since his childhood. Try as he might to twist his wrists free of his captors' grasp, he could not. *They almost seem happy that I'm struggling. I'm giving them something against which to measure themselves.*

His captors shoved him roughly down into the high-backed metal chair. They snapped cuffs over his forearms to hold his hands in place, then strapped his upper arms down and bound his legs. Both men moved with the efficiency of medtechs securing a patient, then stood and withdrew behind him, shutting the door as they left.

Phelan decided against testing his bonds. *These synthetic straps will give but won't break, and I can't do anything about the metal wrist-cuffs anyway. No sense in wasting the energy.*

He quickly took stock of the featureless room. Roughly three meters by three meters, the room and the chair bolted to the floor had been painted in a flat gray. Recessed overhead lights glowed softly and allowed Phelan just enough light to see his reflection in the room's only true feature. He sat facing a mirrored panel that made up the middle of the wall.

Phelan chuckled to himself. *Same color scheme as my cell and the hallway between here and there. The guys who run this home for wayward MechWarriors have no imagination. Still, it is nice to be free of that cell. If I have to spend another month talking to myself, I'll go crazy.*

He glanced down at his right wrist. A bracelet woven from synthetic white cord encircled his wrist. The soft material did not irritate his skin, nor was it tight enough to cause him any physical discomfort, but he disliked it nonetheless. *An ID tag or electronic locator I could understand, but a piece of rope? There's something unusual going on here, and I definitely don't like it.*

Static crackled through a speaker hidden in the ceiling. "Let the record show that this is the first interview with prisoner 150949L. The subject is male and appears to have recovered from the minor injuries sustained during his capture."

Phelan felt a shiver run down his spine as the voice described him in a detached, clinical way. *Injuries?* He felt a twinge of pain back between his shoulder blades, but he ignored it as old anger resurfaced. *I know I must have suffered a concussion because I can't remember anything after I hit Grinner's ejection button. Everything is a blank, including whatever hurt me.*

A harsh white spotlight flashed on and stabbed its beam down from over Phelan's head. A male voice clipped numbers and words off like an automaton. "150949L, state your name."

The voice hesitated, then repeated the request. "150949L, state your name." Though it delivered the words in the rapid-fire pattern of before, the tone had shifted almost imperceptibly from neutrality to a growing hostility.

Phelan stared directly into the reflection of his own eyes. "Phelan Patrick Kell."

An edge entered the voice. "Deception will not help you."

Phelan sat back against the chair, but tipped his head forward to shade his eyes. He already felt heat from the light collecting in his mop of black hair. "I am Phelan Patrick Kell."

"Very well." The tone implied belief that he was still lying, and suggested dire consequences would result, but it moved on. "Where is your codex?"

Phelan blinked at his own reflection. "My codex?"

"Where is your codex?"

The young mercenary frowned. "Explain what a codex is."

"Deception will not help you. We will go on with this until we are satisfied."

Phelan forced himself to unknot his hands. "I don't know what you are talking about."

"Who is your father?"

Phelan's expression eased. "Colonel Morgan Kell, Morgan Finn Kell."

"Who is your mother?"

"Salome Ward Kell."

The inflection change in the voice surprised Phelan, almost as much as his answer seemed to surprise the questioner. "Deception will not help you. Who is your mother?"

"Salome Ward Kell."

Another voice, clearly male, came through the speaker. "Does your mother claim a Captain Michael Ward of the Star League Defense Forces?" The second voice gave off more feeling, and Phelan almost instantly felt a desire to please that person with his answer.

Easy, Phelan. Be careful. This is the standard good guy/bad guy interrogation technique. He stared forward at the glass. "Yes, on both sides of the family. Her father and mother were distant cousins."

The harsh voice snapped a quick question. "What does the name Jal mean to you?"

The irritation in the harsh voice infected Phelan. "How the hell should I know?" Even as he snarled his answer, something nibbled at the back of his mind. "Wait! Jal was Michael Ward's son. Someone said he took off with General Kerensky in his father's place."

Curiosity seemed to fill the pleasant voice's next question. "Are you sure of this?"

Phelan shrugged as much as the restraints would allow. "As sure as I can be of ancient family history. We have it all written down somewhere so I never bothered to memorize it."

The harsh voice returned. "Where is your codex?"

Phelan ground his teeth. "What is a codex?"

Neither voice answered his question. The speaker went dead, and for a second, the irrational fear that he had been abandoned shot through Phelan like a laser bolt. *Get a grip! You've been in solitary confinement for so long that any contact seems like a godsend.* He looked up at his own reflection. *Those questions and answers could have been programmed into a computer easily.*

Phelan grinned to himself and chuckled lightly. *Hell, you were only twelve when you cobbled together that sound-activated synthesizer. When your mother opened the door to your room to check on you at night and the hinges squeaked, the synthesizer made those sleepy sounds and snores that convinced her you were asleep. At least, it fooled her for a week while you learned how to play poker in the bachelor Officers Quarters.*

He glanced at the silvery mirror again. *Nothing in those voices or words that proves them to be human-generated. Especially the harsh one. If that is a human voice, its owner has a serious attitude problem.*

The pleasant voice again crackled through the hidden speaker. "Please forgive the delay. I would like to keep this initial debriefing friendly. Do you think this is possible?"

"Sure."

"Excellent." Phelan heard some clicking come over the speaker —*the sound of fingers on a keyboard?*—before the next question. "You are certain you have no knowledge of a codex."

Phelan shook his head. "It doesn't manipulate a hologram for me. I've no recollection of ever having heard of it at all."

"A codex is a readout of your genetic pattern. It is quite important."

Phelan chewed his lower lip. "I still don't know what a codex is, but I have had some genotyping. I mean, everyone in the mercenary company has. We use it for identifying people in the event of a death. But that's all kept back with headquarters."

"Interesting." The voice seemed grateful for Phelan's frank answer. "You mention being a member of a mercenary company. What is it?"

Phelan rocked back in the chair. "The Kell Hounds." *How odd. Everyone knows about the Kell Hounds.* "I serve in the Second Regiment."

Shocked disbelief flowed through the pleasant voice. "*Two* regiments. This mercenary band has *two* regiments?"

Unfocused dread gnawed at Phelan's guts. *He sounds surprised and unsettled by that news, but the Hounds have had a second regiment for the last nine years. When Katrina Steiner died, her will pledged enough money to raise another regiment for the Hounds. The original bequest left to my father and his brother by Arthur Luvon, Katrina's husband, was how they formed the original Kell Hounds. Katrina's money doubled the Hounds' size and gave us far more financial freedom than we'd known before.*

He looked up at the mirror and forced himself to keep his expression as relaxed and friendly as appropriate under the circumstances. Behind his eyes, though, his mind had already dropped filters in place to keep from spilling damaging data until he could assess the threat his captors posed. Phelan had assumed, when taken and imprisoned, that he was a captive within an internecine Periphery war. He was not so sure now.

The pleasant voice had regained its composure. "You said you served with a mercenary band with two regiments. Are those Battle-Mech regiments?"

Phelan nodded earnestly, ignoring the cold sweat running down his spine. "Yes. I know, that makes us one of the smaller merc units, but we try to make up in quality what we lack in quantity." His heart pounded in his ears as he waited to see what effect his lie had on his interrogator.

"And these units are truly that: mercenary? They have no allegiance to a lord?" Doubt had bled out of the voice, but an urgency seeped in to replace it, along with something else.

Careful, Phelan. There's a lot riding on this answer. The young mercenary swallowed hard. "As mercenaries, their loyalty is to their employer first. But," he rushed to add, "many mercenaries will not accept offers from nobles they consider unscrupulous. Many don't like doing crowd control or acting as a police force, either. Mercenaries fight wars and that's it."

The harsh voice returned full of triumph. "But was not your pursuit of the pirates a police action?"

The condescending tone of the question stung Phelan. "You ask that as if pursuing bandits is somehow less than honorable. If it is, why were you out there?" Phelan snorted derisively. "At least my companion and I were evenly matched against our enemies. It would have been a fair fight without your interference."

The mirror shook as something hit it from the other side with a muffled thump. Phelan brought his head up and smiled broadly at his unseen interrogators. *If they reacted so well to that small a verbal jab, wait until I really stick it to them.*

The pleasant voice resumed the questioning, but the lighter tone of the queries told Phelan he'd won some respect by nettling the owner of the harsh voice. Though the harsh voice did not return as the session wore on, Phelan realized from the way some of the questions were phrased that Hothead—as Phelan mentally tagged him—was still in the room and listening. Phelan's defenses came up whenever he heard a hostile question, which happened often enough to make him give away very little information.

The middle-aged man leaned against his high-backed chair. His left elbow rested on the chair's arm, his left hand stroking his white moustache and goatee. As his blue eyes followed the lines of text flowing up over his data terminal, the monitor's amber glow brought golden highlights to his short white hair. As the information ended, he tapped a key with his right hand and shut the terminal down.

He looked up, causing the room's only other occupant to pull himself to full attention. With a slight wave of his right hand, the older man allowed the other to relax. "This is most interesting, Star Commander. Most of the intelligence our people have gathered from the Periphery's inhabitants has been exaggerated nonsense based on centuries-old rumors, wishful thinking, and nightmares. This Phelan Kell, on the other hand, has knowledge and is intelligent enough to conceal it."

The Star Commander nodded in agreement. In the room's muted light, his dark gray uniform appeared black and the small red stars on his collar remained hidden until light flashed scarlet from them. "I agree, my Khan. The physicians who repaired the damage done to him estimate his age to be between eighteen and twenty-three years old, confirming his statement that he is eighteen. As we saw in the battle tapes of the engagement where we captured him, he handles a 'Mech with some skill."

The older man nodded sagely, his left hand again rising to toy with his goatee. "What do you make of his name being the same as that of the mercenary unit? Is he an orphan they adopted?"

The Star Commander shrugged. "Neg, my Khan. It would be impossible for an adoptee to earn a name so quickly, quineg? It would seem to me that he is related to the family that owns the unit. I could further suppose that he is in some disfavor because he was given service in the Periphery. Perhaps, as we have done, the Kell Hounds placed a training cadre out hunting vermin."

"Possible, Star Commander. Very possible." The older man smiled. "Do not reprimand either Vlad or Carew for their performances in the interrogation. Vlad's outbursts were unfortunate, but he has given this Phelan a focus for his own anger. Vlad will continue to be part of the inquiry team for this subject. Carew's surprise concerning the mercenaries caused Kell to be cautious, which tells us he has information he thinks is important. That, too, is valuable."

"Do they continue to question him as is?"

The old man paused for a moment, then nodded slowly. "Aff. Let them work unaided for the next month. By the time the DropShip *Orion* returns here, the interrogators will have collected enough data to alert us to areas where he has information he does not want to give up. At that time, with more experienced people, we will do what we must to learn all that Phelan Kell can tell us."

Kommandant Victor Steiner-Davion adjusted the picture of his family on the corner of his desk. Taken about a year and a half before he left the New Avalon Military Academy to return to the Nagelring, it represented the last time the whole family had been together. Victor, his father, and his hulking brother Peter stood in the back row. His mother sat in front of Hanse, with Katherine on her right, Arthur on her left, and little Yvonne sitting at her feet. Victor centered the portrait between his data monitor and the lamp clamped onto the right side of the desk, then leaned back in his chair to study its effect.

With a frown, he leaned forward to shift the picture back to the other side of the walnut desk. *Is having this picture going to rub it in that I've got a battalion command because of who I am? Renny and the others in my class graduated Leftenants and have lance commands. I'm a Kommandant and get to oversee a whole battalion. The damnable thing is I know I can handle this responsibility, provided I get the chance. I want to be treated like everyone else in the Federated Commonwealth's Armed Forces, but it just ain't going to happen that way.*

A light knock sounded on his door, pulling Victor back to reality. He quickly twisted the picture so its back was to the door, then straightened his uniform. "Enter."

A slender, sandy-haired man stepped into the room and snapped Victor a quick salute. "Hauptmann Galen Cox reporting, sir."

Victor quickly stood, cursing himself for not having done so before Cox entered the room, and returned the salute crisply. He noticed the Hauptmann's restless blue eyes taking in everything, but Cox's face gave no clue to his thoughts. Extending his hand, Victor greeted his visitor warmly. "I am pleased to meet you, Hauptmann Cox. I am Victor Steiner-Davion."

Cox met Victor's firm grip and pumped his arm strongly. It was not a contest of strength, but a comradely welcome that pleased Victor. *No need to prove himself stronger than me, yet no desire to toady up, either. Good. I like that.*

Victor waved Cox to one of the two yellow leather chairs across from his desk, but the Hauptmann demurred. "Is there something I can do for you, Hauptmann?" Victor asked.

"I'm reporting for duty, Kommandant. I am your aide."

Victor pressed his lips together into a thin line. "Hauptmann, don't take this as an insult or any reflection upon you or the impression you've created, but I already told Leftenant-General Hawksworth I don't want an aide." Victor pointed through the open door toward the other Kommandant offices further down the hall. "Just like the others, I'll make due with a clerk."

Cox nodded easily, but Victor knew the man had not surrendered. "Begging your pardon, sir, but the Kommandant is not like the others."

"An accident of birth does not make me different, Hauptmann. I will not have an aide just because I am the Archon's son. Do you understand that?"

The Hauptmann dipped his blond head again and turned from Victor. For a moment, Victor thought he had won—which surprised him—but then he saw Cox close the office door. Victor smiled to himself. *Now we're into the trenches.*

Cox again appraised Victor openly. "Permission to speak frankly, Kommandant."

Victor extended his hands palms-up. "Have at it, Mr. Cox."

"When I said you were not like the others, I was not referring to your lineage. If we assigned an officer to every blue-blood in the AFFC, we'd double the size of the officer corps and drop its efficiency by an order of magnitude. And, just for your information, Leftenant-General Hawksworth had nothing to do with my being here. He respected your wishes and made them known to the rest of the officers here."

Victor leaned forward on his desk. "If the General has not assigned you to me, and if you're not here because of my bloodlines, what the hell is going on?"

Cox's grin grew wider. "I was selected by the regiment's officers to be your aide."

"What!" Victor sank back down in his chair. "Since when did the army become a democracy?"

"Since officers fresh from the Academy are given a battalion command." Cox's grin faded as his look became stern. "Being out here on the Periphery is a joke to people back on Tharkad. Hell, you probably didn't want to be assigned here—which makes you *exactly* like most of the other officers in this outfit. Most of our lance commanders are fresh from school, just like you, and they're full of that graduation glow. For them, this assignment is a chance to show their potential so they can win a more glamorous assignment like guarding the Draconis border or kicking around some Free Worlders."

Victor felt his face flush as he recalled how he'd protested his assignment.

Cox moved toward the chair Victor had indicated earlier, but stepped behind it and rested his hands on its back. "Most Leftenants are easy to straighten out. We get into an engagement with pirates or bandits or a Rasalhague raiding party and step them through the fight. If they don't freeze up or faint at the first exchange, we give them orders and they execute them. That first fight is always rough on them, and generally rougher on the men and women they command, but they survive it if they listen and do what they are told. It's sort of military Darwinism in action."

Cox met Victor's stare head-on. "You, on the other hand, have a battalion to command. That puts more than thirty-five MechWarriors in your hands during a battle. There'll be confusion and there'll be chaos. If you can't handle it, people will die." Cox shrugged. "People don't want to die, so here I am."

Victor found himself sitting with his legs crossed and his arms folded around his chest. "And if I issue an order dismissing you as my aide?"

Cox's grin returned. "I think you'll find that order will get lost in the electronic shuffle around here."

Looking up, Victor felt himself being infected by Cox's contagious grin. *I want to be angry and insulted, but that'll just prove I need the keeper I've been saddled with. I appreciate the regiment's concern, and what's more, I can understand their reluctance to follow an unproven commander into battle. I must earn their respect, so if I want to be treated normally, I guess I have to start now.*

Victor chewed his lower lip for a moment. "So I'm stuck with you, whether I like it or not. Is that it, Hauptmann?"

Cox's grin became broader.

"Then I better like it." Victor stood and thrust his hand forward. "Pleased to have you as my aide, Hauptmann Cox."

Cox again shook his hand strongly. "Glad to be with you, Highness."

Victor waved off the honorific. "This is the AFFC, Hauptmann. Address me by rank or as Victor."

"Yes, sir, Kommandant."

Victor settled back into his chair. "How did they happen to select you for my aide, Mr. Cox?" He saw a strange spark in Cox's eyes, but the Hauptmann smothered it before Victor could identify it. He could guess, though. "This wasn't meant to be your command, was it? My appointment didn't rob you of a battalion command, did it?"

Cox shrugged nonchalantly. "I don't think so, or if it did, it was the best-kept secret on base. I got this position because I volunteered for it."

Victor raised an eyebrow. "You volunteered to nursemaid me? Why would you do that?"

Cox stretched out in the chair. "Well, when we got the news that you were coming to take over Kommandant Sykes's battalion, lots of people started grousing. You know how it works—one guy talks to another and he talks to someone else. All of a sudden what started out as a minor irritation becomes a crisis. It's like the story of the Mech-Warrior who needs to borrow an actuator-wrench to make a repair on his BattleMech. As he's walking back to the supply depot through a rainstorm, he becomes convinced that the Tech won't lend him the wrench. The more he thinks about it, the more worked up he gets. When he finally gets to the depot and finds the Tech, he screams, 'I don't want your damned actuator-wrench anyway!'"

Victor chuckled lightly. "I don't want your damned actuator-wrench anyway! It's been a while since my cousin Morgan Hasek-Davion told me that story, but I understand the situation completely. They had me built up into a monster that was going to get them all killed."

"But only after you'd transformed this unit into a bunch of kiss-ass courtiers waiting on you hand and foot," Cox said with a devilish glint in his eyes. Even as Victor winced, Cox continued. "Anyway, I thought that was getting out of hand, so I looked up your school and service file. Scores on exams never stopped a particle beam, but yours looked good enough to deflect a few. I figured if you were going to get a chance to live up to all that potential, someone would have to cut you some slack." He sat up tall. "Galen the Knife, that's me."

That, Galen Cox, means more to me than you will ever know.

Victor smiled and felt, for the first time since entering the Nagelring, that just a bit of the weight on his shoulders had been removed. "Thanks, Galen. I'll do all I can to be worthy of your trust."

"You'll do better than that, Kommandant," the blond man said, rising to leave. "I've read your file, remember? I hope like hell the rest of us can keep up with *you*…"

Location unknown
Date unknown

Phelan Kell tried to focus his eyes, but the huge disk of light burning above the table to which he was strapped sent searing photon barrages straight into his brain. The backlight was enough to illuminate some of the people standing around and over him, but he could recall no details nor keep track of how many there were. Doing its spongelike best to soak up the chemicals being pumped into him, his brain no longer worked right.

"State your name."

The harsh tone of the voice sparked faint recollections, but Phelan's desire to rebel against the command was fleeting. He managed to speak, despite the clumsy thickness of his tongue. "Phelan Patrick Kell."

"Phelan? Do you know what your alleged name means? Don't nod. Speak. Tell us what it means and why you have it."

"My name is Celtic and means wolf or 'brave as a wolf.'" Phelan's brow furrowed as he tried to remember what his parents had told him about choosing his name. "I was named Phelan for a friend of my parents and Patrick for my dead uncle." Out of control, he giggled, "And I am a Kell 'cause I am."

A wave of vertigo washed over Phelan. *They've juiced me good. I can't let them know what I know*...But stringing together even that much of a logical thought burned up his reserve of defiance, leaving him defenseless.

"Phelan, you have seen service in Rasalhague. How many regiments does Rasalhague have under arms? Include mercenary troops in this total." That new voice expressed a kind of dignified reserve that made Phelan label it the Confessor. *And the other one, that's Hothead*.

Phelan concentrated, letting his hatred of Tor Miraborg fuel his answer. "They have sixteen regiments under arms and a few mercenary companies, but those are employed mostly by independent lords."

Outrage filled Hothead's voice. "Why did you lie about this before?"

Hothead's fury gave Phelan more pleasure than the drugs flowing into his body. He smiled gleefully. "Because fooling you was fun."

The Confessor's voice cut off Hothead. "Phelan, how many regiments does the Draconis Combine have?"

Sadness welled up inside Phelan, pooling dark and heavy around his heart. "I don't know."

A soothing note entered the Confessor's voice. "But you must have an estimate. It must have been discussed during your schooling."

Phelan jerked as though a raw nerve had been hit. "No, no schooling. I don't like the Academy."

"Never mind the Academy. You do have an idea of the Combine's strength? Yes, I thought you would. Just between us, what do you think it is?"

Phelan tried to sit up closer to the silhouette he had assigned to the Confessor's voice, but the headstrap restrained him. Instead, he winked an eye in the voice's direction and dropped his own to a husky whisper. "Officially, the Snakes have 100 line units, but they've rebuilt the DCMS mostly in secret so it's hard to be sure exactly what's going on. My father also said that with the Genyosha and Ryuken training programs, the Combine's troops have become better."

"I see." The Confessor's tone dropped reflectively. "If the Combine's troops are so good, why have they not retaken Rasalhague?"

The young MechWarrior shrugged as best he could. "When Rasalhague went independent, Theodore Kurita fought for the Republic against his own renegade troops. Don't know why. Ask him."

"What about the Lyran Commonwealth? What have they under arms?"

Phelan squirmed uncomfortably at that question from the Confessor. *The Commonwealth is my home!* "I don't know."

Phelan heard a new voice coming from outside the circle of light. "Spikes right to the top of the scale, sir. He is blocking."

"What does his SPL blood level look like?"

"In the seventy-fifth percentile."

89

"Go to the eightieth, but give me a clock so I only keep him there for fifteen minutes." The urgency and command in the Confessor's voice drained away as he again addressed himself to his prisoner. "Phelan, we are all friends here. You can trust me. How many regiments does the Lyran Commonwealth maintain?"

Phelan felt as though he'd been reduced to the size of a micron, then tossed to the winds. The corded wristlet felt like a diamond saw against his flesh. He saw the ribbons that had once been his legs twist together and twist and twist until they knotted up and pain burned in his thighs. Then his neck elongated and his head plunged back down past his feet, hurtling ever faster toward the ground. When it hit, he felt it would splatter like an overripe fruit.

The Confessor snapped a command. "Back SPL off to the seventy-seventh percentile. He has no resistance, no chemo-immunity developed in him. He has a strong will. Nothing more."

Someone snapped his fingers. The sound was like a gunshot to Phelan's senses, but Hothead's voice quickly overrode it. "Tell me, Phelan, what happened to you at the Nagelring."

Phelan's resistance crystallized instantly. "No!"

"Freebirth!" cursed the man tending the interrogation monitors. "What? Are you getting spikes scaling up again?"

"I wish." A series of clicks came from the equipment. "Neg. Not a technical problem. I am getting full cycles off the scale here, not just spikes. He reacts as strongly to that question as someone does when forced out of their sibko."

Phelan latched on to the word *sibko. I know I've heard that before. What? Where? When? Who am I?*

The Confessor's voice helped him refocus himself. "The Free Worlds League has troops. How many regiments does it have?"

Phelan closed his eyes. "Seventy, probably. Andurien lost most of their units when they seceded, in the war with the Capellan Confederation, and then when Thomas Marik took them back into the League. Marik still has to keep troops there to keep the peace."

"And the Federated Suns...How many regiments do they have?"

Phelan frowned. *The Federated Suns and the Lyran Commonwealth have integrated their commands. They want to know about my home!*

"Resistance building, sir. He has linked the Suns with the Lyr-Com."

The Confessor's voice rasped quietly, sounding to Phelan like a knife being drawn from a sheath. "If you cannot tell me about the Federated Suns, we will have to know about the Nagelring."

"No! No, no, no, no, no..." Words falling meaninglessly from his lips, Phelan's consciousness ricocheted around in his skull. *No, no, no, not that.* Shame burned on his cheeks, then his anger broke like a fever and tears rolled from his eyes. *The Federated Suns is too big to hurt.*

"The AFFS has 103 regiments."

"He is still resisting."

Disappointment echoed through the Confessor's voice. "103 regiments and...?"

Phelan tried to hold his answer in, but cracks had developed in the dam he'd tried to build up. "The Davion and Steiner militaries have been merged into one and the whole thing is called the Armed Forces of the Federated Commonwealth."

"Good, very good, Phelan." Someone patted his leg reassuringly. "Keep up the cooperation and we can end this soon. How many regiments does the LCAF have?"

The mercenary's whole body tensed. He tried to withhold the information, but a voice inside his head whispered seductive arguments that gnawed away at his resolve. *What have the Lyrans ever done for you, Phelan? They humiliated you and cast you out of the Nagelring. They murdered DJ with their stupidity. Think of all the times you vowed you would avenge her if you had the force. You don't have it, but they do. All you have to do is tell them what they want to know and your shame will be absolved.*

Phelan felt as if a million fire-ants were marching over his body, feasting as they went. He searched his brain for the information on the Lyran Commonwealth's troop strengths, but instead he ran headlong into reasons why he could not give the Commonwealth up. *My father and mother are fanatical in their devotion to the Steiner family. Victor Steiner-Davion is my cousin. To betray the Commonwealth is to betray them, to betray everyone I love. I cannot!*

The Confessor's voice gained an edge. "Take him up to eighty and back down again immediately."

The mercenary heard the menace in those words and tried to brace himself for the drug's effect, but he could never have anticipated it. He felt a tremor begin at his feet and knew that a wave had begun in the kilometers of ribbon that made them up. Moving up beyond his knees, it built in intensity and coursed through his thighs. He saw his whole body flapping in a technicolor wind. As the power of the wave increased almost beyond endurance, it suddenly broke like a mighty explosion in his brain.

Over Phelan's scream of agony, the Confessor repeated the question. "How many regiments does the Lyran Commonwealth have?"

Phelan fought to resist, but the words had already reached his throat and tongue. "One-hundred fifty-three regiments. The sixty-five coming from Skye and Tamar are questionable in loyalty because the Archon has forbidden them to try to take back former Tamar Pact worlds from Rasalhague."

His body quivered and sobs wracked his chest, but nothing could free him from his bonds or his tormentors. Hothead's evil chuckle underscored and mocked the Confessor's strong voice. "Very good, Phelan. Now we will start again, from the beginning, and make sure everything tallies. Work with us and we will not have to hurt you again..."

Skondia
Federation of Skye, Lyran Commonwealth
31 December 3049

Drenched in sweat, Kai Allard rested his hands on his hips and raised his face to the sky. *These hills really make me wonder about my commitment to running.* He laughed to himself. *On Skondia, running isn't a commitment. It's a sentence!* He snaked his hands under the hem of his red t-shirt, raising it to wipe his face.

When he pulled the shirt down again, he saw her for the first time. Her black hair barely brushed the shoulders of the oversized gray sweatshirt she wore. The black and green body suit underneath hugged her long, well-muscled legs, the design's green elements swirling up her limbs like long blades of grass. With her right heel resting on a park bench, she leaned over and grasped the toe of her right shoe and pulled herself forward to touch her nose to her kneecap.

As she unfolded, she caught sight of Kai watching her and seemed to become self-conscious. Though she smiled, her blue eyes were wary as a cat's. She brought her arms close to her chest, obscuring the New Avalon Institute of Science crest on the sweatshirt, and began to perform waist-twists. "Hello."

"Sorry to startle you," Kai said. "I'd not expected to see anyone else here this early in the morning." He glanced out over the misty green valley where he'd just run. "They've got a beautiful exercise course set up here, but you couldn't tell that from the number of people using it."

He took a half-step forward and saw her drift back easily. He pointed at the tan canvas bag near her end of the bench. "Could you toss the bag to me? I'd like my towel."

Her reserve broke as she lofted the bag to Kai. "How well did you do?"

Kai frowned. "Pardon?"

She smiled and Kai instantly decided he liked that very much. "Your shirt…it's from the Twenty-fifth New Avalon Myriameter Run. How well did you do?"

Kai pulled a white towel from his bag and mopped his face. "Uh, I finished in the fifties."

She lifted her other leg to the bench and began to stretch. "Was that place or time?" Her question came without challenge or skepticism and that pleased Kai.

She's not yet decided if I am a liar or a fellow runner whom she can trust. "Place. My time was 43:35. I should have done better, but I died late in the race."

She laughed easily. "Heartbreak Hill!"

Kai matched her laugh with his own. "You know it? I mean you've run in the race?"

Her black air whipped back and forth as she shook her head. "No, not the race, just the course. I'm not much for competition." She straightened up. "That hill is a killer. It may only be a kilometer and a half back through Davion Peace Park to the finish line, but it might as well be a light year after that hill."

Kai hung his towel around his neck and raised one of his legs to the bench. A droplet of sweat rolled off his nose as he bent forward to stretch out his hamstring. "You're right. The hill is death itself. Still, running through the park, I got a lift from the Silver Eagle memorial."

"How is that?" She shuddered visibly. "That statue is so horrible. That dog's all torn up and obviously in pain. Just as obviously the panther is going to kill it. I found it depressing." Her face screwed itself tight with distaste. "It's so violent I don't see why it's in the Peace Park."

Kai shifted legs and bent forward until the muscle in the back of his other thigh almost screamed. *I remember when my Uncle Dan took me to the park and explained how the dog represented the Kell Hounds rescuing Melissa Steiner from a Kurita trap. Patrick Kell sacrificed himself to make sure his cousin Melissa could escape. The statue deserves to be in the Peace Park because people need to remember that great sacrifice is necessary for great gain.*

Kai looked over at her. "I understand your point, but I differ with it. I think the child the hound is protecting—and the rope rising into the

94

sky symbolizing the child's imminent rescue—makes it a hopeful display." He refrained from bragging about his family's connection with the statue. "In the race, I felt as torn up as the dog looks, but I pushed myself because I knew it wouldn't kill me and because I felt I owed myself the best finish I could muster."

"And I see your point." She stripped off the sweatshirt revealing the body suit's clinging tank-top. The muscles in her bare arms were well-defined and her flat stomach and smallish breasts marked her as a dedicated runner. She tossed the garment down on the bench. "Is it safe here?"

Shifting around, Kai leaned into the bench to stretch out his Achilles tendon and the muscles of his right calf. "Do you mean for you or the shirt?"

She gave him a half-grin. "The shirt. I may be just off the Drop-Ship, but I can take care of myself."

Kai chuckled lightly. "The shirt should be fine. Skondia's criminal element would consider it beneath them. Since this world's penal colony is located on that silvery moon over there, and the ambient temperature is zero degrees Centigrade, they go for the big stuff. An NAIS sweatshirt isn't worth it."

She followed his line of sight to a small silver ball hovering between two jagged mountain peaks near the horizon. "Escaping from there requires more than carving a laser pistol from a block of sodium tallowate." She turned back to Kai. "What do they call it?"

Kai met her gaze squarely. "The crims call it the Last Mistress, but the locals just call it Justice."

She frowned. "That's cold…"

Kai laughed. "No pun intended."

She shook her head emphatically. "No, no pun." She watched him for a moment, then nodded approvingly. "Not many people stretch out like they should after exercise. It's a good thing you're doing."

He nodded. "I don't want to be a tightened-up old man."

She frowned sympathetically. "Is there a family tendency toward that sort of thing? I mean, how are your grandfathers?"

Kai kept the smile on his face, but his mind was racing over his nearest ancestors. *Grandpa Allard is fine. I know it's a common story that he has a rare, untreatable form of Alzheimer's Disease, but that's so no one will try to kidnap him and pump information out of him. His years in the Ministry of Intelligence Information and Operations would make him a valuable resource to enemy intelligence agencies. But my mother's father, he was nuts for years before he finally died.*

After hearing all the things he did, and seeing what Romano Liao—I still can't warm to the idea of her as my aunt—has done to bedevil my mother, I can only hope I take after the Allard side of the family.

"One is dead, but neither had real problems. I just don't want to leave anything up to chance." He wiped his face again with the towel, then stuffed it into his bag. "Well, enjoy your run. Five klicks out, you'll hit a downhill stretch that looks inviting, but save something. Beyond it is a slope that makes Heartbreak Hill look like a speed-bump."

Suspicion crept into her voice. "And after that?"

"The hill's big brother."

"Thanks for the warning," she tossed back over her shoulder as she headed off along the running trail.

Kai watched until her head sank out of sight, then smacked the palm of his right hand against his forehead. *Idiot. She said she was just off a DropShip. She's probably not had time to make many friends and you don't have a date for the Marshal's reception tonight.*

He glanced at her crumpled t-shirt and wished he had pencil and paper to leave a message with it. Slightly angry with himself, Kai started back up the road to the Military Compound and the small house he shared with another Leftenant in the Guards. He stopped at the crest of the hill and searched vainly for a view of her. Then he abandoned his vantage point and retreated home, silently berating himself for not even getting her name.

"Blake's Blood, Kai!" Dressed only in a towel wrapped around his narrow waist, Bevan Pelosi pounded his fist against the door jamb. Steam still drifted from the shower stall beyond him, but his deep voice suffered no competition from the faucet's constant dripping. "How could you let such a woman get away?"

Kai shot his tow-headed housemate a daggered glance. "This is me we're talking about, Bevan, not you. I do not have your vast experience with women. Give me an opportunity and I just screw it up."

Bevan's hair hung in wet ringlets over his forehead but did not hide his frown. "I was thinking about this girl in the shower…"

"Hence the smile on your face," Kai quipped. "And the flush of your skin…"

"Wise guy!" Bevan made a face. "Why the hell didn't you just come back here and write a note, then drive back down to the park and leave it? You could've used my aircar. You know where I keep the keys."

Kai turned from the mirror and raised an eyebrow. "My dear friend, I actually thought of that this morning." Kai glanced at a waste receptacle by his desk. "I would have done exactly as you suggest except that your *guest* from last evening had already taken the keys so she could go out and buy all those things she put into that omelet this morning."

Bevan shrugged helplessly. "And don't think I don't appreciate your helping me eat that thing." He slapped a hand against his flat stomach. "Why is it that women want to fatten me up?"

"They probably want to slow you down long enough to catch you."

Pelosi's grin blossomed like a sunflower. "So many women, so little time…"

Kai turned back to the mirror. *So many women, so little nerve…* He tugged at the collar of his green dress uniform and hooked it shut.

"Is it fixed right, Bevan?"

Pelosi closed his left eye, then nodded. "Don't change the subject, Kai. How long has it been since you've had a date?"

"You mean aside from the time I went out with Pamela's cousin so you could be alone with Pam?"

Bevan ignored the needling and stared wistfully into space. "Pam. Now there was a girl who really knew how to…"

"Cook?" Kai offered wryly. He moved back from the mirror and sat on the edge of his bed. Flipping open a rosewood case, he pulled one of the silver spurs from their bed of ruby velvet. The spur was a simple U-shape with a rowelless spike at the lowest point in the loop. "At least Pam didn't insist on putting quillar in an omelet," he commented as he fastened the spur to the heel of his left boot with a black leather strap.

Leaning against the door jamb, Bevan wrinkled his nose. "This from a man buckling spurs to his boots."

Kai ignored the jibe. "Why'd you stop seeing her?"

Bevan shrugged. "I dunno. She just started grating on me. I think she liked you more than me anyway."

"Not surprising." Kai tucked his trousers into the tops of his black boots. "I paid more attention to her than you did."

"Yeah. I felt pretty embarrassed when you got her that holovid for her birthday and I'd forgotten clean about it." Bevan shook his head. "Wondered why you didn't ask her out after we broke up. I wouldn't have minded."

Kai stood and checked himself in the mirror. "It wouldn't have worked—your permission or otherwise." Kai stared into the mirror but saw only a long line of footprints along a black sandy beach.

As though reading Kai's mind, Bevan smiled sympathetically. "Hey, I know your thing with…ah, what was her name…?"

Kai's face remained impassive and his eyes distant. "Wendy. Wendy Sylvester."

Bevan looked down apologetically. "Yeah, Wendy, right. Well, I know how that ended and that you blame yourself and all, but you can't let it ruin your life. You gotta start living sometime. This girl today, she could have been an omen."

Kai shrugged. "If she was an omen, I already missed."

Bevan opened his arms expansively, lifting his palms to the heavens. "There are plenty of fish in the sea, Kai. You're an eligible officer who also happens to have enough noble blood coursing through his veins to get him invited to the Marshal's reception while us po' folks have to fend for ourselves on this New Year's Eve. There are women in the thousands who'd like to be seen on your arm, or in your bed, if you'd just give it a chance."

Before Kai could respond, Bevan cut him off. "I know what you're going to say, but bottom line is this, Kai: You just have to open up and give yourself a chance. Hell, today's the day."

Give yourself a chance. Somewhere deep inside that phrase struck a chord in Kai. *Why spend your life avoiding things because you know they'll turn out badly? You know you got along with Pam because she was with Bevan, which meant there was no pressure on you. You couldn't screw that up. Give yourself a chance.*

"So resolved. As of January 1, 3050, Kai Allard will give himself a chance." As he offered his hand to Bevan, a whisper of dread passed through him. *Let's hope the gods of retribution do not notice your boldness. If they do, you will reap what your temerity richly deserves.*

"Yes, sir, I think it was three years ago we last saw each other." Kai smiled as he took Leftenant-General Andrew Redburn's hand and shook it. "As I recall, it was at the anniversary party for my Aunt Riva and Uncle Robert. I enjoyed getting to see both you and Misha." He looked around. "Is she here?"

Andrew shook his head. "No, but she sends her love. She asked me to thank you for that kind hologram concerning her last book…" Andrew Redburn's deep voice and ready smile reminded Kai of when the Leftenant-General—then just a Major with the First Kathil Uhlans—had brought his family to Kestrel for Dan Allard's wedding. He'd made it his duty to ride herd on all the children present to keep them from getting underfoot during the preparations. Kai remembered fondly more than one colossal wrestling match where Victor Davion, Phelan Kell, Andrew's son Thelos, and he had been wolves to Andrew's bear—complete with roars and growls and playful swats on all sides.

"I meant every word," Kai said. "She and Jay Mitchell are the only historians around who have any sense for accurate battle reportage. *Freedom's Bloody Price* really brought to life Rasalhague's battle against the renegade Kurita forces during the Ronin Wars. The tactical descriptions of the battles read logically, and her judgment of the Gunzburg debacle placed the blame where it belongs: on the mercenaries and the politicians equally. I very much enjoyed the book and felt I had to tell her so."

Andrew smiled and light glinted from the medals and campaign ribbons on the broad, black breast of his Uhlans' uniform. "Your message arrived right after the book had been damned in a review, so your comments were most welcome."

"Then I'm doubly glad I wrote to her. I just hope Misha is the one to chronicle any battles where I find myself. I know the victors write the history, but having a sympathetic historian in your corner can't hurt at all."

"Excuse me."

Kai felt a jolt as he heard her voice and felt a tap on his shoulder. He turned from Andrew and stared straight into the deep blue eyes of the woman he'd met that morning. *Maybe Bevan was right. Maybe she is an omen!*

She wore a black evening gown whose bodice was sewn with ebon sequins in a starburst pattern that flashed with the lights as she moved. The string of pearls around her throat matched her earrings and had enough of a blue tint to complement her eyes and dark hair.

"You forgot your bag," she said with an impish smile.

"What?" was all Kai could think of to say.

She laid her hand on his arm. "Your bag. The one with your towel in it? You left it on the bench. I waited after my run, thinking you might come back for it. There was nothing with your name so I couldn't call you. I took it home and planned to get out to the trail early enough tomorrow to give it back to you."

Kai felt his cheeks flushing and turned back to Andrew just in time to see a bemused smile spread over his face. "We met this morning, General. Out running. I would introduce you, but I…"

Andrew winked at the woman. "No need. Dr. Lear came in with us yesterday. She's being transferred to the Tenth Lyran Guards and I met her on the way down to Skondia. It's good to see you again, Doctor."

She nodded her head. "And you, General."

Andrew glanced at Kai. "Allow me to perform introductions. Leftenant, this is Dr. Deirdre Lear."

Kai took her hand and raised it to his lips. "Most pleased to make your acquaintance formally."

"And, Dr. Lear, this is Leftenant Kai Allard-Liao."

Her smile froze, then dissolved into a thin, colorless gash in her face. She blinked once or twice, as though searching for words that would not come. She clawed at the back of her right hand, raking nails across where Kai had kissed her, then turned abruptly and vanished into the crowd.

Kai's jaw dropped open and concern puckered Andrew's brow. Both men looked at each other, then looked away like friends who had both seen a ghost, but would not admit it to the other. Hair rising on the back of his neck, Kai tried to see if he could catch any glimpse of her retreating form, but the milling crowd had swallowed her whole.

Kai rubbed his right hand over the back of his neck. "I wonder what that was all about?"

Andrew shook his head slowly. "I have no idea. I do know she became a doctor because her father was a MechWarrior who died in battle when she was only a child. She's not much on violence, though she did mention having a black belt in *aikido*."

Kai nodded. "That doesn't surprise me. *Aikido* teaches one to use his opponent's energy against him. It is the ultimate in non-violent self-protection. You don't hurt your foe. He hurts himself."

"Perhaps she didn't realize you were a MechWarrior," Andrew suggested. "But then, she would have known that from your uniform. Maybe it's that she has no fondness for nobles—it's not unheard of."

Kai chewed his lower lip. "Perhaps." *Whatever it is, she was hurt and hurt bad. Isn't it enough that I have to live up to my family's reputation? Now I have to work against something that someone else did. What good is it to give myself a chance, if it's just going to blow up in my face?*

The next morning Kai found his bag on the bench, but Deirdre was nowhere in sight. He searched the bag for a note or some other sign from her, but found nothing.

He slumped down on the bench. *If Bevan was right and she is an omen, 3050 is going to be a very bad year.*

JumpShip Dire Wolf
Star's End, Periphery
15 January 3050

The sour smell of sweat-drenched sheets met Phelan Kell as he fought his way to consciousness through the black fog filling his mind. Thousands of questions asked in hundreds of different ways by a legion of voices continued to echo through his brain. In counterpoint, he heard a single, agonized voice answering them again and again, and in the end, always surrendering valuable truths. Like the stench of his bedding, Phelan recognized the voice as his own.

No, dear God, I couldn't have told them all those things! I've betrayed everyone and everything that means anything to me. His stomach heaved, though Phelan couldn't tell whether his nausea was from self-loathing or the after-effects of the drugs they had used on him. Weak, trembling, and gasping for breath, he lay on his cot and stared into the darkness of his cell. *The fact that it was drugs that made me talk doesn't make my action any less hideous or damaging.*

A searing oval of light outlined the door to his cell and gave him a moment's warning to close his eyes. Light still bled through his eyelids, stabbing needles of torment straight into his brain. Thought moved so slowly that by the time Phelan realized he could raise his hand to shield his eyes, the door was already closed and someone had flipped him onto his back. A hand grabbed his left wrist and deftly rotated his forearm upward. A tug extended his arm, then something sharp lanced into the vein at his elbow.

A chemical flood swept through his body and blasted away the sludgy residue of the myriad interrogation sessions. As the voices and questions faded, Phelan felt a jolt travel through him. His eyes snapped open on command, eloquent witness to the fact that brain-to-body messages were once again traveling express instead of over the local routes of the past two months. He flipped his wrist over and caught hold of the person who had been holding him.

A hand chopped down into the middle of his forearm, numbing the entire limb, then surrounded his thumb and peeled his hand away with the ease of a child removing the rind from a naranji. *I may be in command of my body,* Phelan thought, *but I've still got no strength.* He opened both hands and let his arms drop limply to the bedding.

"That was a wise choice." It was a woman's voice, but somehow that didn't surprise him. Her voice was husky, but as matter-of-fact and emotionless as her handling of Phelan's attack.

She lifted his right hand up by the cord around his wrist and positioned it to cover his eyes. "I am going to bring the lights up slowly. Keep your eyes shaded because the drug I just injected into you will dilate your pupils somewhat."

Light mutated the entire ceiling from an infinite black plane through stages of gray and tallow to a luminescent white that filled every corner of the small cell. Phelan hooded his eyes, but greedily drank in every detail of his surroundings as the light unveiled them one by one. His ragged cot all but filled the tiny room. The commode opposite the hatchway he recognized instantly as the peculiar design suited to zero-gravity use. *That means I'm still on a DropShip.* In the corner next to the hatch, Phelan saw a gray woolen blanket wadded into a ball, and sympathetic pains in his back dredged up memories of more than one night spent curled up with it like a child.

Phelan looked up at the woman, twisting around so he could orient her properly to the dark cell. For a moment, he had trouble reconciling the sleek beauty standing over him with the beefy image he had formed in his mind, based entirely on her strength at manhandling him earlier. She wore her white hair very short and combed behind her ears. Though her expression was serious, her pert, upturned nose gave her an incongruous air of amusement.

She wore a navy jumpsuit and no other no other decoration except for a single earring in her left ear. Formed in a star pattern, it had been enameled to the color of fresh blood. Four of the eight points on the star were enlarged, with the southernmost point almost four times the length of the others, giving the whole design a dagger-like shape. As she moved toward the door, Phelan saw that the shoulder patch on her uniform matched the earring's design.

She clipped the lighting remote control to the jumpsuit's hip pocket and folded her arms across her chest. "I should have expected this."

Phelan swung his legs over the edge of the bed and sat up. Another wave of nausea swept over him, and he gripped the edge of the cot to keep from falling over. He shook his head to clear it, but that only increased his discomfort. There was nothing to do but wait for the dizziness to pass. When it finally did, he carefully turned his head to look at her.

"What should you have expected?" The hoarse, croaking quality of his voice surprised him. *What have I been doing, gargling razor-blades?* He shuddered as another memory bobbed to the surface of his mind, recalling the terrifying hallucinations that had driven him from his bed to the corner. *I must have been screaming for hours...*

Irritation played across her face. "I cannot take you to see the Khan looking like this. You will have to be made presentable." She frowned deeply. "By rights, I should take you down with the other bondsmen, but you are supposed to be in isolation. All praise be to the Khan, but why did he give me *this* job?" She wrinkled her nose, then seemed to decide on a course of action. "The others will not like it, but that is their problem, quineg? Let us go."

Phelan unsteadily gained his feet, then reeled over to the cell's opposite wall. The cool metal felt good against his spine and helped hold the nausea at bay. He pressed both palms against it and levered himself away from the wall. "Where am I? Who are you? Where the hell are you taking me?" He folded his arms across his chest. "Answer me, or we're not going anywhere."

She arched an eyebrow in surprise, and the corners of her mouth curled up in a grin. "It is up to the Khan to answer your questions, Phelan Kell, if he so desires. You must go to him, and it is my job to get you there. I can understand, after all you have been through, your desire to exert some independence. But that is not to be. You must ask yourself if you will go willingly or if you want me to carry you."

Phelan opened his mouth to snap out a retort, then stopped. *You're as weak as a kitten and she's as strong as a tiger.* His shoulders sagged down. "You mean that we can do this your way or the *hard* way." She nodded and he shuffled forward. "Lead on."

Wordlessly, she waved Phelan through the door, then guided him down a hallway. Cool and clean, it, too, was lit by glowing ceiling panels. Phelan noticed that all the other hatches in the corridor stood open, making him wonder if he were the only prisoner, or if he had mistaken his status. He looked around for any sign that might be a clue to where he was, but he saw only a triangular shield with three links of a chain painted across the upper edge.

Its meaning eluded him until they reached another stretch of corridor curving around like the hub of a wheel. Other corridors shot off like spokes, and at the entrance to each, Phelan saw more shields painted with symbols. In addition to the earlier shield and chain image, he noticed a shield with a hexagonal device, one with a small red star, and one showing a blue and white striated ball. The woman led Phelan to the corridor marked with this latter symbol.

Icons! The shields are simple icons that indicate what sort of things can be found further down the corridor. Phelan smiled to himself, pleased that his brain had started to function in something more than a random pattern. *I haven't a clue to what the hexagon means, but I bet the chains mean prison. The red star and the colored ball are anyone's guess.*

Phelan quickly pierced the secret of the blue-white ball as he moved down the corridor. The aroma of food started his belly rumbling, and several of the doorways on his right were emblazoned with shields showing wavy lines that looked like spaghetti gone mad. *God alone knows what that symbol is supposed to be, but unless my nose isn't working, there's food around. If the ball corridor contains a place to eat, maybe it indicates living quarters or personnel services.*

As they continued along the corridor, something else nagged at Phelan's mind. *If all these doors with tangle-string icons lead into the galley, that's a fairly big room. That means there are lots of people aboard this Drop Ship. And so its got to be a big one—probably a* Behemoth *Class.*

A bit further along, his guide stopped before a door on the left that withdrew up into the wall. Phelan caught the flash of a shield and a V-shaped symbol with a big ball in the middle and two smaller balls on either horn. He stepped into the room and around a partition, then winced at the bright light reflecting from the white tile walls and silver metal mirrors on the left-hand wall. As his eyes accustomed themselves to the light, he frowned. *What in the world is this place?*

Two of the three people in the room glared at him as though he had interrupted some sacred ceremony. Phelan felt a shiver run down his spine, but he quickly identified it as more than a normal uneasy feeling about wandering into a place where he was definitely unwelcome. *I got used to that on Gunzburg. Here, it's as though I'm not even human.*

The three people present were so unusual in shape and appearance that Phelan wondered if *they* were human. Furthest away was a naked woman seated on a narrow bench that sagged deeply in the middle. It was not because she was fat, though Phelan guessed she would tip a scale at 150 kilos, but she was *huge!* Pale flesh stretched over thick muscles, and Phelan realized her physique was better than that of Kell Hound members who lifted weights in their spare time. *Her shoulders are broader than seven of those lockers! She's two-meters thirty if a centimeter.*

The woman looked over her shoulder at Phelan, her brown eyes cold. He saw her measure his limbs and study the muscles of his nearly naked body like a predator deciding if the prey would be worth the effort needed to kill it. Then she simply resumed braiding the long, red queue snaking down from the back of her head. *If she and I never tangle, I won't mind at all. Where do they find 'Mechs to fit someone like that?*

The man nearest Phelan looked equally strange. Between him and the amazon, they could have made three normal-sized individuals. A shock of yellow hair covered the man's large head, but his naked body seemed far too small to be attached to his neck. Still, the well-defined muscles hinted at a strength and power that belied his actual size. The man never turned to look at Phelan, but watched him with bulging green eyes in the mirror.

When Phelan locked eyes with the third person in the room, it felt as though he'd stabbed a metric incritometer into an electrical outlet. Pure hatred smoldered in the man's dark eyes. *What the hell is eating him?* The man wore a long, loose blue shirt, but Phelan guessed they were about the same size. *Our hair's the same color, but he's got a widow's-peak. If not for that and his brown eyes, we'd almost look like brothers.*

The middle man turned his molten stare on Phelan's guide. "Get him out of here. Take him down to the shearing pens."

She shook her head. "Neg. I am taking him to see the Khan and he must be cleaned up."

The amazon looked over. "But here, Ranna?"

Ranna raked slender fingers through her snowy hair. "Yes, Evantha, here. He has to remain isolated from the others." She shot Phelan a glance. "You couldn't have expected me to take him to my cabin to clean him up, quineg?"

"Certainly not that, Star Commander," mocked the middle man. "You should have taken him to the kitchens. They have tubs there for cleaning the grime off vegetables." The flesh around his brown eyes tightened. "Do what you will. I do not care. I am done here."

Something in the man's voice sparked recognition in Phelan, but he couldn't place why. As the man tucked his dark blue shirt into his trousers, Phelan noticed a flash of silver at the man's waist, and anger shot through him. "Hey, that's my belt buckle!" The mercenary reached his hand out for the onyx and malachite wolf's-head Tyra had made for him.

Phelan never saw any of the punches, but he heard and felt them well enough. The first blow caught him on the side of the head, over his left temple. It snapped his head around and started him going down. A left jab slammed into his stomach, doubling him over and blasting his breath away. His legs collapsed as though he were a rag-doll. The final hammershot smashed into his left ear and drove him into a row of gray lockers. Phelan hit hard and bounced to the ground.

"Vlad!"

His head ringing, he barely heard Ranna shout the name, but he felt the menace overshadowing him withdraw. The world spun around him, and his lungs burned with the need for air. He tried to breathe, but his lungs refused to work. Shaken as he was, he understood why he couldn't breathe, but that did nothing to ease his panic. *Air! I need air!*

The small, blond man knelt beside him and rolled him over onto his back. He grasped the waistband of the shorts Phelan was wearing. Lifting up, he forced Phelan to arch his back and some precious air seeped into the mercenary's lungs. He continued elevating and lowering the mercenary's middle while looking up at Phelan's assailant.

His expression furious as a thundercloud, Vlad looked ready to spit. "Do not gaze upon me in that fashion, Carew!" He shifted his gaze to Phelan's guide. "Nor you, Ranna. I will not be spoken to in that tone of voice by an inferior, nor will I suffer the likes of him touching me. This buckle is mine!" He thrust a finger at Phelan. "He was my kill and I took the buckle by right. It is the least I am due, given the Khan's uncharacteristic action."

Ranna brought her chin up. "You forget yourself, Vlad. The Khan has not often exercised his right to claim what his people have won, but it is, nonetheless, his *right* to do just that. Your action brings shame on the sibko. You were raised for better."

Ranna's stinging rebuke brought color to Vlad's cheeks. He stared at her, then looked down abruptly. Without another word, he stepped around Carew and left the room. As the door shut automatically behind him, Carew and Ranna both sighed.

Having his lungs working at least marginally had put out the fire in Phelan's chest. He stared at the door and spat hair and dirt from his mouth. *That voice! The one they called Vlad was one of my interrogators. He was Hothead.* Phelan's fingers itched to throttle the man who had battered him, but the quivering weakness of his limbs left him no illusions about his fighting ability. *I've been juiced up for days and weeks—probably months—and been kept cramped in a small room with no chance to exercise at all. Back in trim, I might be able to do something, but damn, he moved* fast. *And he hit hard, too.*

Carew shifted around to get his hands under Phelan's right arm as Ranna came over and grabbed his left. They heaved him to his feet, then plopped him down on the bench. Evantha stood, gave Phelan a disgusted look, and stalked deeper into the room. The mercenary steadied himself, then looked up and found himself staring at a stranger in the mirror.

His beard had grown out a ruddy shade of auburn that did not match his coal-black hair. His hair, which he had always worn longer than most MechWarriors, had become a thick, matted tangle. In fact, if not for his left eye slowly swelling shut and the thin ribbon of blood running down his neck from where Vlad's last punch had torn the top of his ear, he would not have recognized himself.

Carew glanced from Phelan's reflection to Ranna and back. "You are supposed to make him look presentable? I pray, for your sake, that you can work the same magic on him that you did on your command exams."

Ranna's left hand moved so quickly that Phelan only saw a blur as she struck at the smaller man's neck. Carew's right hand came up in an attempt to bat her blow aside, but he missed. She laughed. "You are getting slow, Carew. I could have have killed you there, quiaff? I, however, decided to spare you."

The smaller man shook his head. "Just wait until the next simtime when you face me, Star Commander. Still, I owe you my life. As I am so little, I trust a little favor will suffice to redeem it, quiaff?"

"Aff." She smiled wearily. "You wash and I dry?"

Phelan began to feel offended. *I wouldn't mind their talking about me as though I'm not here except that they make me sound like a sinkful of dirty dishes.* "Excuse me, but I have been known to wash myself in the past."

The big-eyed man smiled. "Imagine that! And are you any better at it than you were at defending yourself just now?"

A low growl rumbled from the mercenary's throat. "Well, I do have more practice at washing than I do at getting beaten up."

Ranna and Carew shared a laugh. "Good. You have spirit," she said. Turning to Carew, she asked, "Will you help? It is for the good of the sibko!"

He sighed heavily. "Aff. We use your supplies and your scissors and your razor."

"Bargained well and done."

Phelan shook his head. "Why do I get the feeling the two of you would rather take me to whatever passes for a laundry on this ship and toss me into a washer?" As he saw an expression of enlightenment spread across their faces, he held up his hands. "Honest, I won't be any trouble. Let's just get this over and done with."

Phelan, dressed in the olive-green clothes Ranna had obtained for him while Carew cut his hair, ran his left hand over his clean-shaven face. *Glad to have the beard gone. It made me look too old.* Unbidden, the image of his father's bearded face came to him, along with an overwhelming sadness. *How long have I been a captive? They must think me dead. I have to get word to them somehow. Why is there never a ComStar Acolyte around when you need one?*

With his back against the rear wall of the turbolift, Phelan watched the numbers flash by as the box carried Ranna and him toward the nose of the ship. The number of decks, each marked with its own shield icon, surprised the mercenary. *That's twenty decks serviced by this lift alone. To get onto the top dozen decks, it looks like you have to type a code sequence into that number pad. If the lifts on this ship function like those on other DropShips, and don't run the length of the ship to preclude breaching and atmosphere loss, then this one is really big.* The thought that it might be larger than a *Behemoth* flashed through Phelan's mind, but he dismissed it immediately as impossible.

The elevator slowed to a stop. Ranna punched a number sequence into the keypad, and each stroke was answered by a melodic tone. The door slid open and she pulled Phelan out of the box. Leading the way down a corridor, Ranna moved so quickly that the Kell Hound had little time to study his surroundings. When she stopped finally, Ranna stood before a door painted with a shield showing another device. Central to it was the silhouette of a wolf's head that looked surprisingly like the Kell Hound crest and the belt buckle Tyra had made for him. Beneath it was a row of five red stars similar to the design of Ranna's earring. She stood at attention and Phelan aped her as the door opened.

"Come in, please." The speaker, a tall, slender man with closely cropped white hair, gestured them into the room hospitably but without enthusiasm. He was smiling slightly, but Phelan took no comfort in it. Something flickered over the older man's expression as his gaze swept over Phelan's swollen left eye and the patch of crusted blood on his ear, but he said nothing.

Phelan followed Ranna into the room, and the door whispered shut behind them. Right hand snapping up to her brow, Ranna stopped just inside the door and saluted the Khan. He returned her salute smartly, then smiled genuinely at her. "I trust you did not mind being asked to conduct this man here."

She shrugged, the gesture coming just stiffly enough to betray a gram of resentment. "As I am not required to perform my duties at this time, I must find new ways to serve."

The Khan accepted her explanation graciously and turned to Phelan. "You look both better and worse than when I last looked in on you."

Phelan smiled politely as his mind raced and tried in vain to match the Khan's voice with any of those that had interrogated him. "I'm clumsy."

The Khan arched a white eyebrow. "Then when Vlad placed himself on report for assaulting you, he was in error?"

Phelan's head came up and he studied the Khan carefully. *Is this whole meeting going to be filled with testing and intrigue? What could I possibly tell him that his people have not already drugged out of me?* "Were I not so clumsy, I would have either avoided setting him off or I would have avoided his fists."

The Khan's blue eyes narrowed, then his face brightened and he waved Phelan deeper into the suite with one hand. "Forgive me. You have had quite enough questioning in the past months, quiaff? And I keep you standing here in the foyer like some Point being reprimanded. Please come in and meet my other guest."

As he moved forward at his host's invitation, Phelan noted that the Khan's quarters seemed to fit the man perfectly. At first, Phelan thought the rooms sparsely furnished, but then he noticed that everything had been selected for quality, as though the Khan would fill his living space only with the finest. Phelan imagined that the decorations and furnishings were probably the victors of a long weeding-out process. He could easily see this man discarding something before bringing anything new into this place.

A somber gray carpet and warm maroon walls lent the room a studious air. Yellowish light shown down from recessed ceiling lamps, illuminating the glass and gray steel shelving and tables. The couch and pair of chairs looked comfortable but were not matched in either color or design. The shelves held a few mementoes and two or three holographic books, but Phelan could identify none of them.

The only decoration mounted on the walls hung over the couch. It was as large as his own chest, and Phelan recognized the emblem as similar to the shield emblazoned on the Khan's door. The only differences were that this one actually was a shield and there were no stars beneath the wolf's head. Instead of the stars, Phelan saw a small square balanced on one point fixed to the shield. Moving closer to it, he made another startling discovery. *Damn, that looks like it was pounded out of 'Mech armor!*

Any further thought about what the device was or how it was constructed fled from Phelan's mind as the Khan's other guest turned from one of the shelves where he had been browsing. "Greetings, Phelan Kell. It does, indeed, appear that stories of your death were greatly exaggerated."

Despite the shock, the young mercenary immediately identified the man by the scarlet sash on his white robe. *What in the seven hells is a ComStar Precentor doing here?* Stunned, Phelan gaped at the white-haired old man, then recovered his poise. "Peace of Blake be with you, Precentor…"

The Precentor adjusted the patch over his right eye, then squinted at the mercenary with his good one. "Yes, I can see it. You are a Kell."

Something in the way the Precentor spoke made Phelan uncomfortable. "You know my father?"

The Precentor hesitated for a moment, and Phelan sensed him swallowing whatever his first response would have been. "Know him? No, not really. In my capacity as Precentor Martial, I have studied him and I have grown to respect him greatly. I even met him long ago, but I doubt he would remember me or the meeting."

Phelan started to ask the ComStar official if he could get word of his survival back to his parents, but the Khan's entry into the room stopped him. Smiling politely, the Khan opened his arms to welcome his guests. "Allow me to perform formal introductions. Phelan Kell, this is Anastasius Focht, the Precentor Martial of your ComStar. Precentor, this is Phelan Kell."

The young mercenary acknowledged Focht with a nod of his head, then looked expectantly at the Khan. The Khan met Phelan's gaze. "And permit me to introduce myself. I am Ulric, Khan of the Wolves. You were taken by an advanced raiding party sent out by my clan, and brought here to my JumpShip, the *Dire Wolf.*"

The news that he was on a JumpShip shocked the Kell Hound even more than his previous attempts at estimating the size of what he'd believed to be a DropShip. *JumpShip! That's impossible! Jump-Ships are nothing more than a bridge module mounted on the body of a Kearny-Fuchida drive. Maybe they have a shuttle docking bay, and the Cu has those agrodecks, but that's it. A JumpShip with decks and facilities for lots of people. Oh, Phelan, this is decidedly worse than a little blizzard-stalking on Tharkad.*

Phelan recovered himself quickly and wanted to offer the Khan his hand, but sensed that Ulric would have rejected the gesture more as a matter of form than from any distrust or dislike. "Sir, if I might, would it be possible for me to communicate a message to my family that I am still alive? No, please, it need not contain any military intelligence—my interrogation and that first battle were enough to tell me you are invading the Periphery and consolidating it. I just don't want my parents to suffer."

Ulric shook his head, but Focht answered the question. "I regret, Herr Kell, that even with the Khan's permission, I could not transmit such a message. The Primus sent me as an envoy to these remarkable people. My mission is diplomatic in nature, and I cannot ferry messages back and forth, regardless of their content." The Precentor smiled and half-turned to the Khan. "The Khan has shown me battle-tapes of your encounter with their raiding party. As you have seen, their military technology and skill are impressive."

Focht's words smothered the hope in Phelan's heart. Bile burned in his throat as he nodded agreement with the Precentor's comment. "Impressive, indeed." His head came up. "I've never known of another organization in which a soldier would put himself on report for assault."

Ulric frowned. "If you damaged another's property, you would tell the owner, quineg?"

Half-hearing the question, Kell nodded. "Yes, but…Wait a minute, *property?*"

The calm on Ulric's face did not suggest that anything was out of the ordinary. "In capturing you, Vlad earned a claim on you. I exercised my prerogative as Khan." The growing look of horror on Phelan's face didn't alter Ulric's explanation in the least. He grabbed Phelan's right wrist and brought the corded bracelet into view. "Simply speaking, Phelan Kell, you belong to me."

Orbital Space, Thule, Rasalhague Province
Free Rasalhague Republic
7 March 3050

Tyra Miraborg glanced at the auxiliary monitor on her cockpit control monitor. It showed a small icon representing her *Shilone* fighter dead-center on the screen and slowly rotated a vector-graphic sphere around the craft. Three small triangles with identification tags appeared near her ship to mark the position of her wingman and the other two pilots in her flight. Further on along her line of flight, a large orb remained tantalizingly distant.

She smiled, barely feeling the added pressure of the neurohelmet's padding against the corners of her mouth. *We'll be home soon enough. Back aboard the* Bragi *and off to another system. I should have known that joining an honor guard company would mean spending most of my time doing ceremonial things, but I didn't expect extended tours of duty guarding the Defense Minister as he toured the systems the Periphery pirates had attacked.*

Anika Janssen's voice called to her through the speakers built into the helmet. "I've got nothing unusual, Kapten."

Tyra turned her head to the right and saw Anika's *Shilone* pull parallel to her own fighter craft. The wing shape of the craft made it one of the few AeroSpace Fighters suited to both atmospheric and deep-space combat. *Shilone* pilots, as a class, referred to their craft as "boomerangs." "That, darlin'," one of Tyra's first fight instructors had told her, "is because *Shilone* pilots always come back after a mission."

Sure, and ComStar never loses a message. Tyra keyed her radio. "Roger that, Valkyrie Two. I'm clear. What about you, Ljungquist?"

"Clear as the day after a weekend off," laughed Sven Ljungquist.

"Valkyrie Four reports no trouble. He's been watching our six. No one has crept up on us."

"Roger, three." Tyra touched a finger to the DropShip icon on her auxiliary screen. In an instant, the DropShip replaced her ship in the center of the screen, depositing the icons marking her flight down at eight o'clock on its scanner sphere. In addition to painting her screen with the *Bragi*'s sensor data, the computer opened a direct line to the flight's home ship. "Valkyrie Flight reporting all clear."

"Roger, Valkyrie Leader. You should be home in time for supper." The male flight controller lowered his voice. "The food's not going to be anything like the meal I had two nights ago in Sovol, Tyra. You should have accepted my invitation."

Anika cut into the line before Tyra could answer. "Löjtnant Tviet, would you mind sticking to business? We are in a hostile theatre of operations."

Tyra heard Tviet's acknowledgement of Anika's rebuke and the radio went dead. She thanked Anika silently, but the all-too-familiar feelings of regret and anger began to boil up within her again. She fought to keep her mind from wandering off on these unhappy tangents. *You made your decision and that is that. You decided to decline Phelan's offer and sign on with this company because that made the most sense. You couldn't stay on Gunzburg, that's for certain.*

A red light flared on her radio control panel, and she punched it automatically. As though reading Tyra's mind, Anika spoke with her friend over the private frequency they shared. "Tyra, you can't keep kicking yourself, because it's not your fault. What happens, happens."

Tyra nodded and glanced over at Anika's *Shilone.* "I know you're right, Nik. There's nothing I could have done about Phelan's death, even if I *had* signed on with the Kell Hounds. Phelan's unit didn't have aerospace cover, so I wouldn't even have been there."

"That's more like it." A mixture of relief and exasperation echoed through Anika's voice.

Tyra glanced again at the sensor scan from the *Bragi,* but it remained clear. Throughout this "public relations" tour, she had been hoping the pirates that killed Phelan would stage a raid so she could get a shot at revenge. *That's stupid. Just the sort of thinking to get me killed.*

Tyra keyed her mike. "Thanks, Nik. I'm back. When we hit the *Bragi,* remind me to give Tviet a lesson in the definition of the word *nej.*"

"Roger."

Tyra saw something new appear on the scanner screen. Four

small red triangles appeared at the outer edge of the DropShip's scan. Her combat computer brought the secondary monitor up and started flashing the different silhouettes and performance profiles for all aerospace fighters and shuttlecraft that matched the incoming data. The computer alternated between the *Stuka* and the *Corsair* models but could not make a final decision.

Tyra touched the icon representing her ship, and the scanning computer shifted back over to her own instrumentation. It cut down the range of the scan, but gave her combat capability which, all of a sudden, seemed a good thing. She keyed her radio to the DropShip's control frequency, but patched her flight's tactical channel into the feed.

"Valkyrie flight here, *Bragi*. We have four UAC on the screen." She looked at the monitor again. "They're coming in on a vector that might have looked to you like our heat shadows, but I've got them on my instruments. Please confirm."

Tyra increased vector thrust on the right side of her ship, moving it to the left and away from Anika's craft. She watched as one of the four ships following her flight aped her maneuver. *Whoever they are, they're good! It takes some tight flying to pass yourself off as the IR shadow of an aerospace fighter traveling through a helium cloud.*

Tviet's voice answered Tyra's call, but gone was the cockiness of their earlier communication. "Ah, roger, Valflight. We're getting some jammed transmission from Thule itself. We don't know what it was, but chances are it has something to do with hostile actions on the planet."

"Roger, *Bragi*. Do we engage the people on our tails? I have them about a hundred myriameters behind us."

"Negative, Valflight. We are clear to the JumpShip at the nadir point. Just watch them."

Tviet's words came slowly, with pauses between them that told Tyra the controller was getting lots of input from sources other than her ship. She glanced at the auxiliary monitor and saw the four unidentified aerospace craft split formation and pick up speed. *Here they come!* "Be advised, *Bragi,* we are under attack and moving to engage. Valkyrie Two form up on me. Three and Four hang together and take the pair vectored at 256 degrees and closing. Luck."

"Skill," countered Ljungquist.

Tyra kicked her thrusters in and vectored their output to pull her through a tight turn that stood her ship on its left wing-tip. While in space she didn't have to worry about friction and air turbulence, but inertia still affected her and her craft. Her flightsuit pressurized itself

114

to prevent blood from draining from her head as she pulled four gees coming around, but she knew that even the suit would not keep her from blacking out if she maneuvered too quickly.

Set on her new course—racing back through the space she had just patrolled—Tyra brought each of her combat systems up. The computer drew a picture of the *Shilone* on her primary monitor and illuminated each weapon as it came on line. "Forward long range missile launcher, check," Tyra mumbled to herself. "Forward heavy laser, check. Wing-mounted medium lasers, check and check, and aft arc short-range missile launcher loaded and ready." A red crosshair painted itself on her helmet's faceplate and tracked with her right eye as she looked around. The armrests of her chair slowly rotated ninety degrees, presenting the trigger buttons for all her weapons. *Keep the crosshairs on the target, in space or on the sensor display, and poof, it's gone.*

Like the ground-pounding BattleMechs, AeroSpace Fighters relied on a holographic display of sensor data. Though 'Mech pilots had only to orient themselves within a two-dimensional battlefield, fighter pilots had to deal with enemies in a full three-dimensional theatre. That meant their holographic displays formed a bowl with the area toward which the fighter's nose pointed as the center. When a gold ring flashed around the whole display, it told the pilot that the computer had gotten a lock-on to a target in the aft arc.

Tyra's computer still could not decide if the ships she and Anika were hurtling toward were *Corsair*s or *Stuka*s, which was disturbing. The *Stuka* was a heavily armored fighter boasting all the weapons she had, but more of them. The *Corsair,* while lighter in weapons and armor, had superior handling capabilities that made it an elusive enemy. *Still, if I can get into its aft arc, it's vulnerable.*

"Is your computer *schizing* out on you?" Anika asked, apparently having the same problem with hers.

Tyra tried to answer confidently. "Yeah, something has definitely addled its little silicon brain." She felt a shiver course up her spine. "Figure on *Stuka*s but pray for *Corsair*s."

"Roger." Static shot over the open channel for a second, then came Anika's voice again. "What the hell are Davion fighters doing out here? Did I miss a declaration of war? I mean, did Prince Hanse Davion get married again or something?"

Tyra knew that *Stuka*s and *Corsair*s were key Federated Suns military spacecraft, but something told her that these fighters were not from the Federated Suns. Before she could say anything to Anika, lights blazed to life on her command console. Then came the keening alarm resounding through her cockpit. "I've got a hostile radar lock on me! Juke left high!" Tyra shouted.

She sideslipped her *Shilone* right, which jammed her shoulder into the left side of the cockpit. That dropped her fighter directly beneath Anika's craft, with only twenty-five meters between them. As the computer updated its sensor data, painting one image over the other, Tyra boosted thrust to the right vector. The *Shilone* rocketed off to the left, streaking up beyond where Anika's *Shilone* had been while Anika executed a similar move that took her high and to Tyra's right.

The warning lights died. *Good. Mixing our silhouettes, then ripping them apart confused it.* She punched her right fist against the targeting computer. *Why the hell did they get a lock on me and I didn't reciprocate? This is not the time for my computer to go out on me.*

She glanced at the auxiliary monitor, dropping the visually guided crosshairs onto the scanner image of the lead enemy craft. In the flick of an eye, she armed her long-range missiles and waited for the dot in the center of the crosshairs to light up, confirming a sensor lock. Instead of the dot, she got a running meter clicking off the distance separating her target from the LRM's effective range. *What? They had a lock on me at three times effective range. Who the hell are these guys?*

She opened a radio channel. "Valkyrie Three, bogies might have advanced target capability. Advise caution."

She heard the sensor lock sirens blaring through Ljungquist's reply. "Roger. Kinda busy here, Val One." His voice slurred its way through the next sentence as he put his *Slayer* through a high-gee maneuver to shake the lock. "No, dammit. Arrgghh!"

A sizzling pop snapped through the radio speakers. Before Tyra could find out what had happened to Ljungquist, the computer gave her a lock onto her target. Her right index finger hit the trigger beneath it, and the LRM pod mounted beneath the cockpit spat out a score of missiles in rapid-fire succession. The missiles streaked away until their rockets seemed little more than stars in the distance, then a series of explosions cast light into the void. *Hit!*

She knew better than to hope one volley of LRMs had destroyed her enemy, and she gained quick confirmation of that fact as both aerospace fighters shot past each other. Instantly, her computer stopped its vacillation between *Stuka* and *Corsair* fighters. It settled on neither and instead filled the secondary monitor with a digitized visual representation of the craft she faced.

The craft had definitely been built along the lines of a *Stuka*. The rectangular body and stubby wings supporting large weapons pods

116

were unmistakably those of an STU-K5. It also had the forward stabilizers, located beneath the dome-covered cockpit, which added stability to the aerospace fighter when forced into atmosphere. Slight variations in the outline of the weapon canisters on the wings suggested, however, that they carried even more weapons than the standard complement of twin heavy lasers, which did not please Tyra at all.

What did please her was the ruined armor on the *Stuka's* nose and the gaping, fire-blackened hole where the computer reported a short-range missile launcher should have been. *Good! In a tight fight, that will be to my advantage, though his lasers are more than enough to destroy this thing. And not only is it packing more weapons, but its performance profile suggests it has more armor, too.*

Most intriguing, the visual image showed the craft's crest. At first glance, it looked to Tyra like a polar bear silhouetted against a black moon. *No, that can't be right. No bear has six legs. And why is there a white star in the middle of the moon?*

Tyra kicked her *Shilone* around in a split-S, sending it arcing up and off to the right and then rolling the craft back around, its nose pointed one-hundred-eighty degrees from where it had just been. She tried to get another weapons lock onto the enemy fighter, but it had pulled a similar move, sending their warbirds straight at each other again. Tyra, seeing that the abbreviated range of the battle would give her heavily armed enemy the advantage, let the *Shilone* continue its slide to the right. Then she brought the craft over and around in a broad barrel roll that looped her around her enemy's line of attack.

She armed another weapon as her scanners reported her foe nosing up abruptly and rolling in an Immelmann. *Fancy flying, but real risky. You gotta be woozy from the gees you've just pulled.* She looked at the icon of the craft behind her, then when the rim of her display disk pulsed gold, hit the switch beneath her left thumb. *Here's where you earn your pay.*

Four SRMs shot straight in on their target, hitting the enemy fighter just as it completed its roll. The missile explosions marched in succession up the nose of the fighter and onto the cockpit canopy. Tyra's combat computer updated the picture of her enemy by ripping holes in armor and denting the crystalline cockpit dome.

The pilot reacted to the attack after only a moment's hesitation. During that moment, the craft continued its roll, so the pilot increased thrust to bring the craft down and to the right. Tyra jerked her fighter up onto its left wing, then feathered the pitch controls to bring up the nose. The maneuver slammed her down into her seat and ground her

117

teeth together, but she hung with it. Boosting the thrust from her right wing, she sent the *Shilone* spinning back down to where it dove like a hawk on the fleeing raider craft.

Shimmering, multicolored balls danced before her eyes as she brought the *Shilone's* nose back up. *My dive arc is steeper than his. Gotta come up to target...*She pressed her left foot down, vectoring more thrust to that wing, which brought the left side of the craft up and around by fifteen degrees. *Hold it! Hold it!* Her *Shilone* swung in behind the raider as though being towed on a string. *Now!*

Tyra fired all her forward weapons at the enemy, and in turn, took damage from the medium laser he fired back into his rear arc. The scarlet beam of light slashed a blackened scar through the armor on the right side of the *Shilone's* fuselage. Tyra's combat computer updated the status of her ship, but no warning lights flashed or sirens sounded. *Clean bill of health.*

The nose-mounted large laser pumped kilojoules of energy into the enemy fighter. The ruby beam swept over the fuselage like a spotlight, but concentrated its attack on the left rear-thrust port. In combination with the medium laser mounted on the *Shilone's* left wing, it fused the port shut, instantly bouncing the enemy fighter to the left. The *Shilone's* other medium laser sliced armor plates from the aerospace fighter's right wing, but did little more real damage than melt the moon and bear insignia from its surface.

Tyra rode her fighter over to the left, relentlessly tracking the enemy. *With the left vector port gone, the pilot can't easily turn right. I've got him!*

Before she could lock her weapons onto target for another savage assault, the piercing wail of warning alarms filled her cockpit. "SRM lock!" She stomped down with both feet, engaging the overthrusters and hurtling her craft forward. Smashed back into her seat, she overshot her intended target and tried to pull another wingover to cut out of her current vector. Just as the *Shilone* began to react, the trio of SRMs launched by the raider's wingman hit.

One blasted into the surface of her left wing. The explosion rocked her craft and blew chunks of armor from the *Shilone*, but the inertial reaction to the blast actually helped her bring the fighter over on her intended maneuver. The other missiles slammed into the engine in the *Shilone's* aft. The computer dropped her power output by 7 percent and flashed two small icons against the *Shilone's* outline on the primary monitor.

A wave of heat washed into the cockpit to tell her what the computer silently displayed. *Great. Two heat sinks hit. I lose speed*

118

*with the engine damage and now this baby will slowly roast me. Well,
I won't have to worry about that if this new raider gets a lock on me
again.* "Nik, where are you?"

"On him, Cap. Break left. Three, two, one…missiles and lasers
away!"

Tyra rolled her *Shilone* to the left, and Anika's fighter shot
through the area she'd just left. As her ship corkscrewed through space,
Tyra saw a series of explosions on the ship Nik had been chasing.
Righting her craft, Tyra radioed a quick congratulation to her wingmate, then looked at her sensor screen and found her quarry. Easing
back on the thrust, she sent another flight of SRMs from her rear-arc
launcher at him.

The missiles missed their target, but forced the pilot further left
in his wild attempt to elude them. That pulled him even with Tyra only
thirty meters off her left wing. The pilot actually tossed her a salute,
then began to pull up. *Of all the…salute this!*

Tyra sent a microburst of ion thrust through her right yaw control
and cut all acceleration thrust. Unfettered by atmosphere, the *Shilone*
rotated on its vertical axis, tossing Tyra forward against her safety
belts and the left side of the cockpit. The fighters continued to sail
along in the same direction, but suddenly Tyra's craft brought all
weapons to bear on her foe.

The raider whipped his ship over on its left wing and vectored
thrust through the belly ports to pull away. Tyra's targeting system
locked onto this new heat source and flashed the dot in the crosshairs.
Without thinking, Tyra triggered all three lasers through the forward
thrust port. Armor vaporized at the lasers' touch, and the half-melted
vector louvers spun away amid clouds of ionized thrust. The hellish
beams stabbed up into the body of the craft itself, but at first, Tyra
could not tell if they had done any damage at all.

Almost as if her attack had not taken place, the raider's nose
continued to pull out of line. The unbridled thrust pouring through the
forward port stressed laser-heated stabilizers in the fighter's body, and
warped the metal out of shape. As the aft belly thruster pushed the ship
forward, the nose thruster just pushed it *away*. Like a wax model in
unbearable heat, the fighter began to bend in the middle, then the nose
snapped off right behind the cockpit. The two halves slammed into
each other, crushing the cockpit like an eggshell, then spun off in a ball
of twisted metal and fused ceramic armor.

"Val Two, this is Val One. I'm free. Where are you?" Tyra looked
anxiously at her scanner. It registered two enemy craft and three
friendlies, including herself, but the added heat pouring into her

cockpit had temporarily fried whatever circuit painted the identifier tags on the scanner icons. "Who did we lose?"

Another of the enemy craft winked out of existence before Anika answered. "Sorry, Cap. Needed to concentrate there. I have minor damage to a vector thruster, but I'll survive."

"Valkyrie Four reporting. My target is breaking off." Karl Niemi's voice carried no emotion with it. "Sven lost it in the first exchange. He took damage to the cockpit and was in and out thereafter. He did box one in for me and I got him."

Tyra felt a lump rise in her throat. "Damn! He was a good man. How are you doing?"

"I'm leaking fuel, but I should be able to coast to the *Bragi*. I've plotted a return vector. If I can't land in the bay, I'll punch out. I can't raise the ship, so I'd appreciate it if you'd radio and have a rescue team standing by."

"Roger." Tyra looked down at the frozen image of the black moon and six-legged bear insignia on her secondary monitor. "Anybody know what pirate unit this crest belongs to?"

Giddy with having survived, Anika called out, "Does it matter? They die like other pirates. Whoever they are, we fight them just like we fight everyone else."

Tyra felt her mouth go dry. *New pirates in new machines? I think we're in for the fight of our lives.*

Smoke coiled like oily black ropes against the red dawn sky. Scanning the horizon, Yodama knew it was more than just the heat churning out of his *Phoenix Hawk's* fusion reactor that made the sweat pour down his face. *First Battalion must be in the fight of its life! If that's the petrochem refinery burning, it means they've fallen back to their final line of defense.* He pushed his 'Mech forward, but only with the most powerful sense of doom.

As the disk of the sun appeared over the line of low hills between Shin's forward lance and the First Battalion's last stand, it flooded his infrared scan with white fire and so he shifted sensor modes over to vislight. While the computer was cycling through, a quick flash on magscan made him punch a button and switch the scanners back to magnetic anomaly detection. The computer painted, plain as day, humanoid silhouettes against the background of the vector-graphic landscape.

Shin stared at the display. *Another puzzle. They've given this flank over to infantry in metallic IR-baffling equipment!* Shin opened a radio link to Hohiro Kurita. *"Sho-sa,* I have infantry detected on magscan at 500 meters. We have been anticipated." He keyed a feed of his sensor data over to Hohiro's *Grand Dragon.*

"Are you certain, *Tai-i?"* Hohiro's voice was calm, despite the possibility of ambush. "Check the magnification on your scan. Could they be 'Mechs?"

121

"It's normal, *Sho-sa*. I would guess they're infantry with Inferno missiles meant to slow us down." Even as he spoke the word, Shin experienced a jolt in the stomach. Inferno rockets, fired from a handheld launcher, exploded in a fiery flood of jellied fuel that clung to a 'Mech like burning honey. Besides making a 'Mech an easier target for heat-seeking weapons, Inferno hits spiked the internal temperature of a 'Mech high enough to bake the pilot inside his war machine.

"I think you're right." Hohiro's voice remained confident despite the bizarre nature of the raid. "I'll move the rest of the unit south of that position while you and your lance scatter the infantry. Join us as soon as possible, but be wary. Who knows what other surprises these raiders may have for us."

"*Hai*," Shin replied smartly, all the while experiencing the same uneasiness he'd felt at the first staff briefing on the raiders coming in toward Turtle Bay. The raiders had popped in at a "pirate point," an arrival point much closer to the planet than most astronavigators felt safe plotting. They had obviously intended the raid to be a surprise, as it would have been except for an emergency oxygen run by a crew mining the rings. They had spotted the incoming DropShips and tight-beamed a warning to the planet.

That warning, however, had preceded the raiders' own radio message to the surface by only minutes. The raiders identified themselves as the "Smoke Jaguars," a name never previously associated with any Periphery pirate band. They wanted to know how many units the planet offered in defense, and took it easily in stride when told they were facing the Fourteenth Legion of Vega. The raiders then reported their targets and said they were only going to attack with two clusters. Shin didn't know what a cluster was, but their 'Mechs had been ripping the hell out of First Battalion.

He keyed the radio frequency open to the rest of his lance. "Arrow Lance, shift to magscan and drift north-northeast. We're to harry those infantrymen and drive them back. Be careful. They may have Infernos." As his men acknowledged the order, Shin moved his *Phoenix Hawk* out to the battalion's left flank. Massive jump jets, looking like a folded pair of wings, clung to the back of the eleven-meter-tall 'Mech. The war machine carried a pistol-like large laser in its right hand and each arm mounted a medium laser and an 50-caliber machine gun for anti-personnel use.

Using the joysticks on both arms of the command couch, Shin dropped the crosshairs for his weapons onto two of the hidden raiders. *I hate to see 'Mechs warring on infantry, but I can't let my people be broiled alive in their machines. Maybe most of those groundpounders*

122

will run if a couple get hit. Swallowing hard, Shin tightened his middle fingers on the firing studs and sent the familiar thrumming of machine-gun fire echoing up into the cockpit.

Tracer rounds burned white lines from the weapons to their targets hidden in brush. The magscan in the cockpit scored both volleys as direct hits and shifted the target icon from standing to prone, but Shin was sure some of the brilliant tracer rounds had lanced up and away as though ricocheting from their targets. *But that's impossible! Must just have hit some rocks behind them or something. A 50-caliber round will go through any body armor a man can wear.*

The other targets glowing like fireflies on his tactical display did not move and run as he had hoped. He swung the crosshairs onto two more human icons and pulled the triggers. Bullets burned into the targets, but one of the two targets seemed to jump away from the stream of projectiles. Leaping up, the icon bounded across the com-puter-generated landscape like a triple-jumper.

Stunned, Shin glanced back at the first two targets he had hit. Both were back up and bouncing across the battlefield like gazelles. With the same foreboding he'd felt earlier, the MechWarrior snapped his sensors over to magnified vislight. *May the Dragon have mercy! What the hell are those things?*

They looked like men in form, but their mottled gray and black flesh and the abnormal thickness of the armored plates on their bodies marked them as utterly alien. With no necks to speak of, their heads looked like lumps raised from the shoulders and breastplate as an afterthought. A dark V-shaped viewport passed for the mechanical creature's face. Thick cylindrical structures reinforced the forearms, but clearly served more than a strengthening function. The right arm ended in the muzzle of a laser, while the left forearm boasted an underslung machine gun muzzle. The left hand consisted of only a thumb and two abnormally thick fingers, and the feet looked like nothing so much as overlarge, bifurcated hooves melded onto the legs of a smaller creature.

Only when the double-barreled, back-mounted missile launcher lipped flame and sent a missile at his *Phoenix Hawk* did Shin realize he was looking at a suit of infantry armor instead of a living entity. The missile exploded against the *Phoenix Hawk's* left breast and spalled off armor. A tremor ran through the 'Mech on impact, but Shin barely noticed because his mind was running riot.

Without thinking, he impaled the armored figure with crosshairs and hit one of his medium lasers. The ruby beam struck the target and blasted it back as armor vaporized. The figure tumbled over and over again, grasses and bushes along its haphazard line of retreat bursting into flame as it passed. The figure rolled to a stop on its face, with the now-detached missile launcher continuing to tumble several meters further on.

"Arrow Lance, be careful. These are not normal infantry."

"Roger that, *Tai-i*," said Arishige Shimazu from the cockpit of his *Firestarter*. "The machine guns just seem to make them mad."

Shin spitted another figure with a medium laser. "At least the lasers keep them…" His mouth went dry. The infantryman he'd hit first with a machine gun burst and then with a laser bolt struggled to his feet. The gray and black jaguar-like spotting had been burned from the front of his armor, revealing shiny metal where some of the armor had melted and run, but the figure moved with no real difficulty. Dropping to one knee, it extended its right arm and sent a laser bolt flying at the *Phoenix Hawk*, burning away some of the 'Mech's head armor.

Unbelieving, Shin stabbed a large laser toward the little man and mashed his thumb down onto the firing button. The scarlet beam slammed into the humanoid metallic shell, pouring kilojoules of energy into it. The form wavered like an image seen through rippling water, then vanished as the hellish beam totally consumed it.

The smoking hole left where the figure had stood did nothing for Shin's piece of mind. *I'm forced to use a heavy laser against that thing, but there's nothing left to show I destroyed it! It could have jumped away. Hell, there's not even any proof it was there in the first place!* Shin saw the quartet of glowing impact sites the computer added to the outline of his 'Mech on his status monitor. *Nothing but the damage done to me!*

More and more of the little infantrymen popped up over the hilltop to surround Shin's embattled lance. As the raiders closed in, their bouncing gait made them tougher to hit. Worse, as he would track one of them to blast it with his energy weapons, two or three others were targeting his 'Mech with impunity. Damage sites dotted Shin's 'Mech like flea-bites, while his efforts to hit his attackers were almost as fruitless as swatting at such diminutive insects.

"Yodama, help!"

Shin whirled his *Phoenix Hawk* at the panicked sound of Harunobu Mori's voice. The infantrymen had swarmed over Mori's *Locust* like ants pulling down a grasshopper. One of the *Locust*'s bird-legs had crumpled beneath withering assaults, and two of the armored figures clung to the other leg, pumping bolt after bolt of laser fire from their right arms into the 'Mech's other hip joint. Three of the infantrymen hammered the 'Mech with their free hands, stripping off sheets of armor as they burrowed into the *Locust*.

Shin swept machine gun fire over the infantry. The bullets failed to penetrate the armor, but the sheer kinetic force knocked several from their precarious perches. One of the figures hung on somehow to the 'Mech's good leg, but the bullets blasted a hole in the blocky backpack that had once mounted a missile launcher. Lightning geysered out as a detonation shredded the figure's back. The infantryman fell limply to the ground, then Mori crushed it as his 'Mech struggled back to its feet.

Suddenly, a form blocked Shin's viewport. Clinging to the *Phoenix Hawk's* head with one hand, the raider pointed his laser at the viewport and triggered it. The red beam slowly began to eat through the polarized glass, while the raider began to beat his armored head against the viewport in anticipation of breaching it.

Shin jammed both feet down on the jump jet pedals of his command couch. Ion jets ignited with a sharp jolt, kicking the forty-five ton 'Mech off the ground. As it rocketed skyward, the figure slipped away, returning Shin's view of the battlefield below, and granting him a look at the conflict being fought beyond the hill. For a moment, Shin almost wished the figure had kept him blind.

Below him, the infantry had reestablished its hold on the *Locust*, and smoke was beginning to boil from holes torn in the 'Mech's flesh. Malcolm Yesugi's *Stinger* was down, with a dozen raiders working furiously to tear it apart. Shimazu had moved in with his *Firestarter* to help clear the enemy from Yesugi's 'Mech, but a half-dozen of the armored fleas gnawed at it despite repeated baths in ion-flame.

Beyond the hill, the Fourteenth Legion of Vega lay in tatters. As Shin had guessed, the petrochem refinery had, indeed, been put to the torch. Flaming rivers of thick, blue-black liquid gushed from the ruptured sides of storage tanks. The First Battalion had obviously created the rivers in desperation because they knew no 'Mech could wade through a flood of fire without overheating. Their fiery moat should have warded their flank and directed the attack to an area more easily defended, but the trail of mechanical carcasses told a different story.

Somehow the raiders managed to get through the flames to hit the undefended flank! Shin stared at the raider 'Mechs but couldn't identify them. He glanced at his auxiliary monitor and met the disturbing sight of the computer flipping back and forth between several different 'Mech designs in its effort to correctly label the raiders. Looking up again at the horrible tableau, Shin saw one of the raiders emerge from the flames, rivulets of burning oil running off its legs.

The raiders, about two dozen 'Mechs, pressed forward. They chased the remnants of First Battalion back into the ranks of Second Battalion, then engaged the Kurita reinforcements at the extremes of long range. Seeing two 'Mechs go down in the initial barrage, Shin had the sickening feeling that one of them was Hohiro Kurita's *Grand Dragon*.

Once more, the armored figure hauled itself up over his viewplate like a malevolent ghost and resumed working on the glass. Again, Shin punched down on the pedals to boost himself even higher, hoping to shake the man. An explosion at his 'Mech's back accompanied a flashed warning on his status monitor. Something had blown out the left jump jet, letting the right jet send the 'Mech into a lazy pirouette.

Dammit! There must be another one of them working on the jets! Shin gasped involuntarily as the figure on his view plate began to pound his head against the glass with renewed intensity. *Two hundred fifty meters up and falling fast! If the drop doesn't kill me, he will!*

Shin slammed his fist down on the eject button. Explosive bolts around the faceplate detonated in unison. They blew the faceplate out, wrapping the armored figure in shards of glass. The invader spun up and away, for a heartbeat allowing Shin to believe he was rid of his tormentor.

Hanging on by one hand, the armored raider swung back down, his steel-shod hooves clanging against the lip of the cockpit. The figure bounced up and down, its silhouette resembling nothing so much as an excited ape. It may have been trying to speak, but the warning klaxons blaring in the cockpit drowned out the sounds. The creature raised its right hand and pointed the laser at Shin, making his intent loud and clear.

Fire filled the spherical cockpit as the ejection rockets on the back of Shin's command couch ignited. Inertia jammed Shin back down into the couch's thick padding as the rockets catapulted him free of the doomed *Phoenix Hawk*. He hurled through the sky, spinning and whirling uncontrollably, which told him he'd struck the raider in the exit from his 'Mech. The wet stickiness running down over his thighs also told him the raider had not missed his dying laser shot.

The couch's gyrostabilizers kicked in and brought an end to the chair's wild ride. Using the foot pedals, Shin turned the chair and directed it down in a small meadow about five hundred meters from where the infantry continued to dismember his lance. He slowed the chair for landing and saw his *Phoenix Hawk* hit the earth.

His ejection had snapped the 'Mech's head back and imparted a slow backward spin to the humanoid machine. With all the aerodynamics God gave the average mountain, the war machine flipped end over end, then landed on its head. The body crushed the cabin like an empty eggshell, then the 'Mech's broad shoulders hit. Inertia splayed its arms out, grinding clenched fists into the earth and causing the 'Mech's sturdy legs to telescope down into the torso. Fire spurted from all the growing cracks in the *Phoenix Hawk* as the legs speared the fusion reactor, then the limbs shot up from the doomed 'Mech on jets of ion fire. As the legs spun away, the rest of the 'Mech exploded, sowing the battlefield with mammoth shards of half-melted ceramic armor and jagged slivers of ferro-titanium skeleton.

Arrow Lance's 'Mechs, by dint of their size, weathered the blast easily. Debris from the *Phoenix Hawk* washed over them with all the damage of a summer shower. The smaller raiders, however, suffered as armor sheets twice their size sliced through them and bone fragments impaled them. Even those that survived the shrapnel storm fell prey to the explosion's shockwave. It knocked them flying, freeing their captives.

Shin grounded the command couch and popped the restraints holding him into it. He pulled off his neurohelmet, then looked down to see how much damage the raider had done with his last shot. *I don't feel any pain, just blood. That's got to be bad.*

He was right. The wound was horrible, unsurvivable. Blood covered him from the lower part of his cooling vest, down his legs, and into the tops of his boots. Already black flies buzzed around him, and in his shocked state, he could barely summon the strength to shoo them away.

Fortunately, the blood was not his.

Weakly, Shin grasped the armor-sheathed left arm and lifted it away from his waist. The smooth metal felt almost warm and fleshlike, and the fingers remained curled around a small piece of weather-stripping from the *Phoenix Hawk's* face. A slight dent near the upper arm showed where the command couch's leading edge had hit it during the ejection. Extending up beyond the shoulder, half of the thing's head armor and a broad plate from its chest had been pulled free. Without looking inside at the pieces leaking blood, Shin threw the arm into the long, green summer grasses and climbed out of his chair.

He grabbed the back cushion and yanked it free of the couch. From behind it, compressed into flat packages, he pulled a survival pack, a forest camo jumpsuit, a gun and gunbelt, several clips of ammo, and a cylindrical, diatomic water purification pump. He laid each out on the seat of his couch, then stripped off his cooling vest and bloody shorts. Using several handfuls of grass, he managed to scrape off most of the blood, then pulled on the jumpsuit. After fastening the water pump to it, he shrugged the backpack on and belted the gun around his waist.

Ready to depart, he reached into the command couch's cavity and pulled out his *katana*. The sword measured a little over a meter, including hilt, and weighed no more than two kilos. The black lacquered wooden sheath showed no decoration, but Shin knew that under ultraviolet light, ghostly purple calligraphy would show up to identify the sword as belonging to a member of the Kuroi Kiri. As he was not a graduate of one of the elite military academies, Shin did not wear a wakizashi sword as well. *I am entitled to this one blade, but as my* oyabun *put it, "Two swords are for show. A blade's work is best done alone."*

Holding the sheathed sword in his right hand, Shin started away from his command couch and almost immediately stumbled over the discarded infantryman's arm. He dropped to one knee beside it and turned it over. *That's odd. The whole limb has gotten cold! It feels like the armor is chilling itself. And down inside here, a membrane has irised down, and what's this black, sticky stuff leaking all over? It almost looks like a tourniquet to stop the arm from losing blood. It's as though the armor is protecting it so the limb can be reattached... that's impossible—but no more so than anything else I've seen today. And it means...*

At the sound of grasses rustling behind him, Shin came up in a whirl. The *katana* flashed from its sheath and swung down in a glittering silvery arc. A last-second adjustment to account for the raider's incredible height guided the slash through the side of his neck and splashed crimson over his shoulder. The raider staggered back, and failing to steady himself because of his missing arm, fell awkwardly to his back.

Bile burned Shin's throat. The black, tar-like substance he had seen on the discarded arm coated the raider's exposed flesh with a thin membrane, but leaked a little blood around the cut. New jets of black fluid pumped from the portion of the helmet still in place. It oozed down over the raider's face and head, filling the wound and choking off the flow of blood. Shin heard a hissing and saw clear fluid spurt into the air. The raider moaned in concert with it, then smiled insanely. Eyes and teeth stark white amid a dripping black face, he rolled to his feet.

Shin dropped the sword and pulled his pistol. Unlike most of his compatriots, he preferred a heavy slug-throwing weapon to a lighter

128

needle-shooter. Holding the gun rock-steady in his left hand, he aimed at the raider's exposed left breast and pulled the trigger twice.

Both slugs hit and jerked the raider half around, but did not stop him. Shin shifted his aim up, sighting in on the exposed eye. Seeing the pupil as big as a saucer, he guessed the raider's armor was pumping him full of painkillers. *Whatever this guy is, he's not in pain. I hope like hell the body works the same way as ours.*

The first shot to the head dropped the raider to his knees, but it took the rest of the clip to kill him dead. Even with such massive trauma, the armor continued to pump the black synthetic flesh out to fill the wounds. Besides sealing the body in a black cocoon, it injected more drugs, then sprayed out some other clear chemical that killed the flies starting to land on the black skin.

Shin stared dumbly at the raider and its armor until the sounds of battle brought him back from his confusion. He knelt and fastened the arm to his pack. *I have to take this with me. With its arm torn off, that thing survived a 250-meter drop to the ground and tracked me to this spot where it took eight rounds to kill it—if I have killed it!*

He glanced back over his shoulder at the black curtain of smoke that had risen to hide the sun. *These are no Periphery bandits, that's for sure. I don't know what they are, but if they decide to take every world in the Inner Sphere, who can stop them?*

Trell I
Tamar March, Lyran Commonwealth
13 April 3050

Kommandant Victor Steiner-Davion ducked his *Victor* and sidled it left through the subterranean lagoon as the raider 'Mech stabbed its left weapons pod at him. The *Marauder*-type pod spat the artificial lightning of a particle projection cannon. The azure bolt sizzled over the *Victor's* right shoulder, drilled into a massive icicle clinging to the cavern ceiling, and split it with a thundercrack.

Despite the frost covering his Mech's viewplate, the intense blue of the energy weapon lit his cockpit like a strobe. Concentrating on the computer-created landscape of magscan data, Victor dropped his autocannon's gold crosshairs onto the enemy 'Mech's outline and punched the trigger button with his thumb. There was a loud scream like that of some mechanical banshee, and then Victor saw his volley hit its target.

The storm of depleted uranium shells again burrowed into the raider's left shoulder, pulverizing what little armor remained over the joint, then stripping the myomer muscles from the ferro-titanium bones. The bones themselves bent, twisted, and then finally snapped under the savage assault. The arm flew away, pulling taut the ammo chain to the autocannon, then popping it apart and continuing on its cartwheeling flight.

Victor grinned as his computer assessed the damage to his enemy. When he'd first encountered the unusual 'Mech, the computer had tried to tag it as a *Warhammer*, then as a *Marauder,* and then as a *Victor.* Realizing he'd never seen its like before, Victor commanded the computer to record all the data on the machine under the name "Thor," which he chose because the 'Mech had a heavy autocannon in one arm and a PPC in the other. *Thunder and lightning... just the stuff the god Thor used to toss about.*

The *Thor* swung its PPC arm in Victor's direction, but never managed a shot. Sending two flights of SRMs from the leg-mounted launchers of his *Crusader*, Galen Cox pummeled the *Thor*'s arm. SRM explosions blasted shards of armor deeper into the dim cave, and more important, knocked the gunnery pod wide of its target. Once again, the raider's PPC shot missed the *Victor*. It vaporized another icicle, but the cavern's bitter cold converted the mist into snow, which fell into the steaming lagoon.

Thanks, Galen. I owe you. Victor tracked the off-balance *Thor* as it tried to withdraw. Cutting to the left, it slammed into a huge stalagmite and bounced back while the megalith slowly tottered, then fell. As the *Thor* drifted involuntarily into Victor's sights, he triggered his autocannon. The weapon's whine filled the cockpit, and heat levels in the cramped quarters increased, drenching Victor in another layer of sweat.

The autocannon slugs ripped a scar down the *Thor*'s left thigh, then lanced sparks from its knee. Shrapnel peppered the water and some of the shells, having blown entirely through the joint, skipped off the water, and ricocheted deeper into the Thunder Rift complex of caverns. The *Thor*'s knee buckled, then twisted and locked again. Metal fused with metal, keeping the 'Mech upright, but reducing the knee to a solid, immobile joint.

"Kommandant, we have trouble." Galen kept his voice calm, but Victor heard the urgency in his voice. "I mark two more of these *Thor*s and two of what I'm calling *Loki* —'cause of its utterly mad configuration—in the Antechamber. It looks as if these Jade Falcons work in configurations of five, not lances of four like we do. I would suggest his lancemates are on the way."

"Roger, Galen." Victor glanced at his sector scan. *These new 'Mechs mean Galen and I are cut off from our rendezvous with the battalion in this direction. We'll have to backtrack through the Smugglers' Stroll to the Dragon's Lair.* "We could have had him, you know. Let's back off."

"Yes, sir."

Galen started his *Crusader* moving back, and the *Thor* mirrored the retreat. When Galen reported his *Crusader* in position to cover the *Victor*, Davion worked his way through the hot-spring-fed, underground lake. Feeling somewhat safer with a palisade of stalactites and stalagmites between him and the raider, Victor opened a radio channel to his aide. "If we hadn't submerged ourselves when we first picked up those reports of a scout moving through here, do you think we would have gotten him?"

Galen's reply came after a moment or two of thought. "If he'd been running on magscan, he would have seen us and had us at a disadvantage. He must have been using infrared scanning, and the hot water helped us dissipate our heat signatures. If we hadn't ambushed him, I think we'd have been in trouble. Despite all the shooting he did in that fight, he never heated up."

Victor nodded to himself. *If not for Cox keeping him busy and a couple of lucky shots from me, that monster would have eaten me alive. As it is, I've lost chunks of armor over my chest and right leg. The armor on Galen's* Crusader *has likewise been reduced to paper-thinness over his right torso and left leg. These raiders are tough, but at least they're not invincible.* "I agree, Mr. Cox. I'm going to radio Leftenant-General Hawksworth and see if he can give us a clear route to the battalion."

Victor punched two buttons on his command console and opened a tactical frequency directly to the regimental headquarters. "Badger One to Den Mother, come in. I need a new vector to the front."

General Hawksworth's voice sounded tight with tension. "Negative, Badger One. You are to return to the Den immediately. That goes for Badger Two as well."

Victor frowned. "Say again, Den Mother." Victor toggled a radio filter on and off, letting static break up the communication. "I'm getting static here. Please repeat."

"Don't play games with me, Badger. I know all about filter switching when you hear orders you don't like. That trick got old with Redburn on St. Andre in the Fourth War. Repeat, report to the Den immediately. I want you here."

Victor swallowed hard. "Roger, Den Mother. Reporting home immediately."

Victor left his BattleMech standing next to a *Leopard* Class DropShip. He clambered quickly down the rope ladder from the cockpit and tossed his neurohelmet to a startled Tech as he sprinted to the low, squat building that served as the regiment's brain center during times of battle. Like a lean greyhound, Galen Cox followed on Victor's heels.

The cavernous room resounded with echoed fragments of desperate radio reports and requests for reinforcement. In the eerie glow of radar screens and holographic display units, the communications specialists looked especially haggard. They nodded in concert with demands for support, then punched buttons to shift the calls to others who could better deal with the problem.

As Victor pulled on a parka over his cooling vest, he saw why Hawksworth had called him back to the base. *Someone has to organize this place. We can't mount a defense with everything running riot the way it is here.* He spotted Hawksworth hunched over a tactical display unit and cut straight through the crowd toward him. "Kommandant Davion reporting, sir."

Hawksworth listlessly returned his salute. The normally jovial man had been drained of all good humor. Strands of white hair fanned down over his brow and sweat dripped from his nose. "No beating around the bush, Kommandant. You saw that *Leopard* out there?"

"Yes, sir. I left my *Victor* beside it."

"Good. Get on it." The Leftenant-General looked up past Victor. "You too, Cox. Both of you. Get the hell out of here."

"No!" Victor's shout cut through the din filling the room. "I will not go! My battalion is out there getting cut to ribbons. I won't abandon them."

The General straightened up, fire returning to his eyes. "You will do as I order, Kommandant! You and Hauptmann Cox will get aboard the *Hejira* now and let it take you to the JumpShip *Strongbow*. You're leaving."

Victor clenched his fists, but refrained from slamming them into the tactical display table. "No. You can't send me away. If you do, we'll lose this fight."

"We'll lose it anyway." Hawksworth thrust a trembling finger at the tactical display. "We're falling back on all fronts. The circle is tightening around us like a noose. These Jade Falcons hit at incredible ranges and pick our defenses apart. I've got more casualties in the first three hours of fighting than I've had in the four years I've been on Trellwan. And they're only fighting us with three dozen 'Mechs and some crazy infantry unit in body armor."

Victor felt his heart begin to pound as Hawksworth spouted his litany of disaster. "Think, Leftenant-General! Do you want to be remembered by history as the man who lost Trell I, or do you want praise for defeating these *invincible* raiders?"

Muscles bunched at Hawksworth's jaw. "I'll be known as the man who lost Trell I. There's nothing I can do about that now." He met Victor's cold gray stare without flinching. "But I will *not* be known as the man who got Hanse Davion's heir killed."

"NO!" Victor stabbed a finger into the older man's chest. "Don't do that to me, General. Don't use my father against me. Don't be a fool." Victor looked down at the holographic map. "Galen and I met and blasted one of the raiders here in Thunder Rift. The terrain and obstructions bring everything down to a close range, and our people can fight that way. Pull units back into that cavern complex and into the Black Mountain foothills. We have to adopt guerrilla tactics to defeat these people, and we can do it. Dammit, man! Fight them! And let me fight them, too!"

"I'm sorry, Victor. If we had known, if we had more time, your plan might work. Hell, it might yet work, but I can't bet your life on it." The older man looked up. "You'll get your chance. And when you do, I pray you have more courage than I do. Good bye, Highness." To Cox, Hawksworth added, "Get him out of here."

Before he could say anything, Victor felt himself spun about. Galen Cox's fist flying toward his chin formed the last vision of Trell I that Victor Steiner-Davion ever saw.

Myndo Waterly directed the attention of the Precentors to the center of the chamber. "We received this transmission from our facility on Balsta yesterday. I have reviewed it once and now present it for your edification. The message is relatively short, and in the Precentor Martial's style, somewhat succinct."

She clapped her hands once, sharply, and the lights in the bowl-shaped chamber dimmed. Directly above the gold-star insignia of ComStar worked into the floor, the image of the Precentor Martial flickered to holographic life. The image only showed him from the shoulders up and had been so enlarged that his eyepatch was the size of an aircar's steering wheel.

"The Peace of Blake be with you, Primus. I bring you greetings from Ulric, the Khan of the Wolf Clan. He has graciously consented to the transmission of this message, provided I release no useful military data. He does not suspect us of duplicity, but prefers not to give the appearance of breaching his own security."

Focht adjusted the patch over his right eye. "In the three months I have been here, I've been given freedom to monitor virtually all operations that are military in nature, while being kept out of harm's way on Ulric's flagship. The Wolf Clan fields a superior military force in both tactics and equipment, which has made short work of opposition. They have been inordinately fair in accepting surrenders, and the only plunder they take from conquered worlds is in the form of slaves—

though they call them bondsmen. Besides becoming an involuntary workforce, these captives also play the role of hostages against the good behavior of the people of their former homeworlds."

The Precentor Martial dipped his head in a bow, then lifted his head and gazed out of the hologram at the Primus. "My attempts to discern their intent have been met with polite evasion, though some interest has been expressed in our assistance. I have heard strange references to a massive migration following the invading forces, but Ulric denies it. Still, there is a curious lack of common folk aboard the ships I have visited. This is definitely an army on the move. And on the move quickly.

"Though they attempt to hide it, there is an apparent rivalry between the different groups in the invasion force. Representatives of other clans are present on Wolf ships, and the Khan of Khans, the ilKhan, resides on Ulric's flagship even though the ilKhan is of the Smoke Jaguar clan. Despite the distance between his clan and the Wolf clan, Leo ilKhan is in daily contact with his people and apparently directs their efforts in the Draconis Combine."

Focht rubbed at his good eye, then allowed himself to smile. "The Clanspeople are an interesting lot. Many are good-natured, though all are cold and competent when in battle. Trading verbal barbs and other forms of surrogate combat are popular here, and bondsmen see their share of abuse, but the damage done is rarely serious. And even what we consider a serious injury is of little consequence to these people. I have heard of a broken spine being repaired, and one Medtech even commented that he could have restored my eye if he had been present at the time I lost it."

The Precentor Martial glanced out of the frame, then nodded. "I will be permitted to contact you from our next site. The Wolves have agreed to leave our stations operating in exchange for a promise that we kill all military intelligence being sent out by partisans. I have given such orders to the facility manager here, and he has further passed the order to the other worlds the Wolves have taken. Ulric understands, of course, that you have the final authority on that. If you choose to overrule my action, Ulric will order that the ComStar facilities be isolated, but he will respect our peaceful sovereignty."

The image vanished, plunging the room into darkness for a second or two before the lights came up. Myndo surveyed the faces of the First Circuit members and was pleased at the shocked expressions. *They knew I had sent the Precentor Martial as my personal ambassador to the invaders, but they did not expect me to authorize him to offer them intelligence to further their conquests.* She smiled benignly.

"Comments?"

Ulthan Everson, the burly Precentor from Tharkad, lifted his hand slightly. "By touching his face during that transmission, Focht let us know he was being monitored. In light of that, I am surprised that Ulric allowed him to speak so frankly about the taking of slaves and the political divisions between the clans."

Diminutive and fragile behind her crystalline podium, the Precentor from the Capellan capital of Sian shook her head in disagreement. "Could it not be, Precentor Tharkad, that Ulric wished us to know that he is a power to be reckoned with even if he is not the ilKhan? That Ulric has this Leo in his power suggests a compromise somewhere in the past. Why else would the Khan of Khans consent to command his clan from a flagship far away from the battle?"

Myndo smiled as Sharilar Mori, the woman who had succeeded her as Precentor of Dieron, accepted Precentor Sian's challenge. "I would suggest, Jen Li, that the answer to your question is of greater concern to us than any political infighting in the invader camp. The fact that Leo is in *daily* contact with his forces—forces operating over 130 light years from him—must imply that these clans have Hyper-Pulse Generators, and are well versed in their use."

Myndo lowered her eyelids, which gave her face a catlike air. *HyperPulse Generators are what give ComStar power among the Successor States. It is the HPG that allows us to send instantaneous messages between planets up to 50 light years apart. We alone know how to make and operate them, and thus everyone else is dependent on our services. Through us flows great power because we have control of communications between the stars.*

The sleeves of his scarlet robe flopping down around his wrists, Everson leaned forward on his podium. "I do not think we have to worry about these invaders as a rival to our services, Precentor Dieron. The Jade Falcon clan has already taken ten Steiner worlds, including the deep strike at Trell I. And the Wolves who are so politely hosting the Precentor Martial have taken the worlds of Icar and Chateau. This is more of an emergency than any competition they might offer our Order."

Gardner Riis, the lanky, platinum-haired Precentor of Rasalhague, also stared harshly at Sharilar. "I, too, must direct your attention to the worlds that have been taken. Between attacks by the Wolves and the Ghost Bears, the Rasalhague Republic has lost eleven planets. The military threat is paramount."

Myndo raised a hand, letting the sleeve of her gold silk robe slide down to her elbow. "Cease this squabbling so that we can review the

137

facts of this invasion and assess its true danger." She nodded at Everson. "We begin with you, Precentor Tharkad. What have these so-called clans taken and how have they done so?"

Everson's blue eyes darkened. "In a crescent from Barcelona up and around the rim of the Lyran Commonwealth, the Jade Falcons have taken Barcelona, Bone-Norman, Anywhere, Here, Bensinger, and Toland. Their thrust forward, which took place only two days ago, added Steelton, Persistence, Winfield, and Trell I to that list. The conquest of the last four worlds is not complete, but it appears inevitable. The Wolves, as I mentioned earlier, have taken Icar and Chateau."

The Primus turned her cool gaze on Everson. "Precentor Tharkad, Trell I was the world where Davion's first-born was stationed. What news of him?"

Everson addressed himself directly to her. "Leftenant-General Hawksworth evacuated Victor Davion about four hours into the battling and the invaders let him go. His DropShip is heading for the JumpShip *Strongbow,* which is expected to leave the system sometime tomorrow." The Primus looked at him, measuring the man. It was almost as though she knew what he might say, but she nodded for him to continue. "Apparently the Prince suggested a strategy to Hawksworth before being sent off, and the General has put it into play. The plan will not keep the Jade Falcons from taking the world from Steiner, but it will make it a costlier victory. Aside from that, the situation is very dark."

Bidden to speak by a gesture from the Primus, Riis recounted the losses for his state. "The Wolves have taken Skallevoll, Outpost, Svelvik, Alleghe, The Edge, New Caledonia, Balsta, and St. John. The Ghost Bears have taken Thule, Damian, and Holmsbu. In their March 7 attack on Thule, they missed a prize by sending only one flight of aerospace fighters to harry a DropShip heading outsystem. The Rasalhague Minister of Defense was aboard the ship, and his death would have utterly crippled the Republic."

Huthrin Vandel ran his fingers back through his black widow's-peak. "From the list of captured worlds, Precentor Rasalhague, one would think the Rasalhague Republic has no defenses at all."

Riis bristled at Precentor New Avalon's remarks, but restrained himself from an angry protest. "You seem to find this all so amusing, Vandel, but I daresay you would be singing a different tune if the Federated Suns had been invaded." He glanced up at the Primus. "The invaders have ripped through Rasalhague's troops rather easily, but are magnanimous in accepting surrender. The only exception to this rule concerns mercenaries. The clans, especially the Ghost Bears, seem to take a dim view of soldiers selling their services for money. There are no reports of prisoners being executed, but the clans have stripped captured mercs of their 'Mechs, effectively ending their careers."

Myndo cocked her head, but the utter confidence of her expression belied either curiosity or distress. "How has this affected other mercenary units? Do they hold firm or do some prefer retreat?"

Riis shrugged. "Most remain on garrison, probably because they are not aware of all the facts. As you know, information about the invasion has been limited in its publication. We of the First Circuit must surely have the best view of what is actually occurring. As you have instructed, only the government officials of each nation should know the extent of his losses, and each of them should imagine that only their area is hit. The general populace is not yet alarmed, and most believe that the loss of communications with a few rim worlds is nothing more serious than a raid by Periphery pirates."

Sharilar Mori laughed grimly. "I would say, Precentor Rasalhague, that if you truly believe Theodore Kurita and Hanse Davion have not guessed at the scope of the invasion, you are not fit for the position you currently hold. Neither of them is so foolish as to imagine that an invader of such might and skill would be daunted by borders drawn on a map or decided by treaty. I concede that none knows how far the invaders have come, but they can venture a very good guess."

Sharilar looked up at Myndo. "The Draconis Combine has lost seven worlds to the Smoke Jaguar clan. Because habitable worlds are more widely spaced in the region of the Combine bordering Rasalhague, the Smoke Jaguars did not have so broad a front to assault or they would probably have taken even more planets. Richmond, Idlewind, Tarnby, Bjarred, and Schwartz fell easily. Rockland, a garrison planet on the Alshain border, made more of a fight of it, but the battle did not last long. On Turtle Bay, the Fourteenth Legion of Vega got ripped up, but did manage to inflict damage on the enemy. In addition, elements of the yakuza have created a guerrilla resistance there that is giving the Smoke Jaguars trouble. Though line units have left the first four worlds, the conquering troops are still on Turtle Bay two weeks after their initial victory."

Myndo folded her arms, slipping her hands into the voluminous sleeves of her golden robe. "What of Hohiro Kurita? Has there been no word?"

Sharilar shook her head. "My people have not located him or his body. It is possible he is among the throng of captives the Jaguars have taken, but we cannot get anyone in to see them. No matter our claims of neutrality, the local garrison commander claims his orders come from the ilKhan and he has not been given leave to grant the prisoners any visitors."

"Returning Theodore Kurita's son to him could win us many concessions from him, or even the Coordinator himself," the Primus said. "Is it possible for our ROM team to break Hohiro out of prison?"

Sharilar frowned. "The Adept in charge of the ROM cell says it is not. He points out that the prison housing the captured MechWarriors is the toughest maximum security facility in the Turtle Bay system. In fifty years, only one person ever escaped from it. He was shot in the stomach during the attempt and has not been heard from since he plunged into the Sawagashii River just outside the prison.

"Aside from that, Primus, to attempt such a rescue would easily poison our relationship with the clans. If it turns out that they cannot be stopped, the gratitude of Theodore and Takashi Kurita would be worthless."

Myndo smiled approvingly. "Well-spoken, Precentor Dieron. We must remain always a step ahead of events. In the meantime, what is your estimate for how long this yakuza resistance will last?"

The slender Precentor from the Draconis Combine shrugged. "I have no way to judge this. My informants cannot or will not travel among the yakuza. We have been unable to gauge their strength, but unless the yakuza have a storehouse of weapons and munitions hidden away, their resistance cannot last. They will cause trouble, but they will never drive the invaders from Turtle Bay."

All the Precentors turned to Myndo now that the reports seemed to be complete, but she was looking at Ulthan Everson, her old adversary. She smiled, as at some secret amusement. "Yes, Precentor Tharkad?"

Fingers intertwined, Everson rested his hands on the podium. "I believe, Primus, that the Precentor Martial said Ulric expressed interest in our offer to share intelligence with the invaders. But have we abandoned our own mission of leading humanity back into the light? How does aiding a formidable, *possibly non-human,* invader in his conquests help us to achieve our own mission? These clan creatures wear civilization like an ill-fitting mask. Our message of spiritual prosperity can mean nothing to them. I do not see the logic in your offer to help them."

"My old friend," Myndo said, and Everson reddened at her patronizing tone. "I believe this course of action is the most logical under the circumstances and *does* advance our cause."

She smiled, as though in innocent wonder, which seemed to

140

deepen his distress. "First, in exchange for military intelligence, the invaders will allow us to remain on their conquered worlds. We will be permitted to act as an interface between the populace and the invaders. In short, we will become a benevolent class of administrators able to restructure the worlds, including all governmental, and more important, educational systems to indoctrinate the people with our message. To wit, ComStar is the savior of all mankind and only through us can mankind rise again."

She ticked off another point on one finger. "Second, we can direct the invaders at targets that we want destroyed for our own purposes. We can prompt the Smoke Jaguars to shatter Luthien and decapitate the Draconis Combine. We can turn them toward cold Tharkad to eliminate that half of the Steiner-Davion axis. With Thomas Marik sympathetic to our cause, we can keep the invaders *away* from his holding until they have spread themselves thinly enough to be defeated."

Her voice dropped with the last point. "Third, and oh so final, giving the clans military intelligence means that they will become dependent upon us. We will become their eyes and ears, so that on the day we cut them off, they become blind and deaf. By that time, the Precentor Martial will have learned enough to enable him to defeat these hordes. And so all mankind will rejoice as ComStar rises up to destroy the alien invader."

She smiled cruelly. "In short, ladies and gentlemen, the Clans and their invasion are a means to an end. I will use them and then discard them. Thereby, and in our own time, the dream of the Blessed Blake will come true."

Book III

Heart of the Beast

Edo, Turtle Bay
Pesht Military District, Draconis Combine
16 April 3050

Shin Yodama clutched the threadbare blanket tightly to himself.
The sewer's damp chill soaked up into him through the stone ledge
where he sat. Moisture condensing on the tunnel ceiling dripped down
with a dreadful monotony, but he tried to use it as a kind of mantra.
Anything…anything to take me away from this place.

Two men grumbling next to him broke his concentration. "Why
do we follow the Old Man if he is content to keep us down here like
rats? These invaders are not a storm that will blow over. I do not think
the Old Man has the will to fight them."

"He may be content to die down here in the darkness," the other
man said, "but I am not. I want to be staring up at the rings when I go."

Both men fell instantly silent as someone splashed through the
knee-deep stream and approached the forward guardpost. Shin drew
his pistol, but kept it hidden by the folds of the blanket. The figure
approaching through the gloom sped on, seeming unmindful that he
was rushing into danger.

As the man pulled parallel with his position, Shin eared back the
hammer on the pistol. "Who goes there?" he demanded.

The figure stiffened, his terror apparent. "Azushi Motochika," he
gasped.

"Where the hell have you been?" Shin asked, putting his pistol
aside. "We were certain the *Muen no Daineko* got you."

The man shook his head and confidence replaced the fear in his

145

voice and silhouette. "No. The Smoke Jaguars did not get me, but I got them!" Motochika chortled with self-important glee. "Did you hear that explosion earlier?"

Shin nodded. "We assumed it was the Cats trying to seal another of our ratholes."

"No, one of the sewer rats struck back at the Cats. I planted a bomb at the Meibutsu club. It exploded and I think it got all of them. There were a dozen in there. I saw them go in. I counted them."

The other two men whooped with joy and pounded Motochika on the back, but Shin just stared in disbelief. "What about the others in the club? What about *our* people in there?"

Motochika hesitated, but another of the men answered for him. "What do they matter? They were collaborators. They deserve what they got."

Shin launched himself from the ledge and pistol-whipped the speaker down into the sewage stream. "Idiot! They are our *people*! Without them and their support, we are nothing! We survive on their generosity because they believe we can drive the Smoke Jaguars away."

Before the echoes of Shin's outburst could fade, the heavy thunder of a BattleMech marching overhead smothered the sound. The three other men cringed in terror, the wet one pressing a hand to the gash Shin's gun had opened on his cheek. Shin looked up, the Mech-Warrior in him not letting him show fear. He pointed at Motochika.

"You! Come with me. We're going up to see what the Cats are doing. You two stay here." Without further ado, Shin set off down the tunnel, then along a side passage running north. His course took him beneath the streets that the 'Mech trod above. When the 'Mech stopped, however, Shin continued on until he came to a set of rusty iron rungs set into the wall. He let Motochika catch up with him, then pointed up. "This leads to an abandoned building that should be just up the street from where they're standing. You go first."

Motochika mounted the rungs enthusiastically at first, but slowed as he reached the surface. He timidly pushed the trap door open, then crouched at the edge before waving Shin on up. Shin, who had waited in the shadows below the surface light's reach, joined the yakuza bomber and crept across the room to a broken window that looked out onto the street.

It was warmer up here, but Shin felt colder than ever at the sight of the BattleMech he had tagged *Daishi*—Great Death. It was surrounded by five armored warriors like the one he had been lucky enough to kill in the field two weeks earlier. Each had a boxy missile

146

launcher on his back, clamped firmly to the assembly Shin believed to be a power pack for the armor and its weapons. Instead of relying only on their right-hand lasers, the infantry carried heavy rifles, too. The yakuza MechWarrior noticed how the rifle's trigger-guard assembly fit neatly over the laser muzzle, probably to somehow amplify the laser's energy.

The *Daishi* 'Mech towered above all but the tallest building in this slummy *burakumin* section of Edo. Though its legs and torso might have belonged to a humanoid model, the LRM launcher on its left shoulder looked like a multi-eyed auxiliary head and its arms were little more than bundles of gun-barrels. Shin recognized the weapons as large lasers, small autocannon, and medium lasers, with three more medium laser ports dotting the front of the 'Mech's chest.

One of the armored warriors stepped forward. "People of Urama-chi precinct, we have traced a criminal to this place. He committed the most wasteful and careless act of planting a bomb in a place where civilian and military personnel were present. The explosion caused great loss of life—both to our people and to yours. This will not continue."

The infantryman pointed to the hovel nearest the *Daishi*. "If the individual responsible is not turned over to us in the next two minutes, everyone in this house will die."

Shin cuffed Motochika roughly. "Fool, see what you have done?"

The younger man looked at Shin as though the MechWarrior were mad. "You don't expect me to go out there, do you? I struck a blow for our freedom. They're bluffing. They won't destroy that house."

Shin stared hard at the man beside him. "You best hope they don't. If they do, and if you refuse to turn yourself over, I'll shoot you myself and dump your body in the street."

As the deadline neared, faces appeared in the windows and doorways of the street, including the house designated for destruction. The Smoke Jaguar infantryman bowed in the direction of the street, then turned toward the dwelling. At the same time, the *Daishi* swung its elbows back and locked its weapons down on the wood-scrap and tar-paper hovel.

Motochika turned away, but Shin grabbed a handful of his hair and forced him to look out the window. "Watch!"

At the large laser's hellish touch, the hovel exploded into an instant bonfire. Crackling flames appeared from everywhere at once, rising above the *Daishi*'s head, then dropping down again as a hail of autocannon slugs flattened the building. A woman, her hair and clothing aflame, dashed screaming from the door, but one burst of laser bolts from the invader infantryman silenced her cries forever.

The acrid scent of singed hair and burning flesh made Motochika tear away from Shin's grasp and vomit in the corner. Shin ignored him as the *Daishi* stepped forward and snuffed the flames beneath its flat metal feet. The infantry spokesman again addressed the street.

"People of Uramachi precinct, we have traced a criminal to this place. He committed the most wasteful and careless act of planting a bomb in a place where civilian and military personnel were present. The explosion caused great loss of life—both to our people and yours. This will not continue."

The soldier pointed to the next hovel. "If the individual responsible is not turned over to us in the next two minutes, everyone in this house will die."

Shin's mouth went sour. "The same words, Motochika, and the same gestures. Are you going to take responsibility for your actions, or are you going to let more people die?"

Motochika, still holding himself on hands and knees, looked weakly over his shoulder at the *Kuroi Kiri* MechWarrior. "No one else has dared to strike at them as I have. The Old Man authorized expeditions to steal weapons and supplies from them, but we have never hurt them. While he has been content with thievery, they have been kidnapping our people. If I am the only man with true courage, I cannot allow myself to be sacrificed because no one else will actually *fight* these invaders!"

Shin fought to control the fury Motochika's words aroused. "What courage does it take to plant a bomb and kill innocents as well as the guilty? You are nothing more than a common murderer! And how is it you claim courage when you huddle here like a whipped cur? There must be more than courage. There must be intelligence and honor in your actions. You are a child striking out blindly, then expecting others to take responsibility for your mistakes."

A bright spark of orange caught Shin's eye from the street, and almost instantly he knew what would happen. He leaned over and grabbed Motochika by the collar of his leather jacket. "This is courage. Watch and learn."

A bald-headed, saffron-robed Buddhist monk walked down the rubble-strewn street toward the Smoke Jaguars. He held his hands pressed together just below his chin and bowed to the lead infantryman. "You will forgive me for not appearing sooner. I had sought to deny my fate. I planted the bomb you described. You need punish no

148

one else."

Without hesitation or remorse, the infantryman swung his laser rifle around and triggered it. The bolts stitched their way up the monk's body and knocked him flying. He finally rolled to a stop, smoke rising from the black crater where his face should have been.

The Smoke Jaguars then turned and walked away as though nothing untoward had happened. Shin released Motochika, letting him slump against the window casement, then crept across the floor to the trapdoor. "Were I like you, Motochika, I would shoot you. But it is not my place to challenge the Old Man's authority. I am going to him now to ask for his judgement. If you are the man you claim to be, then follow me."

Deep beneath the streets of Edo, the Old Man held court in a dusty, dimly lit room. Though small and skeletally frail, he was still possessed of great power. He stared mercilessly at Motochika's kneeling form, then lifted his gaze up enough to include the entire audience in his displeasure. From his position off to the side, Shin felt insulated from the Old Man's ire, but embarrassment and shame radiated from the other yakuza in the room.

"So, Motochika Azushi," the Old Man spat out, "you presume to know what is best for us in this war against the Smoke Jaguars? You have had a revelation that gives you wisdom beyond your years? You have fathomed my thinking and believe you know the perfect strategy? You have decided that I am a doddering old fool who knows nothing? And this prompts you to plant a bomb that kills more of our people than it does of the enemy, and then you allow a blameless monk to pay for your action? Have you less pride than you have brains?"

The Old Man drew a knife from the sleeve of his black silk kimono and tossed it to the kneeling hoodlum. "Use this."

Motochika looked up, horror clawing lines of terror in his face. *"Hara-kiri?"*

The Old Man shook his head scornfully. "If I had wanted you to slit your belly, I would have scraped the knife dull against the stones and then given it to you. No. Prove to me your remorse."

Motochika took up the knife in his right hand. All the fingers of his left hand he curled into a fist except for his littlest finger. He pressed that hand to the stone floor, then laid the blade's razored edge against the top joint. He looked up before proceeding.

The Old Man's eyes narrowed. "You caused the death of blameless people."

149

Motochika moved the knife down to the second joint. Keeping his head up, he sliced the blade through his own flesh, then brought his fist over, snapping off the severed part of his finger. Shin felt as though he'd been punched in the stomach while some of the other wartime yakuza recruits reeled away, but Motochika made no sound. He hugged his maimed hand to his chest, then offered the severed joints and the bloody knife to the Old Man. "Excuse me, *oyabun*. I will not fail you again."

The Old Man nodded, then looked up at the others. "Many of you assumed I would do nothing to hurt the Smoke Jaguars, but you are wrong. I have had another, greater concern and I have been long in deciding how to acquit it." He glanced at Shin. "As you know from our compatriot, Yodama, Hohiro Kurita was lost in the fighting, but we have seen no proof of his death. This is because he is not dead. The Smoke Cats have him in their prison. We will get him out and return him to the Coordinator."

Someone in the crowd gasped aloud. "But that is impossible. They are holding their prisoners in Kurushiiyama. No one ever escaped from there when the ISF controlled it, and the Cats have only increased security. We will die in the attempt."

Shin saw many others nod in agreement. *That prison*—Kurushii-yama—*is a legend even on Marfik. It is aptly named Pain Mountain. After what I have seen in fighting the Cats, if they want to keep people in, it's not likely we can get them out.* Still, Shin was not inclined to bet against the Old Man.

"Why am I surrounded by children?" the Old Man asked in disgust. "Do you not remember any of the stories? Kurushiiyama surrendered a prisoner once before. Its walls have yielded in the past, and will yield again. We will see to it."

A tall man crouching just behind Motochika shook his head. "The story of that escape is an old-wives' tale. The prisoner was gut-shot. He may have escaped the walls of the prison, but he died in its shadow and the Sawagashii River carried him away."

Pity and scorn playing over his face, the Old Man unknotted the *obi* on his kimono and fully bared the left side of his chest. He pointed to the bullet wound scar that obliterated part of the dragon tattooed across his chest and abdomen. "This is where they shot me as I was clearing the last wall."

He let the rest of his kimono fall away, revealing the tattoo on the right side of his body. Like a grand mural running from shoulder to waist, the multi-colored tattoo depicted the story of a young man's journey from captivity to freedom. At his shoulder, the saga's hero

150

escaped the confines of a dark, lightning-struck mountain. At the foot of the mountain, he fought and killed two demons, though one managed to stab him in the belly with a fiery spear. Finally, blood leaking from the wound, the hero swam a river and took refuge in a seasonally dry storm tunnel until he could regain enough strength to leave the sewers.

"You see, my friends, it is possible to beat Kurushiiyama. The route I used to escape had been deemed the secondary one because we saved the first and best for a mass escape. Our first duty is to the Dragon, and saving Hohiro will acquit it perfectly. After that," the old man smiled cruelly, "the Cats will be ours to play with."

20

Prince Hanse Davion leaned forward across the briefing table and stared at the holographic map of the Lyran Commonwealth. He reached over, took his wife's left hand in his right and gave it a reassuring squeeze. "Are you certain four more worlds are under assault? They only hit the first dozen two weeks ago! Is it possible?"

Justin Allard, standing halfway down the table, nodded slowly. "It looks as though the troops that conquer the worlds are not the same ones used to garrison the worlds. Once the populace is disarmed, the invaders are most willing to work with local authorities to maintain order. This frees up the shock troops to move on to hit forward targets."

Melissa Steiner Davion studied the map. "If their first wave took twelve worlds so easily, why did they only attack four in this wave?"

"That, Archon, is a question I cannnot answer." Justin nodded to Alex Mallory, the tall, slender man seated at a data terminal opposite him. Alex hit a number of keys, and the map dissolved in favor of some grainy images of bizarre 'Mechs engaging in combat. The picture zoomed in on the green falcon crest on one 'Mech's chest. As soon as that picture stabilized, another crest—a wolf's-head—appeared beside it.

Justin pointed to the crests. "The majority of worlds taken from the Commonwealth in the first wave were captured by troops wearing this Jade Falcon crest. Icar and Chateau fell to the Wolves. Their 'Mechs are similar, but we have seen no combined operations. They appear to share a similar origin, yet the two forces are not working together."

Alex brought the map back up, then focused it down on the rim sector where the invasion had begun to nibble away at the Commonwealth. Invaded and conquered worlds burned green on the map, while bright blue pin pricks of light represented the Commonwealth's other worlds. "The four new invasion sites were hit by Jade Falcon troops alone. Reports have come in slowly, but we think the Jade Falcons concentrated their attack forces from the ten worlds they took to attack the next four. There is even a possibility that they reinforced Trell I because Leftenant-General Hawksworth's guerrilla tactics still appear to be giving them some trouble."

I pray to God you survive, Hawksworth. I want to pin a medal on your chest for being smart enough to get Victor out of there. Hanse's blue eyes narrowed. "How long can the Twelfth Donegal hold out?"

Justin's face darkened. "As an effective fighting force? Not much longer. Their 'Mechs have to be virtually out of supply. Their energy weapons will continue to work as long as there's fuel for the fusion engines, which is no problem on a world producing hydrogen, but the lack of repair facilities and missiles will put them at a great disadvantage. I'd be very surprised if they survived even a month more."

Alex nodded in agreement, but added a caveat. "Trell I does have a couple of hidden supply stations within Hawksworth's operational area. They were part of our advance line of supply when we feared the Ronin renegades would come through Rasalhague and hit our worlds. Hawksworth knows where they are. If he can reach them, he'll be able to resupply and maintain a good defensive position. Of course, any pitched battle against the 'Mechs these invaders are using would be foolish, at best."

Hanse leaned back in his chair as the others settled into silence. *We always expected an invasion, but I expected Kurita or the Free Worlds League to launch it. We never dreamed of an attack by invaders from beyond the Periphery in 'Mechs the like of which we've never seen... In their first wave, they almost robbed me of my son and then they sliced a chunk from my wife's realm. So far, the only way to combat them is with the desperate tactics of guerrilla war. That could work in isolated cases where the conditions of a world are favorable, but it cannot throw the invaders back.*

The Prince took a deep breath. "But who the hell are they?"

For the first time in Hanse's memory, the Secretary of Intelligence let frustration flash over his face. "I don't know, Highness. So many theories have been put forward, but we don't have enough information to sort the fact from the fiction."

Melissa folded her hands in front of her, and tapped the tip of one thumb against the other. "Are they Kerensky's people come back?"

Justin looked at his aide, and the slender man hit a few keys on the computer, summoning another holographic image above the center of the table. "We cannot be certain, of course, but their unit organization points away from a Star League genesis. As you know, we organize our troops on the old Star League four/three system: four 'Mechs make a lance, three lances make a company, three companies make a battalion, and three battalions make a regiment—with the battalion and regimental command lances adding up to about two dozen 'Mechs."

The gentle click of keys brought up another table of organization beside the first. "As nearly as we can extrapolate from the data gathered by your son and Hauptmann Cox, the invaders work on a system based on the number five. Five 'Mechs make up a lance, and five of those units make up the next highest unit, and so on."

Anger knotted Hanse's eyebrows together. "So, if it's not Kerensky descendants, then who?"

Justin interlaced his fingers behind his neck and shot a glance at Melissa. "Perhaps it has some connection to the time, some forty years ago, when Katrina Steiner disguised herself as the pirate the Red Corsair, while she, Morgan Kell, and Arthur Luvon escaped into the Periphery to elude Alessandro Steiner's assassins. That was when they found a Star League-research center on an uncharted planet that had recently been ravaged by pirates. Many of the items they brought back after the year in hiding remained mysterious for decades. You know, of course, that this is the origin of the Black Boxes that helped us circumvent the ComStar Communications Interdiction during the Fourth Succession War. Until the pirates overran them, that small reseach station had been able to continue experimenting and learning while the rest of the Inner Sphere went into a technological decline because of centuries of war."

Melissa chewed her lower lip for a moment. "So you're suggesting that if there was one research station that escaped discovery all those years, there could be others?"

The Secretary of Intelligence nodded emphatically. "There could be thousands more, Highness, but it only needed one—one that engaged in weapons research. The 'Mechs these invaders have are definitely built along the lines of our BattleMechs. They just happen to be more powerful and run a lot cooler. Getting more power out of a fusion engine and creating better heat sinks are two of the prime focii

154

for research at the New Avalon Institute of Science. It could be that the invaders just had a three-century head start on us."

Hanse's right hand convulsed down into a fist. "And they started from a level of technology we have yet to reach. What do you think happened then, Justin? Could a base able to produce such powerful 'Mechs fall to Periphery bandits who now turn their resources against us?"

"Probably not." Justin shrugged helplessly. "All we can say for certain is that whoever they are, their technology supersedes anything from the days of the Star League. Other than that, all we can do with our current information is continue to guess."

How can we grapple with an enemy who outguns us and outmaneuvers us when we can't figure out who they are and what they want? It's like wrestling with smoke. "Your ideas have merit, and I know you'll keep working on the problem. Identifying the invaders is of paramount importance."

"Of course, my Prince."

Davion's blue eyes flicked up and met Justin's dark gaze. "Have we had *any* word from General Hawksworth?"

"No, Highness. It is believed he destroyed his Black Box just after sending Victor away. We are not certain if any of the supply depots have a working model. If they do, a message could be on its way to us now." The spymaster knotted his fists in frustration. "Even if he had sent us a message, it would take over a week to reach Tharkad. And if he sent it here to New Avalon, it would take almost a month."

The Archon leaned forward. "He hasn't been able to send a message out through ComStar?"

Justin shook his head. "Either the invaders have quarantined all ComStar outposts, or else ComStar is working with the invaders so they won't interfere with their business of running messages between the stars. We know ComStar is filtering some messages because the news that Victor escaped Trell I came more quickly through a message by Hauptmann Cox to his family than did Victor's priority message to the Court."

The Prince frowned deeply. "If ComStar is filtering messages, we'll never be able to learn the true extent of the invasion. We cannot be certain if or where our enemies have been hit."

Justin smiled briefly and glanced at Alex. "I think, my Prince, that we have beaten ComStar at their own game." He nodded to his aide. "You came up with this brainchild, Alex. You explain it."

Alex nodded and summoned a stream of data to replace the map. "ComStar, for reasons known only to its leaders, has chosen not to broadcast news of the invasion. I suspect they want to avoid panicking the public until the various governments have had a chance to react to the threat. Regardless, they have continued to supply commodity and production reports from all the worlds that have been hit. For all intents and purposes, things look normal out there."

The clack of keys summoned another line of data and a variable matrix below it. "To keep anyone from twigging onto their deception, ComStar has composed the figures from data collected over the last seventy years. The figures look correct because they once were correct. I compared the numbers with our database for the same reports. It took some work, but I think I figured out the pattern. Someone at ComStar is sloppy and hasn't varied their algorithm. By using it on the data they're supplying for other likely target worlds, I think we can pick out where the invaders have hit Rasalhague and the Draconis Combine."

The map returned as Alex worked his magic on the computer. Instead of just presenting the Lyran Commonwealth's rim worlds, he expanded the map to show likely invasion sites in Rasalhague and the Combine. "As you can see, things are going best for the invaders in the section of Rasalhague nearest the Commonwealth border. I believe this is the area being rolled over by the Wolves. ComStar's data on the five worlds from Csesztreg through New Bergen to Leoben has just started to look like it's been doctored, so I would guess they've ony recently been hit. Closer to the Combine, and in the Combine itself, things are moving more slowly."

"Are the invaders meeting any resistance in the Rasalhague Republic?" Melissa asked. "They lost thirteen planets in the first wave, which is a much higher percentage for them than a dozen worlds is to the Lyran Commonwealth."

Justin pointed to one world on the Rasalhague rim. "The strike here at Thule could have crippled Rasalhague's ability to fight, because their Minister of Defense was on a tour of the rim at the time. We thought he'd been killed, but he appeared in a recent news holovid from Rasalhague itself. Our sources have given us independent confirmation of his survival, though rumors had it that the invaders almost got him."

The Archon arched a brow. "That's interesting. The Jade Eagles strike at Trell I where our son is stationed. Invaders strike at Thule while the Minister of Defense is there, but just miss him. I notice they also hit Turtle Bay. As I recall, Hohiro Kurita is stationed there, is he not?"

The spymaster nodded gravely. "Unless Hohiro was moved

offworld just before the assault, he was on Turtle Bay when it came. We have no reports that he escaped, and so it is conceivable that he was killed in the fighting. Even without first-hand information, there are indications that matters did not go well for the Combine in that region."

Justin looked over at Alex. "Bring up the Combine's recent troop movements." As the map image drew back, then focused in on a section of the Combine/Commonwealth border, icons representing military units formed neat little columns below. "As you can see, Theodore Kurita is exercising his authority as Gunji no Kanrei. He is shifting troops away from the Dieron Military District and sending them back on their own supply ships. He will be able to deliver twenty crack regiments to oppose the invaders by the end of the summer. He is also shifting troops up from the Rasalhague border, but there are not really enough of them to do more than slow the invaders' advance."

As Alex added animation to the troop movements, a gross area of weakness appeared in the Combine's border defenses. The Prince stared at it like a chessmaster studying a board. *If Theodore completes his troop movements, he leaves the Combine's belly open for a strike that could cripple it. Caught between the invaders and our forces, the Combine would be crushed once and for all.*

He looked up. "How did we get this information?"

Justin pressed his palms flat to the table and leaned forward. "Half of it came through agents we have on the various bases that are giving up troops. They did not know what to look for until we gave them very specific orders, however. We were seeking confirmation of intelligence obtained by an agent on Luthien. We believe that agent has blown his cover, but the Gunji no Kanrei has not seen fit to eliminate him yet."

Hanse leaned back and steepled his fingers. "Then you think Theodore Kurita may have leaked us this information about his own weakness?"

Justin hesitated for a moment, then nodded. "Yes, Highness, I do." He took everyone in with his glance. "He would never admit weakness, but his letting us see his intended troop movements could imply that he believes the invaders are a greater threat to the Successor States than we are to each other."

Hanse took a deep breath and let it out slowly. *This would be a perfect opportunity to destroy the Combine—and more than one of my Field Marshals will encourage me to do it. But, if Justin's right about Theodore's intentions, I shared the Kanrei's view of the invasion. What good is defeating an enemy if I cannot build upon that victory? It would be foolish.*

Hanse turned to his wife. "What do you think?"

"It strikes me, beloved, that Theodore must be as concerned about his son's fate as we were for ours until we heard that Victor had been evacuated. You know that Kurita will prosecute a war with the invaders as well as anyone in the Successor States. If we were to attack him, he would be forced to divide his effort, and that would spell disaster for his war against these strangers. One look at the map makes it clear that once the invaders have broken the Combine, the Federated Suns is next. If troops we now have assigned to the Combine border could be shifted rimward, they could be used to hold back the invasion into the Commonwealth."

"As always, your analysis is most valued and most accurate," Hanse said with a smile, then turned to Justin. "Do you concur? Do we move our troops from the Isle of Skye out to face the invaders?"

Justin nodded. "Our JumpShip assets are in position to move quickly. We can deliver troops to the rim more quickly than the Combine can. I've already sent orders for mercenary units under contract to head toward the rim. If we're lucky, they can form a firebreak to slow the invaders."

"What about the Eridani Light Horse?" Hanse asked. "Are they willing to move before the ink is dry on the new contract?"

"Yes, sire. I had confirmation of compliance with the orders from them earlier today." Justin half-closed his eyes. "I also had a request from my brother Daniel to move the Kell Hounds toward the rim. I don't know where Dan got the information, but there seems to be no question that the invaders were responsible for Phelan Kell's death out in the Periphery. I gave him permission to move both regiments to Sudeten, as I thought that would be a good rendezvous world for whatever forces we're going to send north."

The Prince smiled appreciatively. "Excellent thinking. Any word from Jaime Wolf?"

"No reply to the message I sent two weeks ago. I do know, however, that Epsilon and Zeta Regiments have been withdrawn from their duty posts in Andurien, and Thomas Marik is rather upset that he was not warned about it. They appear bound for Outreach."

"I see." The Prince sat forward, resting his elbows on the table. "Wolf's calling his people home for some kind of meeting, I suspect. When they make a decision, we'll hear about it." Hanse paused as he studied the map. "Issue orders for the First Kathil Uhlans and all the Deneb, Arcturan Guard, Lyran Guard, Royal Guard, and F-C Regiments from Skye March to depart for Sudeten. Let Morgan know he's in charge of this Army group and route Victor to Sudeten. We'll move troops from the Crucis March up to reinforce the Terran corridor and Skye."

The Prince caught himself as his wife's silence and the flash of pain in Justin's eyes finally registered on his brain. "Forgive me, Justin, for asking you to issue that order. I know your son is in the Tenth Lyran Guards."

The Secretary raised his head proudly. "I am certain he will serve you well, my Prince."

"Of that I have no doubt, Justin Allard." The Prince's eyes narrowed. "But I recall a time twenty-three years ago when I told your father to order another man to kill you. Both he and I knew that issuing such an order was the only way to keep you alive while you were under cover, but I know how difficult it was for your father. I never imagined I'd have to put anyone else through that again."

Melissa looked up at him. "Then why do you put yourself through it?"

Hanse took her hands in his. "I can order Victor to meet with Morgan on Sudeten with a clear heart. You and I know that he would never accept being left out of the planning. He would be there—with or without orders, so forbidding him to join the fight would do no good. I think it is better to let him *know* we have confidence in him than to have him imagine we do not."

JumpShip Dire Wolf, *L-5 Orbit*
New Bergen, Rasalhague Province, Free Rasalhague Republic
3 May 3050

Phelan Kell jabbed Griffin Picon in the side with his elbow. "Don't watch me, Griff. Watch the *stravag* door!"

The shorter, broadly built blond man grunted with the blow and turned his attention to the closed portal to the bondsmen's dormitory. "You're learning to curse in the Clanner's tongue quickly enough, Kell. Come a time we won't be able to tell you from them. How much longer will it be?"

"Not long, and if you'd been cursed as a malingerer as much as me, you'd quickly pick up the words, too!"

Griff laughed. "Yeah, that Vlad really has it in for you, doesn't he?"

"Quineg, Griff. You're supposed to end a question like that with "quineg" if you want to speak like a Clanner."

"And you are not to use contractions, Phelan," the pirate reminded him. "And, all quinegs aside, that Vlad's hatred for you goes bone-deep."

"All because I ruined the paint job on his 'Mech." Phelan snapped a chip down into the circuit board, then fitted it inside a gray petrochem box just slightly larger than a pack of cards. He slid the cover from beneath the corded loop on his wrist and settled it in place with a click, then palmed the device. "There. Got it."

Griff glanced back over his shoulder at the mercenary. "You sure that thing will work?" After a moment's hesitation, he added,

"Quiaff?"

Phelan crossed to his bunk and slipped the slender box inside his mattress. "Aff. I fixed up two of their audiosensitive locks on a work detail last week. Their Tech was so impressed with my skill—" Phelan rolled his eyes to heaven—"that he even showed me how to burn eproms down in the workshop."

The former Periphery pirate made no attempt to hide his confusion. "Eproms?"

Phelan half-smiled. *So much of what the Clans have on this JumpShip is lostech in the Successor States. I've heard of burning programs into computer chips, but that's only because of my father's friend, Clovis Holstein. Clovis showed me how to do it, but the machine he used was a monster with only a quarter of the features of the one down in the maintenance bays here. With equipment like that, it's no wonder their 'Mechs are so superior to ours.*

"An eprom is a computer chip. It holds the program—the information and instructions—that makes machinery work. What I did was to create a program that will cycle through all possible lock combinations, starting with two numbers and working up until the lock opens. The little lights on the box show you how many numbers are being checked in the current series."

Griff shook his head. "You amaze me, kid. In my day, all I had to know about chips was that if one went bad in my 'Mech, I had to steal a whole board from another machine to make it right. But you say that thing will get us into the bondswomen's area?"

Phelan nodded solemnly. "I have to do some soldering next time I'm in the shop and get some power cells for it. But after that, if the door has a lock, this will open it."

Griff clapped his hands once, sharply. "Yeah! Won't everyone be happy to hear that? I haven't seen my little Marianna in far too long... What's wrong?"

The young MechWarrior forced the sour look from his face. "I don't mind you knowing about this lockpick. You're responsible, and I appreciate your keeping the others off me when Ulric transferred me into this dorm." Phelan looked around at the large room filled with bunks whose blankets were a shade deeper than the prison gray of the walls and the cold metal deck. *Tossing me in with this pack of pirates could have been a mistake, but I don't think Ulric makes many of those. I suspect he wanted to see if I could survive in this viper pit.*

Phelan sighed. "I just don't want Kenny Ryan getting his hands on it. His turbolift doesn't quite make it to the bridge, if you know what I mean. He'd want to use my lockpick to get into the armory or the

'Mech bays or the bridge, which would cause real trouble."

Griff's green eyes widened. "It could get us into those places?"

The Kell Hound nodded. "As I said, if it has a sonic lock, this will get you in. Still, those places have guards and are very secure. I wouldn't mind if Kenny got his head toasted by a laser bolt or two, but I'd hate to think of the other casualties...You and I both know he wouldn't have the guts to go alone. The only reason Kenny became leader was because he saw which way you all wanted to go and jumped out in front."

The door suddenly opened, cutting off any comment from Griff. Ranna's smile died a little at seeing the pirate, but not completely. "Phelan," she said, "the Khan requests your presence."

Phelan stood up quickly and straightened his jumpsuit. He didn't realize how hard his heart was pounding until he noticed the bemused expression on Griff's face. That made Phelan blush, and the pirate smiled even more broadly. *She's smart and pretty and a MechWarrior, and, dammit, I like her. Why should I be embarrassed? I'm not betraying them, am I?*

Griff winked at Ranna. "Now don't keep him out until all hours. The boy needs his rest if he's going to do his work."

Ranna tried to look stern, but her eyes revealed amusement. "Work. Now that is a novel concept for you. I thought the lot of you were supposed to be painting Storage Bay Seven. I can check on that."

Griff held up his hands. "I was just heading down there." He glanced at Phelan. "Don't embarrass us, kid. Remember not to slurp your tea."

The mercenary smiled cruelly. "Don't worry, this ain't the Periphery. They actually give us cups."

Griff laughed and slipped past Ranna at the door. The Clanswoman kept the disapproving look on her face until he had passed, then her facade also dissolved into laughter. Phelan threaded his way between bunks and followed her out into the corridor.

"Do you know what the Khan wants, Ranna, or do I just have to wait and see?"

She shook her head, then tucked her hands into the pockets of her navy jumpsuit. She fished around for a moment, her expression becoming annoyed. Then she patted her chest pockets, still not finding what she sought. "How could I forget my remote?" she asked irritably, more to herself than Phelan. She turned to him as they reached the turbolift. "We'll have to take a short detour. I left something in my quarters."

She punched the button summoning the lift. Once inside, she

directed the box up four levels, punched in the entry code, then ushered Phelan along a corridor marked by a shield and a blue-white ball icon. When they came to a door marked by a wolf's-head and a single, red dagger-star beneath it, she keyed a series of five numbers into the lock panel. Tones sounded out, but came too quickly for Phelan to identify them. The door slid to the left, then shut silently after they entered.

Phelan looked around. *The room is smaller than the Khan's suite, to be sure, yet doesn't feel cramped.* The foyer, with a mirrored closet to the left and hatchway into a lavatory to the right, opened onto a small living room. A drafting table took up the far left corner, and surrounding it, Phelan saw pens, pencils, brushes, paints, and other artist's tools. Paintings hung on each wall, and though they used different colors and were of vastly different subjects, Phelan noted elements of style that bound them all together.

Ranna passed through a hatchway in the living room's right wall and disappeared into what Phelan assumed was her bedchamber. He crossed to the far wall and stared closely at a landscape in tones of purple and red. The use of blurred lines gave the impression that the subject of the painting was a hellishly hot place. Above the highest mountains, the cold blackness of space and the brilliant, diamond-like stars looked like a sanctuary, but somehow Phelan read a reluctance to leave the world for the boundless void between the stars.

She called to him from the doorway. "Do you like it?"

"I'm not sure that I'm supposed to like it. It reminds me of the first time I shipped out from Arc-Royal with the Hounds and realized what it meant to be leaving the world where I was born. I was only five at the time. I felt enthusiastic because it was a great adventure, but I also didn't want to leave my grandparents and cousins behind." Phelan turned to face her. "I wanted to go, but I also dreaded it, quiaff?"

Ranna nodded. "Aff, I think I have some understanding. That is a landscape from the world where I grew up. I felt great sadness in leaving. But you mentioned cousins..."

Phelan smiled sheepishly. "Well, that's what I called them. They weren't first cousins, of course, because I didn't have any—I mean, that was years before we found out about Chris. They were just the folks I grew up with on Arc-Royal."

She smiled as what he was saying finally seemed to dawn on her. "Ah, your sibko. I can understand why you were reluctant to leave them. Fortunately for me, my sibko has traveled with me, or I with it, as it were."

The Kell Hound looked over at Ranna and shook his head. "Somehow I wouldn't have figured you for an artist." Ranna started to object, but he held up his hand up to forestall her complaint. "What I mean is that the atmosphere around here seems more suited to military than to artistic pursuits. Of course, you're different than the others—I can't imagine Evantha or Vlad painting or writing poetry, if you see my point."

The thought brought a smile to Ranna's face. "Aff, maybe I get your meaning, but I am not sure. You have to understand that I grew up with them, so I am blind in that area. It is hard to be sure how I could be different."

Easy, Phelan. This discussion could get you into lots of trouble. He shrugged, then lifted his right wrist and pulled at the cord binding it. "Except for you and the Khan, everyone else looks no further than this wristlet when they look at me. You see the person I am, for better or worse. Without your help, I might not have survived this long."

A devilish gleam lit her azure eyes. "Oh, I do not think that is true, Phelan Patrick Kell. Perhaps I look beyond your bondcord because you seem different from the other bondsmen."

Phelan raised an eyebrow. "If I may be so bold…how, why?"

She leaned easily against the hatch's edge. "The Khan's interest in you first opened the door, I believe. At first I resented being assigned to nursemaid you, but now I do not find the duty so odious…"

"There is a God…"

"That is one of the things I like about you, Phelan. You have a wit and express it easily. You don't seem to be plotting your escape, but I know you are smart and dangerous enough to have that idea somewhere in your head." She saluted him with a nod. "Most of all, your sense of independence seems to set you apart from the others. You are so much a MechWarrior that the bondcord will forever chafe your spirit."

He half-closed his eyes, considering her words. *She's right. I would love to escape this tin whale, or at least get a message out. Have I given myself away, or is she just very good at sizing up the opposition?*

He forced himself to smile easily. "I thank you for your insight."

"And I thank you for yours as well." She returned his smile. "I have to ask you about something you said before. You knew your grandparents, quiaff?"

"Sure. Grandpa Kell's still alive. He's slowed down a bit at age eighty-seven, but he still manages his holding. Grandpa Ward died in the war before I was born, but Grandma Ward is alive and lives on Arc-Royal."

Ranna's eyes narrowed. "Eighty-seven years old? You have to be joking."

Phelan shook his head. "Nope. He'll be eighty-eight this October."

"Amazing." Something squeaked in the room behind her. Half-turning, Ranna held out her hand and made little cooing sounds. "Nothing to be afraid of, Jehu." A dark creature scuttled its way onto her arm and perched on her shoulder.

Phelan blinked twice and pointed at it with his left hand. "What in hell is that?"

Before Ranna could answer, the creature leaped from her shoulder and spread its bat-like wings. Long tail whipping through the air to steady it in flight, the furry animal flew straight at Phelan. It swooped low, then arced up and landed on his forearm, wrapping its prehensile tail around his wrist. It flapped its wings twice to steady itself as Phelan got used to its weight, then it loosened its tail-grip and walked up to his shoulder.

Its face, hind parts, and tail made it look like a small primate, but the wings marked it as a creature apart from monkeys and apes. It chattered melodically on his shoulder and gently wrapped its tail around Phelan's neck like an old friend draping his arm over the mercenary's shoulders. Red and white stripes of fur on its face made it look comically fierce.

Ranna stared at him. "That is incredible. Jehu never takes to strangers. What did you do?"

Phelan shrugged gently so as not to disturb Jehu. "I don't know. I don't even know what Jehu is, so I can't imagine what I did to inspire his trust."

"Her," Ranna corrected him. "Jehu is a surat. They are native to one of the worlds beyond the Periphery. They are intelligent and highly domestic, which puts them two steps above most of the lifeforms in the Periphery."

"Hey, be careful. You pulled *me* out of the Periphery."

Ranna bowed her white-maned head. "Present company excepted, of course. After all, Jehu likes you, which means your lifeform is clearly superior." She looked at the surat. "Jehu, go to bed. Eat later."

Jehu unfurled her wings and hugged Phelan's head, an experience he found much like being smothered with a musky sweater, then leaped into the air. Ranna turned sideways and slipped out of the doorway as Jehu swept her right wing up and banked through the opening. Ranna smiled at the creature, then guided Phelan out into the corridor. "Keeping Jehu is my one luxury."

Reaching the turbolift, Phelan punched the button on the wall. "Yeah, pets are special."

"Do you have one, quiaff?"

The mercenary shook his head. "Had. He was a dog named Grinner. A mongrel with even some wolf blood in the mix. Called him Grinner 'cause he always had his mouth open in a leer that could turn into a bark or growl or a big, wet slurp with his tongue." Phelan smiled, but sadness crept into his eyes.

Ranna followed him into the lift, then laid a hand on his forearm. "What happened to him?"

"He died." Phelan swallowed, trying to choke back the lump in his throat. "We were on station in the Free Worlds League, very close to the border with the Capellan Confederation. Chancellor Romano Liao had sent a Maskirovka assassin to kill Dan Allard—he was a Major at the time—and his family. Dan is Romano's brother-in-law, and that witch decided to kill his whole family to get at Justin Allard, Dan's brother and husband of her sister Candace. The assassin got the wrong house, and assumed I was one of Dan's kids."

"Grinner came at him like a shadow. He never growled or barked, just leaped and took the man down. I woke up when they crashed into my nightstand and I heard the vibroblade, but it was all over by then. Grinner ripped out the assassin's throat, but the assassin had carved my dog up." Phelan rubbed his hands against the chest of his jumpsuit. "He never even whimpered. Just kept grinning with those bloody teeth until he died."

Ranna took Phelan's left hand in both of hers and gave it a squeeze. "Your grief is mine. I..." She looked up into his green eyes and hesitated, then looked down again. "I am glad you were not hurt."

"Yeah, that was definitely the up-side of the whole experience." The Kell Hound sighed heavily. "I named my 'Mech 'Grinner' after the dog. Always was a good omen until I ran into Vlad."

She squeezed his hand again. The lift door opened, but she kept hold of his hand even after they'd stepped into the corridor. Phelan tried to read her expression as their fingers drifted apart, but her profile revealed nothing. *Does she just feel sorry for me, or is there something more there? I'll admit to being confused and not a little gun-shy after Tyra. No, it must be just pity, nothing more. Remember Phelan, you are an outsider and a bondsman, and these people ultimately are your enemies.*

Jump Ship Dire Wolf, *L-5 Orbit*
New Bergen, Rasalhague Province, Free Rasalhague Republic
3 May 3050

Instead of taking him to the Khan's personal quarters, Ranna guided Phelan through a deck he had not visited before. Here the shield icons were more fearsome, especially one of a human figure with both arms raised above its head, a lightning bolt in each hand and another showing a single eye hovering above crossed laser rifles. The corridor itself was kept dim, and a line of red lights at the juncture of bulkhead and deck showed them in which direction to travel.

Phelan realized it had be a command center of sorts. The dim lights obviated the necessity of adjusting one's eyes to the darkness common in briefing rooms. More important, the martial icons could only mean that behind these doors were the nerve centers for the various branches of Clan service. Phelan guessed that the ship had reached some new system and the Clansmen were about to take it.

The mercenary's pulse began to thunder in his ears. *Why would the Khan want me present during an invasion? Even if I can't escape, why expose me to military intelligence that I should not see? I would occasionally like to be told what is expected of me. The novelty of living like a rat in an experimenter's cage is wearing thin.*

Ranna opened a door whose icon was a single eye, and led the way into a comfortably appointed chamber. Once inside, Phelan saw several JumpShips through a large, round viewport into space. Fixed to the walls, maroon leather couches provided comfortable seating. Each of the walls, save the one to his right, was decorated with holo-

167

graphic battlescenes.

The whole right wall was made of glass and looked out over the *Dire Wolf*'s battle bridge. Below, dozens of Clan officers of both sexes stood around an area containing the largest holographic display Phelan had ever seen. It covered an area at least six meters in diameter, and the images rose more than three meters above the deck to the ceiling. Beyond it, running the length of the rectangular room and side to side, hundreds of data terminals flickered with green or amber light. Down at the far end of the bridge, a giant portal looked out onto the planet under assault.

Walking within the images, Phelan recognized Ulric, but could not identify the dark-skinned man walking with him. "Ranna, who is that with the Khan?"

She frowned slightly. "That is Leo, the ilKhan. He is a Smoke Jaguar and the current Khan of Khans. He is the invasion's leader."

Phelan looked over at her. "You don't much care for him."

She shook her head. "He is the ilKhan, and I do as he commands. But he is determined to interfere with the Khan's assault of the planet. The Khan wanted either Star Colonel Lara or Star Colonel Darren to lead the attack, but the ilKhan has forced him to use Star Colonel Marcos instead of Darren."

Phelan matched names to the individuals Ranna pointed out from their vantage point. As Leo and Ulric left the holographic area, the Precentor Martial joined them. Then two other individuals entered the display unit. Star Colonel Lara wore her blond hair midway down her back and her fingernails painted black. Marcos joined her, confidently smoothing his jet black hair against his pate. Both looked fit, and to Phelan, far too young to be Colonels.

"What is that thing where they're pacing around?"

Ranna looked at Phelan curiously. "That is a full-sized holotank. Its computers coordinate all the different datafeeds to create a three-dimensional map of the planet below. It can even get down to a one-to-one scale, though it loses some resolution at that point. Mostly it is used as a tactical display, but similar units are used for simulator combat to train the Elementals—our armored infantry. Evantha is an Elemental."

The mercenary watched the two Star Colonels stalk around the holotank. "A Colonel should be commanding a regiment, which means about one hundred-thirty 'Mechs and assorted support personnel. It's going to take more than one regiment to capture a whole planet. Why doesn't the ilKhan just send both of them?"

Ranna hesitated just long enough for Phelan to know she was

leaving something out of her answer. "New Bergen—I believe that is what you call the world—has said they only have two regiments to oppose us. Each Colonel will bid for the honor of taking the world."

"Bid?" Phelan didn't understand at all. "Your 'Mechs might be good, but this isn't a game…"

Ranna look at him with steel in her blue eyes. "No, Phelan, this is not a game." Tension filled her voice and body. When a large data monitor mounted on the wall flashed to life, her head whipped around and she watched the scene below intently.

In the holotank, the Star Colonels shook hands, then left the display. Ulric nodded to Lara and she said something, but the sound did not make it through the window. Behind her, fifteen eight-pointed, red dagger-stars lined themselves up on the wall-mounted data display beneath an icon that Phelan decided represented the *Dire Wolf*. At the same time, a small device clipped to Ranna's belt beeped and a red LED lit up.

Ranna smiled wolfishly and rubbed her hands together. "Yes, open with everything and see how he cuts it."

Marcos thrust a fist in the air and shouted something, but again the sound was lost to those in the observing room. Beneath the line of stars that materialized when Lara spoke, another line appeared, but this one had only fourteen stars. Lara immediately replied to Marcos, and two of the stars vanished from her line. Marcos countered and Lara matched him, leaving each row equal in length at a dozen stars.

Phelan looked over at his companion. "What just happened?"

The Clanswoman held her right hand up to forestall another question. "Preliminaries, that is all. They are both at twelve stars and it is Marcos's bid."

Marcos turned and huddled with a couple of other Clan officers, including Vlad. Phelan saw the Precentor Martial say something to Ulric, which brought a nod from the Khan and a sour look to the ilKhan's face. Lara watched her adversary through the holotank and waved off advice from her supporters.

Marcos turned and grinned confidently. He offered a bid that removed three of the dagger stars, replacing them with three small, five-pointed, blue-white stars and three green, four-pointed dagger-stars trimmed in silver. The ilKhan saluted that bid, and Marcos stared at his opposition.

Lara's return bid swept away three of the dagger-stars, but put nothing up in their place. Marcos looked stricken, and the blood drained from the ilKhan's face. Ulric nodded a silent salute to Lara, and the Precentor Martial matched the gesture.

"No!" Ranna looked down at the device on her belt as the red light died. Anger and frustration warring for control of her face, she slumped down on the couch beneath the window. "Why bid *my* star away?"

Phelan folded a leg beneath himself and sat beside her. "What's the matter? Can't you explain any of this to me?"

She turned to him, staring angrily as though she didn't recognize him. Then her mood softened to take him in again. "Lara and Marcos were bidding to see who could take the world with the least amount of equipment and personnel. Each of the red dagger-stars represents a Star of 'Mechs. The small blue-white stars represent a Star of Aero-Space Fighters, and the green dagger-stars are Elementals. Marcos's bid substituting three Aerostars and three Elemental stars for three 'Mech stars surrendered him no power. Lara realized Marcos had hit the low end of his confidence, so she dropped herself down to nine 'Mech stars. It gives her room to maneuver if she runs into trouble on the planet, and will be a great victory if she does not."

Phelan frowned. "What do you mean by 'room to maneuver'?'"

Ranna looked at her hands. "Lara can call down forces equal to Marcos's last bid without surrendering any booty to him. With his agreement—something she is not likely to get—she could call down forces equivalent to her opening bid, but she would have to concede all sorts of things, making the victory worthless to her."

"Oh." The mercenary peered at Ranna, trying to pierce the veil of dejection. "Why are you upset? I thought you wanted Lara to win the bidding war."

"I did." She showed him the device that had been clipped to her belt as though in answer to his question. "It is just that the last 'Mech Star she bid away was mine. While she is down there fighting on New Bergen, I will still be up here."

"Sorry. I didn't realize I was such poor company. I can see how you would prefer combat to…"

Irritation knotting her brows, she cuffed him playfully. "It is not that. But I want to be part of the invasion. This is the first assault since I tested into Star Commander and I want a chance to prove myself."

Phelan covered her hands with his. "I understand."

The door to the observation room slid open to admit Khan Ulric. Ranna and Phelan both stood immediately. If the Khan noticed their physical contact when he entered, he gave no sign. The Precentor Martial, a step behind him, did notice, but controlled his reaction perfectly.

The Khan pointed toward the battle bridge. "Did you see what happened, Phelan? Did you understand it?"

Phelan took a deep breath before answering. "I watched. I believe I understand. Your commanders bid against each other to see who can accomplish an objective with the least amount of personnel and equipment. I can see how it forces each to be as sharp as possible because, I assume, success in a mission breeds opportunity for more missions. What I don't understand is why you wanted me to watch this"—Phelan searched for the appropriate word—"ritual."

The Khan spitted Phelan with a steady stare. "I wanted you to watch because I want you to understand. I want you to understand because I want you to see how we think and operate."

The mercenary frowned. "I am honored, but how does that make me more valuable to you?"

"You underestimate yourself, Phelan. The ilKhan has decided that because our next target lies near the border of our attack zone and that of the Ghost Bears, I will have to bid against Khan Bjorn for the right to take it. You are acquainted with how your people make war, and from what the Precentor Martial tells me of your background, you possess a most unorthodox military mind. I want you to help me prepare my bids. Our next target is a ripe plum, indeed, and I mean to have it."

Ulric reached out and clapped the younger man on both shoulders. "With your help, Phelan Kell, Rasalhague will be mine."

Edo, Turtle Bay
Pesht Military District, Draconis Combine
7 May 3050

Crouched in the darkness of the storm drainage tunnels beneath Kurushiiyama, Shin Yodama adjusted the light sensitivity of his mirrored faceplate. The device, which had been given only to the yakuza's "wet" team, concentrated the available light streaming in through the small, round drainage hole above them. With the amplification, the meager light pouring down through the drains dotting the tunnel's spine looked like harsh spotlights.

Shin glanced at the luminous time display on the upper left corner of the faceplate. Above, the time slowly increased toward midnight. Below, seconds and minutes clicked down as the deadline for their attack approached. Shin smiled, trying to fool himself out of the nervousness that had his stomach churning. *We're here a full minute ahead of schedule. Three minutes and counting.*

The wet team had approached the prison by swimming beneath the Sawagashii River, then located the ferrocrete tunnel where the Old Man had found temporary refuge after his escape years ago. It led deeper into the prison, and was designed to carry water from the monsoons and other storms to the river. The two-meter-diameter tunnel had long been dreamed of as an escape route, but all the drains leading down into it were too small to admit any prisoner, and no one had the equipment to break through the ferrocrete that lay between him and the path to freedom.

Shin watched as two of the dozen-man team placed the explosive

172

charges in a circle around one of the drains. *Those shaped charges should blow up and out with enough force to open a hole for us to climb through into the cell blocks.* The MechWarrior glanced up at the drain. *I hope the yakuza who volunteered to get themselves incarcerated so they could get word to the Legion's people will be able to get out again.* Motochika had been first in line for that duty.

To reassure himself, Shin dropped a hand to the curious weapon he had been given for the assault. Mated to the body of a laser rifle, the barrel and action of a pump-fed shotgun clung to the underside of the laser's barrel. For the sixth time since entering the tunnel, Shin looked at the pulse duration selector for the laser and held himself back from increasing it to a full half-second. *If a .25 second bolt can't melt its way through something, the shotgun will just have to knock it down.*

Mindful of his encounter with an armored infantryman half in and out of his armor, Shin had filled the bandolier hanging across his chest with heavy slugs. That the shotgun would eject to the right and cross his line-of-sight bothered the left-handed yakuza a little, but he dismissed the concern as trivial. *If that's the worst thing that happens to me in this operation, I will be doing fine.* More practically, Shin drew confidence from the bandolier's heavy weight and the fact that the thigh pockets of his black fatigues bulged with power packs for the laser rifle.

As the last minute counted down on the clock, Shin and the rest of the team moved back down the tunnel. *Thirty seconds to the blast. The yakuza outside the prison should start their rocket barrage soon now. The Inferno missiles should shake up these invaders a bit and even provide us some illumination. If they miss their deadline, we just switch the explosives over to remote...No, there they go.*

The thunderous rumble of SRM and Infernos exploding against the prison walls and gates reached the tunnels below Kurushiiyama. As flames soared high into the sky, enough light flickered down through the storm drains to nearly blind the team waiting below. As the last second vanished from his faceplate clock, Shin ducked his head, screwed his eyes shut and clapped his hands over his ears.

The force of the explosion bounced him a meter back down the tunnel, but he recovered his balance almost instantly. Uncoiling like a snake, he darted forward. In the shower of dust filtering down from the hole, Shin saw the twisted ends of the metal bars that had formed the tunnel's skeleton. Letting the rifle swing back on its shoulderstrap, he grabbed a bar and pulled himself up into the the dark confines of the prison laundry.

Others also clambered up and out of the hole, then spread out to form a perimeter. Firelight streamed in through the barred windows, dispelling all but the most dense shadows. Shin pointed one man to check a line of washers that had been tumbled over like dominoes in the blast, then sent others forward toward the doors. When his scouts reported all clear, Shin moved the team out.

We're in the lowest level of Katana Block. Up the corridor, around the corner to the stairwell, through the checkpoint, and we reach the Gallery. Blow the bar-locks and everyone is free. Shin moved to the front of the group. He stopped at the end of the corridor, glanced quickly around the corner, then waved the others onward. Another man dropped to one knee at the base of the stairs while Shin swept past him, taking them two at a time.

A flash of motion caught by the faceplate's enhancement of his peripheral vision gave him enough warning. Shin launched himself into a rolling dive that took him to the stairs' first landing. He ignored the grinding pain in his back as he somersaulted on the bandolier. Reaching a sitting position, he slewed himself around so that his back slammed into the landing's far corner, pounding pain through him again.

Needles of laser light burned yellow-green flames in the bricks just above his line of travel. In the laser rifle's backlight, Shin saw the hulking shadow of a man silhouetted between the stair railing and the building wall. Shin swung his own weapon into line with the apparition, then jerked the shotgun's trigger and hit the laser's firing stud.

His laser bolt caught the Smoke Jaguar just above the waist of his dark green jumpsuit. The shotgun slug slammed into the laser rifle, destroying its energy coils in a brilliant electric-blue flash, then ricocheted into the invader. It entered his chest just above the laser wound and spun the warrior away into the wall. The Smoke Jaguar hit the bricks hard, then rebounded and cascaded limply down the stairs to Shin's feet.

Two more yakuza ran up the stairs. One knelt beside the Smoke Jaguar and checked his throat for a pulse, while the other dropped to Shin's side. "Are you hurt?"

Shin shook his head, then rubbed his right hand against the left side of his chest. "The gun was just seated wrong. It recoiled into my ribs." He rolled forward and scrambled to his feet without assistance. He straightened up slowly, then pumped another shell into the shotgun's action. "Wait! What are you doing?"

The man who had knelt next to the invader had drawn a knife from his boot. "He still lives!"

Shin felt a hollowness in the pit of his stomach. He nodded to the man, who then cut the Smoke Jaguar's throat. Shin motioned to another member of the team to move up the stairs and pointed toward the steel door set back from the top of the stairs. As the man unlimbered a portable rocket launcher, Shin carefully deployed those yakuza who had not already taken up their assigned positions. "Go!"

The armor-piercing rocket's depleted-uranium tip punched through the door like a bullet through an apple. Two meters beyond the thick steel slab, the rocket's warhead exploded within a narrow rectangular chamber. A jet of fire stabbed back out of the entry hole to scorch the stairwell wall, then subsidiary flames created a reddish-yellow corona around the door seconds before it tottered from its tracks and smashed flat against the ferrocrete floor.

Smoke billowed from the chamber beyond the door. The upper half of each wall had been blown out by the blast, sowing glass shrapnel through the guard chambers on either side of the security checkpoint. Through the smoke and beyond, Shin saw into the Gallery.

Two yakuza moved in low, then lofted anti-personnel grenades into the guard stations. Twin explosions sounded one after the other, and some of the barbed, plastic flechettes from the grenades bounced out to the stairs. One of the two men rose up and took a step forward, then hesitated for a fatal second.

Three scarlet laser bolts shot through the smoke and punctured his chest. Energy only partially spent, they burst through the back of his black tunic, igniting cloth as they did so. The yakuza spun around, collided with the railing at the top of the stairs and pitched head over heels. His body landed with a wet thud at the bottom of the stairs and lay very still.

The blood-streaked Smoke Jaguar in the guard's chamber disintegrated in the withering hail of return fire. Dozens of little fires burned like votive candles in the wall beyond his position. The furthest-forward yakuza stayed low and moved through the checkpoint. His appearance on the other side of the doorway brought a cheer from the inmates while more detonations shook the building from outside.

"Yamato, prepare to blow the bar-locks." Shin waited until Yamato had climbed through the empty windows to the guard station before he charged into the Gallery. Even though he'd studied plans of the building to where he found himself wandering through it in his dreams, the reality of it shocked him. *This is a wastebin for humanity!*

Rising up to a height of ten tiers, the Gallery formed a gray, cold ferrocrete canyon separating dark walls dotted with even darker holes. Arms and legs jutted between prison bars like insect appendages hanging from the mouth of a lizard. Thousands of voices echoed through the room, filling it with a murmuring chaos that drowned out all but the sharpest explosions from outside.

Shin darted toward the staircase leading to the upper levels of the cell block. A shotgun blast blew the lock from the wire-mesh door. Shin ripped it aside and sprinted up the stairs. *Hohiro is in Cell Seventeen, Tier Three.* Another shotgun slug mangled the lock on Level Three and gave Shin access to the tier's balcony.

People jammed the doorways, stretching their arms out to claw at him and draw him closer, desperation on their faces. *They all want to be free, but they're terrified they'll never make it. We've got to get them out.*

He found the mouth of Cell Seventeen and leveled his gun at the inmates choking it. They melted back, leaving Shin a clear view of Hohiro seated on a cot. He'd raised himself up on his elbows and had an expectant look on his face, but the circles under his eyes and the bloody rag wrapped around his right leg gave the yakuza the true story of Hohiro's condition.

Shin stepped to the balcony and raised his right hand. Someone down below relayed the signal to Yamato. A sharp flash of light preceded the report of an explosion and the resulting alarm signal. A series of metallic clicks sounded up and down the cell blocks, and inmates quickly pulled their limbs back through the doors. The steel-bar portals slid back throughout Katana Block, and the denizens of the cells poured out.

Shin fought his way through the press of prisoners into Cell Seventeen. He pulled his faceplate back onto the top of his head and seated himself on Hohiro's bunk. Pulling free the medical pack from its straps at the small of his back, he smiled at his *Sho-sa.* "Sorry we could not come for you sooner."

Hohiro laughed with relief as tears rolled down his ashen face. "I am glad you came for me at all. Even when word got through that something was going to happen, I couldn't believe it. I should have known you would come up with something."

Shin shook his head. "I am merely the servant of a master craftsman, doing what I have been told." He ripped open the leg of Hohiro's prison togs up to mid-thigh, then pulled a white adhesive patch from the medical pouch. He pressed it to Hohiro's leg, just above and behind the knee. "That's for the pain. Can you walk?"

Hohiro nodded, the tension lines around his eyes beginning to ease. "I can walk, maybe run for a short distance."

"Good. Bare your right forearm." As Hohiro complied with the command, Shin slapped a blue patch to the crook of his elbow. "You'll sleep for a week after we get out of here, but this stuff should keep you going until then."

Screams and the sounds of gunfire echoed up to the cell. Hohiro grabbed Shin's arms, the second drug having already sharpened his reflexes and increased his strength. "What's going on?"

Shin freed himself from Hohiro's grip. "I don't know. Crawl along the balcony to Cell Fifteen and wait for me there." The yakuza pulled his faceplate on again, fed three more shells into the shotgun, and ran to the cell's entrance. What he saw below brought him up short and took his breath away.

Marching relentlessly through the milling throng, a Smoke Jaguar in a bulky suit of powered armor lashed out right and left with his arms. Even a glancing blow crushed bodies and sent them flying deeper into the crowd. Short bursts from the laser burned swaths through the inmate population. The Gallery was so packed that none could escape, try as they might to flee, and people involuntarily filled in the body-strewn path behind the warrior.

Without thinking, Shin brought the laser rifle to his shoulder and triggered two shots. The bolts hit the Jaguar's head and the hump on his gray-spotted back, but failed to breach his armor. Like the cat whose skin he wore, the invader spun quickly, then bent his legs and launched himself up toward the third tier.

The railing collapsed beneath the invader's armored bulk, but impeded him just enough to make landing awkward. He landed on all fours, but his bloody left foot slipped on the ferrocrete decking as he started to get up. The shotgun slug from Shin's rifle hit the Smoke Jaguar in the right shoulder, further unbalancing him. His arms windmilling wildly, the armored figure pitched back off the balcony.

Before he could slip out of sight, his left hand clawed the ferrocrete like an anchor. Shin saw the gray form swing back and forth twice, building momentum, then the right elbow bit into the deck. As inexorable as the sun rising at dawn, the invader hauled himself up.

Shin's hand dropped to the laser rifle's pulse-rate selector and dialed it all the way up. At point-blank range, he sighted in on the dark, glassy V in the middle of the figure's lump-like head. His finger squeezed the firing stud, and the sustained bolt sliced through its target. The figure, smoke curling up from its single, shattered eye-piece, jerked, then fell back. It smashed into the tier below, then whirled end over end into the waiting crowd.

Nervous sweat misting against the inside of his faceplate, Shin stepped back and moved down to Cell Fifteen. Hohiro was leaning

177

against a bunk as Shin entered. "Now what?"

Without stopping to reply, Shin studied the cell's back wall. From the lower right-corner, he counted five cinderblocks out and five up. As he popped his power pack from the laser and snapped a new one in place, he offered the *Sho-sa* an explanation. "When the contractor built the prison, the yakuza put pressure on him to seriously modify the original design. Various cells, with numbers and levels determined by use of the lucky number five, had escape routes built into them. They were never used because once their secret was revealed, all would be shut down."

The yakuza triggered a dozen laser bolts. The five-cinderblock pattern in the center of the wall dissolved into smoke and ferrocrete dust. The hole in the wall sucked much of the smoke down. Hohiro walked over to it and peered in, but carefully avoided touching any of the still-glowing rock.

He looked back over his shoulder at Shin. "This gets us out?"

"Yes. We climb down and take the first crosscut shaft heading north. That will dump us out in the Uramachi area. From there, the Old Man will get us aboard a fast shuttle heading up to a *Scout* Class JumpShip hidden in the Rings." Shin forced himself to smile. "After that, it's up to your father's people to get us home."

Hohiro nodded and touched one of the hole's melted edges. "We can go now." More screams sounded from the Gallery. "What about them?"

Shin's eyes narrowed. "We live to serve the Dragon. Those who escape will join the Old Man's underground army." Muscles bunched at the corners of his jaw. "Those who don't...Well, it's up to us to see they are avenged."

Kai Allard turned and tossed the small petrochem case to the next man in line as the stream of cargo continued to flow from the small shuttlecraft's cargo hold. His shoulders ached just a little, but somehow the simple repetition and physical exertion felt welcome. *I hate being cooped up in a DropShip, especially a troop transport ship. Granted, all of us moving from the* Viper *to the* Gibraltar *means the ship will be overcrowded, but there will still be more room to move around than on the* Overlord *Class ship.*

"Leftenant Allard."

Kai turned at the sound of the voice and began to smile at Leftenant-General Redburn, when the guy next in line turned and shoved the next parcel at him. The sharp edge raked across the back of Kai's right hand, gouging out a bloody gash. "Youch!" Kai caught the package in his left hand and passed it along, then took a step back and inspected the damaged hand.

The trooper looked stricken. "Sorry, sir…"

Kai shook his head and Andrew Redburn reassured the soldier. "Not your fault. I shouldn't have broken the rhythm of the line."

Kai sucked at the cut, then watched as blood refilled the wound. He clapped his left hand over the back of his hand to stop the bleeding, then grinned at Andrew. "You will forgive me if I don't salute, sir?"

Andrew nodded and draped his arm over Kai's shoulder. "I was up on the officers' deck waiting to welcome you with the rest of the

179

Tenth Guard officers, but you weren't there. Leftenant Pelosi told me you'd come over with a cargo shuttle and were helping out. I should have known…"

Should have known what, sir? That I wanted to help load and unload cargo, or that I wanted to avoid shipping over in the same shuttle as Deirdre Lear? Kai shrugged. "I assumed that the faster we unload the *Viper*, the sooner we can be on our way toward the rim. I just wish the *Gibraltar* had room for our BattleMechs."

Andrew grimaced. "That is a desire we share. Unfortunately, the JumpShip assigned to carry the *Viper* blew a helium seal. Without liquid helium to supercool the Kearny-Fuchida drive, there's no way the ship can make the jump to Surcin with the rest of the armada. I wouldn't worry, though. We have more ships coming through Arcturus and their 'Mech bays will be free. *Yen-lo-wang* will catch up with you soon enough, but if worse comes to worst, I know of a half-dozen 'Mechs available to a promising young officer."

Kai smiled broadly. "Thank you, sir. In that event—in any event—I'll do everything I can to justify your confidence in me."

"Excellent." Andrew gave Kai a hearty slap on the back. "The reason I wanted to speak with you concerns your battalion's new Kommandant."

Kai nodded. *I didn't wonder that they left Kommandant Smitz behind on Skondia. He'd already agreed to resign his commission and take over command of the Skondia Home Defense Force's Second Regiment. I wonder who will replace him?* A nagging fear bubbled up into Kai's throat. "You're not going to make me his aide, are you? I mean…I still have my lance to command, don't I?"

Redburn chuckled softly. "You sound just like I did when they told me I was being transferred to the Kittery Training Battalion. No, you'll not lose your lance. I wanted to talk to you about your new Kommandant because I would like you to speak up for him in the informal meeting of the battalion staff. There are bound to be some doubts about him, but they are baseless. I know I can trust you with the sensitive information needed to debunk them, and I know you'll be discreet."

Kai slowed his pace. "I don't believe you would set me up, General, but I just want to make sure what you're asking. I'm more than willing to help ease a man into his command, but I won't support an idiot who'll get us all killed. This new Kommandant is not someone who got his commission just because of his noble blood, is he?"

"You tell me," Andrew said, watching Kai carefully. "It's Victor Steiner-Davion."

The younger MechWarrior's jaw shot down, then snapped shut again. "Forgive me, General. I thought he was with the Twelfth Donegal Guards?"

"He *was*. It's probably not much of a secret that some heavy raiding has gone on out toward the rim."

Kai nodded, a lock of black hair slipping down onto his forehead. "That's why we're all heading out there."

"It was *heavy* raiding, Kai, and Victor's unit no longer has command integrity. We believe they're still fighting a guerrilla-type action. Victor and his aide, Hauptmann Cox, escaped the world because Leftenant-General Hawksworth ordered them away."

The younger man's eyes narrowed. "That's not the Victor I know. He'd never leave." *Perhaps he's changed since NAMA...*

Andrew rubbed his right hand over his chin. "Victor is the same: Cox had to knock him out to get him offplanet. That fact, I am afraid, might count for little with the Tenth Lyran Guards when they learn that the Twelfth Donegal Guards have ceased to exist as a military unit. Morgan Hasek-Davion and I both have the utmost confidence in Victor, but we also know how spooky troops can get if they perceive their leader as an albatross."

Kai glanced down. *If Victor's work at the New Avalon Military Academy was any indication, he should be a strong leader. He'll probably make us do things we'd never have thought possible. Better yet, things the enemy won't think possible.* "Sir, I've no doubt Victor will be an excellent leader for us, but I'm not sure it's me you should be talking to. Hauptmann Meisler is my company commander, and the other two Hauptmanns tend to set great store by what she says."

"I've already had a word with Rachel and she promises to keep an open mind on the matter. She recalled that you'd known Victor at NAMA and said it would be an honor to have one of the officers who defeated the La Mancha scenario in her command and the other as her CO." Andrew's smile broadened as Kai blushed. "In my days at Warriors Hall on New Syrtis, I would have strangled either or both of you for doing so well."

I know I should feel complimented, but my victory skewed the curve on that test, putting Wendy on the alternate list for the Davion Heavy Guards. He shook his head. "To call what I did a victory is to pervert the word and take away from Victor's solution to the problem."

Andrew folded his arms across his chest. "Surrounded by four heavier 'Mechs and managing to destroy three of them is certainly a victory in that no-win situation. What you did hadn't been done before and it worked."

181

The Leftenant frowned. "It worked, but only for a little while. Instead of shooting first, I ran. I knew the *Phoenix Hawk* I'd chosen for the test could outdistance the 'Mechs the computer controlled. I just strung them out and picked them off one by one. In my last fight, that's when the computer ganged up on me. I got cocky. I should have pulled out and found another way to split up those last two 'Mechs." As he spoke, Kai pounded his right fist into his left hand and started the cut on the back of his hand bleeding again. "Victor's solution destroyed the enemy BattleMechs and got him out of there safe and sound. Even though I punched out successfully, I would have still been at the mercy of that last *Quickdraw*."

He sucked at the cut again, then looked up at Redburn. "I ran. No one had ever done that before because no one had ever been afraid in that test before."

The General smiled benignly and shook his head. "You really don't understand your gift, do you? Everyone goes into that test terrified, the same as you. You alone recognized your fear and found a way to beat it, and beat the scenario. People who start shooting when faced with overwhelming odds do not have long or particularly noteworthy careers. Of you, on the other hand, I expect great things."

Andrew glanced at Kai's hand. "Why don't you go get that patched up in sick bay, then meet me up in what passes for the officer's lounge on this monster. Marshal Hasek-Davion mentioned he would be sending a message to Prince Hanse and suggested you might want to put in something for your father. He also extends an invitation for you to dine with us this evening."

"Yes, sir," Kai said, saluting crisply. "My pleasure."

Kai showed the gash on his hand to the orderly just inside the sick bay's hatchway. "It's really nothing."

The young man shook his head. "Best to be sure." He pointed back toward a hatchway leading deeper into the ship's hospital. "Just go through there and sit in Alpha Berth. The doctor will be with you in a minute."

The MechWarrior crossed the small antechamber and hopped up onto the examination table, his hand smearing a bloodstain on the white paper that covered the table. Kai looked down at the cut on his hand and gently probed it with his index finger, which started some new blood oozing.

"Think we'll need morphine?"

At the icy tone of voice, Kai straightened up. "No, Dr. Lear."

None too gently, she picked up his right hand and examined it. "The cut's not bad, but your hands are filthy." She picked up his left hand and looked at the black dust coating it. "Using this hand to stop the bleeding is about as safe as cauterizing a shaving cut with a laser rifle."

"Well, Doctor, I saw no need to wash my hands before getting cut, and I came down here immediately afterward." He tried to get her to smile with one of his own, but it didn't work.

"Well, then, I guess the rumors about you are true—you are special. Imagine being able to get dirty and injured up on the officers' deck. I thought that impossible."

"I wouldn't know." Kai slid forward and off the table. "I got cut down in the cargo bay unloading luggage and supplies from the *Viper*." He pulled his hand from hers. "The damned case that cut me was probably yours."

She cocked her head and frowned. "You were where?"

The MechWarrior matched her cold stare. "I was down in the cargo bay unloading the supply shuttle. I flew over here from the *Viper* in it." He looked away. "I wanted to stay away from the other shuttle to prevent having a 'scene' with you."

Deirdre took his right hand again, this time more gently, and directed him to a sink fitted with a transparent plastic hood. "Foot pedal controls the waterflow. Use the stuff in the green bottle there and wash the cut well."

"I've used a Zero-G sink before, Doctor." Kai squeezed some of the gelatinous green scrubbing compound onto his left palm, then added water and rubbed until foam covered his hands. The foam had started out as greenish-white, but most of it had taken on an ashy tint. Kai rinsed his hands. Even before Deirdre could direct him to do it, he soaped them up again. He took special care to clean the cut, then rinsed and presented his dripping hands to her for inspection. "Do they pass?"

She bit back her first answer, then nodded. She opened a cabinet beside the sink and pulled out a pump-spray bottle filled with a vile yellow liquid. It moved in the clear container with a viscosity somewhere between water and spit. "This will sting."

"Of course."

"Touché, Leftenant." She hit the sprayer's trigger and coated the back of his hand with the mustard-colored disinfectant. Kai's hand jerked involuntarily, but she held on and gave it another spray. "I'm sorry. This will help seal the wound. It's not bad enough to require staples." She looked at it more closely. "I think I'll use a butterfly bandage to draw it together. That, or—"she glanced up at him, her voice sympathetic—"you could have a small scar after it heals."

Confusion ran through Kai's mind. *I don't understand how there's so much anger in your voice one moment, only to have it vanish the next. You hate me for some reason, but your role as a medic overrides that personal feeling.* "A bandage will be good. If nothing else, it will remind me to be more careful."

"A good idea at any time." She replaced the bottle in the cabinet and pulled out a small, barbell-shaped bandage. Freeing it from the backing, she stretched it across the center of the cut, then pressed the ends down. The elastic material contracted, tugging the edges of the cut closer to each other. "How did it happen?"

Kai shrugged. "I was helping pass stuff down a line and got distracted by General Redburn."

Deirdre's blue eyes flickered. "Hobnobbing with the brass, eh?"

The MechWarrior stiffened. "No. He sought me out. General Redburn had something he wanted to tell me."

She smiled coyly. "But he is an old family friend, isn't he?"

Does she have some antipathy toward nobles, after all? Kai nodded, feeling uncomfortably like he was stepping into a trap. "He served with my father before the Fourth War."

Deirdre Lear's eyes hardened and Kai read anger and pain in them. *Her coldness toward me has something to do with the war, or perhaps, my father. Didn't Andrew say her father had been a Mech-Warrior who died when she was young? She's not that much older than me, so she probably lost him in the war. Who knows?*

He started to tell her he was sorry about her loss, but something stopped him. *Don't. You don't know anything about her father.* A horrible thought struck him. *Her father might have died in the assault on Sarna—whose defense some say my father planned. Wait. Try to learn about her background. If you say anything right now, it will only make things worse.*

He bowed his head. "Thank you for attending my wound."

"Be more careful in the future," she said, all compassion gone. "I don't want to see you in my hospital again."

25

Black Pearl Base, Sudeten
Tamar March, Lyran Commonwealth
15 June 3050

Unsuspecting, the *Thor* moved across the holovid screen from the left, snow and thin ribbons of ice glittering from its head and shoulders as it traveled through the blizzard. Tendrils of steam drifted up from the fire-blackened shell of the LRM launcher on the *Thor's* left shoulder and other half-melted scars on its body. Where wind-whipped snow actually fell against the myomer muscle exposed on the *Thor's* right arm, arcing sparks converted to vapor as the muscle flexed and moved the PPC side to side in a vain search for prey.

Suddenly, the snow exploded up around the 'Mech's legs. Black dirt and shards of armor sprayed into the air to stain the virgin snow as the buried mine savaged the *Thor's* legs. The giant 'Mech staggered and dropped to one knee. All around it, snow-encrusted Donegal 'Mechs encircled their foe and poured SRM and laser fire into the *Thor*. Under the hideous barrage, the heavy 'Mech tottered and went down...

Victor Steiner-Davion looked up from the holovid view screen as Galen Cox dropped into the seat across the aisle from him. "What is it?" He fastened his seatbelt and shoulder restraints, then jerked his head toward the shuttlecraft's nose. "The crew wanted to make sure you're buckled in. We'll be landing in about five minutes." He glanced at the images marching across the holovid screen built into the bulkhead in front of Victor's seat. "Do you think there's more you can learn from that?"

Anger exploded in Victor's blue eyes, but he held back his rage.

There has to be more I can learn from it. The Twelfth Donegal Guards continued to send us sensitive telemetry as we headed out of the system. These visual images alone give us a better look at the raiders than anything else we've got. He choked back his emotions and nodded slowly. "I hope there is, Hauptmann. Otherwise, so many people will have died in vain."

Galen drew in a deep breath. "Sir, once again I ask that you give my resignation further consideration. I will, at your order, remand myself over for court martial on charges of striking a superior officer."

Victor looked over at the taller man, then shook his head as he strapped himself into the seat. "Yes, Hauptmann, I have considered your request and I apologize for keeping you on the hook for so long. Your resignation has been rejected." He glanced down, no longer able to maintain eye contact with his aide. "I admit that I blamed you for preventing me from trying to help defeat the invaders on Trell I. But no victory on that world would have been possible. I realize that now. As nearly as we know, all resistance to the Jade Falcons ended weeks ago. Even implementation of my plan early on wouldn't have changed that."

Victor raised his hand to forestall any comment by Galen. "Furthermore, I realize that your action probably spurred the men and women of the Twelfth Donegal on to even greater acts of heroism. Their radio chatter makes it clear that they were trying to draw the invaders' attention to themselves and away from me. Many died trying to help me escape. I must do all I can to make good their sacrifice.

"The fact that my father cut orders for me to attend this meeting in no way guarantees that I'll get a combat assignment. My parents would probably like to see me in a staff position with the First Kathil Uhlans. Morgan, on the other hand, might assign me to another line unit, but what general will take the chance that Hawksworth refused?"

Cox nodded. "Damned if you do and damned if you don't…"

Victor opened his hands, then crossed his fingers. "Real close, but not 100 percent yet. If I can come up with an operation that is sound and has merit, Morgan might just give it to me. Remember, he wasn't that much older than I am now when the Uhlans assaulted the Capellan capital. Morgan won't let me throw away the lives of men and women in some vanity assault, but he will listen to reason."

"Looks like quite a reception committee waiting for you, Kommandant."

Victor turned around on the long escalator and looked through the building's glass wall at the five men standing in the blue carpeted visitor's lounge. "Guess it's old home week." He noticed Galen looked somewhat puzzled. "You know who they are, don't you?"

Galen shrugged sheepishly. "I'm afraid I haven't kept up with my reading of Burke's Peerage, Highness." Galen thrust his chin forward. "Perhaps I should just have you knock me out and get me through this."

Victor shook his head, then surreptitiously indicated the first man in line. "You see the one in the black and gold uniform, with the long red hair?"

"Do you mean Marshal Morgan Hasek-Davion?" When Victor looked back and shot him a nasty glance, Galen laughed lightly. "I'm bound to know the supreme commander of the armed forces in which I serve, after all."

"True," Victor said. "The man next to him is Leftenant-General Andrew Redburn. Before helping Morgan form the First Kathil Uhlans, Redburn commanded the Davion Light Guards Delta Company in the Fourth War."

Galen's blue eyes focused distantly. "The St. Andre drop on Cochraine's Goliaths? I remember that being cited at the War College of Tamar as a classic action of maneuverability and surprise defeating larger 'Mechs. Didn't he also handle the defense of Gan Singh?"

Victor nodded. "3042. Some House Marik troops decided it was time to nibble on the Sarna March to see how badly we'd been damaged in the 3039 war against Theodore Kurita. Andrew convinced them, quickly and forcefully, that any weakness on our part was a figment of their imagination."

Galen rubbed his hand over his unshaven chin. "Yeah, I remember that now. I was just coming out of the War College. O.K., so that's who he is. Now what about the two next to him? Those aren't AFFC uniforms."

Victor looked along the line to the next two men. Both wore similar uniforms of red jackets and black trousers tucked into knee-high boots. The jacket was double-breasted and shaped as a hound's-head with ears that rose to each shoulder and a muzzle that fastened down at the jacket's waist. The older MechWarrior had four ribbons sewn onto the hound's left ear to represent the unit's commendations. He also wore spurs on his boots, marking him as a product of a Federated Suns military academy. The younger man wore no spurs and his jacket showed only one unit commendation ribbon.

"The older man is Lieutenant-Colonel Daniel Allard. He's the commander of the Kell Hounds and the brother of Intelligence Secretary Justin Allard."

Galen squinted at the mercenary. "That's Dan Allard? He seems like he's been around forever."

Victor shook his head. "The white hair is throwing you off. He takes after his father and went white early. He's only in his fifties, though he's been with the Hounds for over thirty years. He was there when they rescued Melissa Steiner in the *Silver Eagle* incident. Morgan Kell appointed Dan as the Kell Hounds commander when he retired eight years ago."

"And the other man? Who's he?"

Victor hesitated for a moment. "That's my cousin, Christian Kell. He's a Major with the Hounds and commands the First Battalion."

Galen rested a hand on Victor's shoulder. "You say that as though trying to convince yourself he *is* Christian Kell. Now me, I thought Morgan Kell had only one son—the one who died out in the Periphery last year."

Victor bowed his head. *How well you put it, my friend. I do have a hard time believing Chris is Chris because I see so much of his father in him.* "Phelan was Morgan Kell's only son. Christian is Patrick Kell's son, but Patrick never knew it at the time he died. Eight years ago, Chris showed up at a world the Kell Hounds were garrisoning and presented Morgan with a verigraphed message from a woman who had been Patrick's lover. It said Christian was Patrick's son."

Galen raised an eyebrow. "The Kell fortunes are known to be vast, and that would have been right after your grandmother left a huge legacy to Morgan Kell. They had him genotyped to verify the claim, didn't they?"

"Yes, though it was hardly necessary." Victor's senior by four years, the tall, slender mercenary towered over him by twenty centimeters and outweighed him by fifteen kilos. In the way he wore his black hair and in the structure of his features, Victor saw a familiar face, but it was of a man who was older and who had died several years before his birth. "Only his brown eyes mark him as different from his father. I only know Patrick Kell from holovids, but the resemblance is eerie. My mother considers it the clearest proof ever offered of reincarnation, notwithstanding the fact that Christian was born almost a year before his father's death."

"Huh." Galen smiled quizzically. "Where did he go to school? Rising to Major so quickly means he must be hot."

Victor took pride in Galen's respectful tone. "He doesn't talk about it much, but he was raised in the Draconis Combine, speaks Japanese fluently, and is reported to be every bit the demon his father was in personal combat. When he arrived, Morgan retired and took

Chris to the Dragoons' world of Outreach. For the next three years, Chris studied with the best. Rumor has it that Jaime Wolf even offered him a commission with the Dragoons. He entered the Hounds as a Lieutenant, but worked his way up to Major through his action during the Ambergrist Crisis."

"That's a fast crowd waiting for you." Galen nodded toward the last man in the group. "In that company, the last guy must be Death personified."

It took Victor a moment to recognize him, then he nodded. "Correction. This is the guy Death is afraid of. That's Kai Allard-Liao. He's Dan's nephew and Justin's son. You can't tell it by looking at him, or even by listening to him, but Kai is one of the sharpest tactical minds ground out by any of the Academies since his uncle or Morgan Hasek-Davion graduated. He's got an intuitive grasp of military situations that's unbelievable. In combat simulations, he moves a 'Mech like it's grafted straight into his brain."

Galen's eyes narrowed. "I hear a 'but' lurking there somewhere. What's the down-side?"

Victor shrugged. "Given the chance, any chance at all, Kai will second-guess and berate himself into indecision and inactivity. And the damnable thing is that it's not just a lack of self-confidence. He knows he's smart, but just can't allow himself to think he'll be just as smart tomorrow or the next day or the next month. When it works, his analytical ability is uncanny at picking out the weaknesses of the enemy."

"He sounds to me like the type of man you bring in to assess a situation in toto, then confine his part of the operation to a narrow field in which he has little room to assess what he must do."

An astute observation, Galen. "I think you may well be right."

Victor bent and hefted the small bag of supplies given him by the *Hejira's* crew. Stepping off the escalator, he nodded to Galen. "Now that you know who they are, let's go meet them."

Rounding the corner in the circular jetway tunnel, Victor smiled and stripped the glove off his right hand. He stepped into the receiving lounge, then stopped and saluted sharply. "Kommandant Victor Steiner-Davion reporting for duty, sir." Behind him, Galen Cox stopped and saluted as well.

Marshal Morgan Hasek-Davion returned the salute crisply, then extended his hand to Victor. They shook hands, then embraced in back-slapping hugs. "It's good to see you safe, Victor."

Victor nodded, then pulled back away from his cousin. "This is Hauptmann Galen Cox. He's the reason I'm here." Victor rubbed his

189

jaw. "He has a foolproof method for dealing with officers who are foolish."

Morgan shook Galen's hand, then turned to the others in the greeting party. "You know General Andrew Redburn, of course."

Victor saluted Andrew, then shook his hand. "It is good to see you again, General."

Andrew chuckled lightly. "The last time was when they coerced me into giving a speech at the Nagelring."

"And an excellent presentation it was." Victor looked up and met Andrew's gaze. "It started me thinking about warfare in a different way, bringing home the awesome power we command in a single BattleMech."

Victor moved along to the next man in line and offered him his hand. "Hello, Colonel Allard."

The white-haired mercenary took Victor's hand in a strong grip and pumped his arm warmly. "I'm glad to see you here. I didn't think they could keep you away, but I was afraid someone might be foolish enough to try."

Victor took pleasure in Daniel Allard's sincere greeting. "Thank you, Colonel. I'm glad no one was so foolish as to try to keep the Kell Hounds away." With that, Victor extended his hand to the other Kell Hound.

"Greetings, Major. Very good to see you again."

The haunted look around Christian Kell's eyes vanished as he bowed, then took Victor's right hand into both of his. "I'm surprised to see you here, cousin. There were rumors that you were out in Trell's caverns with a cutting torch and survival knife while the invaders were still crawling over that planet."

Victor laughed and shook his cousin's hand. Chris knew that Victor would never willingly have left his station. "Crazy rumors, I guess, but I do want another go-round with the Jade Falcons. I owe them for the Twelfth Donegal Guards, and we both owe them for Phelan's life."

Chris nodded. "A debt we will repay in full."

Victor smiled gravely, then freed Chris's hand and turned to Kai. "I'm glad to see you here, Kai. These Jade Falcons are unbelievable."

Kai glanced down sheepishly, then met Victor's gaze and warm handshake. "I'm glad you're here, too."

Having greeted them all, Victor became more businesslike. "What's the agenda?" he asked Morgan. "How much time have we?"

"I don't know exactly," Morgan said, "but we're scheduled to meet here over the next eight weeks to study all the data we have on

190

the invaders. By the end of that time—and sooner, if necessary—we'll have gathered the troops and supplies needed to implement whatever plans we come up with."

Victor looked up at his cousin. "Will I get a command?"

Morgan showed him the barest hint of a smile. "You've already been transferred to the Tenth Lyran Guards at your present rank of Kommandant. Whether or not you'll see combat depends upon what you and the invaders do over the next two months."

Victor nodded grimly. *Well, then, I'll just have to prove myself. I may have been born heir to the Lyran Commonwealth and the Federated Suns, but here and now is where I begin to earn the right to rule them.*

"Let us go, gentlemen," he said, pointing to the door. "We have a war to plan and to win."

26

JumpShip Dire Wolf, *Rasalhague 7 Darkside*
Rasalhague System, Rasalhague Province, Free Rasalhague
   Republic
7 July 3050

Water dripping from his face, Phelan Kell straightened up from
the sink and stared into the eyes of Kenny Ryan's reflection in the
mirror. Behind the pirate chieftain, a half-dozen Periphery bandits
stood in a rough semi-circle blocking entrance to the lavatory. Further
back, Griff Picon watched the whole scene with an amused look on his
face.

Phelan turned slowly. "Sorry, Kenny. My dance card is full." He
pulled the towel from his shoulder and wiped his hands.

"Funny, Kell." The small, unkempt man narrowed his rat eyes.
"Real funny. You won't be doing much dancing if we decide to take
your kneecaps off." The men backing Kenny smiled coldly.

"Oh, I get it." Phelan smiled courteously. "You had a thought, a
real thought and you decided to let me in on it. That's real swell,
Kenny, and very considerate of you, but I'm not interested." He turned
back to the sink full of soapy water, but a hand on his bare shoulder
spun him back around again.

"You don't get the picture, Kell." Ryan's cruel expression and
greasy brown hair reminded Phelan of a wet rodent. "You've got an in
with that Ranna and you're getting special treatment. You're going to
help us get the same, or we'll make sure she doesn't think you're so
pretty anymore. Got it?"

Ryan started to jab a finger into Phelan's chest, but he never completed the move. The mercenary grabbed the front of the pirate's jumpsuit, hoisted him up, then turned and jammed him, butt first, onto the sink. Warm water splashed everywhere and soaked up through the seat of Ryan's pants. Phelan's left hand slipped up to grab him by the throat and jam his head back against the mirror. Then he half-turned to address Ryan's henchmen. "If any of you interfere, you'll never visit the bondswomen again! Your choice. Walk away now or look forward to being your own best friend for a good long time!"

As the knot of men at his back dissolved, Phelan returned his attention back to his captive. "I suppose this has been coming for a long time, quiaff, Kenny? I was hoping you'd behave and maybe even learn how to survive here with the Clans. I guess you're just too stupid to do either."

Phelan released the pressure on Ryan's throat, letting some of the reddish-purple color drain from his face. The pirate knotted his face in a ferocious leer, but his sputtering voice betrayed his fear. "Y-you've done it now, Kell. I've held them back from killing you or hurting you because I told them you'd be useful. No more. You're a dead man."

The mercenary slapped Ryan once, hard. "Don't try to scare me, you jackal. Those monosynaptic, evolutionary anomalies think with their gonads and I just convinced them—without much of a struggle—that my goodwill is their passport to paradise. You also decided, when I first joined this little community, that I could be physically intimidated because of how weak I was back then." Phelan's eyes burned angrily. "Back then, I was coming off months of chemical interrogation. Now I'm back in form, and perhaps even a little bit better, thanks to Ranna and Khan Ulric. I've half a mind to tear off your head and spit down your neck just to prove it to you."

"Go ahead." Ryan locked both of his hands around Phelan's left wrist. "If you think you can do it, go ahead. You'll find me a little bit more difficult to kill than you think."

The young Kell Hound laughed to himself, then released Ryan and took a couple of steps back. "I'm not going to do it, but not for the reasons you think. You haven't learned the first thing about these people, or our status among them, have you? You don't realize how important it is for me to stay in their good graces, do you?"

"What are you doing that's so special, aside from sucking up to the Khan?"

Phelan let the barb pass without comment. "What you should understand about our masters is that each jump is taking us deeper and deeper into the Inner Sphere."

Ryan cackled contemptuously. "Delicious! And soon High-and-mighty Hanse and Teddy-bear Samurai will be joining us here!"

Phelan snapped Kenny's head back with a slap, denting the mirror. "Idiot! This isn't some holovid drama or staged Solaris championship. People are dying in droves. The Clanspeople are toying with us. They only send down enough troops to make it a good fight. You remember how quickly they went through your people! That's happening all across the Inner Sphere."

The pirate tugged unconsciously at the braided cord encircling his right wrist. "Why should I care about that? Why should I care whether or not the others are getting what I got?" He spat at the floor.

The scorn in Ryan's voice echoed through Phelan's head. *He's right, quiaff? It's the arrogance of the Successor States—the same sort of blind stupidity that got DJ killed—that's making them vulnerable to the Clans. You can see, just from working with Ulric and Lara on the Rasalhague bid, that the Clans are not invincible. Others should be able to see the chinks in their armor, too, but they're too busy hanging on for retirement or studying up to win that next promotion. They just don't think anymore and you don't owe them a thing.*

He shook his head to clear away such thoughts. "Civilization is dying around us. The Clans strip away the best and the brightest from the worlds they take. They impose martial law. They're crushing Rasalhague and destroying the hopes of millions. Someone has to stop them."

"So that's how you rationalize collaborating with them, quiaff?"

Ryan's use of the Clanner term shook Phelan. *Is the desire to stop the Clans enough to justify betraying my own people until I can accomplish my goal? Am I trying to atone for the breaches of trust I committed under interrogation, or am I helping Ulric for other, more personal reasons? I can't hide behind the fact that they're attacking Rasalhague, where the people despise mercenaries. I've helped Ulric plan a campaign that will not lose. Am I playing Judas to the Successor States to avenge myself on Tor Miraborg and my peers at the Nagelring?*

He swallowed hard. "As things stand now, no force can defeat or even slow the invaders because no one knows enough about them. Each of the Clans has its own way of pacifying the planets it takes, and the Wolf Clan seems to be the least harsh. In fact, when they move, the Wolves leave little more than a token garrison force to work with the existing governmental structures to maintain order. Conquest by the Wolf Clan is probably no worse on the ordinary people of a world than being conquered by a rival lord in the constant warring among the Successor States.

194

"There's another thing, too." The mercenary met Ryan's gaze. "Right now the Precentor Martial and I are the only people who have a rapport with the invaders. We're the only ones learning how to deal with them on a personal basis, which means we could act as intermediaries between the Clans and the rulers of the Successor States. We might just be able to bring this war to a close sooner so fewer people have to die."

Ryan spat on the floor. "You're a dreamer...and a captive. They're using you. And when they're done with you, they'll discard you like a spent shell casing."

"You may be right, but at least I'm trying." Phelan glared at Ryan. "I don't like thinking of you and me as members of the same species, but we're on the same side in all this. And, yes, I might be betraying part of the Successor States to the invaders, but I'm giving it over to the Wolf Clan. If the Wolves become ascendant, then maybe I'll be in a position to exert some influence."

Kenny Ryan ground his teeth together. "I was wrong. You're not a dreamer, you're a fool. Paint whatever face you want on it, Kell. You're a traitor to your people."

Unbridled fury ripped through Phelan as Ryan's words hit home, but it was directed as much at himself as at the Periphery bandit. *No! It's not like that!* "Think whatever you want, Kenny. It doesn't matter to me. I may not owe the people of the Inner Sphere anything, but I'll be damned if I'm going to stand by and see these Clansmen slaughter innocents."

Phelan stood next to Ulric in the holotank, while the rolling landscape of Rasalhague's northern continental mass stretched out in all directions around them. As they walked forward, new terrain scrolled up over the rounded horizon. In response to a command Ulric had given upon entering the tank, the world remained lit as if it were only several hours past dawn no matter where they stood.

Phelan pointed to the south where a thick tropical belt girded the world's equator. "This is the first thing you can discount that the Ghost Bear's Khan is not likely to ignore. Scale up to one meter equals fifteen kilometers." As the computer complied, flattening out the horizon and increasing the resolution of the topography, a large urban settlement on a narrow bay materialized. "That's Firebase Tyr, home to the Third Rasalhague Freemen. They're a tough BattleMech regiment with some battle experience. They're normally based on Kandis but were recently moved here to reinforce Rasalhague. However, they won't be much of a factor in your battle."

Ulric frowned. "Explain."

Phelan smiled. "Ages ago, when people first settled on Rasalhague, they ran into a little problem with a virus native to the planet."

The Khan nodded and rubbed his hand across his jaw. "Yes, the Fenris Plague. I had forgotten about that. Surely they have conquered it, quiaff."

The mercenary nodded. "Yes, soon after the world was colonized. But over time, the strains became less virulent as they mutated. The deadly form of the Fenris Plague ceased to exist centuries ago, but milder cousins of the virus still crop up. Each year, starting in July, the new virus gets its start in the tropics and works its way around the world. The Freemen have been scattered around to keep all the troops from getting sick at once. Most of the unit is on leave during virus season, which is just as well because the tropics are unbearable during that time anyway."

The Clan leader shook his head. "What do you think are the chances the Freemen will have been recalled to oppose us?"

"The chances are about fifty-fifty because the government has a problem. If they recall the troops to Tyr, many of them could get sick because they have developed no immunity. If they move equipment out to staging areas so the Freemen have their BattleMechs, the chances of the current virus being spread around the world that much faster are incredible. Furthermore, even if the Freemen are scattered around in company-level units, they're not likely to be much of a threat because they'll be reacting to your strikes. Their transport network isn't likely to be very quick, especially if you control the skies."

Ulric nodded in reluctant agreement. "That brings us to another point: aerospace superiority. The report from the Ghost Bears indicated that the aerospace regiment of the First Rasalhague Drakøns was an elite unit that could give us considerable difficulty."

"The report was correct in its assessment of the Drakøns. Even so, I think there's a way to neutralize them."

The Khan watched Phelan closely. "Yes?"

Phelan rubbed his sweaty palms against the breast of his jumpsuit. "Drakøns are the Elected Prince's Honor Guard and bodyguard regiment. They are formed along the lines of Davion Regimental Combat Teams and consist of Rasalhague's most elite warriors. Their strength is deceptive, especially in aerospace fighters, because of how they're organized. 'Mech companies have four lances, not three, and missile support lances often have five or even six BattleMechs in them."

196

The mercenary clasped his hands at the small of his back. "As I understand your unit organization, a single BattleMech, two Aero-Space Fighters, or five of your Elementals are called a Point, and five of those make up a Star—a unit roughly analogous to what I call a Lance. The Drakøns' aerospace company, unlike others in the Successor States, puts four fighters in a lance, not two. That means a full regiment runs with 108 fighters, a formidable force, no matter what technological advantages you have over them."

Ulric nodded, conceding the bondsman's last point. "As you noted in the last briefing session, the extended range of our weapons does not work well in tight fights, which are exactly what Inner Sphere pilots are used to. So how do we eliminate the flying Drakøns?"

"I said *neutralize,* not eliminate." Phelan took a deep breath. "Elected Prince Haakon Magnusson of Rasalhague was an old anti-Kurita revolutionary from Alshain. In his fighting days, they called him the Silver Fox. Actually, he's not that old, but his career as a terrorist on behalf of Free Rasalhague predates independence by many years. He's uncomfortable with pitched battles. In fact, the hit-and-run fights that have given the Ghost Bears problems are a result of his people using their old tactics against them.

"The Drakøns are his bodyguard and are as loyal to him and his Ministers as the Smoke Jaguars are to the ilKhan. The way to pull the flying Drakøns off is to give them a mission: getting the Silver Fox to safety. If you don't hit Reykjavik in the first pass because, operating on mistaken information, you assault Asgard, the new capital they are building, the Silver Fox will have a chance to bolt. He'll head for a JumpShip at the nadir jump point, believing that as long as he has his freedom, he can one day throw you back."

Ulric smiled appreciatively. "If Magnusson escapes and our AeroSpace Fighters shadow him, the Drakøns will have to stay with him all the way to ensure his safety. They'll end up jumping out with him."

The Kell Hound nodded. "Not only that, but his survival means other worlds in Rasalhague will not capitulate easily. You've developed a good method of bringing conquered worlds to heel by permitting them a certain amount of sovereignty. That's a salve to the egos of the Rasalhagians, and makes them far more cooperative. I gather, from some of the reports I've read, that the Ghost Bears and Smoke Jaguars haven't learned the technique yet."

Ulric interlaced his fingers, then pressed them together against his lips. "Let us just say that their philosophical outlook does not allow them the flexibility that could assist their quest." He closed his eyes for a moment. "That would leave us with the Drakøn ground forces and the First Rasalhague Freemen to deal with."

"Right. The Freemen should be easy to handle. They're stationed on the south polar continent, which is in the middle of its winter right now. Though they're specialists in cold-weather fighting, and reportedly revel in battles that take place in the continual dark and blizzard conditions of the winter, the icy flatness of the terrain make them extremely vulnerable to the extended-range capabilities of your 'Mechs. I would suggest BattleMechs with large complements of energy weapons because the cold can affect missiles and the loading mechanisms for projectile weapons on even the best machines."

"I concur," said the Khan. "What about the Drakøns?"

Phelan sighed heavily. "They're good, and they have infantry and armor support. I think the only thing you can do is to slug it out with them. Perhaps your armored infantry can harry the armor and slow it down. The Drakøns might accept free passage from the planet so that they can join the Prince, but I think that has only a slim chance of working. Slightly better might be an offer to make them part of your garrison here, especially if you threaten to bring in your own mercenaries to do the job if they don't agree."

The Clansman beamed suddenly. "An excellent suggestion. That is just what I might do if I win the bidding." Ulric looked away, already concentrating on the battle he would wage with Bjorn of the Ghost Bears. Almost as an afterthought, he asked, "Anything else, quineg?"

"Aff, Khan Ulric." Phelan saw by Ulric's reaction that he had expected a negative response. *I can't let happen to Rasalhague what happened on Turtle Bay.* "I know of something that will guarantee you win the bidding." For the first time, Phelan saw uncertainty on the older man's face, and it worried him. *Have I overplayed my hand? Have I made myself a danger to him and the Clans?*

Ulric's features settled into an impassive mask. "What is it?"

Now or never. "Bid away the *Dire Wolf*."

The mercenary's answer brought a momentary look of shock to the Khan's face, but it faded quickly. "You do not know what you are suggesting." Even as Ulric spoke, his gaze flicked over Phelan, seeming to reassess what the bondsman had become.

Phelan straightened up. "I believe I do, Khan Ulric." The Kell Hound suddenly found his mouth going dry. "I saw the holovid of the *Sabre Cat,* the Smoke Jaguar flagship, lasing Edo to put an end to the riots there. I watched as missiles leveled buildings and lasers stabbed down from high orbit to melt the streets. The Sawagashii River boiled away to nothing! In a matter of minutes, a city of over a million was reduced to a charred, glassy scar on the face of the planet. How can you say I don't know what I'm asking?"

"Even the ilKhan believed that a prison break and six weeks of riots were not enough to justify that sort of retaliation." The Khan's eyes focused beyond the holotank. "I give you my word that I will never so level a world."

Phelan's hands convulsed into fists as Kenny Ryan's words echoed in his mind. "I know that and I believe it, or I wouldn't have helped you plan your assault on a free world. The problem is that I don't know that about Bjorn." The mercenary forced his hands open and rubbed at his temples. "I know the *Dire Wolf* is capable of the same planetary bombardments and assaults, and I know it's been kept like an ace in the hole in case you run into something you can't handle."

His head came up and his hands dropped back down to his sides. "I requested and got information on Bjorn. His holograph showed four-pointed gold stars on his collar where you wear the red dagger-stars. Ranna told me the red dagger-stars indicate someone who is a MechWarrior and that the gold stars are worn by those who come up through the Orbital Craft branch of your services. That tells me that Bjorn, no matter who or what he has advising him, is going to be dependent—consciously or unconsciously—on DropShip and Jump-Ship resources.

"Because Rasalhague actually does lie in your invasion zone, you will bid first. I know that the winner of the bidding has the right to bring down as much force as he offers in his first bid, and I know the first few bids are preliminaries to set the stage for the bidding war." Phelan felt the pulse pounding in his temples, but made no attempt to control his anger. "If your bid does not include the *Dire Wolf,* Bjorn will have to eliminate the *Ursa Major* from his first offer, or he will concede defeat with the opening bid. You'll put him off balance from the start. He'll never get back on line quickly enough to oppose you effectively."

The Khan's face hardened. "This is not how things are done. There is a formula to the bidding. You are asking me to violate the tradition that governs our ways."

"That's right. I remind you, however, that it was my reputation for unorthodox action that made you ask for my assistance. There it is. An unorthodox action that will win you the right to take Rasalhague."

"I will do this." Ulric's cerulean eyes became slits. "And I will endure whatever are the consequences of such an action but only if you will give me something in return."

Phelan hesitated. "What can I give you? I am your bondsman. You already own me."

The Khan shook his head slowly. "I have made you privy to military secrets and classified material. To obtain your help, I have made you a severe threat to the invasion and to the Clans. So much so that whether I succeed in the bidding or not, I believe the ilKhan will ask me to destroy you." A pain flashed through Ulric's eyes. "It would not please me to do so."

I've blundered onto my own vibramines! A sickening void centered itself in his stomach. *I was foolish to believe Ulric would not have recognized what sort of monster he'd created by giving me the data needed to help him.* "The assault will be as bloodless as possible?"

Ulric nodded. "Once the world is pacified, you may accompany me on an inspection."

"Well-bargained and done." Phelan swallowed past the naranji-sized lump in his throat. "I give you my word, as a MechWarrior, that I will not attempt to escape or communicate what I know to anyone without a directive from you. Before you owned my body, now you own my *soul*."

27

Black Pearl Base, Sudeten
Tamar March, Lyran Commonwealth
12 July 3050

Kai Allard, seated at the far end of the briefing table, shifted uncomfortably. *I never should have let Victor talk me into attending this liaison meeting. He should have brought someone like Renny Sanderlin...If I'd known that going to meet Victor when he arrived would get me placed in one of the strategy groups, I might not have been so anxious to see him right away.*

From the head of the table, Morgan Hasek-Davion acknowledged with a nod Dan Allard, Chris Kell, and General Adriana Winston of the Eridani Light Horse. "Thank you for the briefing on mercenary resources and readiness. I share your concern about the the way the invaders seize the 'Mechs of mercenaries they capture. I cannot indemnify you against losses in the name of the Federated Commonwealth, but I am willing to use my personal resources and influence to help restore BattleMechs to those who've been Dispossessed. This is obviously not a guarantee that everyone will return from the battles with a 'Mech—I cannot reward foolishness or incompetence—but I don't want to see good MechWarriors fall into the ranks of the Dispossessed, because of the whim of some enemy commander."

Daniel Allard smiled grimly. "Understood, Marshal, and greatly appreciated."

Morgan looked down at the far end of the table. "Victor, may we have your report from the Junior Officer Strategy Group."

Victor stood, sliding his chair back from the end of the table. "As directed, we studied all the information currently available on the invasion. As we all know, the invaders have superior 'Mechs that outgun us and are heavily armored. Their range extends well beyond that of our 'Mechs, which gives them an almost unbeatable advantage on the ground. In the air or space, however, our aerofighters can reduce this range advantage because of superior mobility over ground-bound 'Mechs, but the increased weaponry and armor still causes problems."

Victor punched a couple of keys on the keyboard he'd plugged in at his end of the table. Over the middle of the black briefing table, a computer-generated hologram came into focus. The left half of the object appeared in vector graphics, with a series of notations pertaining to design appended. Shiny metallic flesh coated the other half, giving the image a more humanoid appearance.

"Besides improved 'Mechs, the invaders have these armored infantry soldiers. Because they can jump significant distances and are exceptionally hard to kill, we've taken to calling them Toads. From the little we can see in holovids, the armor makes the infantry personnel immune to at least one shot with anything under a PPC or heavy autocannon in damage potential. We have nothing even roughly analogous to this branch of their army, and the Toads have actually destroyed scouting lances on their own."

Andrew Redburn, seated at Morgan's right hand, lifted a finger to draw Victor's attention. "Have you a rough equivalency rating worked out?"

Victor looked down. "Kai?"

Even though he knew the answer, Kai typed furiously on his noteputer. The machine's answer reconfirmed the numbers floating around in his head. "We estimate a point-two efficiency rating. That means a battle between one twenty-ton *Locust* and five Toads should leave 50 percent casualties for each side. When the *Locust* has been destroyed, only two Toads will be dead." He glanced at the noteputer again. "This evaluation includes the following assumptions, however. First, that the Toads would be using nothing heavier than their SRMs and small lasers, and second, that the *Locust* pilot had significant trouble targeting the Toads because of their high mobility."

Victor resumed his briefing. "Despite the apparent superiority of their weapons and forces, we were able to come up with some strategies. Leftenant Allard produced these ideas through analysis of the available data. I'll leave it to him to explain the information."

Kai shot Victor a surprised look. His mouth going dry, he stood up slowly. *Please, God, don't let me screw up.*

"I, ah, didn't realize I would be doing more than answering questions today, so I haven't prepared a briefing document in advance. Remember, please, that all of this is really preliminary work. I mean, It's been checked over, but I've not had a chance to review it in light of the new data that may have come in over the last three hours, so I..."

Morgan Hasek-Davion raised his right hand. "At ease, Leftenant. We'd just like to hear some of your observations. God grant us enough time that we won't have to fall back on strategies still in the gestation stage."

"Thank you, Marshal." Morgan's words reassured him, but Kai's heart continued to pound and his voice trembled slightly. His glance flew toward his Uncle Dan, who smiled encouragment. After typing a request for information into his noteputer, he took the keyboard from in front of Victor and called up a chart that replaced the Toad image over the center of the table.

"This is a chart of the apparent range advantage the invader's weapons have over us. As you can see, the ratio is roughly three to one —what we can hit at 100 meters, they hit at 300 meters. Their weapons are probably not more powerful than ours, but they can do damage at longer ranges because of better targeting systems."

Kai hit another button on the keyboard and two new columns sprang up next to the ones indicating effective range. The new columns stood roughly the same height. "These columns indicate the mean number of targets any one pilot shoots at in an exchange of fire. You can see that our pilots average 1.312 targets per salvo, while the invaders average 1.097 targets per salvo. That may not seem like a significant variation, but it is. Looking at the modal data for our troops, based on figures from as far back as Galahad 3026, our pilots seem more comfortable with selecting more than one target in an engagement. Though this might be attributed to the closer range of battles typical of the Succession Wars, the invaders may prefer to concentrate on one foe to the exclusion of others. We must bear in mind, of course, that our universe of data for the invaders is limited, at best."

Chris Kell looked over at Kai. "Do you mean they prefer to fight one-on-one like the Kurita warriors—issuing challenges and the like?"

"No reports indicate challenges offered or accepted by the invaders during a battle," Kai replied, his anxiety beginning to fade. "It's my guess that the invaders have a highly coordinated method of attack. More likely, the unit commander allots targets, and the warrior considers it a matter of pride to finish off his own foe. We've seen them allowing a lancemate to personally finish a target even though it might be quicker for the whole unit to kill off the enemy."

The young MechWarrior typed another order into the computer. The chart reorganized itself into holograms of several items. "Because of this tendency to fight against only one foe at a time, and because of their increased range potential, it struck us in the Junior Officers' Group that decoys and sensor overloads could be effective against the invaders. It would mean modifying some anti-personnel type weapons and their distribution over fields of engagement.

"The first item here is the standard M-1423 pop-up mine. When stepped on, the mine shoots its charge into the air and then explodes. Normally, we include a shrapnel device and set it to explode a meter above the ground to kill infantry, but that would be ineffective against the Toads or 'Mechs. But if we use a white phosphorus explosive that would detonate ten to twelve meters above the ground, the explosion should burn out infrared scanner cells. Other charges filled with magnetized chaff and even paint could block magscan and vislight scanning devices."

A hastily typed command magnified the second item. "This is a standard training-course decoy. Back on Skondia, these are used to project the images of tanks and 'Mechs on the live-fire range. Seeding a battlefield with these, especially if they're modified to cycle on and off from within a 'Mech, would give the illusion that our forces are much larger. It would also give the invaders a legion of targets, only a few of which are legitimate. If nothing else, it would distract them and create difficulties in selecting targets. At best, a phantom army could soak off Toads or even a lance or two of 'Mechs long enough for us to withdraw or even lure the invaders into ambushes."

General Winston frowned. "Given their improved technology in a number of areas, how can we know these decoys would fool their 'Mechs?"

"Good question, General." Victor smiled easily. "A report from Barcelona described the Jade Falcons ripping the local militia training course to pieces. Someone had left it up and running as they evacuated the base—more by mistake than because of any plan."

Chris Kell smiled wolfishly. "How'd they do?"

Victor sobered immediately. "Good enough that I'd prefer they shoot at decoys than at me."

Morgan leaned back in his chair. "Interesting. By equipping our own 'Mechs with override programs, the decoys wouldn't distract *us*. Also, by having some decoys functioning only on IR or magscan levels, we could create even more confusion." He grasped the arms of his chair and leaned back with a satisfied expression. "Thank you for your analysis, Leftenant. It gives us good material to work with. It would definitely require some preparation, though, which brings us to the biggest problem identified by the Senior Officers' Group. We have to know where the invaders will strike before we can go into action against them."

Kai, halfway into his seat, straightened up again. "Forgive me, sir, but that is not wholly true."

Morgan hesitated, then nodded quickly. "I see your point. All of these things could be deployed by air before we actually meet their forces. I stand corrected. Still, finding the enemy and learning where they will strike is a major problem."

Kai opened his mouth, then looked back at Victor. "Go ahead, Kai," Victor encouraged him. "It's your idea and one I support fully."

Kai swallowed hard. *Why you believe in me I'll never know, but it means more than you can imagine.* "Forgive me again, Marshal, for speaking out of turn."

"No, go ahead, Leftenant. This is why we have these meetings. Perhaps our ossified brains missed something."

"Well, sir, we identified the same problem—that is, of having no way to anticipate when and where the invaders will strike. The action in the rimward area of the Commonwealth has provided us no pattern for attacks. The first wave hit twelve planets, then the next reduced itself to four. It's hard to say what the logic of that is, so we decided *not* to try to anticipate."

That admission brought startled looks from all the senior officers and mercenaries, but Kai plunged on. "We all know that the concept of a 'front' in interstellar war is really a myth. Supply lines do trace themselves through various systems, but because of the vast number of stars never deemed worthy of colonization, there are countless other recharging stations for Kearny-Fuchida drives all over."

Kai looked to his uncle. "Colonel Allard will recall, I believe, that the Kell Hounds used an uncolonized star as a recharge point twenty-three years ago in the rescue of the *Silver Eagle*. Marshal, you and General Redburn will also recall using uncolonized stars during the First Kathil Uhlans' invasion of the Capellan homeworld. Because of the threat of a drive failure, most transit routes are planned through inhabited systems so help can be obtained in emergencies, but we all know that's not the only way to get around."

"This has already been stated, Leftenant," General Winston broke in impatiently. "It's because of such systems that we have no way of knowing where the invaders will strike."

Kai nodded enthusiastically. "Agreed. The invaders hit us on inhabited worlds because they know that's where they'll find us. Conversely, the only places we know to find the invaders are on the worlds they've already taken. Because there is no front, we can ignore the worlds they've targeted in their current push, and hit the worlds they took most recently. We have to hit them where they are, and if we start to cut them off from wherever their supply bases are, their offensive will have to turn back on itself because they'll be losing ground every time they take a new world."

"It stands to reason that they'd use their best troops as their vanguard," Victor chimed in. "Their elite troops are conquering worlds, not garrisoning worlds already taken. We have to assume that their garrison troops are not as good as the conquerors. If we pit our elite units against their chaff, and avoid getting our good units ripped up by their elites, we can slow down their juggernaut."

Dan Allard winced. "What if their garrison troops are as good as their elite troops?"

"Then all the planning we do is for nothing." Kai shrugged helplessly. "They'll just rip us up, no matter what."

Morgan steepled his fingers and watched the two junior officers at the far end of the table. "Your analysis and strategy are interesting, and at the very least, unusual. Not bad for just over a month of study and work. By the end of our time here, I expect a working proposal concerning this strategy, including likely units to be used and a suitable target."

Before he could issue any more instructions, a knock at the door interrupted him. A staff aide entered the room and handed the flame-haired Marshal a small yellow slip of paper. Morgan read it, then dismissed the aide with a brusque nod. He waited for the door to close before speaking. "Our time to plan has been cut down, my friends."

Kai felt a cold set of talons rake up through his middle. *What has happened? What have the invaders done now?*

Morgan pressed the paper flat against the tabletop. "I need your final reports in fourteen days. No less. The invaders have just hit Rasalhague."

28

*1st Rasalhague Drakøns Briefing Room, Reykjavik North
Rasalhague, Rasalhague Province, Free Rasalhague Republic
12 July 3050*

Tyra Miraborg shook her head. *I couldn't have heard him right.*
Raising her hand, she stood as Överste Siggurson acknowledged her.
"I'm not sure I understand what you just said, Överste."

The hawk-nosed leader of the Drakøns moved from the glare of
the overhead projector at the center of the amphitheatre. "What don't
you understand, Kapten? I thought I explained it all quite clearly." The
irritation in his voice ridiculed her question.

Tyra lifted her head proudly, and glared down at him. "I fully
understand the desperate situation of our forces, Överste. I understand
how devastating is this attack on the Republic's capital. What I do not
understand is why you're ordering the aerowing to stay out of the
battle." She looked at the other aeropilots in the room. "You've already
given your MechWarriors their assignments and sent them out. But
then you call us in to say that we're to stay out of the fight! That, sir,
makes no sense!"

Siggurson laughed coldly. "Spoken just like the daughter of the
Iron Jarl. Don't worry, Kapten. You'll get plenty of opportunities to
win yourself medals in the future."

Fury shook Tyra. "Sir, that is *not* my concern at all." She spread
her arms to take in all of the pilots in the room. "We're warriors,
dammit, and it's our right and our duty to be attacking this enemy. We
deserve the right to make sure that our comrades, earth-bound though
they might be, do not fight alone."

Siggurson let the others pilots murmur their agreement with Tyra's sentiments, then cut off all discussion by slapping his wooden pointer against a front-row chair. The pointer splintered with a sharp crack that produced immediate silence. "Let me answer your unspoken question, Kapten: Did I send out my troops with the mistaken impression that they would get air support? The answer is that those troops know you will not be there to cover them. In short, the other half of the Drakøns know I'm sending them out to die. It wasn't any easier telling them that than it is to tell you that I need you alive."

The Överste waved his left hand back at the image still projected on the wall. A map of Rasalhague's northern continent, it showed where the invaders had landed and gave approximations of their strengths. "You can see everything as well as I can. The invaders have erroneously selected Asgard City, instead of the true capital of Reykjavik, as their target. We can now deploy our ground troops to intercept their troops as they return to the capital, but they will have to pay very dearly if they hope to take it. And the reason our people will fight so hard is because the enemy's error gives you the opportunity to evacuate the Silver Fox from Rasalhague.

"If he lives, the Republic lives. If the Republic lives, then our sacrifice is not in vain."

Tyra heard both the bitterness and the plea for obedience in Siggurson's voice, but she could not leave it alone. "Överste, it will not take a whole aero regiment to fly cover for the Elected Prince. Give him a company. Let the rest of us help you."

Siggurson shook his head. "No, and that is final. We might not need a regiment to get Prince Haakon off the planet, but we might well need that regiment to ensure his safety in the systems through which he'll have to travel. The hopes and dreams of billions will be in your hands. May the gods speed you on your way and safeguard each and every one of you."

"Tighten it up, Val Four." Tyra glanced at the tactical readout on her auxiliary monitor. "Stay with us, Marnie, or you'll be left behind."

"Roger, Kapten."

I hope you meant that, Löjtnant Ingstad, because this is no time for solo missions. The Wolves might not be after us on this outward run, but we're the folks who have to make sure it's clear for the Silver Fox to escape. I don't like the mission, but I'll be damned if I'll let it fail. Tyra flipped the radio over to the frequency she shared with Anika Janssen. "Clear to you, Nik?"

"Roger, Kapten. I'm clear on a vector to the Fox's bolt hole." Frustration tinged Janssen's words. "I know what Ingstad is thinking, and I bet you and Karl are thinking it along with her. We're supposed to safeguard the Prince so he can get away, but I don't like the idea of leaving the rest of the Drakøns behind, no matter what Siggurson said. Dammit, they may be ground-pounders and mud-marchers but..."

"...They're *our* ground-pounders," Tyra completed the sentence. "I know. I don't like it either. Let me see if I can do something about it." Tyra switched the radio to the taccom frequency. "Valkyrie Flight reporting in. Rakblad vector is clear."

"Roger," a distant voice crackled back through the speakers in her neurohelmet. "We have Viking Flight five minutes behind you, then Fox Flight will appear. Rendezvous in fifteen minutes, Vector Ressjuka for outbound travel."

"Affirmative, Taccom. Valkyrie Flight transferring from eight thousand meters to the deck to continue sweep." Tyra crossed her fingers and tried to keep anxiety from her voice. "Can you authorize mission status transfer, Taccom?"

Weariness filled the radio operator's voice. "You and every other pilot in this aeroforce...No can do, Valkyrie Leader, but you'll do it even if clearance isn't given, won't you? I am ordered to forbid you to change heading to two-seven-one and drop to Nape. I am further ordered not to tell you that twenty-five kilometers out we have a reported contact. Be careful and be back in fifteen."

"Thanks, Taccom. You can set your chronometer by us." Tyra opened a frequency to the three other members of her flight. "Heads up. Change to course two-seven-one and glide on down till the trees tickle your undercarriage. We want to go in at 800 kph, which makes contact just over two minutes off. Stay close. We'll have time for a couple of passes. You get hit and come back here. We're out on Ressjuka vector in fifteen minutes, and I don't want to leave anyone behind. Got it?"

Tyra got three positive responses, then stood her *Shilone* on its left wing and pointed its nose at the ground. She watched her air-speed indicator as the wing dropped like a rock toward the planet below. Feathering her thrust vectors, she trimmed the craft's tendency to shift pitch in atmosphere, then pulled its nose up to transform the steep dive into a glide that sent her streaking across the face of the planet.

Once down on the deck, Tyra engaged the Nape guidance system. Under computer control, the *Shilone* raced 500 meters above the landscape that spread out beneath her like a rumpled blanket. The forests became an evergreen blur that seemed to stretch on forever except when the computer bounced her up and over a gray granite ridge. Even within the close confines of her cockpit and neurohelmet, the roar of wind rushing past reached her and set her heart beating faster.

As her flight came over the last mountain barrier and moved down into the Asgard Valley, Tyra switched off the Nape computer and engaged the tactical computer. Once again, a holographic composite representing the battlefield below filled the space between her and her instruments. The targeting light appeared on her faceplate and the armrests rotated until they filled her hands with triggers. All her weapons systems came on-line and reported 100 percent operational.

"Nik, you and I go in first. Val Three and Four, hang back, then follow us."

Tyra kept her hands steady on the triggers as the *Shilone* glided in like a hawk over a meadow. She took the fighter down to twenty-five meters above the ground, flying more by feel than conscious process. The neurohelmet enabled her craft to use her own kinesthetic sense to keep it skimming the valley's golden, grassy carpet. Then, suddenly, targets appeared on the holographic display at more than three thousand meters out.

At 800 kph, extreme range passed to close range in the blink of an eye, but that hardly mattered. Tyra hit the firing buttons for her three lasers. The ruby beams raked the 'Mechs massed below, vaporizing armor and setting the grass ablaze. Over the invaders, Tyra boosted the *Shilone's* nose into the air and punched out a flight of the aft-arc short range missiles. As they exploded among the 'Mechs, she rolled the fighter, then swooped up and out of her enemy's range.

Excitement filled Anika's voice. "Beautiful, Tyra. They didn't expect us, and they didn't have time to track us. We left some armor hanging, but they're still heading toward Asgard City."

Tyra leveled out at a kilometer and turned to watch Karl Niemi and Marnie Ingstad make their passes. Both *Slayer*s flew over the terrain like vultures racing to a carcass. Laser bolts stabbed through the cloud of ashen smoke surrounding the invaders. Because of the smoke, Tyra could not make out any actual damage done, but a roiling ball of golden fire erupting out of the smoke told her that at least one invader's fusion engines had exploded.

As both fighters banked up and out of the smoke, she opened the radio channel to them. "Great shooting. Nik, crossing pattern at point-one klick. Three and Four, set up for a similar run, but rotate it thirty degrees. Go now!"

Anika's fighter slipped from its position on Tyra's left wing and

210

spiraled around until it appeared half a kilometer below her and off her starboard bow. Tyra dropped her *Shilone*'s nose and began a slow turn to the left. Set up at ninety degrees to Anika's angle of attack, she leveled her dive out and came in at 500 meters.

She let a full flight of LRMs announce her arrival. The invaders fired back along the missiles' flight path, but Tyra had closed so much ground in that short time that their counterattacks passed beneath her. Even as a couple of invaders realized their error and started to adjust their aim, she began her strafing run. She held her right thumb down on the firing stud and tightened up the first two fingers of her left hand on the trigger buttons under them. Ruby lasers slashed through the smoke, and subsidiary explosions told her she'd found vulnerable targets within the enemy host.

Two seconds later, as she pulled up the nose of her *Shilone* and the invaders started to track her ship, Anika shot through the smoke at right angles to Tyra's line of attack. Her raking laser fire provided more than enough distraction for the MechWarriors attempting to knock Tyra from the sky. Then, as the invaders maneuvered to kill Anika, the twin *Slayer*s made their passes. In a dozen hearbeats, whole and unscathed, Valkyrie Flight reformed at eight thousand meters and raced to the east.

Tyra keyed her radio to taccom, but left the line open to allow the rest of her flight to hear what she said. "Taccom, Valkyrie Flight confirms contact at heading two-seven-one. We rolled out the welcome mat for them and showed them just how the Republic feels about them."

The controller summoned a weak laugh. "Obliged, Valflight. Överste Siggurson wants to know what made you think you could violate his orders?"

Tyra's eyes narrowed. "Tell him it was bad blood." She looked at her navigational computer. "Valkyrie Flight on heading oh-eight-nine for the Ressjuka out vector. Give 'em hell."

"Roger, Val Leader. We'll make you proud. Rasalhague out."

211

Reykjavik, State of Islandia
Rasalhague, Rasalhague Province, Free Rasalhague Republic
17 July 3050

Smoke drifted raggedly along the streets, snaking its way from small bonfires through the hollow shells of buildings. Bricks and mortar lay frozen in the dawn light. The bricks' color reminded Phelan of dried blood and the gray mortar of the ashes he saw everywhere. *My God, they actually had to fight their way into the city!*

The captive MechWarrior followed a step or two behind Ulric as Star Colonel Lara guided the Khan and his entourage through the conquered capital. She walked at Ulric's right hand, while the Precentor Martial accepted a place of honor at his left. A dozen of the giant Elementals formed a pocket around the visitors, but only two of them wore their metallic armor. In addition to Phelan, Clan MechWarriors trailed behind their leaders, including a smug-looking Vlad.

Lara pointed out a rough semicircle of buildings that marked the perimeter of destruction. "The Drakøns made a last stand in this area. We had not planned to be so destructive, but the tight quarters of the city made things difficult. And many of our people wanted to get it over with quickly after the strafing run their fighters made on us near Asgard."

Phelan heard her words but could find no relation betweeen what she said and the scene before him. These buildings had not merely been blown apart. Rather, they looked like vegetables that had succumbed to rot. What had once been sharp angles had melted into curves. Buildings, their walls liquified by lasers and particle beams, had sagged in on themselves. Blackened by fire and streaked with red

212

where new flows of fluid brick ran down the surface, the buildings might have been some flaccid fungi wilting in the sunlight.

And those weren't even the intended targets! The scraps and bits of Drakøn 'Mechs still visible seemed to Phelan far too few for this to have been a major battleground. *I've seen the aftermath of a dozen battles, but this scene looks more like a thoroughly scavenged scrapyard.* The largest concentrations of 'Mech debris were small hovels the refugees had thrown up, using armor shards for walls and roofs to protect them from the chill of night. Beyond that, the stripped skeleton of a 'Mech's hand pointing loosely off toward the north was the only real clue that 'Mechs had fought and died here.

The Precentor Martial uttered Phelan's question for him. "Did any of the Drakøn pilots survive, quiaff?"

Lara nodded. "Affirmative. Most, in fact. We decided early on that it would be best to base our occupational forces on cooperation with the Drakøns, who will be our ambassadors to the people on Rasalhague." She smiled at Focht. "Of course, we will work through ComStar's good offices, as usual, to facilitate the restructuring of the society."

Across the street, Phelan saw a small knot of people standing around a fire inside an old petrochem drum. Their mismatched clothing contrasted sharply with the green jumpsuit and synthetic jacket he wore. Through holes in their trousers and burned patches on their coats, he saw that most of them wore several layers of rags to ward off the cold. The haunted look in their eyes revealed the state of their hunger and their hopelessness.

"Forgive my presumption, Star Colonel," Phelan found himself saying, "but what provision has been made for the people whose homes were destroyed?"

Lara started to answer, but glanced at Ulric first, who gave her a slight nod. "We have housed the vast majority on the west side of the city. The facilities we are using were in disrepair, but they are adequate until things can be rebuilt." The Clanswoman pointed to the people skulking around the ruins. "These people have refused to report to the facilities, and therefore, will not receive support."

Phelan suddenly remembered a fragment of information. *Camps on the west side of Reykjavik...Wasn't that something described in Misha Auburn's* Freedom's Bloody Price? "Would you be referring to the Kempei Tai barracks over on the other side of the Oslo river, quineg?"

"Aff. I believe that name was associated with the place."

Phelan made no attempt to disguise his shock. "The Kempei Tai barracks was an ISF—Kurita secret police—reeducation center before Rasalhague became independent. The FRR maintained it as a reminder of man's inhumanity to man. Fully a quarter of the people sent there never returned. Is it any wonder these people refused to be herded in there?"

Before Lara could frame an answer, another incident demanded the group's attention. While everyone in the Khan's entourage had been distracted by the discussion, one of the refugees, a ragged man stinking of sweat and with soot-stained face and clothes, approached the group. He tugged on the Khan's sleeve. "Please, sir. You must help us…"

Vlad lunged forward and bowled the vagabond aside with a backhanded slap. The refugee reeled away, stumbled, and rolled awkwardly into a crouch. Though he held up his hands and ducked his head in submission, the Clan MechWarrior kept on coming. A solid kick to the chest lifted the older man from the ground and dumped him on his back a couple of meters away. Stunned, arms and legs splayed out, the refugee offered no resistance and no threat, but that did not slow Vlad at all.

Phelan grabbed the Khan. "He'll kill the old man. You have to stop him!"

Ulric's steel blue gaze jolted the Kell Hound. "Do I?"

"We had a deal." The mercenary's eyes blazed. "This was supposed to be as bloodless as possible!"

Ulric turned and stared at where Vlad stood beating the beggar senseless. "If it concerns you, then you deal with him."

Like a warhound slipped from its leash, Phelan dashed forward. His left hand closed on Vlad's left wrist, locking the bloodied fist at the highest point of its arc. Before Vlad could disentangle his right hand from the old man's silvery hair, the mercenary slammed his right fist into the Clansman's ribs. He let Vlad tear his left fist free, then buried his own left hand in the invader's midsection. Vlad brought his left arm down to cover his side and stomach, but it did not help him. Phelan's right fist arced up and over Vlad's left shoulder and snapped his head around with a crisp shot to the jaw.

As Vlad dropped to the pavement, Phelan felt massive hands on his shoulders. Without thinking, he drove his right elbow back into this new opponent's stomach. The rock-hard muscles gave a bit and the hands began to tighten. The mercenary cranked his right fist up in a short hammer-arc, mashing thick lips against white teeth. At the same time, he twisted to the right, slipping his shoulders from the hands gripping them. His right hand dropped down, then shot back up, catching the Elemental on the point of her jaw. Evantha's eyes glazed over and she pitched onto her back.

A right hand exploded on Phelan's left cheek, but he'd already begun to pull back his head, lessening the effect of the blow. His own right hand shot across his body and hit Vlad in the stomach with a short jab. The punch forced a grunt from the Clansman and brought him up short. Vlad's right hand came in again, but Phelan faded back before it and guided it beyond his face with his left hand. Then the mercenary delivered his own right hand in a jab that came straight from the shoulder. Vlad's nose collapsed with a crack, then his legs turned to water and he sank to the ground.

Phelan pivoted on his right foot and looked back at the Clanspeople. On his left hand, Evantha began to stir, but on the right, only the rhythmical rise and fall of Vlad's chest and the slow trickle of blood from his nose gave any indication that he still lived. Sucking in cold air painfully through his clenched teeth, the mercenary surveyed the damage he had done. "He has, my Khan, been stopped."

Ulric's face betrayed nothing. "So he has."

Phelan eyed the rest of the Clanspeople with an open challenge on his face. A couple of the infantrymen met his stare, then bowed their heads in a silent salute and looked away as their comrade moaned in pain. Their reaction, for a moment or two, struck him as curious, then he unraveled the myriad meanings of that simple gesture. *In this martial society, what I have done is nothing short of a miracle. For me to beat another MechWarrior is within the realm of possibility because that is what I am. But to beat someone whose area of expertise is hand-to-hand combat, that is special, indeed. It does not matter to them that she was taken by surprise—it is her error for underestimating me. In their eyes, that does not diminish what they must consider an incredible victory.*

He flexed his fists, then exerted control over his breathing. He felt his muscles begin to tremble as the adrenaline started to wear off. He bowed deeply from the waist—more in Kurita fashion than anything he had learned in his time with the Clans—and addressed the Khan. "I request leave, Master, to take this man back to his people."

The Khan narrowed his eyes. "You know we will be leaving here an hour before sunset—approximately 1800 hours local time, quiaff?"

The Kell Hound nodded solemnly. "You know I will be there." *Always testing, aren't you, quiaff? What do you want from me? I have given you my word that I will neither escape nor betray your secrets.*

Ulric smiled wolfishly. "I had no doubt." He unfastened the strap on his chronometer and tossed the heavy steel timepiece to Phelan. "Here. This will keep you from being late."

The mercenary caught it and strapped it to his left wrist. "Thank you."

The Khan nodded. "You are my personal envoy to this man and his people, Phelan. Persuade them that the old days are no more. Encourage them to go to the camps so we may rebuild their homes. It is for the best."

Phelan stared after the Khan as his party, including the two Elementals bearing Vlad and Evantha, walked away. *I don't understand you, Ulric, Khan of the Wolf Clan. And that scares me. But what scares me even more is the feeling that, before long, I will understand you far better than either one of us has sense enough to dread.*

The steel anchor monument against which Phelan leaned was cold, but he never noticed as he stared out at the broad Oslo River. River gulls, with their blood-red bodies and black wings, hovered above him, screaming. He wanted to pick up a rock and scatter them, but couldn't muster the energy to do so.

"What is the matter, Phelan?" Ranna startled him as she gave his shoulder a squeeze from behind. "You are not an easy man to find. I doubt I would have if that family you brought to the refugee center hadn't mentioned something."

"I guess I didn't want to be found...Not right now." Ranna pulled back, but he reached out to catch her hand. "No, I didn't mean it that way. It's just..."

Ranna sat down beside him on the base of the anchor monument. The chilly air had brought a rosy glow to her cheeks and made her hands cold. She let him sandwich her hands between his for warmth, then smiled. "You do not have to talk about it if you do not want to."

He chewed on his lip for a moment, then shook his head. "I just keep thinking about the old man and his family. When I helped him up, he looked at me like I was the second coming of God. He babbled on at me in that Swedenese of theirs, and I just smiled and helped him over to where his family was standing around a fire. His son, who's at least ten years older than me, treated me like his overlord. He translated what his father was saying about the fight and he made it sound as though I'd taken a 'Mech regiment—a Cluster to you—all by myself."

A devilish look flashed through Ranna's blue eyes. "To hear the infantry tell it, you did more than that."

Her remark brought momentary life to Phelan's dour expression, but he wasn't deflected from his train of thought. "All the while they were praising me, all I could think about was how I helped sell this world to Ulric. I gave him the tools to outbid Bjorn."

"And that helped these people more than you know, Phelan. The Ghost Bears would have made bombing runs against the Drakøn

216

positions in the city, and their pilots believe quantity beats quality when attacking the enemy."

"I know that, dammit, but it doesn't make it any easier feeling like a Judas." He turned to stare into her eyes. "When someone writes the history of the conquest of Rasalhague, I'll be cast as Stefan Amaris the Usurper."

Ranna jerked her hands from his. "Do not say that. You are no Judas and certainly not an Amaris. Your motive was not personal greed." She jabbed a finger back toward the burned-out section of the town. "You jumped a trained warrior to defend an innocent man. Many of the refugees saw what you did, and many followed you when you led the man's family to the shelter. The risk you took meant that those people will at least be warm tonight. They will have food, too, and soon their homes will be rebuilt."

She lifted his head to meet her gaze. "What happened to these people would have happened with or without your help. Aside from those we choose to join us, life here will return to normal."

Phelan turned away. "You make it sound as if being made a bondsman is an honor…"

Ranna took in a deep breath, then let it out slowly in a wispy white vapor. "There are many things you have not learned about us because you have contact with only one part of our society. You see only the martial branch because we are the vanguard of the Clans. I cannot explain it all to you right now, but you're right—being made a bondsman *is* an honor. Those taken are selected to join our Clan and that is one of the greatest honors a person can know in life."

Phelan frowned. "But I have joined the Wolf Clan as chattel, not as a person."

"You do not understand…All that matters is that you are part of the Wolf Clan." Frustration knotted her fingers into fists.

Seeing that the discussion would continue to run in circles, Phelan reached out again and gathered her hands into his. "I don't want to fight with you, Ranna." He shrugged sheepishly. "Maybe I'm just homesick, after nearly a year on DropShips and JumpShips. Having solid mass under my feet and feeling real gravity again…Even the gulls, with their red and black coloring, make me think of my unit." He turned to stare out over the water. "I feel so alone."

Grasping Phelan by the wrists, Ranna pulled him to his feet. "As long as I am here, Phelan Kell, you will never be alone. As a Star Commander, I've been given a suite at the Hotel Copenhagen. Come share it with me. Let me show you that you truly do have a home in the Wolf Clan."

Book IV

Head of the
Beast

Marshdale, Kagoshima Prefecture
Pesht Military District, Draconis Combine
21 July 3050

Shin Yodama tugged on the ends of the sash at his waist, pulling the quilted robe tighter. The sound of angry waves crashing against the cliff-face below, and winds howling around his tower deepened the sensation of cold gnawing into his bones. *To think I talked myself into enduring eight weeks of JumpShip transit because I thought a tropical paradise waited at the other end of the trip! Marshdale is certainly not that. If I'd known, I might have suggested we just continue on to Luthien, no matter what our orders said.*

Eighth of ten planets in the system, Marshdale never passed close enough to either of the binary system's stars to warm up. However, the gravitational forces working on it squeezed and stretched the planet regularly. That created enough friction between tectonic plates to warm the oceans sufficiently to sustain life and create the ground-hugging clouds of fog that shrouded the planet. The earthquakes produced as a byproduct of this gravitational torture required that all buildings be massive, but tremors were so common that long-time residents ignored all but the truly violent ones.

Shin steadied himself against a heavy, oaken table as the ground shifted beneath his feet. *Hell, even a DropShip bucking turbulence is more stable than this planet.* Still clinging to the table as the tremor passed, he realized suddenly how tired he was. *I guess getting Hohiro here and then the debriefings kept me too busy to see how close to the edge I've been. I've been pushing myself and my luck quite a bit. I also*

*know I don't like having been kept in virtual isolation here. And I want
to know what has been going on with the invasion and what has
happened to Turtle Bay since we escaped.*

A knock sounded at the heavy wooden door. "Enter," Shin
snapped irritably. At the sight of the man who stepped through the
doorway, Shin's jaw dropped open. He bowed so deeply that he almost
bashed his face on the table and held it. "Excuse me, Gunji no Kanrei!
I did not mean to be rude." He slowly straightened up.

Theodore Kurita returned the bow, then shut the door, which
remained guarded by two of his uniformed men. "I heard no rudeness,
Shin Yodama. The door stripped all emotion from the word it let pass
through."

Shin's nervousness began to drain away, and he tried to smile.
*Had I used that tone with Takashi Kurita, I would have regretted it, but
not so with Theodore.* "You are most kind, Highness." Shin glanced
down at the floor, not wishing to compound his earlier error with ill-
mannered staring. "What may this humble servant do for you?"

The heir to the Dragon smiled, looking suddenly youthful. Only
the scar over his left eyebrow and the wrinkles beginning at the corners
of his eyes hinted at his fifty-three years. Aside from those minute
clues, the tall, slender man could have passed for a MechWarrior half
his age.

The Kanrei pointed to a chair and waved Shin to it. "You have
already served me more faithfully than many of the warriors in my
service." He raised his left hand to the scar on his brow. "You have
been with me for as long as this scar. Marfik, Najha, and now Turtle
Bay. You have done enough in any one of those places to satisfy most
men for a lifetime. And now you have saved my son."

The yakuza shook his head. "Forgive me, Kanrei, but I have only
done my duty. I saved my commanding officer, which is what any
other would have done in the same circumstances and with the same
resources. Praise and thanks should go to the *oyabun* of the *Ryugawa-
gumi* in Edo. Without him, both Hohiro-*sama* and I would be dead."

A shadow seemed to pass over Theodore's face. "I would do this
thing, were it possible. Unfortunately, the city of Edo was razed by a
planetary bombardment. The Smoke Jaguars decided that if they could
not control the populace, they would wipe it out. Everything is gone."

In his mind's-eye, Shin saw the Old Man's castle evaporate in a
wave of flame, and his stomach roiled in response. "How could they
do that? How could they kill a city?"

The Kanrei closed his eyes. "I do not know. My source said the
Jaguar commander was most arrogant and wished to make an example

222

of Edo."

"I will confirm their arrogance," Shin said. The debriefers may have told you that I witnessed the destruction of a hovel calculated to make the people turn over a terrorist to the invaders. When a Buddhist monk confessed to the crime of planting a bomb, they killed him, then left. They had seemed concerned with the unnecessary loss of life, but my judgment must have been wrong for them to have destroyed Edo."

"Apparently, the *Ryugawa-gumi* made life unpleasant for the garrison troops once the front line forces left for new conquests. Instead of sending elite troops back down to restore order, they used their orbital fleet to destroy Edo, and at the same time, broadcast its destruction to the other major urban centers on the planet." The Kanrei swallowed hard. "Resistance, as you might imagine, ceased overnight."

"What I have told you is, of course, strictly confidential. I have spoken of these things to you because I know that you are the most trustworthy of men. I also felt I owed it to you to tell you about the *Ryugawa-gumi*."

"Thank you, Kanrei. I am honored by your trust."

The Kanrei clasped his hands behind his back, and gave Shin a searching look. "Were it within my power, I would grant you any wish as a reward for rescuing my son from such danger. However, with you and Hohiro being our only sources of first-hand information on this enemy, I must ask instead for your continued service in this crisis. I ask also that you pardon the seeming ingratitude."

Shin smiled warmly. "The only reward I desire is the opportunity to serve you well. Your need and my desire are matched horses."

The Kanrei bowed his head. "Come. The others have arrived and we must discuss strategy."

Theodore and Shin moved through the dark halls of the castle, following the guards, whose heels clicked smartly against the cold stone of the arched passages. The castle, which had been built from native materials on a blueprint from an ancient structure on Terra, felt gloomy and sad to Shin.

Millennia ago, armored European knights would have marched through passages just like these, on their way to plot battles and grand strategies. Now, centuries later, we do the same, the only difference being that our armor has grown too large to tread within this structure. Did Moorish invaders seem as unstoppable to the Knights of Castille as these Clans do to us?

When they came to a broad, curving staircase, the Kanrei and Shin descended into a more brightly lit room. Opposite the stairs, a roaring fire blazed in a hearth that appeared larger, to Shin, than his whole room. Two oaken tables built of well-weathered wood flanked a holographic display unit. Technicians sat at either input station on the briefing unit, while a host of officers were gathered around the tables.

Spirits of my ancestors! This is an incredible collection of military leaders. If the Clans struck this place, they would decapitate the Combine in one stroke. Though Shin could identify units and ranks from uniform insignia, he recognized only one other officer aside from Theodore and Hohiro. *There was no way he or his unit would stay out of this, thank the gods.*

The officer was seated near the end of the table toward which the Kanrei moved. Slightly built and smaller than average, the MechWarrior yet possessed so much power of personality that a number of the less secure officers shot occasional glances at him or behaved as though his gaze was somehow scalding. He greeted Theodore with a nod.

Narimasa Asano, leader of the Genyosha. Shin glanced at the triple-bar insignia on Asano's collar. *It is true, then, that he has refused elevation above the rank of Tai-sa, despite the Genyosha now comprising two full regiments. It is said that this is his gesture of respect for the man who formed the unit, Yorinaga Kurita, but I have also heard that it is to make the Genyosha equal to the Kell Hounds. Either way, I'm glad we have the Black Ocean warriors with us.*

Theodore directed Shin to a seat beside Hohiro, then began his briefing. "To be sure that all of us are current, let me run down the situation as we understand it. In their latest push—which we have termed the 'Third Wave'—the Smoke Jaguars hit six of our worlds. These worlds are: Jeanette, Chupadero, Kabah, Coudoux, Hanover, and Albiero. The Ghost Bears hit Schuyler. We also have unconfirmed reports from our agents in the Rasalhague Republic that the Clans have taken a significant number of worlds there, including the capital."

Shin felt as though someone had punched him in the stomach. *The Clans took Rasalhague! If they can muster the force needed to take a capital world, is it possible for us to gather the strength needed to defend one?* He glanced at the map of the Draconis Combine one of the Techs produced on the display and saw that the wedge of worlds under assault by the Smoke Jaguars, which extended through to Terra and beyond, included Luthien in its swath.

The Kanrei let the seriousness of Rasalhague's loss sink in for a moment before continuing. "The only good thing about all this is that our estimate of Ghost Bear resources and the amount of firepower they used to take Schuyler indicates that they did not participate in the conquest of Rasalhague. Though Schuyler is the first of our worlds that the Clan has taken, we need not fear, at least in the short term, that the resources of the weapons factories on New Oslo will be turned against us."

Hohiro looked up at his father. "Kanrei, has anyone managed to identify these Clans?"

Theodore shook his head. "Their identities remain a mystery. A number of theories have been offered, but none seems satisfactory. One speculation is that their use of BattleMechs means they are the Star League army returning. This theory must be balanced against the reality of those very BattleMechs, which are more sophisticated than any known in the Star League-era. And one must also wonder, if the invaders are, indeed, descendants of Kerensky's force, why they are attacking the Successor States?

"As we have seen, the Clans hit hard and move on swiftly. Many believe that they are only the edge of a mass migration into the Successor States. Something like the barbarian invasions that swept parts of Terra two millennia ago.

"Long before Stefan Amaris murdered the last First Lord of the Star League, the Inner Sphere was surrounded by Periphery realms. Sometimes, these became known to us only by accident. It is, therefore, possible that one or more other nations exist beyond the realms we know about. The idea that a leader created in the mold of Genghis Khan could unite or conquer a legion of small states and weld them into an army able to take on the Inner Sphere does not seem far-fetched. At the very least, it suggests a human origin for the hordes invading us, which I find preferable to any alien explanation."

Shin's head came up. "And if the invaders are another sentient form of life?"

The Kanrei smiled warily. "In that case, I will take comfort in the fact that you, in your assault on Kurushiiyama, managed to kill some of them." He looked around at the others in the room. "That is but one instance proving that our foes are vulnerable to our weapons. They die the same as we do."

At a glance from Theodore, one of the Techs hit a few keystrokes, changing the display to side-by-side views of Hanover and Albiero. "The garrisons on Hanover and Albiero were given orders for dealing with the invaders that differed with the rules of engagement we followed previously. When the invaders asked our garrison commanders what units they would use for their defense, our officers either refused to give any information, or—in our tradition—gave the

225

invaders a complete and detailed report on the unit's proud history. In both cases, the Smoke Jaguars arrived in sufficient force to overwhelm our troops in short order. The only units that performed beyond the norm were newly formed regiments whose history did not reflect the caliber of MechWarriors in them."

He glanced at Asano. "Those units were created and trained along the lines of the Genyosha and the Ryuken. Their commanders avoided the clean and crisp battles the Smoke Jaguars desired in favor of something more like the hit-and-run tactics of bandits. Though our forces eventually succumbed, partly because of supply problems, their tactics did manage to reduce the advantage of range the invaders have over us."

Something in Theodore's explanation struck a chord in Shin. *When the Smoke Jaguars came into Uramachi looking for Motochika, they accepted, at face value, the monk's confession that he had planted the bomb. They didn't seem to even consider the possibility he might be lying.* "Forgive me for interrupting," he said, "but from what you say, the invaders inquire what forces we will use to defend a world. Taking the information on faith, they then act upon it. Wouldn't that mean that they could easily underestimate unknown and untested units? It seems to be part of their arrogance, as in the example of the monk who confessed in order to save others."

"The very point toward which I was heading," the Kanrei agreed, bringing a flush to Shin's cheeks. "As *Chu-sa* Yodama has pointed out, the Jaguars appear to be guileless when requesting information. They do not expect deception. It would be dishonorable to lie to them, but recently, I had occasion to change the unit names and designations for the troops on Hanover and Albiero. I permitted the commanders of those garrisons to provide histories of their units that included only actions under their new names. This may have contributed to the invaders' confusion about which were veteran and which were green units."

So intently was Shin listening to Theodore's reasoning that he missed, at first, the rank designation used to address him. Then, suddenly, the word hit him: *Chu-sa! Lieutenant-Colonel! It must have been a mistake. A jump of two ranks...Impossible!*

Theodore looked over at Shin. "Yes, *Chu-sa* Yodama, you have been promoted. Your commanding officer recommended the promotion and I will have none less than a *Chu-sa* serving on my staff. I hope my need and your desire are still matched horses, for we must work together to stop the invaders."

His words took Shin's breath away. *I have been catapulted well above my station in life. Amida grant me the skill to be of service, and the wisdom to know when my time has come.* "Your will be done, or I die in harness, Kanrei."

"Good." A gesture from the Kanrei brought a graphic concerning troop strengths and losses up on the display. "On Hanover, things went exceptionally well for us. Our forces, using supply caches hidden in the Worldspine mountains, were able to oppose the Smoke Jaguars very effectively. Their downfall came when the invaders brought down reinforcements and flanked our people. The resulting battle, which occurred during a blizzard, inflicted heavy casualties on both sides. Our commander surrendered only after the enemy agreed to treat his warriors honorably."

Another casualty report replaced the first. Unlike its predecessor, the loss column for the Combine's forces dwarfed that for the invaders. "The Hanover battle ended about twelve hours before the Albiero assault began. The Smoke Jaguars there brought down a bit more materiel than expected and managed to pinpoint our troops' supply caches. An ambush at one of those sites destroyed the command company for the regiment, which led to a collapse of resistance. Still, some units did continue guerrilla action, which hampered the general pacification of the world."

"If they got word out in twelve hours," Narimasa Asano began carefully, "either the Clans are using ComStar, or they have Hyper-Pulse technology themselves. There is no other way for a message to travel that fast between stars fifteen light years apart, unless they used a JumpShip to relay the message."

Theodore shook his head. "No JumpShip was used. As we cannot rule out ComStar involvement, all operations from now on will go out under sealed orders. That the enemy has his own HyperPulse Generators is a simpler solution to the mystery, I think. Capturing one, and the means to operate it, would be a boon, but that can only come after we defeat our enemy. And defeat him we will."

The Kanrei grinned proudly. "At the rate the attack waves have been coming, we have approximately two months before they move on. That gives us the time we need to set up Operation *Sakkaku*— Illusion. We will gather our most elite units under new designations on Wolcott, a world they are certain to hit in the next thrust. We will prepare hidden supply depots and occupy the most defensible points on the world. We will be ready for them."

Shin frowned. "How do we know they will not sense a trap? Why wouldn't they simply bypass Wolcott in favor of more meekly de-fended planets?"

The Kanrei watched Shin like a hawk. "Oh, they'll know it's a trap, but they will come anyway. When they discover our bait, they will trap themselves. Remember how arrogant they are."

The Kanrei smiled sagely. "How, after all, can they resist Wolcott when they learn the defenders are commanded by the two people who escaped them on Turtle Bay?"

Black Pearl Base, Sudeten
Tamar March, Lyran Commonwealth
21 July 3050

Victor Steiner-Davion shook his head. "God above, I hate waiting."

"Don't worry, Vic. Your plan's a good one," said Kai Allard, seated next to him outside the briefing room. "It will work. They have to approve it."

"Excuse me...I thought you were Kai Allard, the eternal pessimist?"

Kai looked sheepish, then grinned weakly. "Victor, I may have my own problems with self-confidence, but I'm not such a slouch at seeing someone else's strengths. That was a great idea that your Hauptmann Cox came up with of me running the Jade Falcon forces in our last simulation. There I got to exploit all the flaws I saw or imagined in our strategy."

Victor snorted. "Yeah, and you wadded up our forces and tossed them aside like they were tin soldiers."

Kai shrugged. "But that was *supposed* to be a worst-case scenario. We had our forces scattered and with major casualties on the landings because of freak storms and enemy aerofighter action. Everything that could go wrong *did* go wrong, but you still managed to pull a regiment and a half back out. The disaster was controlled, and at the very least, the wealth of enemy data we would gain in such a case is justification enough for the operation. We can't discount the value of intelligence."

Victor laughed softly. "Spoken like a spymaster's son."

Kai laughed as well. "Hey, it runs in the blood. The point is that this assault has a higher-than-normal chance of working. I won't bet on how many days or hours we can hold Twycross after we take it, but I know it will slow the Jade Falcons' advance in the future."

The door to the briefing room slid open, and Leftenant-General Andrew Redburn appeared in the doorway. "We have some questions. If you will accompany me…"

Vic rubbed his right hand against his stomach and got up slowly. Kai looked at him with concern. "What's the matter?"

Victor rested his hand on his friend's shoulder. "No big problem, but I think the butterflies in my stomach just got issued BattleMechs."

They entered the room, and as the door slid shut behind them, took their places at the far end of the table. As in the previous briefings, they faced Morgan Hasek-Davion, with Leftenant-General Redburn to their left and the mercenary leaders on their right. Kai took a seat and pulled the keyboard over. Victor chose to stand.

Morgan tapped his fingers against the black cover of Victor's battleplan. "Before we start, I'd like to say that all of us are impressed with the extent of the work you and your team have put into this document. It is clear and concise. We especially appreciate the extensive adversarial testing you did on it. This is work I would have expected from a cabal of hoary old veterans, not young officers like yourselves. Commendations have been recorded for those who contributed in this effort."

Victor smiled and bowed his head. "Thank you, Marshal. We are most grateful that the work was of interest." He paused for a moment, then met Morgan's malachite stare. "I sense a 'but' in there somewhere."

"You do, indeed," said Morgan in a low voice. "This plan calls for the allocation of four Regiments: the Tenth Lyran Guards, both Kell Hound regiments, and the Ninth F-C RCT. Moving those units and the necessary support materiel and personnel will take 45 percent of our available JumpShip and DropShip resources. That severely limits my ability to move forces to the worlds the invaders are likely to hit in their next wave."

Victor frowned deeply. "But we agreed, in a meeting two weeks ago, that it was foolishness trying to defend all the areas the invaders could possibly hit. It's a guessing game that we can only lose."

"Just because we know we *can't* defend all the worlds doesn't mean we don't have to *try*," Morgan corrected him. "This is more than just a military conflict, and you know it as well as I do. Ryan Steiner, for one, would be happy to pull the Isle of Skye out of the Common-wealth. If he were to hear that we'd made no effort to protect worlds in the Tamar March, he and his wife might decide to secede and negotiate their own pact with the invaders. That would neatly cut us off from the Federated Suns—a move you would agree is counter-productive."

"Believe it or not, cousin, I did take that into consideration," Victor said, wishing that someone had strangled Ryan Steiner at birth. "We chose Twycross as a target for many reasons, most having to do with terrain and other significant combat factors. Though the political considerations of Twycross are given short shrift in the report, they did weigh in favor of its selection. The world is, after all, a Command center. How can Ryan fault us for trying to take back an important world in the Tamar March?"

The Marshal said nothing. He leaned back in his chair and studied Victor for a long moment.

Victor slammed his right fist on the table. "Dammit, Morgan, don't look at me that way! I'm well aware of the political implications of what we're doing here. I know this battleplan reads like some storybook warrior's grand plan to defeat enemy hordes and I can see in your eyes that it worries you. You think we put this together because we're a bunch of green warriors who think war is a game where we can win glory. It's not so."

Victor looked up at the ceiling and forced himself to breathe slowly so he could regain control of his anger. "More times than I can count, I reviewed the holovid transmissions sent to the *Hejira* as it traveled to the rendezvous with the *Strongbow*. I know by heart the names of every man and woman in my old command, and I know who was still alive when I left, and who died. I've run millions of scenarios through my head to estimate who could have survived and for how long. That process, that torture, has purged from me any thoughts of glory in war."

Pressing his palms flat against the table, he leaned forward heavily. "Next April, I celebrate my twenty-first birthday. From that time on, I will be of age and eligible to rule the united Federated Commonwealth. My mother has guided the Lyran Commonwealth with strength and wisdom. My father is a military genius who engineered the conquest of the Capellan Confederation. I have one hell of a lot to live up to if I'm ever to lead and unite both of these nations. I have to earn the respect of my people, and I have to prove I'm capable of doing whatever is necessary to protect them."

Some of the vehemence drained from his voice, but none of the

231

pain. "I believe you once told my father that, given a bucket of water, you'd storm the gates of hell for him. Well, I confess to wanting a bit more than that in the way of resources for my little battle. I've picked a world notorious for brutal weather and a treacherous terrain because most of the population lives underground and will be out of the way. I also imagine that the Jade Falcons will leave behind as few troops as possible because Twycross is really a station where troops should be *sentenced* to serve."

Andrew Redburn flipped open his copy of the plan. "Though the Diabolis storm will provide superior cover, the Ninth F-C isn't going to appreciate being asked to move with it."

"Nobody would," Victor agreed. "Running around in that giant sandstorm is not going to be fun or easy, but it will give us the edge we need. Besides, the Ninth has trained in storms just as fierce as the Diabolis." He hesitated for a moment, then continued, somewhat subdued. "They just aren't that *big!*"

Dan Allard leaned forward and rested his clasped hands on the table. "For the record, Highness, I have reviewed your plan with Chris here and Lieutenant-Colonels Brahe and Bradley. We're agreed to the plan. Furthermore, I have been assured by Janos Vandermeer that there does, indeed, exist a pirate point close to Twycross III. Because the fourth planet in that system is a hot gas giant, he also believes that we can recharge the JumpShips there at approximately half-efficiency. With ion engine assist, we could jump back out within a week."

"Twycross is also an important BattleMech production center, Marshal." Victor quickly controlled the smile on his face. "We can use its stores and facilities to help maintain our force."

"How long can you hold Twycross?" Morgan asked.

Victor sighed heavily. "I don't know. Obviously, that depends on how long it takes for the Jade Falcons to notice we took it, and what they send back to retake it. My forces can either defend it, pull out, or even jump further back toward the rim if we recover sufficient supplies in the assault. The net effect is that the Jade Falcons will have to pull line troops away from their invasion force to hunt us down. Suddenly, they'll have to play the same guessing games that we're playing."

Morgan steepled his fingertips in a gesture Victor had learned, after long years of associating with his cousin, to fear. Before Morgan could pronounce sentence on the plan, Victor made one last plea. "Morgan, remember what you told me back on Tharkad this time last year? You reminded me that my father held you back until the time was right. I understand your reservations and I respect them, but you weren't much older than I am now when you formed the Uhlans and did the impossible. My plan isn't impossible. It can succeed, and I am ready to make it do so. Trust me in this…please. Give me this chance, or else take out a gun and shoot me, because my future rides on this plan."

Morgan looked down and closed his eyes as he rubbed the fingertips of his left hand against his forehead. Silence settled over the conference room. To Victor, it seemed that time slowed to a tortoise pace. *Please, Morgan, you must let me go!*

Morgan exhaled heavily, then opened his eyes. "Revise your plan to increase ammunition supplies to sufficiency for six weeks of pitched battles. Boost estimated personnel numbers to 120 percent of current and give them two months' worth of supplies to help cover refugees along the way. Append a plan for evacuating civilians offworld and add a list of tentative strike sites and routes heading back out toward the rim and toward the enemy flank. Also, we need a full listing of possible pirate points and recharge times for all available escape routes."

His gaze flicked up to meet Victor's blue eyes. "You will personally prepare papers to indemnify the Kell Hounds for their losses. Your rules of engagement will stress minimization of civilian involvement. I want triple redundancy on your warning system for the Ninth F-C so they don't blunder out of the Diabolis into a Jade Falcon ambush. Prepare and include a plan for the isolation of the ComStar facility in Daubton."

Victor blinked at Morgan. "It's a go! You're giving me this assault?"

The Marshal nodded once. "Your plan's not flawless, but the gain outweighs the risk. Of the plans I've to consider, it's the best."

Victor looked down at Kai, flashing him a smile, then returned his attention to Morgan. "I can't thank you enough…"

Morgan held up his right hand. "Don't thank me. Even though Colonel Allard will be the force commander, I'm making you responsible for the lives of every man, woman, and child on Twycross. That is an awesome burden, but it's only a taste of what you'll assume when you take the throne. Twenty years from now, after the assault has been forgotten by all but a few historians, then decide if you want to thank me or not."

Victor Steiner-Davion narrowed his eyes. *Truly spoken, cousin.* "In twenty years then, Morgan."

After the meeting was dismissed, Victor caught up with Kai in the hallway outside. "Well, we did it. We're on for Twycross." Kai's subdued nod started alarm bells ringing in Victor's head. "What's wrong? Don't tell me you've got butterflies now, after it's all over."

Kai shook his head. "No, it's not that. When they had me do some resource-checking, I saw that my 'Mech hasn't arrived yet, and won't in time for it to catch up with us." He looked over at Victor. "Due to some bureaucratic snafu, I'm *Dispossessed!*"

That word stabbed through Victor like a knife. *Dispossessed! Is there a fate worse than being a MechWarrior without a 'Mech?* He shuddered.

"I can transfer command of my lance to Leutnant Abel von Rhemmer," Kai went on. "He just joined the Tenth from the Nagel-ring. He ought to do okay."

"The hell you say!" Victor grabbed Kai by the shoulders and turned him around. "Listen here. We worked out this plan with you in it, at the head of your lance. Dammit, we have your whole battalion slated for crisis management because some of your people are best at thinking on their feet—and you top that list, my friend."

Kai hung his head. "I appreciate the pep-talk, but that won't get *Yen-lo-wang* here any faster." His head came up. "But don't worry. I wouldn't miss this for all the worlds in the Tamar March. I'll be there, in the command post or wherever else you want me. I'm not trying to weasel out, just facing facts."

"Kai, the facts are these: I want you there, and I want you in a 'Mech at the head of your lance." Victor frowned. "What the hell good is it being the son of the Prince of the Federated Suns and the Archon of the Lyran Commonwealth if I can't get a friend a 'Mech?" He sighed. "It's not likely to be *Yen-lo-wang*, but it could be something similar. Don't you worry. I'll find you a war-horse."

Kai smiled gratefully. "Do I have to wait twenty years to thank you?"

Victor laughed, draping his arm over Kai's shoulder and steering his friend down the hall. "Yeah. I think that's a good idea. That way we're both certain to still be around."

"I'll be there, Highness."

Victor smiled to himself. *And with your help, Kai, so will I.*

JumpShip Dire Wolf, *Assault Orbit, Engadin VII*
Radstadt Province, Free Rasalhague Republic
30 August 3050

Phelan Kell flopped down on his bunk in the dormitory and groaned as his legs stretched out. "God, I'm exhausted."

Griff, walking past, slapped Phelan on the thigh. "She's keeping you up nights, eh?"

Irritation flashed over Phelan's face, but he let it slide. "No, that's *not* the problem. It seems Engadin has a Home Defense Force just bristling with Inferno missiles in hand-held launchers. There are apparently stockpiles all over the place on numerous little satellite assembly plants. They're giving Star Colonel Marcos absolute fits, and Lara's been having me go over intelligence reports to advise her what sort of support she should allow Marcos in the assault."

Griff stared incredulously at the Kell Hound as he dropped onto his own bunk. "One commander is rationing supplies for a rival?"

The mercenary shrugged. "It's a screwy system, but it doesn't seem to have slowed their advance any. In fact, as I hear the rumors, the other three Clans are madder than hell about the Wolves getting their fourth wave off a month ahead of everyone else. Also, the Wolves are deeper into the Successor States than the others. It's all really weird."

"To put it mildly." The older man smiled and winked at his friend. "With them keeping you so busy, I thought you'd want to spend what little free time you have with Ranna." He smiled sheepishly. "I was going to appropriate your lockpick and make a run over to the women's quarters."

"I've only had one real chance to speak with her but Vlad made sure he found something else for me to do instead," Phelan said gloomily. "I don't know where she is now."

The Periphery bandit leaned forward, elbows on his knees. "Your voice is saying something different than your words."

Phelan sighed. He knew he had to trust someone, and maybe talking it out would keep him from blowing it all out of proportion. "I don't know if it's a problem, really. I mean, I think things are going very well between Ranna and me, but every so often something happens that just doesn't feel right. When I suggested getting together, she said she wanted time to herself."

Griff frowned. "That can be a good sign and a bad one. You haven't been having any other…problems, have you?"

"No, all systems are go," Phelan said with a laugh. "Though I have to admit a few instances of automatic shutdown because of overheating and sensory overload."

"Is the problem that you're only a bondsman?"

"Maybe, but I don't think so," Phelan said. "What it could be is more insidious than that. Unlike most of the others, Ranna isn't just a death-machine pilot. Remember I told you about her pet, Jehu, and the paintings? She's…we're…intense, I guess you'd call it passionate, in a way that's got to be more alien to her than to me. I think she finds that intensity incredibly seductive, but at the same time dangerous."

"So what lures her also repels her," Griff grunted.

"And the tug of war is ripping her up. What's worse is that I don't think she sees it clearly, and so she's got no way of dealing with the conflict." Phelan shrugged. "Of course, this is all pure speculation about a problem that may not even exist. The real explanation is probably a lot simpler."

Griff chuckled evilly. "Yeah, she's probably just found a younger stud from that last crop of bondsmen captured on Rasalhague."

"Yeah, there you go." The Kell Hound gave his friend a withering look. "And I suppose that's why you want the lockpick? Going to properly welcome the new women to our little community?"

"Service with a smile. It's a tough job, but someone has to do it." The bandit's voice dropped in volume. "And I have another little covert mission to perform. Kenny and I want to leave Vlad a token of our appreciation for giving us a double-shift to unload junk from Rasalhague into the storage holds of the *Dire Wolf*. I'd invite you along, but I don't think you need any more reasons for Vlad to hate you."

"No, I think I'll pass on that," Phelan said, rolling over on to his right side. Snaking his left hand beneath the mattress, he pulled out the small box. He handed it to Griff. "I'm not so sure visiting Vlad is a good idea. You might want to reconsider it."

Griff shrugged. "We'll see."

"Whatever." Phelan lay back down on his cot, his right forearm across his eyes. "Have fun."

"Yes, mother. Don't wait up."

Phelan bolted upright as Griff ripped his mattress back and tossed the lockpick beneath it. All through the dormitory, ex-pirates dove into their beds and pretended to be fast asleep. Griff let Phelan's mattress flop back down, then hopped onto his own cot and draped the blanket over himself.

Phelan blinked twice, then peered through the gloom at his friend. "What the hell happened?"

"Nothing." Griff slammed a fist angrily into his pillow. "Just go to sleep. It's better if you don't know."

Kenny Ryan's voice cut through the darkness. "Tell him, Griff."

Ryan's weaseling tone and Griff's quick denial told Phelan that whatever had happened, it was a disaster of major proportions. "Dammit, Griff, don't leave me hanging. You used my lockpick, and that means I'm involved. What happened?"

"Tell him, Griff, or I will," Ryan insisted.

"No, you son of a bitch. No!" Griff rolled over onto his side to face the young mercenary. "We went to Vlad's room. We opened the door. He was there. End of story. Now go to sleep."

Phelan stared at Griff. "Did he see you?"

"No. It was dark. At most, we were silhouettes in the doorway. There, now you know what happened. Go to sleep."

Before Phelan could ask another question, Ryan's voice broke in. "Tell him all of it, Griff. Do it, or I will, and you know I'll enjoy it."

Phelan heard the squeaking sound of Griff's teeth grinding together. "Vlad wasn't alone…"

"What the hell difference does that make to me?" Phelan said, but he wondered why Kenny Ryan should be so intent on him finding out. *If Kenny wants me to know, it has to be bad…*Then the answer hit him. "No," he gasped. "It can't be…"

"Hey, you guessed it, Kell," Ryan said cheerfully. "She was there with him and they weren't discussing troop movements." His voice dropped conspiratorially. "You didn't tell us she was a screamer, Kell."

The mental image of Ranna and Vlad coupling as light from the hallway splashed over them seared into Phelan's brain. All his own recollections of their times together became bitter, acid memories. The softness of her flesh under his hands became the caress of a thousand razor blades. Her cries of pleasure became mocking laughter and the love he had imagined in her eyes became contempt. *I've been an idiot! Ulric has been using me, Vlad has been using me, and Ranna has been using me. I'm a tool, nothing more. It satisfies Ulric to have my counsel from time to time. It satisfies Vlad to make my life miserable. It satisfied Ranna to...*

The deep ache in the pit of his stomach kept him from finishing that thought. He turned to Griff, ignoring Ryan's mocking laughter, and swallowed hard. "Thanks for trying to protect me, but it's better I know..."

Griff reached out to give Phelan's shoulder a squeeze. "I would have found a way to let you down easy, you know. I wouldn't have left you in the dark."

"Let him *down*? Keep him in the *dark*? God, stop it, Griff. You're killing me with these puns."

Griff threw back his blanket. "I'm gonna kill you with my bare hands, you malignant dwarf!"

Phelan saw Ryan's silhouette a few bunks away. "What's the matter? Isn't Kell man enough to fight his own battles, quineg?" Ryan's voice took on a razored edge. "Of course not. If he was a *man*, his little love-bitch wouldn't have found herself someone else, would she?"

The whispered sound of the door sliding open preceded the harsh flood of lights by a half-second. Phelan shaded his eyes and saw Vlad framed in the doorway. His blue jumpsuit was unzipped to the waist and sweat glistened on the mat of curly black hair on his chest. His eyes seemed to burn with fury and his expression looked positively demonic.

"Which of you *savashri* dared invade my chambers?" Vlad snarled. "The rest of you give him up, or it will go badly for all."

Vlad held a black, fifteen-centimeter-long tube in his right hand. As he flicked his wrist away from his body, three meter's worth of flexible black cable uncoiled itself like a languid tentacle. His thumb pressed down on a red stud on the handle, filling the room with a hiss that sounded somewhere between radio static and a rattlesnake's warning. The men in bunks closest to the door backed away immediately and Vlad laughed viciously.

"Who will be punished, children? Will I have to start at random?" He swung the electro-lash effortlessly at one of the bunks. The cable slapped into a pillow, which then exploded into half-melted bits of spongy fiber. As the stink of burned petrochem filled the air, Vlad gestured the men forward with his free hand. "Believe me, I will find the guilty parties and they will pay. Do you answer me voluntarily, or do I have to force the answers out of you?"

Phelan's pain over Ranna changed to anger. *An electro-lash...the kinder cousin of a neural whip. It won't leave you permanently damaged, but it doesn't cause enough pain to put you out, either. Using them on beasts of burden or for animal control—as they were intended—is one thing. Using them indiscriminately on men is another...*

Vlad pointed to one man cowering at the foot of Kenny Ryan's bunk. "You," he said. "Come here."

Phelan threw back his covers. "No, Vlad. Leave him alone."

The Clansman's head came up, and everyone else turned their attention to the mercenary. "You? It is *you* who will tell me who they were?"

Phelan shook his head. "I'm the one you want. I claim all responsibility."

Vlad's cruel snicker accompanied the slow shaking of his head. "No, Kell, this will not work the way you think. The fact that the Khan has claimed you as his own would not stop me from beating you even if you were one of the guilty."

Phelan walked toward the front of the room. "No trick. I'm it."

The Clansman's eyes narrowed. "You weren't even there. Why are you doing this?"

The Kell Hound matched Vlad's angry stare. "I *was* there. Do you want me to describe it to you, quiaff?" Phelan hesitated and his brave facade almost broke. As he moved forward, he saw Ranna standing back from the doorway. Waves of pain at her betrayal threatened to drown him, but he forced himself to play out his hand. "You and Ranna were together, enjoying one another's company."

He forced himself to laugh, and he heard the sound echo with the hollowness of his insides. "And from what I *heard*, you were enjoying each other immensely."

Confusion arced through Vlad's eyes. "You were not there. There were two and neither had your build."

Phelan laughed casually. "How can you be so sure? In the state you were in, it's a wonder you remember anything reliably. Sights and sounds and time all seem to drift away, don't they?"

Anger furrowed Vlad's brow. "Why are you doing this?"

"It's my responsibility. I did it. I'm the one you want." Phelan looked over at the other bondsmen. "No one else will own up to this crime, and everyone else will say I did it, no matter how much you torture them. What's the matter? Did you want more foreplay?"

Vlad's face locked into a mask of fury. "I will break you, you know. You may have thought to save the others, but in the end, you will give them to me. Believe me, you will."

Phelan shook his head slowly. "Do your worst."

Vlad dug a meter-length of white cord from his pocket and tossed it to Kenny Ryan. "Strip him to the waist, then tie his hands to the top bunk rail."

Phelan unzipped his jumpsuit and tied the sleeves around his waist as Ryan climbed to the top bunk. Phelan offered Ryan his hands and the pirate slid the bondcord down to the mercenary's forearm before expertly trussing his wrists together.

"You're nuts, Kell." Ryan watched the mercenary's face, searching for something. "Don't expect me to thank you for this, because he'll make it worse on us when you give us up."

The Kell Hound shook his head. "If you were a *man*, Ryan, you might understand why I'm doing this. I made the lockpick. It's my responsibility. And don't worry, your back will be spared." Phelan glanced back over his shoulder at Vlad. "I can hurt him more by not telling than he can possibly hurt me, and that's enough to keep your secret."

As Phelan turned back toward the bunk, he saw Ranna looking at him incredulously. She met his gaze, then quickly looked away.

The electro-lash wrapped around his chest like a ribbon of molten steel. It tightened on his ribcage and sent fiery tendrils of pain shooting up and down his spine. All his muscles spasmed, then contracted, leaving him to hang roughly from the cord around his wrists. The pure agony shattered his resolve to remain silent, allowing an inhuman wail of excruciating pain to rip through his throat.

His screams stopped when his throat became too raw to make any sound at all.

Some time after that, his torture stopped as well.

ComStar First Circuit Compound
Hilton Head Island, North America, Terra
30 August 3050

Myndo Waterly slipped her hands inside the sleeves of her gold silk gown. "I agree, Precentor Tharkad, that the razing of Edo on Turtle Bay represents an escalation of the conflict that calls into question the wisdom of working with the Clans. I should remind you, however, that the Precentor Martial reported that he expects no more such attacks because the Khan of the Smoke Jaguar Clan lost considerable face because of that incident."

"With all due respect, Primus, and with deference to my colleague from Dieron, I believe you place more importance on social embarrassment than it warrants." Ulthan Everson leaned forward on his crystalline podium. "I would also note that the Clan's jump-capable warships have not been used of late because they have been bid away in the curious game the invaders play before taking a planet. Though you do not mention it, I recall that it was Phelan Kell who planted the suggestion of bidding away a warship, not our agent to the Clans."

Sharilar Mori looked over at the Primus, who nodded permission to speak. "You confuse your arguments, Precentor Tharkad. If the Primus failed to mention Phelan Kell's part in the decision to abandon planetary bombardment, it is because the important fact is that the bombardments have stopped and are unlikely to continue. The Wolf Clan's third and preemptive fourth waves have shown this perfectly.

"As for the role of social pressures in the Clan society, we keep hearing about the pressure to conform and to out-do the others. That

Khan Ulric of the Wolves bid away the *Dire Wolf* in his negotiations with Khan Bjorn of the Ghost Bears cost Bjorn mightily and has elevated Ulric in the esteem of others, including his rivals. In their quest for glory, others have imitated Ulric by bidding away even more than the support of the warships in their contests over who may attack a world. As the latest reports from Engadin indicate, this has created some difficulty. It may not stop the Clans' advance, but it will slow it."

The diminutive Jen Li, Precentor from the Capellan Confederation, agreed. "Aside from the Wolf Clan's advance strike in this fourth wave, the other clans have moved at a pace roughly equivalent to a wave every two months…"

Everson's head came up. "I am neither blind nor unable to read a calender, Precentor Sian."

"Nor do so I suggest, Precentor Tharkad," Jen Li replied coolly. "I meant to call your attention to the fact that our representatives are reporting longer times needed to pacify the planets the Clans have taken. In the Jade Falcon assault in the Lyran Commonwealth, for example, you see a massive initial assault, which is then truncated down in the second wave. That is due, in my opinion, to the resistance on Trell I. Their third wave was bolder, but the population refused to be cowed. In order to be off on the next wave of the invasion, the Jade Falcons disarmed the MechWarriors and aerospace pilots, but allowed the local militias to retain their weapons and engage in police duties. On Twycross, the natives barely noticed the invaders and gave them permission to hold as much of the surface as they wanted. In fact, had the Diabolis not grounded two DropShips, I believe the Clansmen would have left only a regiment and a half of BattleMechs to defend Twycross."

Huthrin Vandel let out a little laugh. "How curious that a regiment now seems barely sufficient to hold a world when, twenty-five years ago, a battalion was considered an incredible force to garrison any one world. These grounded DropShips increase the Twycross garrison to what?"

The Primus herself answered his question. "One ship is believed to hold what they refer to as a Cluster—approximately forty-five—of their front-line 'Mechs. The ship itself appears to be built along the lines of a modified *Overlord* Class DropShip. The other ship looks like an *Intruder* Class DropShip and is home to approximately seventy-five of their armored infantry."

The Precentor from New Avalon nodded thoughtfully. "Including their garrison units, that would mean the Jade Falcons have the rough equivalent of two and a half 'Mech regiments. In terms of our technology, that would give them a strength of roughly six regiments. The armored infantry have to be worth another company. Even taking into account environmental factors that might curb the extended range of their weapons, they are still a formidable force. Interesting…"

Myndo fixed him with a harsh stare. "Are you still with us, Precentor New Avalon? Do you intend to share your ruminations or not?"

Vandel smiled as his head came up. "Well, we have no solid proof, but I expect that a counterattack on the Lyran front is imminent."

Myndo's dislike of surprises showed plainly on her face. "Explain."

"Though the official military traffic has continued with banal reports and typical communications, the personal messages going to and from troops gathered at Sudeten has trailed off considerably. Military officials deny that troops have been moved offworld, but enough DropShips have been blasting off Sudeten to make the invasion of the Capellan Confederation in 3028 look like a field-trip."

The Primus gave him a reproving glare. "Eliminate the hyperbole, if you please."

"As the Primus commands," Vandel said, to comply without complying. "The troop lists we obtained from our Sudeten facilities were impressive, indeed. The Tenth Lyran Guards, the First Kathil Uhlans, the Kell Hounds, and the Eridani Light Horse, just to mention the best-known units, were all present. In addition, I have three confirmed sightings of Prince Victor Steiner-Davion. He has to be smarting from his part in the Trell debacle.

"I had some of my people run an analysis of the situation in the Commonwealth and had it cross-correlated with Victor's Nagelring records and his personality profile. Though he has the cunning for deceptive tactics, Hanse Davion's son seems to favor an aggressive approach. Defending is not his idea of proper military strategy, so I assumed he would agitate for an offensive strike. I then took conquered worlds that could be reached from Sudeten in the time it would take for the Jade Falcons to launch their fourth wave and cross-correlated them with worlds that had environmental and topographical features favorable to the close infighting most familiar to Inner Sphere warriors. The highest probability was for Twycross, with an 87.5 percent factor."

He smiled boldly at the Primus. "None of the information I used was unavailable to the Davion troops. A study of Victor's friends at the Nagelring and the New Avalon Military Academy shows that Renard

Sanderlin and Kai Allard-Liao were both assigned to units—the Uhlans and Tenth Lyran Guards respectively—that are present on Sudeten. Victor has been transferred to the Tenth Lyran Guards, so I assume that unit will be involved in the assault. I would doubt the Uhlans will go because Morgan Hasek-Davion would never put all his eggs in one basket.

"I also believe that the Kell Hounds, perhaps because of the connection between Dan Allard and his nephew Kai, and because of the Hounds' fanatical loyalty to the Steiner bloodline, will be in on the assault. Conversely, Morgan will hold back the Eridani Light Horse. What other units will go I cannot be certain, but the Seventh Donegal Guards seem likely because the climate of their homeworld of Rahne makes Twycross seem pleasant."

Ulthan Everson, smiling from ear to ear, congratulated his longtime ally. "Excellent analysis, Huthrin." Then he turned toward the Primus again. "I would move that we supply the Davion forces with information about the Clan units on Twycross so they will not be taken by surprise."

Sharilar Mori preempted the Primus's summary rejection by raising her hand. "If you please, Primus, I have some information that could have a bearing on Precentor Tharkad's motion. Ulthan, I think you should know that the Draconis Combine is preparing its own trap for the Clans. Word has gone out to sources the Smoke Jaguars are certain to have captured in their third wave that the individuals who escaped Turtle Bay before Edo's destruction are present on Wolcott. The Jaguars have learned, to their chagrin, that one of the prisoners was Theodore Kurita's son Hohiro, and that Hohiro himself will take part in the defense of Wolcott. If the Jaguar Khan is smarting from the loss of face over the Edo incident, this message will sting him further. Theodore might as well have given them an engraved invitation to attack Wolcott."

Precentor Dieron suppressed a smile. "Invitations to come to Wolcott were not issued to the Clans, but they were given to the Eleventh Legion of Vega and the Genyosha. These two units and several less well-known regiments will be on Wolcott masquerading under fictional unit designations and with histories that cover only the most recent exploits of these units. The Genyosha, for example, have been waiting on the Dieron/Skye border and seen no action in the last year, and so the Jaguars will have no solid grasp on what the unit can do. This tactic worked on Hanover, which means the Jaguars will be suspicious of these 'virginal' units, but the desire to recapture Hohiro Kurita and recover some of the face they lost on Edo will probably

244

outweigh their caution."

Everson smiled broadly again. "Excellent. We will teach the invaders a lesson, one they've needed since their invasion began. I can see no reason why we should not offer information to both the Davion and Kurita forces."

"Don't be a fool, Ulthan," the Primus snapped. "If we tip our hand to the Combine or the Commonwealth, they'll know we have established a relationship with the Clans, which they will resent mightily. Besides, we do not wish to jeopardize our deepening link with the Clans. They now permit us to act as intermediaries between their governors and the people of the conquered worlds, though we do not yet have a free hand to rebuild the societies in our image. Because they have not yet asked us for more than trivial information, they feel no obligation to us. That, I believe, will soon change.

"The latest report from the Precentor Martial included hints of friction between the Clans. He suggested that the Wolf Clan's preemptive fourth wave did not sit well with the other groups, especially the Smoke Jaguars and Jade Falcons. These groups have, apparently, demanded a Council of Khans after their fourth wave has been launched and completed. The Precentor Martial believes this is so they will be on a rough parity with Khan Ulric. Ulric, because of his conquest of Rasalhague and because the ilKhan travels with him, will host the meeting, but the Precentor Martial does not yet know which world the Khan has chosen as the site of the meeting."

Myndo's eyes widened like those of a wolf watching a deer struggle through deep snow. "Ulric is the Khan with whom we have the most influence. He has worked more closely with us than any other Khan, and he has been successful. The Smoke Jaguars and Jade Falcons will, before this meeting, run into severe opposition on their fronts. A stiff battle—or worse, a defeat—will hurt their standing and increase Ulric's power. If we cooperate with House Davion or House Kurita, we risk exposure and censure by the Clans. This would deny us access to the most cooperative and potentially powerful of the Khans. And I'm sure you agree it would be foolish to sacrifice any chance we have of directing the Clans against our most hated enemy: Hanse Davion."

Though the look on his face did express total agreement, Everson bowed his head. "I withdraw the motion, but I do wish my colleagues would consider the possibility of helping our kinsmen in their war against these alien invaders. Though we would risk much in playing both ends against the middle, it seems even riskier to assume that we will one day be able to control Khan Ulric. To lay the groundwork for

245

helping the Successor States against the invaders would be a wise precaution."

Myndo watched Sharilar as Everson spoke. As the slender Oriental woman nodded in agreement, Myndo found her own opinion of his suggestion changing. "I find your counsel to have merit. Furthermore, the appearance of ComStar forces to turn the tide of battles in the favor of the Successor States will garner us more good will—publicly and privately—than merely acting as informants. This I will take under consideration."

She smiled confidently at the assembled members of the First Circuit. "Rest assured, my colleagues, that no matter what happens, ComStar will emerge unscathed from this conflict, and Jerome Blake's dream of a united mankind will be fulfilled."

JumpShip Dire Wolf, *Assault Orbit, Engadin VII*
Radstadt Province, Free Rasalhague Republic
31 August 3050

Even before he heard the sharp intake of breath, Phelan Kell knew she'd been the one to walk through the sick bay door. He'd played the scene over and over again in fitful snatches of dreams, but when he heard, then saw her in the small hand-held mirror by his pillow, he forgot it all. *How could he feel anything for a woman who betrayed him, then came to gloat?*

The look of pain on her face reflected more than just horror at the condition of his back, but whatever else it was eluded him. Phelan knew, from examination in the mirror he held in his left hand, that Vlad had done a superior job on him. Somewhere along the line, Vlad had given up the pretense of trying to get information from Phelan, and in his fury, had just beat him. While the lash had curled around to lightning-lick his stomach, the raw scars and bruises there were nothing compared to the snake-pit tracery on his back.

"Freeborn! Oh, Phelan…" She reached out toward him, then drew her hands back, aghast. "It must hurt so…"

Phelan tried to shrug, reigniting scorched nerves all over his back. He gritted his teeth against the pain, then gasped in a breath or two. "Yeah, it does. But I'll live."

Avoiding his reflected gaze, she shook her head. "I have never seen anything so…savage."

"I expect the Khan will sell me off now," Phelan laughed bitterly. "'One bondsman, shop-worn. Will trade for *surat* or best offer.'"

Ranna's head came up, but Phelan let the mirror flop down on the pillow. "What is the matter? Why are you lashing out at me?"

Her question, phrased in a tone of confused innocence, startled him. *How could she ask that after she'd slept with Vlad? Did she think I didn't know? Hell, she heard me describe the whole thing to him... Did she think I didn't care, or that it wouldn't matter to me?*

Phelan drew in a breath slowly and carefully. "Sorry. It's just that I don't like being used. I thought we were friends."

"What? We are friends." She came closer to the head of the bed, entering his peripheral vision on the right. "We *are* friends, Phelan."

"Friends?" Scorn steamed up from his reply. "If that's how you treat friends, I'm glad I'm not an enemy."

"What are you talking about? What did I do?"

"Cut the innocent act, Ranna! I may be a bondsman, but I'm not stupid!" Despite the pain burning on his flank, Phelan twisted around on his left side to face her. "What did you do? You were sleeping with him! Did you think I wouldn't care, or did you just not consider that in the *heat* of the moment?"

She stared at him, utterly uncomprehending. "How can that hurt you? What difference does it make?"

"What difference?" He shook his head. "Am I missing something here? As I recall, you and I were sleeping together."

Ranna looked at him as though he'd lost his mind. "Obviously, you are confused. You have not been able to sleep. I will visit again later."

He flopped back down on his stomach. "Don't bother. Between you and your lover, you've ripped me up enough."

"Lovers? Vlad and me?" She laughed aloud. "It's quite clear your mind is not working at all."

"You were in bed together. They saw you! What the hell would you call it?"

"We definitely are not lovers. Vlad and I were in the same sibko." Her tone challenged him to turn that into some sort of sinister accusation, then her voice faltered. "I was confused about...something...and I went to talk with him."

"But that's not all you did, is it?"

"How can you make it sound like a crime? We were in the same sibko! We grew up together. You would say we are part of the same family." She pleaded for understanding, but her words only made Phelan shudder with rage. She saw it and tried to head it off. "I came here because I miss the time you and I spent together..."

Phelan let out a small cry of pain. "You've done enough to me.

248

Don't you understand? I'm not going to let you do to my insides what Vlad did to my back—at least not any more. Just go. Go away. I don't want to see you again."

He buried his face in the pillow so she couldn't see the hot tears burning in his eyes. He fought to control his sobs and thought he had until he heard the sound of crying. He tried again harder, but the sound persisted until cut off by the hiss of the closing door.

"Are you awake, Herr Kell?"

Phelan looked into the mirror with red-rimmed eyes and nodded at the Precentor Martial. "Forgive me for not rising to greet you properly, but…"

"No offense taken." Focht said, looking down at the mercenary's brutalized back. "I have seen worse wounds in my time, but never on someone still alive."

The Kell Hound managed a weak smile. "If I'd known it would hurt this much, I probably would have preferred to die."

Focht acknowledged the grim jest with a nod. "Those welts look bad now, but I think the scarring will be minimal."

Phelan nodded. "You know what they said at the Nagelring."

The older man's eye focused distantly. "Yes, I do. 'Scars are the proof man can survive his own stupidity.'" His left hand rose to adjust his eyepatch. "Those words have taken on special meaning for me in the past twenty years."

The mercenary sighed. "I hadn't thought of it that way, else I might have arranged for Vlad to give me a lash across the face to remind me of how brainless I am whenever I look in a mirror."

The Precentor Martial steepled his fingers. "Some men see such marks as proof of their own immortality and infallibility. You would be intolerable if you allowed yourself that vanity."

The image of Tor Miraborg swam through Phelan's mind. *Score one for the ComStar warrior*. "I learned long ago that I'm not infallible."

Focht watched him closely in the mirror. "You refer to your expulsion from the Nagelring?"

"You must know the story. You provided Ulric with a datastack on me…"

"All that was included in the packet sent to me," the tall man said with a slight shrug, "but I didn't read it and deleted the explanation before giving it to Ulric."

"Why would you do that, Precentor? You obviously trained at the legendary Nagelring. I should think you would have relished the tale of my disgrace, just as others have." Phelan hesitated for a moment. "Or did you delete it so Ulric would find me more acceptable as a partner in crime?"

The older man smiled sagely. "I am not vain enough to want to see you suffer for the vague judgments of a Cadet Honor Board. Besides, I would have preferred that the Khan choose me as his advisor. In point of fact, I deleted that part of your record because I believed the story should not be told if you did not want to tell it."

"Thank you." Phelan closed his eyes for a moment, then opened them again to meet the Precentor Martial's steel gaze. "It's a simple story, really. A friend of mine, someone I'd grown up with, graduated from the Nagelring as I entered my deuce year at the Academy. DJ—Donna Jean Connor—got a commission from the Fourteenth Lyran Guards and was posted to Ford. She was always good with book learning and regulations—exactly my opposite in that respect—and her help kept me in the Nagelring during my plebe and trey years." He swallowed hard. "I guess I was lost without her there, but the holovids she sent always anchored me and kept me on the right track.

"Well, right before that nasty blizzard on Tharkad in '48, I got word from DJ's father that she'd been killed in action on Ford. With the information he gave me, I was able to crack the Defense Department's computer and get a full report on the incident. It appears that DJ walked her lance into an area where it shouldn't have been because her Hauptmann was giving orders straight out of a textbook. The Free Worlders must have read the same textbook because their aerowing took one pass at the fire lance supporting DJ's recon advance, then came back and ripped her people to pieces."

Phelan slammed his right hand against the head of his bed, then quivered when his back felt as though some creature was gnawing its way through him. His voice became hoarse with pain. "I went a little out of control, but it didn't reach a head until after the blizzard hit. The media were full of stories about snowbound folks, but the authorities had all us cadets out with 'Mechs to stop people from looting. When I heard a report of a group of school kids supposed to be trapped by an avalanche, I decided to help get them out. I rigged up the stuff needed to increase the pick-up on a *Scorpion*'s external microphones, and then headed out northeast of Tharkad City."

The Precentor nodded. "Into the Sigfried Glacier Reserve?"

"Yeah. I got to the area where their air-bus had gone down and started the computer filtering out everything but human heartbeats and the valve pattern sounds of a Hochbaum fusion engine. Within four hours, I found them and had dug down to where they were. I shunted heat from the 'Mech's fusion engine to the outside to keep them warm, and I gave them the food I'd brought. I radioed for help because some of the kids had been badly hurt when the avalanche wrapped the hoverbus around a dolmen, but a new storm front came through and kept all medevac craft grounded."

Focht frowned. "Wait...now I remember something of this story. Most of them survived, but the children and others who'd been hurt did not. The cadet rescuer wasn't named in the story, but I remember his action was criticized because he did not bring proper medical supplies and personnel with him—resulting in the deaths."

"That was it. At the Honor Board hearing, I maintained that if I had tried to obtain the supplies or a doctor, I'd never have gotten permission to make the trip, but the Board blocked that idea at the outset. I got disgusted and refused to attend the trial. They punted me, but the press wasn't allowed to print much about it, out of deference to my father and the Archon." Phelan sighed. "There. Now you know the whole sordid story."

The Precentor Martial nodded. "I do not get the impression that you see the incident as a mistake at all."

The mercenary thought for a moment, then slowly shook his head. "Going out after those people wasn't a mistake. Not thinking ahead about having a doctor with me was. How I could have gotten one and still made the trip eludes me, and has ever since the incident. The rescue at Sigfried Glacier is my own personal 'La Mancha' scenario. No matter what, I can't win."

Phelan rotated the rectangular mirror to give him a taller view of the ComStar official. "But you didn't come here today to ask me about my schooling, did you?"

The older man smiled. "No. I have come on behalf of Khan Ulric. He would have come himself, but after hearing about Ranna's visit several hours ago, he wanted someone from your own culture to explain exactly what happened between her and Vlad."

"Why don't you save it for someone who will care?" Phelan snapped.

Focht went on as though he hadn't heard the remark. "While you were on Gunzburg, you must have found the Rasalhague language and mannerisms peculiar, didn't you? You had to work to express your thoughts to those who did not have a dialect in common with you. Your German came close enough, in some cases, to make you understood, *ja?*"

He pulled up a chair and lowered himself into it. "I recall once, a very long time ago, when I was on Summer. The Lestrade family had instituted the practice of speaking Italian in their home, where I was a guest. I wanted a glass of water, and I wanted it cold. I told the servant I wanted it *kalt*, but the man did not understand me. I pantomimed cold and repeated *kalt* several times. When I thought he had it, I let him go on his way. Imagine my surprise when he returned with a steaming glass of hot water because the Italian word for cold is *freddo*, while the word for hot is *caldo*. He thought I was miming shivers because I was cold and that I wanted my water *caldo*."

"Are you trying to tell me I've somehow misinterpreted Ranna's sexual relations with Vlad? If I follow your hot/cold analogy, she'd have bedded him for my sake."

The Precentor Martial shook his head impatiently, leaning forward as he spoke. "The point is this: what you saw and reacted to as gross infidelity was not, to Ranna or the other members of the Clans, a problem worthy of your concern. In fact, your reaction borders on what these people see as clinical paranoia. They'd probably already have begun chemical therapy to help you over the problem had the Khan and I not talked."

The more the Precentor Martial spoke, the more foggy Phelan felt. "I'm running with a sensor shutdown and zero visibility here. You're making it sound like her having sex with Vlad is no more significant than a pat on the back."

Again the Precentor shook his head. "No, of course not. Intimate physical contact is a sign of affection…"

"That's the first thing you've said that I can follow…"

"But in this society, it does not carry with it the emotional baggage that it does in ours." Focht moistened his lips with the tip of his tongue. "The Clans are an alien society, Phelan. Indeed, I often find myself wondering if they're human at all. To them, Ranna's sleeping with Vlad is just a sign of friendship."

The mercenary's brows knotted together. "You're making it sound as though the concept of love does not exist within the Clans."

"It does, but not as we know and experience it—at least not among the Clan's warrior caste. For them, *esprit de corps*—in a form far stronger than we would acknowledge—would be the rough equivalent of love in our society. What we might call love apparently exists, but it's the *exception*, not the rule."

Phelan shook his head. "Do you understand what you're saying? How do they decide who they want to marry and who they want to have children with? A society can't function that way."

"A warrior society can, Phelan, and apparently does so very well. Their children are born into a sibko…"

The Kell Hound's head came up. "What the hell is that? Ranna used the same word as though it explained everything."

The Precentor smiled indulgently. "A sibko is a group of children born at the same time—many of them from the same families, as I understand it—who are then raised together. They are schooled and tested for the first twenty years of their lives, and those who pass the examinations continue on. When they reach their twentieth birthday, they are subjected to a final test—a true ordeal. If they pass, they become Clan Warriors.

"It should be obvious to you that people who have lived and worked together for so long will build up very close bonds. As they come of age—speaking physically here—it is only natural that they explore their sexuality with those they know best. Sexual activity between members of a sibko is considered as normal as you watching out for your sister, Caitlin."

"Yeah, but the difference is that I never slept with Caitlin!" Phelan shivered. "No wonder you have a hard time seeing these people as human. They even violate the incest taboo."

Focht frowned. "Yes and no. Incest is taboo because of the problems of inbreeding. None of these couplings are allowed to be fertile, so there is no need for that taboo. Think about it. The incest taboo is imposed by society, not by biology. And in this case, it is moot because Vlad and Ranna come from entirely different bloodlines."

"With all the coupling going on, how would anyone know who belonged to whom?" Though Phelan tried to make the remark more caustic, the effort at sarcasm drained him. *She did seem utterly dismayed at my anger...Could it be as he describes?*

Phelan took a deep breath. "If I accept what you say is true—and I'm not sure I've bought the whole package—then Ranna's actions on Rasalhague and afterward confuse me. We were constantly together." He hesitated for a moment, then crashed on ahead. "I'm no Don Juan, but I've fallen in love a couple of times, and this had all the signs of it. It felt good...it *was* good, then she goes to him. She said she wanted to talk with him. If she didn't see sleeping with him as betraying me, I have to ask why she couldn't have talked to me about whatever she discussed with him?"

The Precentor stood. "You mean you've not yet figured that out? As I said before, love is the exception, not the rule, in this society. Such strong emotions are, as you have suggested, very heady stuff... confusing, maybe even terrifying for someone who has not learned to anticipate and cherish them." He pushed his chair back against the wall and stood. "It should be obvious to you, Phelan Kell. Ranna went to Vlad to talk about falling in love with *you*."

253

The Cloisters, Twycross
Tamar March, Lyran Commonwealth
10 September 3050

Dwarfed by the the wind-carved red rock, Victor Steiner-Davion's BattleMech knelt on one knee at the base of the standing stones, which one explorer had dubbed the Cloisters because of the resemblance to hooded monks. A thin cable passed from the 'Mech's flank into the ground at a small, meter-square concrete box.

Inside the cockpit of his *Victor*, Davion studied the holographic display being relayed from his command center along the ground line to his 'Mech. The Ninth F-C had successfully deployed in the midst of the Diabolis and were moving with the high winds as they scoured the landscape. In their wake, at the site of the Ninth's landing and two other strategic points, a legion of 'Mech decoys and a considerable number of vibrabombs had been planted. The decoys had succeeded in drawing the interest of some Clan garrison troops, but the violent sand storms made communication difficult except by landline, to which very few of their scouts had access.

The Kell Hounds First Regiment and the armor from the Tenth Lyran Guards had deployed below his position, in the Plain of Curtains, named after the drifting ribbons of sand that snaked constantly through the broad valley. One 'Mech company from the Tenth Lyran Guards had set up in the foothills of the Windbreak Mountains to block access to the Kell Hounds' rear area through the Great Gash to the east of the Plain of Curtains. The mercenaries' own Second Regiment warded the First Regiment's left flank by slipping into the

Sharktooth Mountains to the west. The rest of the Tenth had been held in reserve to bolster the Kell Hounds First Regiment or shore up either flank, as needed.

Victor frowned as the transcripts of broken transmissions played across his secondary monitor. "Central, can't you clean up the broadcasts from the Gash? I'm not clear if the explosives needed to close the pass have been put in place. I also get the impression that some of the power armor may be active in that area. Please confirm."

Victor waited as the Comcenter's operator hunted up the information. *If the garrison troops come through and accept the Kell Hounds' challenge, as expected, the Diabolis should cap the north end of the plain just after the Falcons arrive. The Diabolis will make fighting tough, but it gives us an advantage by shortening ranges and diffusing energy beams at anything but point-blank range. The infighting will be nasty, but that's what will even the odds.* He glanced at his 'Mech's status report on the primary display. *Good God willing and this autocannon don't jam, I think we can beat the Clansmen and take back this world.*

"Kommandant, I have the information you want. The explosives have been planted to close the Gash at its deepest point. The demolition crews are ready and the vibrabombs placed nearest the explosives have been shut down to prevent a premature, sympathetic detonation of the explosives."

Yeah, once that pentaglycerine is activated, it's highly unstable. It's a good thing this weather prohibits the use of LRMs and SRMs, because a hit nearby could trigger a collapse of the whole pass. If I don't have to bring it down, I'd prefer to keep it open. "Good. Are there confirmations of armored infantry near the Gash?"

The comtech hesitated. "We aren't sure, sir. The Diabolis has moved into the area, which means communications are all fragmentary. Hauptmann Jungblud appears to have some contact at his forward position and has engaged in fighting. Leftenant-General Milstein says it looks to be fringe elements of the garrison force as they move toward the plain. All our other reports say a full regiment and a half of 'Mechs are moving to beat the storm into the plain."

Though the explanation sounded correct, something nagged at the back of Victor's mind. *It's more than my dislike of Morgan assigning Leftenant-General Milstein as my safety valve. I can't have Milstein pull a Hawksworth on me.* "Thank you, Comcenter." He switched over to another channel on the landline. "Kai, this is Victor. Have you been monitoring the situation at the Gash?"

"Affirmative."

"Assessment?"

The hum of dead air filled Victor's neurohelmet as Kai considered his reply. "I think, Kommandant, that the Clans are probing the Gash to see if we've left it undefended. The use of power armor could be an attempt to get through and into our rear. Depending upon the numbers of the infantry, they'll be able to overwhelm our forward company of 'Mechs—especially if they're fighting with Clan 'Mechs—and then blow through our infantry."

Victor winced. "That's likely to be nasty." He glanced at his map and punched a command into the computer that magnified the section of the map nearest the Gash. "We have a mobile hospital unit in Sector 0227. Get your lance over there and report back to me on the situation. The hospital is sitting right on top of a landline junction box, so you should have no problem getting through."

The enthusiasm in Kai's voice survived transmission intact. "Thank you, Vic. Talk to you in an hour."

"One hour. Got it." Victor stopped his hand in mid-motion just as he was about to shift his radio back to the link with the command center. "Kai, be careful. That *Hatchetman* you're riding has neither the firepower nor the armor you're used to with *Yen-lo-wang*. I hope like hell you won't need it, but remember that baby's whole head assembly comes away when you eject, so your torso has to be up."

Kai laughed. "Just like my uncle's *Wolfhound*. Caution noted and appreciated. Will advise as soon as I arrive on scene. Allard out."

Victor switched his radio back over to his command center. "Taccom, Davion here. I've detached Allard's scout lance for a recon of Sector 0227. Patch him through to me when he has a report, but I want you to monitor it as well. I'm going to break off here and head down to the plain. I'll join up with Hauptmann Cox and Alpha Battalion."

"Acknowledged, sir. Leftenant-General Milstein urges you to be careful. ETA of enemy is thirty minutes at their last clocked speed and position."

"Roger. Davion out." Victor hit a button on his console and the fiber-optic landline splice reeled itself back into the compartment on his 'Mech. As his eighty-ton BattleMech rose to its feet, a wind buffeted it. The *Victor* began to sway, but the gyros linked via the neurohelmet to the Prince's own sense of balance steadied the humanoid machine. With the 'Mech's left hand, Victor patted one of the stone monks on the leg, then lumbered his machine forward and down into the valley.

Below him, the Plain of Curtains spread out like a coppery field

256

of fired clay. From his vantage point, he saw the shifting walls of sand that raced over that baked slab. Juggernaut winds twisting into the valley through the mountains drove the sand before them in haphazard patterns. Where they collided, the writhing walls of sand degenerated into red-gold dervishes that battled each other until they collapsed into scarlet piles of dust.

Beyond the Plain of Curtains lurked the Diabolis. The huge, whirling funnel of dust and debris appeared, for the most part, to be a black cylinder. Victor detected motion in it, but because of the distance and the storm's size, the walls appeared to be spinning at a painfully slow rate. Even so, the height to which streaks of red had risen in the black cone spoke of the power in the creeping storm.

I know the winds in there have been clocked at more than 350 kph. The Ninth F-C's inertial guidance system and independent clocks are going to be the only things that drop them in on us on time. Victor glanced at his own clock. *Twenty minutes to engagement.*

He hurried his 'Mech down the trail hammered flat by the feet of many other killing machines, then cut away from the trail about five hundred meters above the valley floor. As he passed a checkpoint, a 'Mech emblazoned with the flaming arrow insignia of a "pathfinder" waved him toward the front of the Lyran Guards formation. There he found Galen Cox's *Crusader* standing beside a *Wolfhound* painted in the red and black of the Kell Hounds.

Victor opened a radio link with the two 'Mechs. "Lieutenant-Colonel Allard, I've sent Kai to check on the possibility of a Clan probe into the area of the Great Gash. They may have some power armor coming through there, and perhaps a lance or two of 'Mechs."

Dan Allard's reply rumbled through the speakers in Davion's neurohelmet. "I'll have Colonel Brahe drop a lance back to cover that chance. The only good thing about that news is that it means they probably aren't going to come through the Sharkteeth. I think I can have Scott Bradley bring the Second Regiment down into their staging areas now."

Victor nodded to himself. "Excellent idea, sir. We just have to make sure make sure they don't commit too soon. We want the Falcons in and engaged with the First Regiment before we surprise them with the Ninth F-C and the rest of the Hounds."

A note of amusement worked its way through Dan's mild rebuke. "As per the plan, Kommandant. Don't worry, I remember." The *Wolfhound* turned from the other two 'Mechs and began the final descent to the floor of the plain.

Galen's 'Mech pointed toward the far end of the valley. "Our spotter at the valley mouth just said the Falcons are on their way. He reports a scattering of their unusual 'Mechs—*Thor*s and *Loki*s and something he tagged *Fenris*—among other, more conventional designs. It appears they don't let their garrison troops use the good stuff."

"Until now, we hadn't given them any reason to suspect that they needed 'Mechs on their conquered worlds at all." Victor glanced at his secondary monitor. "All we have to do is hold them for an hour and then the Ninth will close the trap. We'll have them and will have handed them their first defeat in this war."

"Good God willing and the pass is held," Galen murmured.

Victor turned his 'Mech to face the Plain of Curtains. "Look, Galen...the Falcons' point-lances have found the Hounds."

The undulating curtains of wind-whipped sand played a deadly game of hide and seek with the BattleMechs. The reddish dust all but hid the scarlet torsos of Kell Hound 'Mechs until the Falcons were almost upon them. At point-blank range, the invaders' targeting edge meant nothing, reducing the battle to a contest that would be decided by the opponents' sheer firepower and the strength of their defenses.

The initial exchanges ran in favor of the Kell Hounds. Because of their superior numbers, they concentrated their fire on a single target and were able to cripple it with a salvo or two. The Falcons, in keeping with what Victor saw as their standard battle doctrine, picked out individual targets and attacked them to the exclusion of all others. The Falcon scout groups withdrew quickly at first, but slowed their retreat as the Kell Hounds failed to follow and their own reinforcements moved up.

The Kell Hounds pulled back in the face of the whole Falcon host. When various individual Falcons sprinted out away from their lines, the Kell Hounds shot them up. The Falcon commander quickly reined in his people, and the invaders began a controlled advance, willing to let the mercenaries choose their own time and place to die.

Victor's eyes narrowed. *They'll make their move soon. The Hounds don't have much room left to pull back further. Once they engage solidly, then we can call in the Second Regiment.* A smile lit his face with boyish delight. *I think this is actually going to work!*

Victor saw a blue button blinking urgently on his command console. As a wave of black and red sand washed away all sight of the battlefield, he punched it. "Davion here. What is it?"

Panic filled the comtech's voice. "Leftenant-General Milstein says to pull out, sir. Do it now!"

Victor couldn't believe his ears. "What? Why? We're set to start ripping them up!"

"Kommandant, Milstein here. You have to pull back. Your position is vulnerable, very vulnerable."

Victor's temper flared. "Explain it to me, dammit, man. What the hell has happened?"*We're not going to replay Trellwan here!*

"We just got a clear transmission from Hauptmann Jungblud. His company was hit by armored infantry and 'Mechs—a regiment of each! These were not garrison 'Mechs—repeat, *not* garrison 'Mechs. They were Clan *frontline* machines, Kommandant. Jungblud's company is destroyed and we can't raise the demo teams."

Milstein's voice faltered. "It's over, Highness. The Clans are pouring through the Gash."

Because the winds had sucked away the oily black smoke from
the burning armored personnel carriers, the first clue Kai Allard had
about conditions in Sector 0227 was the SRM that slammed into his
Hatchetman's chest. Fired by one of the half-dozen armored infantrymen, the rocket exploded against the 'Mech's left breast. The resulting
shower of armor shards took away the Lyran Guard insignia, but the
missile failed to hurt or stop the *Hatchetman*.

Kai dropped the crosshairs for his autocannon onto the nearest
figure and jammed his right thumb down on the firing button. The
BattleMech twisted slightly to the right as the autocannon mounted in
its right breast erupted with a hail of fire and metal. The supersonic
slugs blew completely through the infantryman, then ricocheted off
the canyon walls in a shower of sparks.

The enemy's armored suit and its remaining missiles exploded,
but Kai had already turned his attention to other targets. He directed
the medium lasers slung on the underside of his 'Mech's forearms at
more of the metal-covered invaders. One eluded the ruby beam while
the other, trapped between the APC and a small cinderblock building,
just melted away.

Perhaps believing the spindly-legged 'Mech a weak foe, one
warrior in powered armor leaped up toward the *Hatchetman's* head.
He never reached his destination, as Kai employed the most unusual
element of the *Hatchetman's* weaponry. The titanium-sheathed, de-

pleted-uranium blade of the hand-held warclub that gave the 'Mech its name swatted the Jade Falcon from the air like an insect. The warrior flew, arms and legs spreadeagled, into the canyon wall, then slid lifelessly to the ground, blood and black fluids leaking from the rents in his shell.

Like a vengeful god among arrogant mortals, the *Hatchetman* pounced on the remaining Jade Falcons. As the *Hatchetman* crushed the life from one with its left hand, the autocannon ripped yet another apart. The last enemy warrior, aware that he was doomed, launched two SRMs into other APCs. Kai's lasers vaporized him seconds after the vehicles exploded.

Kai opened a radio link with the rest of his lance. "Get up here. Things are not normal. I just had to put down six of their Toads. Keep your eyes open and be careful." He looked out over the chaotic scene. "It's a mess up here."

Located in the middle of a canyon approximately two hundred meters wide and four times that long, the medical station consisted of two large tents on either side of a smaller truck storing the diagnostic machinery and supplies. Because of the high walls around the canyon, the air remained relatively clear, defended from the fury of the Diabolis. Curling around to the east, at a point opposite the hill Kai had climbed to reach it, the canyon narrowed down into the westernmost portion of the Great Gash. From there, the Gash traveled three hundred meters upward at a gentle slope, with the mountain shoulders rising up another four hundred meters on either side of the narrow pass. At the point where the pass began to slant back down to the east, explosives had been rigged to shut down the pass if needed.

Streaming back from the pass and the heights around it came Commonwealth soldiers all tattered and torn. Some ran in panic, with no idea of where they were or where bound. Others, regardless of their own injuries, helped less-fortunate comrades to the makeshift hospital. More than one soldier carried the limp body of a friend in his arms, and Kai knew that there would be no help for many of them.

Kai dropped his 'Mech down to one knee and used its free left hand to corral a soldier. He flicked his external speakers on with the touch of a button. "Report, Sergeant Detloff," he said, reading the man's name from the patch on his uniform. "What happened?"

The man shuddered and seemed to struggle to speak. "They got through us, sir. We finished planting the explosives and all, and then they were all over us." His hand dropped unconsciously to the empty holster on his right hip. "Nothing stopped them."

The images of unarmored men trying to stop the Jade Falcons

261

with small-arms fire sent a shiver of dread through the MechWarrior. "Did you blow the pass?" Even as he asked, Kai knew the answer. *They couldn't have done it. With all those explosives and that much rock moving, I'd have felt it on the way up.* The non-com confirmed Kai's deduction with a head-shake.

Kai opened up the external microphone and increased its gain slowly. The feedback built into a piercing shriek that blasted through to even the most shocked of the warriors in the valley. Flipping it back off, he keyed up his helmet mike. "Get your people into the APCs and other vehicles. You're pulling out. Those of you who can walk should help the others or carry as much of the hospital's supplies as possible."

Focusing back from the eye-slit viewport to his holographic display, he saw the rest of his lance arrive on the scene. "Jeff, Maggie, use your 'Mechs to clear out these burning APCs so they can get to the good ones. Harry, keep your *Hunchback* near the trail leading down. You're point man for getting this convoy out of here."

"Roger, Leftenant." The *Vindicator* and *Trebuchet* moved toward the burning vehicles while the barrel-chested *Hunchback* stood sentinel at the canyon entrance. Though each of the 'Mechs had only one manipulable hand, their terrific strength enabled them to move the damaged APCs easily.

Kai's heart sank as he looked out his viewport. *Oh, no! They're not having trouble, but I'm about to.*

Stalking from the hospital in a blood-spattered surgical gown, Dr. Deirdre Lear headed straight for the *Hatchetman*. Four or five meters from its base, she jammed her fists onto her hips and glared up at the polarized eyeslit. "I don't know who you think you are, but this hospital is going nowhere!" She pointed a finger back at the twin tents. "I've got people in there who will die if they're moved."

The MechWarrior nudged the armored body of a dead Jade Falcon with his ax. "Your people will die if they *don't* move, Doctor."

"You're here with your guns. Protect us until I can stabilize these people."

Kai dropped the *Hatchetman* to one knee and laid its left hand flat on the ground. "Please, Doctor, join me inside the cockpit. I would prefer that our discussion not be aired in public."

A look of revulsion washed briefly over her face, but she conquered her emotions and stepped into the mechanical hand. Kai slowly brought the hand up to shoulder height, with the edge of the palm resting against the 'Mech's left shoulder. "There's a hatch at the back of the neck. I'm opening it now. Please climb around and in." His fingers danced across the keypad on the right side of his command console, opening the hatch with a hiss of pressurized air.

Deirdre entered the cockpit warily. Without turning to face her, he pointed to a jumpseat folded up against the right side of the pilot's compartment. "Please be seated. I apologize for the lack of accommodations: we don't often have passengers."

"I don't plan to be here very long." She sat down, and he felt her angry eyes boring into him.

He brought the *Hatchetman* back to its feet and resealed the hatch. "Please strap yourself in. You can get a headset from the compartment by your right shoulder. Plug it into the jack there and we can talk normally."

She strapped herself in and connected up her headset. "You might as well leave the 'Mech down."

Kai shook his head and concentrated on the holographic display. "I don't think so, Doctor. This is a war zone and a stationary 'Mech makes an inviting target." He flipped his communications system over to the external speakers. "Sergeant, gather as many men as you can. You're going back up there to seal the gap."

The soldier shook his head wearily. "Can't do it, sir. The Leftenant had the magcard that controlled the detonator."

"Where is he?"

The man looked to be on the verge of tears. "I don't know. He was one of the first hit."

Kai frowned, sweat burning into his eyes. "What did you use for explosive?"

Detloff shuddered. "Pentaglycerine. Lots of it. We had to shut down the vibrabombs to keep from setting off a sympathetic blast."

The MechWarrior's head came up. "Then an autocannon burst against the walls or a missile ought to set it off."

"Sure, if you're of a mind to commit suicide." Detloff looked straight up at the *Hatchetman*. "Even an *Atlas* couldn't climb out from under that much rock, much less survive the burying."

Kai slammed his fist against the command couch's right arm. "Dammit, you better get back up there and find that magcard. You have to. Sealing the gap is our only chance to keep the invaders from killing Victor Davion." *Please, God, get Victor away and clear…*

Fire returned to the soldier's eyes. "Yes, sir." He turned and grabbed two other men. They, in turn, recruited several more as they headed off toward a narrow trail up the canyon wall.

Deirdre's cold voice demanded his attention. "Excuse me, but I thought you brought me in here to discuss defending my hospital?"

As Kai turned around, he saw recognition on her face the second their eyes met. "That's what I'm trying to do, Doctor. I'm trying to buy you the time, but the only way to do that is to seal the gap. The Gash has been mined and is set to explode, but they can't set off the explosives unless they get the card."

"You!" Venom burned in her blue eyes. "Let me out of here right now!"

"No! I need some answers, and only you can give them to me." Kai forced his own anger down. "How much time do you need to stabilize people?"

"All of them? Twelve hours."

Kai shook his head. "No way. Fifty percent fatalities in a triage setup. How long?"

Her jaw dropped. "Fifty percent? That's inhuman! How could you even suggest it?"

"I'm just being realistic."

"You're being a monster, a heartless monster." Her eyes narrowed. "I should have expected it. It's in your blood."

Kai stabbed a finger at her. "Stop it. Just stop it now! I don't know why you hate me and"—he hesitated—"I don't care. If Jade Falcon 'Mechs, even a lance of them, are following those infantry up here, everyone is going to be dead! Give me a realistic time figure, and I'll get you that time." As he turned away, a host of orange stick figures appeared on his magscan display and a tortured note entered his voice. "No!"

Deirdre strained at the shoulder straps holding her in the jumpseat. "What? What is it?"

Kai's face closed. "Time's up."

Laser fire from the Toads at the mouth of the Gash burned through the air. Commonwealth soldiers clawed the ground and the 'Mechs returned fire, scattering the Jade Falcons without doing much damage. While people panicked and broke past him, Kai started the *Hatchetman* running toward the Gash. When the enemy infantry resumed their attack, his charging 'Mech became an obvious though elusive target.

"Jeff, get everyone out of here!" he ordered his second in command. Kai dropped the targeting crosshairs onto a manlike outline and directed a withering stream of autocannon shells at it. He watched the shredded body reel away, then shifted his course so the *Hatchetman's* eleven meters obscured the team working its way up the side of the canyon. *Detloff, you better find your Leftenant! I'll buy you that time, if I can...*

Terror flooded Deirdre's voice. "What are you doing? Are you mad? Let me out of here!"

"Wish I could, Doctor. I wish I could. Hang on." Kai stabbed both feet down against the jump jet pedals on the command couch and the 'Mech leaped up into the air. As the gee forces slammed him back down into the couch, he felt as though his stomach had been left on the ground. He watched his altimeter clicking off meter after meter on the scale, then at 30 meters up and 150 forward, he cut the jets. "Lean forward and grab your knees, Doctor. The landing will be nasty."

He hit the jets hard at the last second, and the retroblast knocked over several of the Falcons. The *Hatchetman* landed solidly, bent at the knees to absorb the shock. Then, like a bear beset by wolves, it lunged forward to wreak havoc among the pack of armored figures.

The *Hatchetman's* lasers swept over the invaders, making armor sizzle and run wherever they touched. The autocannon always found a target, and the sheer physical impact of the projectiles often knocked one flying warrior into another. As for the hatchet, it crushed and maimed those it did not cleave through outright as it scythed back and forth through the knotted mass of the enemy.

Kai's initial rush pushed the invaders back into the mouth of the Gash. There, bunched together, he found them less difficult targets. With fist and foot, he crushed them and continued to batter his way through them. He scraped them from his back and shoulders against the pass's stony walls, leaving the glittering broken corpses to mark his trail.

To Kai, a warrior born of warriors, this battle was everything he had ever trained for. Deep in his heart, he knew the moment he jumped his BattleMech into their midst that he would die. Everything he had learned about the Jade Falcons and their fantastic infantrymen told him he was doomed. He also knew that if he could stay alive long enough, he could pull the battle away from the hospital, giving his comrades a chance to escape and Detloff a chance to blow the Gash.

Something seemed wrong, and as the battle continued to work its way, meter by meter, back through the Gash, that realization seeped into his brain. The sheer ferocity of his attack had shocked the Jade Falcons and driven them back. Though their attacks had pitted and ravaged most of his armor, he had given them no chance to think or to plan or to aim. Just as his weapons attacked their bodies, his unquenchable fury attacked their spirits.

They broke and they ran.

The *Hatchetman* charged after the fleeing man-things, but Kai did not truly try to catch them. Even before his 'Mech took the last few steps to the crest of the Gash, his assessment of the battle began to take shape. *You never should have done this. You risked Deirdre's life unnecessarily. You went off without thinking and nearly cost your lord an invaluable piece of military equipment! If your luck ever runs out...*

Cresting the mountain gap, his mouth went bone dry. "Blake's blood! It's all over."

Seated behind him, Deirdre peered down into the gap at the same moment. Her voice sank into a little-girl's whisper. "Oh, God, what have you done?"

Below them, marching upward in two orderly columns, came a full regiment of Jade Falcon BattleMechs. A few of them showed signs of combat, but only in the blistering of paint on the muzzle of a laser or the soot stains near an autocannon's ejection port. The few remaining infantrymen dashed between the legs of their larger brethren, and in a couple of cases, their armor seemed to meld itself to the Battle-Mechs.

Kai unconsciously started his battlecomputer scanning the machines below. He saw matches for the configurations Victor had labeled as *Loki* and *Thor* flash by, but dozens of other designs appeared on his auxiliary monitor without identifiers. A small counter up in the monitor's corner kept track of the number of 'Mechs scanned and stopped at forty-five.

It might as well be forty-five hundred for all I can do against them. I hope like hell Detloff is in position. Kai switched his scanners over to vislight and boosted magnification on the area where the Sergeant and his men should have been to blow the pass. *Oh no!* Instead of Lyran soldiers, he saw two Toads. One of them raised a broken body in a Commonwealth uniform and defiantly tossed it down to the floor of the gap.

With the magnification on his scanner, Kai saw enough to identify the body as Detloff's. *I killed him. I killed him and his men. It's all over, isn't it? There is no way I can win...* As that thought drifted through his head, it dragged along a memory he had almost forgotten. He considered the course of action it counseled, then nodded slightly to himself.

"Doctor, please do exactly as I ask when I ask you to do it." He flipped two switches on his command console. One filled the cockpit with a red glow and the second slid back a panel on the right arm of his command couch. Sliding up and locking into place, an illuminated blue button rested beneath his fingers. "Do you see that panel by your right knee?"

She nodded, then asked in a small voice, "Do you mean the one labeled 'Magnetic Containment Circuitry'?"

Kai nodded once. "Open that panel please. When I tell you to, pull each and every circuit board as fast as you can. There will be sparks and smoke and a siren, but just keep pulling. Don't worry about damaging them. Just get them out of there."

He punched a button on the communications board, setting up a widebeam broadcast to those below. He lowered his voice into a growl and infused his words with a confidence and arrogance he did not feel. "I am Kai Allard-Liao. I am a killer of men."

He opened the *Hatchetman's* arms wide. "This pass is mine to ward. I offer those who wish to challenge me a warrior's death, but I beg an indulgence of those who would accept my offer. Your smaller companions have forced me to exhaust my autocannon ammunition and they destroyed one of my lasers." He brought the 'Mech's hands together to grip the hatchet's haft. "I have only this club with which to defend myself. I will kill you all, alone or in groups."

He snapped off his mike line to the outside. "Get ready, Doctor."

Deirdre stared at him incredulously. "They'll kill us. I thought you wanted to surrender."

Kai's voice came hard and even. "I will do whatever it takes to survive, but I also have obligations and duties to perform. Sergeant Detloff and his people died because I ordered them into dangerous territory to blow the gap. If I surrender, if I do nothing, these super-'Mechs will sweep through, destroy the refugees fleeing from the hospital area, and then will fall on our lines from the rear."

His voice softened slightly, but its intensity did not diminish. "I regret getting you into this. I don't expect you to understand why all this is happening, but I want you to know it's the only way. Before this is over, my hands will be stained with more blood, but better their blood on my hands, then the blood of my friends on theirs."

The radio crackled with a reply to his message. "I am Star Colonel Adler Malthus in command of the Falcon Guards." A 'Mech of the style the computer labeled as a *Thor* stepped forward from the Guards' line. It raised both of its handless arms above its blocky head and crossed the muzzles of its autocannon and PPC. A second or two later, all the other 'Mechs in the company mimicked the gesture, then again aped their leader as he brought the *Thor's* arms back down. "We salute you, Kai Allard-Liao, and assure you that your bravery will live long in the hearts and minds of your conquerors."

Kai laughed lightly as he reopened his comlink. "And I assure you, the memory of your valor will become a story known far and wide through the Successor States." Shutting down the line, he turned to Deirdre. "When he gets within arm's-reach, start pulling—now,

Doctor, do it now!"

The *Thor* marched forward like a butcher at a slaughterhouse. It raised the PPC that made up its right forearm for a blow that would crush the *Hatchetman*, but Kai sidestepped the attack. He brought the hatchet up into the *Thor's* right armpit. For a half-second, Kai thought the resulting shower of sparks merely the reflection of those filling the rear of the cockpit, but armor raining down showed how much damage he had truly done. *Son of a bitch, this thing really works.*

Instantly, a hollow voice reminded him of how inappropriate self-confidence had doomed him in the Academy's La Mancha scenario. Behind him, Deirdre shouted "Clear!" and a wave of heat turned the closed cockpit into a blast furnace. His right hand slammed down on the blue button, then he crossed his fingers and prayed.

The *Thor* had raised both its arms and clapped them together to crush the *Hatchetman's* head between them like some bloated mosquito. Argent fire encircled the 'Mech's neck before the *Thor's* heavy limbs could converge, then the whole cockpit assembly popped upward like a springloaded piece from a child's toy. Secondary rockets ignited, their golden spear of flame impaling the *Thor's* squat head, and shot the *Hatchetman's* head halfway to the shoulders of the Great Gash.

Down below, no longer contained by the magnetic fields that had been destroyed when Deirdre lobotomized the control computer, the *Hatchetman's* fusion engine exploded. Searing white plasma shot from every joint, then melted through the 'Mech's tattered armor flesh. It engulfed and swallowed the *Thor's* arms, then the roiling energy storm convulsed and tore itself apart in a hideous elemental explosion.

The tremendous shockwave touched off the pentaglycerine buried deep in the Gash's walls. Every twenty meters up and out from the detonation's epicenter, smaller bursts sprayed rock and fire across the canyon. Each wave of explosions triggered the next in a staccato succession that pelted the Falcon Guards with stone shards. Even as the *Hatchetman's* head rose through the Gash itself, the racing thunderstrikes buffeted the armored shell. One huge chunk of rock smashed into the cockpit viewport, cracking the glass and peppering Kai's bare thighs with crystalline needles.

Suddenly the explosions stopped and their echoes faded. Kai, seeing the Gash's crack-riddled walls still standing tall, feared the pentaglycerine had failed its task. Yet, as he tried to think of a way to redirect the escape pod at the walls to crash into them and start a chain reaction, a deep, terrible roar rose up to fill the debris-littered mountain pass. A few pieces of rock at the tallest point leaned forward and slowly fell, tumbling end over end toward the ground. More followed, then the canyon walls buckled in the middle and rock flowed like water to fill and obliterate the Great Gash.

Jump-capable BattleMechs leaped toward the sky, but huge plates of black rock smashed them back down to the earth. Boulders careened through the canyon, scattering 'Mechs like toys before a child's tantrum. Jagged-edged dolmen sliced through 'Mechs like knives, then themselves were blown into fragments and dust by the resulting fusion-engine explosions. Thick black clouds choked what had once been the only pass through the mountains and settled like a black shroud over the Falcon Guards' mass grave.

Horrified by the sight, and shaken at having caused it, Kai shut off the screens where his scanners were toting up, 'Mech by broken 'Mech, the damage done. Oblivious to the pain in his bloodstreaked legs and conscious of only the sobbing sounds behind him, he waited for the pod's rocket motor to burn out, then popped the parachute and looked for a landing spot as far away as possible from the Great Gash.

Plain of Curtains, Twycross
Tamar March, Lyran Commonwealth
10 September 3050

The invaders own the Gash! That realization sent a jolt of adrenaline through Victor's system. Vowing silently that the weeks of planning on Sudeten would not be in vain, he banished defeat from his mind.

He put out a quick radio call to Colonel Allard. "Colonel, please don't pull me out." With his left hand, Victor typed a request for information into his tactical computer and watched the data scrolling up his primary monitor. "Commit the *Excelsior*, the *Triumph*, the *Catamount*, and the *Lugh* to Sector 0227. Have them hold the Falcons as long as they can."

Shock and surprise filled Milstein's voice as he overrode the frequency. "Colonel, those are the DropShips committed to evacuating our troops. The *Excelsior* is meant solely to pull Victor out of here. I can't allow any other use of those ships!"

Victor refused to surrender. "If we don't commit them, they won't have anything to pick up."

"Colonel Allard, countermand this order," Milstein hissed. "You are his superior officer. I don't know who he thinks he is, but he is not his father!"

Victor snarled furiously. "You idiot! I'm not trying to be my father." *I'm trying to be something more.* "This is our only chance to salvage this operation."

The static created by laserfire popped through Victor's neurohelmet as Daniel Allard spoke. "Can it, gentlemen. There's a fight going on here. Milstein, commit the ships."

"Colonel Allard, I must remind you that my duty is to ensure that the Prince's son be safe."

Dan's voice came back cold and hard. "Then I suggest you get your ass in a 'Mech and get the hell down here, because all your radio calls are doing is distracting my officer. Have the DropShips hold 0227."

Victor studied the tactical map of the area that Dan shot over to his 'Mech. In an instant, he confirmed the soundness of what the mercenary leader had already decided on for strategy. Dan had selected one of Kai's contingency plans for the assault. He punched a button that sent the map data to Galen and the rest of the Guards. *This just might work.*

Over the tactical frequency, Dan's voice was strong and confident. "Akira, pull your right flank back and push the left flank forward. We have to commit the Second Regiment to turn the whole Clan formation."

"Got it. We'll wheel the Clans back into the opening to the Gash so their reinforcements will have to fight their way past their own people to get at us. Did you copy that, Scott?"

"Roger. I drop down to cap the valley and roll up their edges. ETA, ten minutes and counting down, now!"

"Good. Victor, I'm committing the Tenth Lyran to shore up Akira's right flank."

Victor felt the sour fear of being left out drain away. "Roger. What about the Ninth F-C?"

"Three-quarters of an hour until they step free of the storm. We can't contact them until then. I don't like it, but we have to do this by ourselves."

Victor nodded grimly. "They can be our ace in the hole if the DropShips don't stop the Falcons at the Gash."

"Let's hope we don't need them," Dan said.

"Roger…and Colonel, thanks for the chance."

A low chuckle echoed through Victor's neurohelmet. "Just don't get your butt shot off, Victor! The paperwork would kill me."

"Wilco, Colonel. Davion out." Victor switched to the Lyran Guards tactical frequency. "Alpha Battalion on me. Kommandants, bring Bravo and Charlie up to form our center and left flank respectively. Charlie, you'll be cheek to cheek with the Hounds' First Regiment. We hit, then give ground slowly to allow the Hounds to pull back to the west. Give better than you get and we'll all survive this."

Standing fourteen meters tall and with an autocannon muzzle where its right forearm should have been, Davion's *Victor* strode down from the hills and led the Tenth Lyran Guards into the mouth of hell. Sand curtains swirled like veils in some exotic dance, hiding some things and providing tantalizing glimpses of others. Wondering what dangers lurked within the boiling sandstorm, Victor barely heard the rasp of sand against his 'Mech's face.

The first Jade Falcon appeared on his right as if by magic. The *Shadow Hawk* had already marched halfway past when its pilot noticed Victor and began to bring his 'Mech about. Victor raised the assault 'Mech's right arm and stabbed the autocannon muzzle toward the *Shadow Hawk's* square faceplate. The muzzle flash erased the image of the 'Mech's head from Victor's sight, and the depleted-uranium shells blowing through it matched form to image. The decapitated *Shadow Hawk* dropped backward and vanished within the black folds of a sand curtain.

All around him, Victor witnessed brutal slices of the battle. A Lyran *Quickdraw*, its right arm dangling by the twisted cord of a myomer muscle, stumbled past him. Like a wild animal on a blood trail, the pursuing Falcon *Rifleman* clomped through the battlefield, its sensor wing whirling madly to collect whatever data it could. It stopped and turned its weapons on Victor, twin autocannon pumping shells into his 'Mech's chest.

The *Victor's* battlecomputer redrew its own outline on the auxiliary monitor, adding glowing yellow spots to represent the damage. Davion ignored it and dropped his targeting crosshairs onto the *Rifleman's* blocky body. The autocannon's high-speed whine filled the cockpit as a stream of projectiles shredded the Falcon's right-shoulder armor. Sparks and flames shot out of the joint in blues and greens, and the arm ceased to move, frozen as it pointed straight ahead.

Victor stepped his war machine closer, putting it well inside the *Rifleman's* ability to bring guns to bear. He chopped the *Victor's* left hand down on the *Rifleman's* right shoulder. The blow crushed ferro-ceramic armor to dust. More sparks shot out as the shoulder ground downward, then the whole limb twisted away and fell to the ground.

The *Rifleman* pilot backed up his machine half a step, then twisted to bring the left arm's guns to bear on Victor. As he did so, Galen Cox's *Crusader* stepped through a wall of blowing sand, grabbed the guns in both of his 'Mech's hands, and cranked them up into the air. The *Rifleman's* shots from both the large laser and autocannon passed well over Victor's head.

The *Crusader's* hands pushed and pulled in different directions.

With a metallic scream audible even through the howling storm, the gun barrels twisted out of alignment. The *Victor* pointed its autocannon at the *Rifleman's* right leg, and the Prince thumbed the trigger button. The autocannon shells peeled the armor off the Falcon 'Mech's knee, then blew through the titano-magnesium bones. The *Rifleman* lurched to the right, then fell on its side and rolled over onto its face.

Victor made his 'Mech throw Galen a salute, then turned and moved on in search of more prey. As the afternoon became evening, he continued to hunt successfully. As evening became night, his autocannon exhausted its ammunition and the battle left gaping rents in his armor until there was no one left to fight.

Galen glanced down at his noteputer. "As nearly as we can figure out, the Falcon commander knew something was up when their reinforcements did not come through the Gash. She issued the order to pull her people back so they could slip out of the Plain as evening came on. They did not expect to run into the Ninth F-C and so lost a few 'Mechs there. The Ninth is still pursuing the rest of them, but those damned 'Mechs run very cool, so they're stretching out the range on our people."

Victor nodded. "Yeah, there's no denying they run cool. I've already had a preliminary report on a heat sink taken from one of their machines. They have some sort of double-chambered heat exchanger and a fluid with a thermal retention factor that's seven-tenths of air itself! The Techs think those units, which are about the size of our own heat sinks, probably are 150 to 200 percent more efficient than ours."

"Hard to believe we beat them after seeing what they had going for them," Galen agreed. "The prisoners seem rather shocked at the defeat, too, but they've adapted. Mostly they want to know the name of our Clan so they know to whom they owe their allegiance." Cox laughed lightly. "The guards couldn't decide if we were Clan Davion or Steiner, so they settled on Victor."

Victor sighed heavily. "Just remind everyone to treat them kindly. We don't know when the tables will be turned. Hey, do you think that's them?"

The walls of Victor's tent began vibrating back and forth as the sound of a helicopter whooped through them. Davion shot to his feet, dumping his wood and canvas campaign chair over on its back. Galen's own grin mirrored the smile spreading over Victor's face. Outside, a general cheer and applause rose up, then the tent flap opened.

Kai Allard, his face beet-red, stepped stiffly in, then held open the flap for Deirdre Lear. After she entered the tent, he let it fall shut again and pivoted awkwardly on bandage-swathed legs. He snapped to attention and saluted Victor. Davion returned the salute, then embraced his friend in a back-slapping hug. "You don't know how happy I was when the search and rescue team reported finding you." *I really thought I'd sent you out to die, my friend.*

Victor took a step back and offered Deirdre his hand. "I'm glad you were with him, Doctor, to take care of his wounds."

"I was pleased to be of service, but if I can avoid accompanying a 'Mech into battle again, I will."

Though puzzled by her vehemence, Victor knew this was not the time or place to probe it further. "Please, be seated." He waved his two guests to chairs. "Kai, when I sent you over to the Gash, I only expected you to report, not win the war all by yourself."

Deirdre slipped into a chair, but Kai remained standing. "Yes, sir. I'm sorry, sir."

Something in Kai's voice and eyes hit Victor as all wrong. *He's sounding like he did back at NAMA. What the hell is going on here?* "Kai, we've been friends for too long for you to be calling me sir, and I recognize that tone in your voice. What is it?"

Kai swallowed hard. "I've given this a lot of thought, Victor. I'm resigning my commission, effective immediately."

Victor looked over at Galen and then at Deirdre, whose faces reflected his own look of shock. "What are you talking about? You just single-handedly saved our expeditionary force. You're going to have to hire someone to follow you around wearing an extra jacket to display all the medals you'll get out of this. Hell, there aren't enough honors in the Inner Sphere to reward what you've done."

The wounded MechWarrior held up his hand to stop Victor. "Highness, I appreciate more than you know those kind words, but all that is meaningless. You'll be able to read it in my report, but I'll give it to you in the short form now. Not only did I recklessly endanger Dr. Lear, but I issued unsatisfactory orders to one of the demolition teams. I foolishly imagined that the half-dozen armored infantry in the hospital area were the only ones in the hills. I sent some of our men back up to blow the gap, then I engaged another twenty or thirty of the armored Falcons in my *Hatchetman*. I knew there had to be even more of them somewhere, but I didn't try to warn Detloff or his people. The Falcons slaughtered them."

He turned to Deirdre. "Ask her. She was there. She'll tell you." Kai lowered his eyes, his face flushed with shame. "I as good as murdered those men, Victor. I should have known better. I *did* know better, and I did nothing to save them. I deserve a court martial, not a medal."

Victor looked at Deirdre. "Well, Doctor, is it as he said? Did he murder those men?"

Conflicting emotions washed over Lear's face as she seemed to struggle for an answer. She glanced at Kai, then looked down at her own hands and interlaced fingers. When her head came up, though, she gazed at Victor without flinching. "No, he did not," she said. "Those men were already dead. If he had not organized them and organized the evacuation of the hospital, everyone would have died. At least, in the mountains, they were able to die as men."

Victor glanced over at Kai. "You need time to think this over. Galen, take Leftenant Allard to the hospital."

Deirdre got up and started to follow them, but Victor placed a hand on her forearm and held her back. "Please, Doctor, wait a moment."

"As you wish, Highness." She lowered herself into her chair again. "Is there something I can do for you?"

Victor nodded slightly. "Kai is a good friend of mine, and I want to see things go well for him. He has never been a bastion of self-confidence, and as you just witnessed, he is overly harsh in judging himself. Even if he does not resign from the AFFC, he will never again order men into that sort of dangerous situation without more intelligence and more help for them."

Her eyes went cold and her voice was arctic. "What has this to do with me?"

"All right, Doctor," Victor said, putting an edge to his own voice. "You could tell me that this is none of my business, but I won't accept that. Consider it the meddling of a privileged noble or the arrogance of a MechWarrior—I don't care. What I do care about is my friend. The friction between you two is so obvious, but he's never done anything to you. Why do you hate him?"

She opened her mouth, then stopped abruptly and looked at the ground. "I am a doctor. It's my job, my vocation, to succor the injured. I hate war and warriors because of the destruction they cause…"

"Yet you've become part of the Armed Forces of the Federated Commonwealth." Davion shook his head. "Why?"

Deirdre exhaled sharply, set her shoulders, and stood up. "I joined the AFFC to show my family and my friends that I can be loyal to your father and the state you will inherit. I joined because my family owed a debt to the Federated Suns and I was and still am determined to pay off that debt." She matched Victor's hard stare. "I joined because

I will do anything I can to reverse the horrors for which you hand out medals."

Victor ground his teeth, but he kept his temper in check. "All right, I'll give you that, but we should save the discussion of why war is necessary for another time. Just answer me this, then you can go. Why do you hate Kai?"

"That's easy to explain." A cruel smile twisted up the corners of her mouth. "Let me ask you this, Highness. How might you expect me to feel about the son of the man who murdered my father?"

Invasion Command, Wolcott
Pesht Military District, Draconis Combine
2 October 3050

Shin Yodama gave Hohiro Kurita a confident smile and a wink as the Kanrei's son opened a widebeam broadcast to the DropShips sliding into orbit around Wolcott. "*Konnichi wa,* Smoke Jaguars! I am Hohiro Kurita, supreme commander of the forces defending Wolcott. I learned something of your customs while enjoying your hospitality on Turtle Bay, as did my aide, who assisted my escape from that world. To show that we are not total barbarians, I ask you how much force you intend to use in this attack so I may decide which of my resources I shall devote to repulsing your attack."

Standing behind Hohiro near the windows of the command post, Kanrei Theodore Kurita watched his son with obvious pride. He caught Shin's gaze, shared his smile, then turned to look out the large windows. Just barely visible above the horizon to the east, a red-orange ball was rising into the night sky. Two small black dots moved slowly across its shining face. Following them, its silhouette like an arrow, one of the Clan JumpShips came into view.

Shin frowned. It was too much to hope that after Turtle Bay they would not bring one of their warships into a battle. All his people's careful planning and hard work would be worthless if the invaders decided to scour the planet's surface with the weaponry bristling on that battlewagon.

The crackle of a response over the radio turned Shin to face the speaker mounted high on the wall. "I am Galaxy Commander Dietr

Osis. I fear you have drawn incorrect conclusions from your observations of us, Hohiro Kurita. We have come to take the planet and make it our own, and so we do not require you to bargain away your strength…"

"Come now, Galaxy Commander," Hohiro responded quickly. "You know that things could get nasty down here. I must, of course, defend this world against you, but I don't wish to lose more men than is absolutely necessary. As a fellow warrior, you can understand that. I desire to know how much force you will use in your attack so I can allocate my forces accordingly."

Utter disbelief underscored Osis's reply. "Are you saying you will not commit everything you have in defense of Wolcott? You are willing to use only part of your forces in a battle to decide who will own this world?"

A smile spread across Hohiro's face, but he kept his voice neutral. "I see that you understand my proposition precisely. I will, as has been our custom, forward to you the service records and history of my units. It will not take you long to see that I have cobbled them together from the dregs of our society. Mind you, they have all volunteered to serve, but bold heart alone does not a MechWarrior make. Yes, I am prepared to use only part of my forces to defend Wolcott, provided the details can be worked out."

"Details? Please elaborate."

Hohiro glanced out the window at the JumpShip's silhouette. "You will attempt to conquer this world, a great prize should you win. I, on the other hand, battle for no special prize."

Osis's reply came back warily. "I could offer a promise of no further attempts at conquering your world if you defeat me." The tone of his voice left no doubt in Shin's mind that the Clansman believed Wolcott's sun would go nova before that ever happened.

"I appreciate that gesture," Hohiro sighed, "but such a promise would bind only you. Upon your death or demotion, another attack would follow almost immediately, and certainly without the civility you now show. I had hoped for something more concrete if we defeat you."

"Such as?"

Hohiro crossed his fingers. "Four of your frontline BattleMechs and two dozen of your power-armored suits."

The Galaxy Commander barked a sharp laugh. "Out of the question!"

"Why is that?" Hohiro asked in an offended tone. "You yourself believe the chances of my victory are non-existent. After the battle,

278

when I again escape your custody and make my way back to my own people, I will need an explanation of my actions to save my reputation. Capturing some of your war materiel is an important enough goal that my superiors will understand my gamble. The least you can do is honor me with the illusion that I am a threat worthy of such an exchange."

The radio fell silent for fifteen to twenty seconds, then Osis's voice returned. His answer came slowly as though he knew he would later regret his words. "Very well. If you defeat me, I will see that you receive four of our BattleMechs and two dozen suits of battle armor. I also promise that Wolcott will retain its independence if we are defeated. As for the force I will use, I tell you that it will total no more than roughly half of whatever force you offer."

Shin narrowed his eyes. *With their increased firepower, that should make them about even with us in sheer destructive capabilities. By controlling the battlefield and using terrain to our advantage, we have a shot at defeating them.*

Hohiro, his smile becoming a wide grin, nodded slowly. "It is a pleasure to deal with such a reasonable and honorable man. I will meet you at the head of the Yuutsu—the Blue Devils—in the *numachi no tanima* district fifteen myriameters north of my current position. In four hours? My technicians will transmit the files on the Blue Devils immediately. I will be using both regiments."

"Four hours, then."

"And Commander, don't worry," Hohiro added in one final barb. "If you survive a defeat, I will treat you better than your people treated me."

Hohiro punched a button, immediately cutting off the microphone. He turned to his father. "Well, what do you think?"

Theodore crossed to his son and rested both his hands on Hohiro's shoulders. "You did very well, my son. Osis will be uneasy, wondering if he has been manipulated, and angry at your affront. That should provide him with some serious distractions."

The Kanrei looked at Shin. "*Chu-sa,* if you would be so kind…"

Shin stood at attention. "Kanrei?"

"Please radio *Tai-sa* Narimasa Asano and tell him we will join his newly christened Blue Devils in Swamp Valley shortly." Theodore smiled wolfishly. "In four hours, we will hand the invaders the first of many bloody defeats."

With mist rising from its brackish water and its thick, vine-laden mangrove forests, Swamp Valley reminded Shin of some demon-haunted domain from the terror tales he had listened to so avidly as a child. Gasses bubbled up in great roiling burps, bringing up viscous black sludge. Reptiles, propelled by the slow undulation of their armored tails, swam through the swamp as though resentful of this invasion but secretly waiting for men to leave their metal shells and become dinner.

With his new *Phoenix Hawk* standing next to Hohiro's *Trebuchet* and Narimasa Asano's *Crusader*, Shin studied the modifications to the battlefield, which were certain to distract and confuse the invaders. Within the swamp's leafy green canopy, thousands of metallic streamers hung like tinsel on a Christian Christmas tree. Shimmering silver and gold, the streamers contained just enough metal to make the whole forest magscan as though it were made of steel, effectively hiding the army of 'Mechs waiting within its dark heart.

To further conceal the Genyosha 'Mechs, the warriors had been ordered to shut down the heat exchangers in the torsos and arms of their machines. The only heat sinks left operating were those in the legs. Submerged in the swamp water, they were more than able to dissipate the heat generated by an idling fusion engine. Aside from raising the infrared output for the swamp in general, that precaution made the 'Mechs virtually invisible to heat scans.

All the 'Mechs have been painted with a camouflage pattern that makes them difficult to see in the swamps, and the radar jammers will take that scanning mode away from them. Shin looked through the swamp to the vast delta downstream of his position. *After they land down there, they'll have to get within spitting distance to see us. The swamp is too wet to burn down, so they'll have to play cat and mouse with us, but on a battlefield of our choosing.*

Two eggshaped DropShips made a pass over the delta, then circled back around to hover over a sandbar. The DropShips didn't lower their landing gear, but remained at approximately ten meters above the ground. The 'Mech bay doors irised open and BattleMechs dropped to the ground in rapid succession. As they hit, they moved out and forward, establishing a perimeter and taking advantage of the little cover offered by sandbars or debris.

Shin marveled at their efficiency. *Their pilots have to be masters to hold a ship that even and level while hundreds of tons of war machines move to the door and jump out. Either they have incredibly steady hands on the controls, or their level of computer control and command integration is beyond anything we can even imagine. And the MechWarriors, too. They jump clear and move to their positions without hesitation. They seem to work in sets of five and with a coor-*

dination that suggests they've undergone intensive training together.

A rain of smaller armored figures followed the 'Mechs out of the hatch, but they and four of the BattleMechs hung back as the other machines pushed their perimeter further out. *Osis honors his bargain. There is our prize, just waiting for us to win it. I am certain he thinks to taunt us with it, but maybe it's we who will have the last laugh.*

Hohiro's voice reverberated through his neurohelmet. "This is it, Shin. I'd wish you luck, but you already have more than enough of it."

With the flick of a finger, Shin brought his targeting computer on line. "Luck will play no part in this, *Sho-sa* Kurita. This is the endgame. You have already beaten the invaders, Highness. Now we just need to remind them of it."

"*Hai, Chu-sa* Yodama. That's what we will do right now."

Shin heard a series of clicks over his headphones, then saw icons move on his holographic display. At the same moment, wickedly fast little hovercraft shot out into the delta from the swamp forest that bordered it on three sides. Little more than a cockpit sandwiched between a medium laser in front and a fan in back, the inappropriately named Savannah Masters closed on the invaders. In datastacks, the vehicles looked worthless because of their light armor and relatively weak weaponry, but their hellacious speed made them deucedly awkward to hit. As they streaked in, their lasers stabbed out at targets but did little more than boil some armor away.

The invaders concentrated their attention and fire on the small hovercraft weaving twisted paths through their formation. That gave the heavier, slower hovercraft in the Yuutsu force a chance to move to the edge of the swamp and launch missile and autocannon salvos at the Clansmen. Armor lances concentrated their fire on specific targets, pounding their foes with devastating amounts of energy and projectiles. Shin saw one *Daishi* splash down on its face, and another 'Mech, one he had designated a *Koshi*, spun to its knees with one arm limply hanging at its side.

Suddenly aware of this new threat, the invaders ignored the Savannah Masters and turned to vent their anger on the Drillson and Saracen hover tanks, but the tanks simply melted back into the forest and vanished from scanner contact. The Savannah Masters, skipping across the delta and sandbars like flat stones flung by some child, likewise took refuge in the forest. Before they had a chance to strike back, the invaders found themselves with casualties but no targets.

The Smoke Jaguars pushed out and started a drive toward the center of the Combine's waiting forces. As the 'Mech Shin had tagged *Hagetaka,* for its vulturelike head and bird-legs, stalked toward his position, it suddenly sank beneath the water. The tops of the twin missile racks on its shoulders bobbed up to the surface for a second, then a geyser of gray water and white foam shot up into the sky. Two subsidiary explosions jolted ripples through the delta and sent debris out to pelt the roiling surface with a ceramic rain. Bubbles and steam rising in a thick rope marked the *Hagetaka's* passing.

Watching the destruction, Shin told himself that dredging out tiger pits and lining them with vibrabombs might be dishonorable, but they had to do it. *As the Kanrei said, "Honor is a thin cloak against the chill of a grave."*

As a second invader BattleMech, this one a *Koshi*, vanished from sight, a blue LED glowed on Shin's command console. Shin reached out and touched a button bringing his weapons computer on line, and the fusion engines shunted power to the *Phoenix Hawk's* large laser and the twin medium lasers mounted on the 'Mech's forearms. *Now we give them a taste of our power, then we melt into the forest just as our armor did before. For the first time, these invaders will know they have a fight on their hands.*

Shin, in concert with the two Genyosha/Yuutsu regiments, stepped his 'Mech forward to the edge of the swamp forest. He trained all his weapons on a *Masakari*. The crosshairs pulsed twice as the 'Mech's squat torso filled the holographic display, and as the invader brought his 'Mech's paired PPCs up, Shin fired all three of his weapons.

The medium laser's bloody beam sliced through the armor shell of the LRM launch canister perched on the *Masakari's* left shoulder. The other one burned a dark scar in the armor over the 'Mech's left breast, slashing in half the gray jaguar icon painted there. At the same time, the invader's particle projection cannons stabbed blue-white bolts of man-made lightning into the *Phoenix Hawk's* left thigh and arm. Armor exploded as the beam's hellish heat instantly converted it to vapor.

Shin fought against the recoil to keep his 'Mech facing forward. The computer cycled energy into the large laser, which coalesced it into a series of luminous green quarrels. The stuttering beam pounded the *Masakari's* jutting head mercilessly, blasting half-melted armor fragments back to ricochet off the 'Mech's broad chest. The war machine staggered slightly, letting the PPCs dip toward the water, then the pilot seemed to regain control of his machine.

Before they could exchange another series of shots, a cloud of beams, missiles, and projectiles from others in the Kurita force slammed into the *Masakari*. Sizzling slugs from a half-dozen auto-cannon drove the 'Mech to its knees. Lasers boiled armor from it, mottling its smooth flesh with wounds that dripped molten ceramics. A swarm of short-range missiles converged on it and bathed it in fire. When the flames dissipated, the smoking, misshapen BattleMech lurched forward, then fell on its face. Hissing clouds of steam shrouded the blackened corpse.

The blue light on his command console died, so Shin backed his 'Mech away to allow the foliage and metal foil to hide him. His last look at the battlefield showed a dozen incapacitated invaders and at least twenty other 'Mechs that had lost the function of one or more limbs. The rest showed signs of damage, though it was mostly armor damage. As for his own troops, Shin spotted two downed light 'Mechs and a half-dozen places where trees at the forest edge had been turned into torches.

None of the invaders moved. *It's finally sunk in that they bit off a tad more than they can chew. This waiting game will get them killed, and their leader is a fool if he doesn't recognize that fact.* Shin studied the delta through some breaks in the tinsel-strewn brush. *What's going on? I don't understand this.*

Out in the killing ground, the majority of the Smoke Jaguars moved their BattleMechs back to a line behind the four 'Mechs and two dozen figures in battle armor. A few war machines checked their downed comrades. Where they found signs of life, Shin presumed, they ripped the pilot's compartment from the 'Mech or otherwise assisted the pilot in escaping, then marched off to join the others until only one 'Mech, a humanoid *Ryoken,* stood between the troops and the forests. That 'Mech raised its arms, which ended in double-barreled large lasers, and Shin heard the crackle-pop of a widebeam radio broadcast in his neurohelmet.

"I am Galaxy Commander Dietr Osis. I freely admit my responsibility in this defeat and absolve my command of any implication of wrong-doing. I salute you, Hohiro Kurita, and your Yuutsu. You chose the time, place, and nature of our meeting. I see now I was defeated before a shot was ever fired." The 'Mech lowered its arms and cracked the cockpit canopy. "Do what must be done and you can claim your prize."

Shin frowned. *Do what must be done? What in the nine hells is he talking about? Does he think we would not grant him the time to kill himself and absolve his family of the shame of his defeat?*

Almost immediately, Hohiro's voice filled his ears. "Shin, you don't think he wants us to arrange a *seppuku* ceremony for him, do you?"

"I don't know, Highness. I am at a loss to suggest an answer."

Out in the delta, a figure appeared on the *Ryoken,* stepping from the cockpit to the 'Mech's broad shoulders and up to the top of its head. The man opened his arms wide and again Shin heard Osis's voice. "Please, I beg your indulgence. I know I deserve your scorn, but I *am* a warrior. Do not break me. That I could not stand."

The hopelessness in Osis's plea struck a chord in Shin, somehow dredging up the memory of the armored soldiers in Uramachi. *This is as strange now as the invaders' actions seemed when they started to raze that ghetto. Somehow I know I should do something for Osis—the desperation in his words tells me that much—but what does he want?* "Highness, perhaps he wants us to take him captive to prove that he has value. Then, with that amount of his honor regained, he will kill himself."

"Yes, Shin, perhaps that is it."

Osis's arms fell to his sides. "I understand. You are right, after what I have done here, I have no more claim to the title of warrior. Please, do not have them destroy my children."

Shin shook his head to clear it. *Destroy his children! We are not butchers! What children is he talking about? What does he mean?*

One of the armored soldiers broke from the formation, and with three incredible leaps, reached the *Ryoken,* then landed on its shoulder. He raised his right arm and triggered the cylindrical laser on his right arm. Osis's headless body tumbled end over end to the muddy water below where huge lizards began to converge on it.

In returning to the ranks of its fellows, the armored figure passed another 'Mech coming out to the fore. A new voice forced itself into Shin's ears. "We regret the oath that prevents us from again attempting to take this world, for there have been few worthy foes in the campaign thus far. With your leave, we will call our ships and depart." Static hissed through a momentary pause, then the voice added, "Do you wish to have the Commander's children destroyed?"

Hohiro's answer came without a moment's hesitation. "No! We do not want his offspring slain. And yes, do call your ships. Leave at once."

Shin immediately shifted his radio over to the command frequency. "*Sho-sa* Hohiro-*sama*, what do you make of that madness?"

"I don't know and I don't understand." Hohiro sounded as unnerved as Shin felt.

"What does it matter, for now, my son?" asked Theodore Kurita.

284

"Let us be content with having accomplished what no one else has been able to do: we have beaten this invader and wrested from him 'Mechs that hold the secret of incredible power. At no time in the history of man has there ever been so great a victory, and in this place and at this time, that is all that matters."

Phelan Kell stepped into the viewing gallery overlooking the *Dire Wolf*'s bridge, fully expecting to find it empty. The presence of another individual snapped him out of the daze in which he'd been wandering. "Forgive me, Precentor Martial. I did not know you would be here." He glanced over his shoulder as the door slid shut. "I will leave you."

Anastasius Focht held his hand up. "No. I am here specifically to see you." The white-haired man smiled and pointed down at the bridge deck where Ulric stood in conversation with the ilKhan. "To see you and to observe from here, as the ilKhan objects to my presence on the bridge."

The younger man tugged unconsciously at the bondcord on his right wrist. "Yeah, everyone's getting testy around here, aren't they? This meeting of the different clan leaders has them all on edge."

Focht nodded thoughtfully, then his hands disappeared into the sleeves of his white robe. "True enough. I would give much to learn what is at the heart of this invasion."

Like an animal with hackles, Phelan sensed danger almost immediately. "It seems to me, Precentor Martial, that you know more about the Clans' true intentions than anyone else in the Inner Sphere except the Clansmen themselves."

Focht smiled distractedly, then clasped his hands behind his back and began to pace the narrow room. "Do not underestimate your own

286

knowledge of their tactics and ways of battle. Yet, neither of us knows what truly motivates these Clans. Someone as intelligent as you must sense hidden purpose in all this."

Phelan nodded as he looked down on the bridge. In addition to the usual complement of bridge officers, he saw even more Clansmen whose clothing patches marked them as members of the Ghost Bear, Smoke Jaguar, and Jade Falcon clans. Most of them, he knew, had arrived a week earlier on three different JumpShips. As nearly as he had been able to determine through overheard snatches of conversation and innocently asked questions, they had come to demand and negotiate the details of a meeting of all the Khans involved in the invasion.

Phelan turned to the ComStar man. "We both recognize rivalries among the Clans, and unless I miss my guess, the early launching of the Wolves' last wave really set the others off. I also gather that the Combine handed the Smoke Jaguars their heads on one world, and that the Commonwealth has made trouble for the Jade Falcons. The Bears have just been slow in consolidating their holdings, all of which means the Wolves, in this warrior society, are top dogs—no pun intended."

Focht's head came up. "Good. Your information is correct, and at some point, I can provide you with some details of the various assaults. For now, let me say that the Kell Hounds were the linchpin of the victory in the Commonwealth."

Well, dammit, it's about bloody time! Phelan smiled more cheerfully than he had in months. "Thank you, Precentor. I owe you one."

Phelan failed to fathom the bemused look that cycled over the Precentor's face. Focht killed it quickly enough as he posed another question. "Have you noticed other divisions within the Clans, one that breaks through Clan lines?"

Phelan gave it some thought, frowning with concentration. "Not really a *division* of the Clans…but I have noted a split in attitude that I attributed to my being a bondsman. Some of the Clansmen seem to accept me freely, or at least view me with curiosity. Others react as though I'm a kind of subhuman. It's like Ulric and Vlad down there on the bridge. Ulric has helped me in return for help, whereas Vlad held me in contempt from the start."

"This dichotomy is not limited to bondsmen, I can assure you." An edge crept into the Precentor's voice as he watched the ilKhan wander around on the bridge. "Khan Ulric felt it would be good for me to observe the formalities of a Grand Council first hand, but the ilKhan banished me as though I were unworthy of such an honor. I don't believe Ulric ever intended for me to attend the Grand Council, but the ilKhan's reaction cost Leo some face and won Ulric a concession for this meeting."

Phelan raised an eyebrow. "What was that?"

"The *Dire Wolf* will be the only flagship at the meeting. The other Khans will have to arrive in smaller JumpShips. Ulric also managed to set the meeting place for Radstadt, a world well in front of anyone else's line of advance. Its selection reinforces the Wolf Clan's superiority in the invasion."

The mercenary chuckled lightly. "Ulric does know how to play political games very well."

The Precentor grunted agreement. "One wonders how to determine when the games end." Focht opened his hands to take in the viewing room. "You and I must both be considered enemies to the Clans, yet Ulric has allowed us to view their activities from here and from the bridge itself. What possible reason would he have to do this?"

The younger man shook his head. "I cannot answer that, Precentor, but I will admit I constantly find myself in testing situations. It almost seems that he lets us watch him so he can watch us and see how we react."

The Precentor Martial turned back from the bridge to face Phelan. "I understand that sense of being constantly tested, and I think you're right about it. I sense, too, that Ulric is keeping something hidden from me. Because he plays his games so well, it's hard to know if he truly intends to keep the information hidden, or whether he wants me to know it is hidden so I can ferret it out. And if that latter case is true, why would he want me to learn something that is supposed to be confidential?"

"Whoa." The Kell Hound held up his hands. "Those kinds of speculations will have you running in such circles that it'll drive you crazy in the end. Even if there is something that Ulric wants you to discover, getting that information won't be easy. In case it's slipped your attention, we're in the middle of the enemy camp and we've both been identified as enemy agents. Furthermore, such spying would take technical expertise and equipment we don't have."

Again a look of amusement spread over the Precentor Martial's face. "As I understand it, you have developed the power to walk through locked doors."

All of a sudden, the boxy sonic lockpick in Phelan's left pocket felt as though its mass had increased a thousandfold. *Why the hell didn't Griff get rid of this thing after Vlad beat me up?* "Wait a minute! We've suddenly gone from an idle discussion of the Khan to a subject that caused me a painful experience. I swore an oath to Ulric that I would not attempt to communicate information about the Clans to anyone. He fulfilled his side of the bargain we struck. I cannot go back on my word."

"Admirable," Focht acknowledged, holding out his right hand to Phelan. "Give me the device and show me how it works. I will do the rest and I will even say I stole it from you."

Three rich tones sounded through the ship, warning everyone of the impending jump to Radstadt. Without thinking, Phelan moved to the couch with its back to the bridge and sat down. "I don't think so, Precentor. It would be a violation of my word to do so."

Focht nodded and sat beside him. "As I said before, your sense of honor is admirable."

"But?"

"But is misplaced here." Focht pulled the restraining straps from the crack between the back and the seat of the couch. "It is vital for us to know the true intentions of people as powerful as these Clansmen," he said, strapping himself in. "You have the means to help me gather this information."

The Precentor paused, smiling and sure of himself. "If you help me in this, Phelan, I will let your family know you're alive."

Focht's offer hit Phelan unexpectedly. Images of his father and mother and sister floated up from where he had carefully tucked them away, overwhelming him with a wave of sadness. He sighed heavily. "Khan Ulric is not the only one who plays the game well."

Remorse seamed the older man's face. "Forgive me, Phelan. I would not have played that trump card except that the Primus herself directed me. Obtaining the information I want is of the utmost importance, and only by making that shameful offer could I convince you of the fact."

The Primus told him to use that tactic on me? This is very important, isn't it? The mercenary fixed the Precentor with an angry stare. "That message would never have reached my family, would it?"

Focht shook his head.

"Do you always do what others tell you to do?"

Focht faced forward and his one eye focused distantly. "There was a time I would have been arrogant enough to say that no one gave me orders, but I have become wiser with age. I realize the importance of my mission among the Clans and I mean to accomplish it." A wry grin twisted up the corners of his mouth as he turned to the mercenary.

"In case it has slipped your attention, the Clans are rapidly conquering the Inner Sphere. Knowing what they want means we can find a way to appease them or defeat them."

Phelan raked the fingers of one hand through his hair, then covered his face with both hands. *Focht is right. I have to decide if I owe more loyalty to my family and my nation or to the man who claims to own me. Stated like that, it's an easy choice, so why am I having trouble making my decision? Why does part of me think the Inner Sphere deserves all this? Does DJ's death and my getting punted from the Nagelring still anger me so, or is it that this warrior society is so seductive because of the way it forces its people to be their best? Can I allow myself to be infatuated with a society that has, as its main focus, destruction?*

The idea of betraying Ulric conjured up more unease and more questions. *Could it be that the Khan has thrown us together so we can discover secrets about the Clans that could aid our own people? He's given me almost as much information as Justin Allard carried away from the Capellan Confederation in the Fourth War, and he certainly has to acknowledge ComStar as a possible conduit for information going to the enemy. The Wolves are trying to have as little effect as possible on the worlds they conquer. Could Ulric be secretly working against a war he does not believe is right? And if so, are the two of us his tools for getting that information to the Successor States?*

Phelan's hands fell away from his face as he reluctantly made a decision. "All right. I'll help you."

The Precentor held out his hand, but Phelan shook his head. "No, not right now and not this device. Give me some time to figure out what sort of stuff we'll need so we don't get caught. Hell, security will be very tight during this Grand Council, and if we wait, we might get more information than before."

Focht nodded, then helped Phelan strap himself into his seat as a series of five warning tones sounded. The mercenary glanced over at the large round porthole in the hull of the ship and watched the stars burning there. At the moment of jump, the stars flattened out as though smashed with a hammer. Their light stretched into disks that overlapped and whitewashed the blackness of the void. At the same time, Phelan felt as though he and the ship were reduced from three dimensions to two and then one and then none. For a time too short to be noticed but too long to be ignored, he knew everything because he had become one with reality.

Then the universe unfolded again and gave him back his life and identity. Barely a second had passed since the jump began, but the *Dire Wolf* had traveled over eight parsecs. It materialized at the nadir jump point, and the star about which Radstadt orbited shone down on them.

Through the porthole, Phelan saw another JumpShip materialize

290

and then another. *The other Khans arrive promptly,* he found himself thinking, as more and more JumpShips appeared. *Wait! Those aren't Clan ships. God in heaven, what's happening?*

Warning klaxons blared loudly. Blast shields irised down to cut off the mercenary's view of the space surrounding the *Dire Wolf* so Phelan slapped the release on his safety belt's buckle and turned to watch the bridge. Below, crew members scrambled and sprinted toward battle stations. Vlad took up a position at a scanner station on the bridge's starboard side. The holotank surrounded Ulric with countless images of ships large and small, and the wall-mounted viewscreens used during battle-bidding flashed to life with a tally of the forces available to the *Dire Wolf.* Below that, in a small box in the corner of the screen, a list of the forces being brought to bear against the *Dire Wolf* scrolled off the bottom, yet continued to flash as the sensors located more threats.

Phelan looked at the old man beside him. "We've been ambushed!"

"By the other Clans, or someone else?"

The mercenary shrugged. "I don't know that," Phelan growled, "but there's one thing I do know. This is where we find out if the Wolves are really as good as they seem."

The horn mounted in the wall just above her berth on the *Raven* blasted out a call to battle stations just after the last wave of nausea from the jump passed over Tyra Miraborg. *What in hell could it be? We've been leapfrogging our way between uninhabited stars for two months now. There's no way they could have tracked us or anticipated our arrival at Radstadt! If some idiot decided we're due a drill, I'll have his head!*

She jerked to her feet, then leaned heavily against the cabin bulkhead as her head swam. She swallowed hard and fought to clear her head. The second the vertigo began to fade, she pulled open the door to her clothes locker and stepped into her scarlet flightsuit. While zipping up the front of the garment and fastening the velcro tighteners on her wrist, she slipped into flight boots that snapped shut around her calves. She grabbed her gloves with one hand, and stepping into the corridor, pulled the door to her cabin shut behind her.

All the other pilots in the Drakøns raced toward the aft launch bays on the *Vengeance* Class DropShip. Tyra, seeing a bottleneck near the lift to the upper two launch decks, headed up a service ladder. One level up, she swung off it and tumbled to the deck as the *Raven* detached itself from the JumpShip that had brought it to this battlefield. The DropShip's engines sent a tremor through the hull and filled the ship with a low growl.

Tyra scrambled to her feet and dashed over to where her *Shilone* waited in the launch bay. She hauled herself up into the cockpit, pulled on her neurohelmet, and snapped the cable coming from it into a socket by her left shoulder. As she struggled to pull on her safety straps and fasten them across her chest, the sounds of a mission briefing already underway came over her helmet speakers.

"We have four, repeat, four invader JumpShips already in-system. One is the size of their planetbusters. The other three are smaller ships. The big one must be their flagship. That is priority target for the fleet…"

Great, just great. We don't get to fight them on Rasalhague when we're all in top shape. We wait to engage the enemy until two months of hiding in space has frazzled everyone. Even as Tyra's anger began to flare, she struggled to curb and channel it. *No, this is not the time to get so mad you can't see. You've got your wingmate and your flight to worry about, and you've got some damage to do to that flagship. Act now and complain later.*

She punched a button on her console and flash-started the engine. The cockpit canopy slid down into place. At her right hand, a number pad's keys lit up. Because a flash-start did not allow for the computer to cycle through the full series of recognition signs and countersigns to ensure that the pilot was assigned to this particular craft, Tyra had to type in an eight-digit number code she herself had chosen to safeguard her machine. *Zero-four, two-eight, three-zero three-six; the day my father lost the use of his legs. It's a date I'll never forget, yet no one else would ever expect me to use it as my code.*

In response to the numbers, the engines throttled up to full power and the weapons computer came on line. It filled the cockpit with a holographic display of the battlefield outside and painted the targeting sight over her right eye on the faceplate of her helmet. The trigger handles rotated up and locked in position, and her auxiliary monitor reported all weapons loaded, armed, and ready.

Tyra opened a frequency to launch control. "Valkyrie One ready for launch. Request go!"

"Go granted."

She punched both feet down on the thruster pedals. The *Shilone* lunged forward, then sped down the launch alley. The metallic walls became a solid silver blur as the square black hole at the end of the runway grew like a mouth intending to swallow her ship. As her velocity indicator climbed past 700 kph, her ship shot free of the *Raven*.

The sight of so many JumpShips, DropShips, and AeroSpace Fighters in one place threatened to overwhelm Tyra's senses. *This is*

*the Götterdämmerung! So many people, so many war machines, so
much death. I've waited a long time for this, for a chance to avenge
Phelan and prove myself to my father. Beware, invaders, you are mine
now.*

Tyra suddenly realized that the enemy had not launched their
fighters. Only the largest ship seemed to have launch bays, though
their presence could not be utterly discounted on the other ships.
*Fighters are going to be most vulnerable as they leave the launch bays.
If I can get in close, I can do some serious damage.*

Before she could put her thoughts into action, Anika Janssen's
Shilone appeared on Tyra's starboard wing. "The biggest target is
bound to be the easiest to hit, eh, boss?"

"Right, Nik. Stay close. If either of us is hit, we break off, right?"

"Roger."

Tyra spiraled her *Shilone* down away from the *Raven* and kicked
it into a long dive toward the invaders' flagship. Without gravity to aid
it, the fighter picked up no speed as it streaked toward the massive
JumpShip, and because of the battlefield's proximity to the orange-
yellow star at the center of the solar system, Tyra had to increase power
to maintain her speed. Anika's ship lagged behind by a few hundred
meters, but slowly caught up to reach Tyra's side when they engaged
the first flight of fighters from the flagship.

"Nik, fire once, then punch it. We'll burst by them, drop an SRM
volley, and leave them to the others." Tyra flipped her radio to a
broader tactical channel. "Valkyrie One, here. We need some assist in
sector Alpha Xray Two Four. Enemy fighters, two by two."

"Roger, Valkyrie One. Fenir Three and Four on our way."

"And Aesir One and Two as well, Valkyrie One. Save us
something."

"Roger." Tyra launched a full volley of long-range missiles, then
brought the *Shilone*'s nose up to carry the ship above the LRM's line
of attack. The missiles shot down at the nearest of the invader
aerofighters, spattering the boxy craft over its nose and right wing.
Tyra stared at the icon representing that fighter on her holographic
display, then tightened her fingers on the trigger buttons. The large
laser shot from the *Shilone*'s nose and burned a furrow through the
armor on the invader's aft turret while the ruby beams from the wing-
mounted medium lasers did more damage to the craft's nose and right
wing.

The invader's return fire shot wide and low, leaving Tyra's ship
intact. She sensed that her enemy was an inexperienced pilot and an
easy kill, but she stayed with her original plan. *All the fighter kills I get*

will mean nothing if we can't take out that big ship. She stomped on the foot pedals and cranked the *Shilone*'s speed up to 1800 kph. Depressing the thumb button on the left joystick dropped a flight of SRMs to discourage pursuit as she dove hard on the flagship.

All around her, DropShips that had detached themselves from their JumpShips likewise shot toward the invaders' fleet. Outside the grip of planetary gravity and free of a buffeting atmosphere, those ungainly, bulbous craft became lethal weapons-platforms. Bristling with missile launchers and laser muzzles, the DropShips rode argent ion flames down toward the invaders' fleet. In more than one case, the ship's captain had opened the 'Mech bay doors, allowing BattleMechs to stand in the opening to add their token firepower to the ship's weapons rather than remain helpless inside their cocoons.

As her *Shilone* swept in on the largest invader ship, Tyra realized why it had been described as a planetbuster. Dozens of DropShips studded the wasplike ship like metallic warts rising from its glossy black flesh. They had docked with their jets pointing toward the interior of the ship, which meant all of their weaponry could be brought to bear on the attackers. In addition, the JumpShip itself boasted numerous gunnery turrets and missile launchers. From various ports on the DropShips and the JumpShip, Clan BattleMechs crawled out and clung to the hull, hoping for a shot at a fighter that strayed too close.

Tyra angled thrust deflectors to take her in a long loop toward the JumpShip's bow. With Anika on her tail, she stood the *Shilone* on its right wing and dove down toward the hull. She launched a volley of LRMs that splattered themselves against the bridge's closed blast shields, then hugged the artificial landscape and began a long strafing run down the ship's spine.

Almost instantly, she recognized a flaw in the ship's design. A narrow valley ran down between the two parts of the hull that had been built up for DropShip docking. By taking her aerofighter to the deck, she flew low enough that the DropShips could not target her craft for fear of doing damage to the JumpShip itself. The valley, while not wide on a planetary scale, provided her just enough room for maneuvers that made hitting her ship very difficult. In her first run, Tyra knocked out two PPC turrets, and toward the end, she bobbed up out of the valley to pepper the hull of a DropShip with a flight of LRMs.

Her ship sped past the JumpShip. *Dammit, no solar sail to waste. That would keep them here for a long time.* She checked her display and saw Anika had likewise survived the trip down the JumpShip's back. "Split-S, Nik, and we make another run."

295

"Roger, I'll go right. And this time," her friend demanded, "I go first."

"Lead on, Nik. I'm right behind you." Tyra vectored thrust to the right, carrying her fighter high and to the left. She brought the right wing up, executing a quick turn, then dove down to the spine level on the JumpShip, following Anika's *Shilone* in on the run. They both resisted the temptation to send a flight of missiles up into the Jump-Ship's exhaust ports because they knew the ion thrust would vaporize the warheads before they could do any damage.

"I'm getting a reading up front, Tyra. No more turrets. We took them out. Must be a mudbug crawled down here to stop us." A trace of anxiety seeped into Anika's voice. "No, dammit, it's two of them! Going in high, you cut them off at the knees!"

Anika's aerofighter pulled up, and Tyra saw laser beams lance down from her comrade's fighter. Cerulean bolts of PPC lightning shot back up from the target, carving armor from Anika's nose and left wing. Her ship drifted upward and out of sight as Tyra's *Shilone* swooped like a hawk over the BattleMechs anchored to the hull against the JumpShip's thrust.

The LRM flight she used to announce her arrival badly battered one of the two 'Mechs. The explosions knocked the war machine from its broad, flat feet and bounced it off the solid valley wall. Arms and legs flailing, the 'Mech rebounded from the crushed wall and careened off into space. Something exploded on one of its shoulders, the blue sparks playing hob all over its flesh as it, too, drifted up and out of Tyra's sight.

The second 'Mech stood its ground. Her computer informed her that the BattleMech had already taken damage from Anika's run, but somehow that did not matter to her. *I don't care what you have or what condition you're in, you're mine. For Nik and for Phelan and for all the Drakøns who died on Rasalhague.* Without conscious effort, she stared hard directly at the center of the 'Mech's broad humanoid chest. Ignoring the PPC fire just over her head, she let the 'Mech have everything her fighter could offer.

The trio of lasers focused dead-center on the BattleMech's chest. The glowing hole they opened spat out hot shards of armor and internal structures. The 'Mech's heat silhouette flared like a supernova. An internal detonation plumped the lean torso out into that of an old man, then the armor buckled as golden claws of fire sliced their way through its middle. As the upper half of the 'Mech evaporated in the fire from its fusion engine, its legs flew out to career back and forth within the valley's narrow confines.

296

Tyra pulled up to avoid the fireball and ran head-on into a flight of SRMs from a nearby DropShip. The missiles exploded against her cockpit, and the flash momentarily blinded her. The jolt shook her as much as the explosions had shaken her ship, but she forced herself to ignore it until she could regain control of her fighter. Kicking in the afterburners, she whirled the craft into a long spiral that took it away toward the JumpShip's bow.

"Tyra! Tyra!"

The urgency of Anika's shout shocked Tyra out of a fog. *My God, zoning out like that in a battle...I must be hit bad.* She recognized a tightness around her right elbow and across her chest, but it took a moment or two for her to realize that it came from her vacuum suit's attempt to localize a breach. The wail of warning sirens suddenly impinged on her brain, and as she brought the primary monitor into focus, she realized her cockpit had been breached. She brought her left hand up to her right shoulder, where it encountered something very hard and came away bloody.

"Tyra, talk to me!"

"I'm here, Nik. How are you?"

"Circuit overload from the PPCs shut my engine down. I'm not having any luck restarting. I'll take it all the way off, then do a full restart. That's not important. How are you?"

"I'm hit, Nik. It's pretty bad." Tyra choked down the lump in her throat. "I love you, you know. I'm glad you can't follow me."

"No, Tyra. Don't do anything stupid. Get your ship over here. I can help you."

"Too late for that, Nik. If you see my father, tell him I made him proud." Tyra cut off her radio and boosted the *Shilone* forward. She flipped off two safety switches. One cut the warning klaxons and the other removed all restraints on engine power. *These ships have more power than a human pilot can normally take. At full power, a pilot will black out, but that doesn't really matter now, does it?*

She laughed aloud and liked the sound. *I've not laughed like that or felt this carefree since Phelan left Gunzburg. How fitting. I'll be with him soon enough.*

Bringing the *Shilone*'s nose down, she let the ship flip over onto its head, then she rolled it over so she could watch the JumpShip's bridge loom ever larger in her viewscreen. *This is it. The Iron Jarl makes another sacrifice for Rasalhague.* Pushing both overthruster pedals to the cockpit floor with her feet, she flew faster than any human ever and kept the *Shilone* dead on target.

JumpShip Dire Wolf, *Nadir Jump Point, Radstadt*
Radstadt Province, Free Rasalhague Republic
31 October 3050

Phelan Kell and the Precentor Martial raced down the corridor toward the *Dire Wolf*'s bridge. Hot on the heels of their escort, they had to use a service ladder to get down from the observation deck, forcing them to head away from the bridge before they could reach it.

As they sprinted down the last thirty meters to the bridge, the whole JumpShip lurched as though struck by some godling's hammer. Phelan stumbled forward, but tucked himself into a roll to absorb the energy. His guide slammed into a corridor wall and smacked his head hard. He slipped to the deck and the Precentor Martial slid nose-up into him.

Jesus Christ, what was that? Phelan shook himself as he unfolded his body and braced for a second impact or subsidiary explosion. He glanced over at the Precentor Martial. "You all right?"

Focht reseated his eye-patch and nodded. "Yes, but our guide isn't. What happened?"

Phelan shrugged as he crawled back to the man's unconscious form. He plucked the radio from his belt and flicked it on. "Damage control, get a team up here to the bridge. We have a problem. And get a medical team up here, too."

"Who is this? Are you calling from the bridge?" Unbridled terror made the words crackle from the radio.

"No. I'm in the corridor outside the bridge. Something exploded in there or hit it."

298

The repair Tech's oath shouted from the radio. "Freebirth! Something opened a hole in the hull. The automatic systems are sealing it, but we have atmosphere loss. Team's on the way. Medical, too."

The mercenary looked up at the Precentor Martial and shook his head. "If you have atmosphere loss, bring up EVA suits and extra oxygen gear."

The Damage Control Officer's voice calmed considerably. "Confirmed, Commander. On the way."

Focht smiled warily. "Commander. That's quite a promotion."

The Kell Hound ignored the irony and concentrated on the greater significance of his promotion. "Damn, most of the *Dire Wolf*'s senior officers were on the bridge. These Clansmen don't take well to surprises and they're always looking for orders from the folks above them. That's why this clown calls me a Commander—because I was giving him orders." He looked up at the one-eyed ComStar man. "Who's going to be giving orders to the folks who are supposed to keep us in one piece?"

Before Focht could answer, the Damage Control Team arrived. Phelan thrust the radio into the Precentor Martial's hands. "See if you can raise Ranna on this thing. Tell her we need to know who's in charge, and if she can't come up with a good answer, tell her she's it." He hesitated. "That is, unless you want the job."

Focht smiled warily. "I think, Phelan Kell, you have assumed that position already."

The mercenary laughed harshly. "Fine. Then consider this delegation of authority. See what can be done."

Phelan turned and crossed to where a Clan Tech had hitched up a piece of diagnostic equipment to the sonic lock beside the bridge's closed doors. "Freebirth!"

"What's the problem?"

"The bridge has been sealed and we have minimal atmosphere," the Tech replied distractedly, "and I have not a clue how long the hull seal will hold. There was a *savashri* short in the electrical systems. The door has given itself a new combination code and I do not know what it is. It was just chosen at random, and if things are still alive in there, it could change again at a moment's notice."

The Kell Hound nodded. "How many digits?"

The Clansman frowned in irritation. "What difference does it make?"

Phelan grabbed the man by his collar and hoisted him off the ground. "Give me an answer, idiot! People may still be alive in there."

"N-nine."

Phelan dropped him and pulled the electronic lockpick from his pocket. He tossed it to the Tech. "Set the switches to nine and hold it against the lockplate." He then turned to one of the other Damage Control Team members. "Give me one of those EVA suits. I go in first. The ilKhan and Khan Ulric were on the bridge. Find them and get them out and to medical facilities immediately, then we pull out any other people we can find."

The Clansmen nodded and prepared their equipment as Phelan pulled on the jumpsuit and sealed the ankles and wrists. *They're so conditioned to take orders that they defer to me because I'm willing to take command. I know I'll pay for this when the crisis is over, though they might accept the excuse of my being a bondsman anxious about my master.* He fitted the bubble helmet over his head and fastened it at the neck. Someone helped him with his boots and gloves, then the Tech at the lock yelped in amazement.

The doors to the bridge slid open. From amid a cloud of gray smoke, two badly burned people stumbled out. Before they'd even cleared the doorway, Medtechs hit them with painkillers and then guided them down the hallway. Phelan grabbed two tanks of oxygen and dropped into a crouch. As soon as the injured were out of his way, he went in below the level of the rapidly dissipating smoke.

Whatever hit us was big or moving fast—or both! With few exceptions, the work stations had ripped free of the deck and tumbled back toward the interior bulkhead. Buried beneath piles of technological debris, Phelan saw arms and legs, but the rivulets of blood leaking from those mounds told him there was no help for the people beneath them. Others lay strewn across the torn-up deck, some of them moving feebly, but Phelan continued past them in his search.

He was in the holotank when I last saw him. As Phelan moved toward the collapsed walls of the display unit, the smoke thinned enough to let him see the hole in the hull. Above and slightly to the right of the main viewscreen, it looked about the size of a 'Mech's balled fist. Jagged daggers of metal pointed inward from the hole, but it was by no means enough to have resealed the hole. *This place must have been sprayed with shrapnel upon impact. What the hell could it have been?*

Pipes running through the hull pumped gouts of a tarry substance over the breach, covering the hole with a glistening black curtain. Some of the dark fluid dribbled down the interior hull, staining the walls black, but most of it clung to the already present layer and increased its thickness. Phelan could see the layer pulled taut where vacuum from outside sucked at it, and he pushed down a momentary flash of panic. He realized that if it were to give, the vacuum would suck him and the others out into space. He looked around the bridge and shook his head. Obviously, anyone not pinned down by debris had flown out through the breach before the sealant had a chance to work. Though the odds were dismal, Phelan knew he would find Ulric.

The repair Tech's voice called anxiously over the radio. "Move it, people. That patch is really stressed. I do not know how much longer the *stravag* thing will hold."

Phelan shot a brief glance back over his shoulder toward the doorway. "Let us know when you have some good news."

The Tech shook his head. "That is the *good* news, bondsman."

Reaching the remains of the holotank, Phelan discovered a hollow beneath the lowest of the curved panels. *Maybe, just maybe…* He dropped to his knees and crawled in. Using the flashlight mounted on his right forearm, he dispelled the darkness and found himself staring at the Khan.

Stravag! Gotta get him air. Phelan fitted the mask from one of his oxygen tanks over Ulric's ashen face and started the flow of oxygen. As carefully as possible, he shined the light around to see if the Khan had sustained other injuries besides a cut on the cheek. *No compound fractures and nothing trapping him. Let's see if I can move him.*

The mercenary grabbed the Khan of the Wolf Clan by the armpits and started to pull. As the Khan's body began to move, Phelan felt some life coming back into the man's limbs. Ulric opened his eyes, and blinked at the glare of the flashlight.

Ulric brought his hands up and grabbed Phelan's arms just above the elbows. Using the mercenary as a brace, the Khan pulled his body free of the holotank. He did his best to stand up, but his knees buckled almost immediately so that Phelan had to catch him before he could fall.

The mercenary gestured to two of the white-suited medics. "This is the Khan. Get him out of here."

Suddenly the radio speakers mounted in his helmet squawked to life. "Everyone, get out of the bridge. The seal is at 110 percent of its maximum stress factor and we have reports that enemy activity is beginning to concentrate in this area. Move! I do not know how long I can hold it."

Phelan started toward the doorway, but saw a pair of legs move weakly. He detoured over to see if he could help, then came up short. *Just my luck, isn't it?*

Wedged partway beneath a curved magnesium girder, Vlad lay on his back with arms and legs splayed out crazily. None of his limbs

301

appeared to be broken, but something had laid his face open on a line from above his left eyebrow down to his jaw. Blood covered that side of his face, but Phelan knew he was alive.

"You, bondsman, move it. We are at 127 percent of max stress. The seal will go any second now."

The mercenary waved off the warning. Kneeling down, he tried to pull Vlad toward the center of the girder's curve, but something had snagged and held the Clansman fast. *It would be ironic if whatever kept you from flying out earlier would prevent me from saving you now.* He reached up under the steel beam, unhooked the MechWarrior from where his belt buckle had been wedged and slid him free.

Grabbing Vlad by the belt buckle Tyra had crafted, Phelan dragged him out from under the metal that had pinned him. Hoisting the Clansman over his left shoulder, the Kell Hound ran toward the doorway as the Tech waved him on. Vaulting piles of debris, he dashed closer to the exit, but five meters from sanctuary, he slipped in a pool of blood and went down.

Vlad bounced from his shoulder and into the doorway, where the repair Tech whisked him out of sight. Phelan tried to scramble to his feet, but his bloodsoaked boots could get no traction. All around him, small pieces of debris began to vibrate and dance as the seal tore away around the edges. Phelan clawed for anything that would pull him closer to the doorway, but nothing gave him purchase. He began to slip, centimeter by centimeter, toward the breach.

Suddenly a huge metal form filled the doorway. The Elemental grabbed the mercenary by the scruff of his neck and heaved him into the corridor beyond the bridge barely seconds before the bridge doors snapped shut behind them. Phelan landed awkwardly in a heap, but the relief at being free of the vacuum's grasp erased any pain or embarrassment he felt.

He climbed to his feet, and with the rippling crackle of parting velcro, he yanked off his left glove. He offered his hand to the Elemental who had saved him. "I don't know how I can ever thank you."

The armored figure reached up and pulled off its helmet. Holding the helmet in the crook of her right elbow, Evantha enfolded Phelan's left hand in a steel grip. "It would have been a waste to let you die."

The mercenary's jaw dropped. "Evantha? After what I did on Rasalhague...Why?"

She shook his hand once, then released it. "You may be a bondsman, Phelan Patrick Kell, but you have a warrior's heart. You have much to learn about us and our ways, but you should realize that we

302

respect you. To let you die needlessly would have been a greater sin than letting you defeat me." Then she let a grin break the fearsome mask she wore. "And it would have prevented me from having the chance to fight you again."

Phelan stared after her as she walked off down the corridor behind the medtechs carrying Vlad away. *She's right. I do have a lot to learn about the Clans. Perhaps that's what Ulric wants... for me to understand why they've come to the Inner Sphere.* His thoughts drifted back to his pledge to help the Precentor Martial unravel the mystery of the Clans. *But what happens when I have that knowledge and how will I be allowed to use it?*

Triad, Tharkad City, Tharkad
District of Donegal, Lyran Commonwealth
10 November 3050

Victor Ian Steiner-Davion smiled as he enfolded Kai Allard's hand in his own. "I'm glad you've decided to remain in the AFFC. Losing you would have been a blow."

Kai shook Victor's hand firmly, but the Prince read doubt in his friend's gray eyes. "I appreciate that, Highness, but I'm not certain it is deserved." As Victor's eyes narrowed, Kai held up his hands. "Don't say I'm being too hard on myself. It's just that sometimes you all try so hard to bolster my confidence that you may err on the other side. I do make mistakes and I had to deal with the consequences of the one I made on Twycross. Thanks for giving me the time to do that."

Victor broke their grip and shrugged. "It was the least I could do for the man who prevented the annihilation of four 'Mech regiments." He opened his arms wide to take in the whole of the throne room where they stood. Green and gold bunting hung from the balustrades and encircled pillars. Even the two *Griffin*s that stood on either side of the Archon's throne had been repainted with the Donegal Guard's crest. "If not for you, all this ribbon would be black and there'd be no celebrations going on. Hell, after the drubbing you gave them, the Clans have pulled back and made no attempt to retake Twycross."

Kai pressed his lips together into a thin, grim line. "I appreciate that latter comment, but you and I both know better than to believe it…"

"You did what had to be done," Victor said, almost sharply.

304

"You're not guilty of any crime. Dr. Lear said it herself: Those men were doomed before you ever sent them up there."

Kai raked his fingers back through his dark hair. "I didn't need to send those men up there at all. I know the properties of pentaglycerine. I knew that an explosion nearby could set it off. I could have used my autocannon or gotten some of the invaders to shoot missiles at me. Those men did not have to die. They could have been evacuated with the others. No matter how I try to look at it, I know their blood is on my hands."

Victor started to frown. "This is basically what you said on Twycross when you resigned. Why the change? Why did you decide to stay with the AFFC?"

Kai pursed his lips, then sighed. "At first I resented your having 'sentenced' me to the medical evacuation ship taking folks off Twycross. My wounds were minor, at best, and even though I'd decided to resign, I still felt responsible for my lance. I was trying to keep to myself on the *Curie*, but word got out somehow about who I was and what I had done."

The Leftenant fixed Victor with a suspicious stare, but the Prince backed off and raised his hands innocently. "Hey, it wasn't me." *Dr. Lear was on the* Curie, *but with orders to stay away from Kai. Though we didn't try to keep Kai's action a secret, it wasn't generally known, either. I wonder...*

"O.K., Victor. I'll take your word for that." Kai looked up toward the ceiling's shadowed spine, his eyes focusing distantly. "On the trip here to Tharkad, many soldiers came to thank me for the sacrifice I'd made to save them. They told me it took great courage to do what I had done. Some of them were soldiers who'd been evacuated from Dr. Lear's field hospital and they thought they'd have wandered around forever if I hadn't come through and given them something to do. They told me I saved their lives and that they'd gladly serve under me again if given the chance.

"Maybe for the first time in my life, I wasn't my father's son, or heir to my mother. They saw me as Kai Allard and they welcomed me not because of my parents or my connections, but because of what I had done for them. They offered to serve with me because of something I accomplished on my own."

"Kai, if you thought I became your friend because..."

Kai shook his head emphatically. "No, Victor, I know you didn't. I'm honored to have a few friends who, like you, persevered enough to get to know me. I should have said that at the start. But even you have to admit that we'd probably not have become friends if the positions of our families hadn't created a natural alliance between us."

"Anyway, those men and women thanking me didn't exactly balance what happened on Twycross, but I realized that I'll never commit that same error again because I know the horror and pain of it. If I resign, however, some other green Leftenant might replace me and make the same mistake all over again."

Kai shrugged. "Therefore, Highness, I withdraw my resignation."

Victor looked at Kai with true joy in his eyes. He knew his friend still had the habit of second-guessing himself, but at least he'd begun to learn to put his actions in the proper perspective. It was a small change, but enough to make a difference.

Victor heard the sound of a door opening behind him and saw Kai jerk to attention. He spun about quickly with his smile growing wider. His mother, Archon Melissa Steiner Davion, accompanied by Morgan Hasek-Davion, entered the throne room through a side door. "Great news!" he told them. "Kai has withdrawn his resignation!"

Before he could say another thing, a third individual entered the throne room through the same door. Dressed in a black uniform, belted at the waist, with red piping running down the legs, the man stepped around Morgan and stood with his fists planted on his hips. His black eyes flashed with an unholy glee and blue highlights played through his long black hair. Both shoulders of his jacket had been embroidered with a wolf's-head design, including actual fur, and the rubies glinting from the wolf's eyes matched the fire in the man's eyes.

"Victor Davion and Kai Allard-Liao. How convenient to find you together."

The man's sarcastic tone made Victor angry. "I am Victor. Whom do I have the *honor* of addressing?"

The man threw back his head and barked a laugh that echoed throughout the cavernous room. "Spectacular!" He turned and nodded to Melissa. "The Steiner and Davion blood has mixed well in this one. Fire and steel. A little tempering and he'll be invincible."

The man looked beyond Victor toward Kai. "And this one, this quiet one, he's one to watch." He winked at Morgan. "You know, back in the days of ancient Rome, they used to put a dwarf in the chariot with victorious generals. During the public parades, as the crowds lavished adulation on the general, the dwarf would whisper reminders that earthly glory was fleeting. An officer that carries his own dwarf with him, one that constantly checks to make sure he *is* right instead of just believing that he's right, that is a valuable man."

Victor turned to watch how Kai took the compliment and was a bit surprised when Kai did not, as he expected, blush. Instead, Kai bowed slightly, then brought his head up and gave the man a wry smile. "Thank you, Major Ngov. That is high praise, indeed."

Victor frowned, looking toward Morgan. "What's going on here? I recognize the uniform—he's from Wolf's Dragoons. Enlighten me, please."

Morgan nodded to Sveng Ngov, and the mercenary smiled broadly at Victor. "It's simple, Highness. Colonel Jaime Wolf sent me to escort your mother, Morgan, Kai, and you to a strategy meeting on Outreach."

"Strategy meeting?" The furrows in Victor's brow deepened. "Why? Last I knew it, Wolf's Dragoons had opted to stay out of this war. Besides, the invaders have left."

The mercenary's smile dimmed. "Times change, Prince Victor, and this meeting is to ensure that *we*, not *they*, control the speed, time, and direction of the change. If we don't, to butcher the old child's rhyme—All the Kings 'Mechs and all the King's men couldn't put the Successor States back together again..."

Palace of Obsidian and Jade, Imperial City, Luthien
Pesht Military District, Draconis Combine
15 November 3050

Shin knelt carefully within the shadows of the garden wall. His black silk kimono rendered him all but invisible, but the garment's fine cloth did little to ward off the cold of the clear Luthien night. Shin welcomed the cold, though, for its numbing effect on the burning of his right side.

He forced himself to control his breathing and drink in the garden's peace. Letting his eyes half-close, he shut out what little light bled into the garden from the rest of the Imperial City, not at all worried that he might doze off. Between the pain and the emotions running riot through him, sleep was the last of his problems.

He lifted his head slightly to study the purple-black outline of the palace that was home to Kanrei Theodore Kurita and his family. Like the Old Man's demesne on Edo, this one was also modeled on ancient Japanese architecture. The central tower rose only three stories, but each was double normal height and the tower had an incredible girth. Shin had traveled in DropShips with less area and mass than this building. He was honored that the Kanrei had granted him a room in this place. *A long way from the slums on Marfik!*

In thinking of his life, everything before the invasion seemed faded and unreal like early holodramas and ancient newsreels. *The invaders were, in many ways, the most honorable of foes. Again and again, they tried to match their forces to ours so that we would not lose too much face, even in defeat. Sometimes they seem downright naive in dealing with us, and since their defeat on Wolcott, we've had no more attacks against our worlds. Could it be, in their way of looking at the universe, that one defeat calls for an end to their assault?*

As quickly as the question formed itself in his mind, he rejected it. *No, that makes even less sense than some of the theories concerning who they really are. What little I've seen of the machines and suits we "earned" from the battle on Wolcott leads me to believe they're human, despite the size of those infantry. That they have BattleMechs says that they ran into humans with 'Mechs at some point, but no one knows how far out Periphery pirates may have ranged. Are they from some lost colony, or maybe the descendants of some charismatic leader who led people off unnoticed to build a martial society?*

Our captives claim to be closemouthed about their past because they say they are now members of the Kurita Clan, yet they won't tell us what significance that has. It's a mystery wrapped within countless mysteries. Now that they've gone, will we ever be able to dig through these mysteries, layer by layer?

The barest hint of boot leather scraping against stone brought Shin's head up sharply. Eclipsing glittering stars, a slender figure vaulted up over the crenelated top of the wall and dropped to a crouch within the garden. As the intruder uncoiled and started to move toward the palace, Shin identified her as female. *No weapons visible...An assassin?*

Noiselessly, Shin picked up a pebble, then stood and moved forward. He whipped the pebble against the garden's far wall. As the intruder turned to identify the sound, he came in at her back, but did not strike her from behind. "Stop!"

Instead of obeying his command, she whirled and executed a roundhouse kick meant to take his head off. Shin ducked beneath most of it, though her heel clipped him and knocked him slightly off balance. Recovering as she came around to face him, he dropped into a fighting stance. Again, moving more quickly than he expected, she grabbed at his right wrist and pain immediately shot up to his shoulder. Though agony numbed the limb, Shin slipped his arm from the kimono's sleeve, ducked, and spun away. As the intruder pulled on the garment, the yakuza let it be stripped from his torso. His movement took him into the center of the garden and left his foe holding the empty kimono.

Doors at both the garden and the balcony levels opened, spilling pale light out into the night. One rectangle trapped Shin and splashed his long-legged shadow against the garden wall. The intruder cast the kimono aside in preparation for another attack, then stopped short and bowed respectfully to him.

Shin's mouth dropped open in surprise. *Fighting one moment, then bowing the next? What's going on here?* As the intruder came up, Shin bowed to her, then tried to recall where he had seen that red wolf's-head insignia decorating the left breast of her tunic. *Wolf's Dragoons? Was it possible? After all this time, the only thing they could want here is the Coordinator's death. If so, why attack the Kanrei's palace?*

The intruder pulled off her black balaclava, which let her long, blond hair spill down over her shoulders. *"Komban wa,* Kanrei Kurita-*sama,"* she offered in flawless Japanese to the man standing on the balcony. "I bring you the greetings of Colonel Jaime Wolf."

The Kanrei rested his fists on his hips. "Colonel Wolf sends greetings to me?" A note of humor entered his voice. "Has the Christian hell truly frozen over, or is this some manner of trick? Do Dragoon envoys always assault the trusted aides of those to whom they bring a message?"

The woman laughed, a lilting sound completely at odds with the deadly menace Shin had sensed from her earlier. "Major Lilith Lang of Wolf's Dragoons, at your service. This is no trick and I would not have attacked Shin Yodama had I known it was him."

Shin stared at her. "What? How did you know...?"

Lilith pointed at the yakuza's chest. "Your history identified you. The left side proclaims you a member of the *Kuroi Kiri* and the right sings of other great deeds."

The light from the palace lit the outlines of Shin's new tattoo. Part of the snarling smoke jaguar face had already been filled in on his shoulder. Its gold eyes glared defiantly at both the mercenary and the Kanrei. Below it, traced in black, was the crumpled form of a dead armored infantryman transfixed with a sword. The trail of stars and jumps made in the escape from Turtle Bay decorated the length of Shin's right arm from wrist to shoulder, and scenes from the prison break bled over from his back to the side of his ribs.

Hohiro, entering the garden through the ground-level entrance, pulled his kimono tight against the cold. "I was unaware that Colonel Wolf had such an interest in my father's men."

"There is much that interests the Dragoons, and much of which you are ignorant, Hohiro," Lilith hissed, her icy tone matching his. She looked up at Theodore. "It is to end this ignorance that I am sent to bring you, your family, and Shin Yodama to Outreach. There is much for you to learn."

Hohiro laughed scornfully, but the Kanrei seemed to consider her outrageous statement for a moment or two. "I would be a fool to travel alone to the headquarters of an enemy..."

The mercenary smiled. "Colonel Wolf predicted that you would say that. He said that you may bring your Genyosha or Ryuken with you if need be, but that he hoped the promise of safe passage from Dechan Fraser and Jeanette Rand would suffice. He also said that his war was never with you or the Combine, it was only with Samsonov and your father. It is because of that vendetta that I could not come here openly. But you must realize that if the Colonel had sent me on a mission of destruction, nothing could have stopped me."

"Well spoken," Theodore agreed. "I shall not need the Genyosha or Ryuken with me, but I would like to bring *Tai-sa* Narimasa Asano."

Lilith beamed up at him. "Excellent. Colonel Wolf said he looked forward to finally meeting *Tai-sa* Asano. Gather your people and shuttle out on a vector to the Ginka orbital factory. We'll radio coordinates to our JumpShip."

Hohiro walked further into the garden and looked up at his father. "This is madness, *sosen*. We've just driven off an enemy and now you deliver us into the hands of another. I don't understand."

The Kanrei exchanged a look with Lilith, then spoke quietly but firmly to his son. "It is not for you to understand right now, Hohiro. You must just obey. For Colonel Wolf to take the risk of sending an envoy here means that his purpose is a serious one. Wolf is no fool, nor is he mad. That's enough for me."

Victor Ian Steiner-Davion stood in the doorway of the hall, awe-struck by the crowd of people filling the room. *If even half the stories I've heard are true, so many powerful people have not gathered in one place since the wedding of my mother and father*. Military leaders moved in and out of small groups surrounding political leaders while members of Wolf's Dragoons—looking as though they fiercely re-sented the service—offered drinks and tidbits to their guests. Perhaps most shocking to Victor was that, with so many important people present, no one noticed his arrival.

The second he caught himself feeling piqued, he smiled. *Recall, Victor, that here you are a very small fish in a big pond. You are neither a political nor military giant—yet—and therefore should be content with having been invited at all*. His thoughts began to drift toward the puzzle he, Kai, and Morgan had tried to solve during the journey to Outreach, but he stopped himself. *We weren't able to figure out why Wolf was calling us together then, so there's no sense wasting brain-sweat on it now*.

Amid the press of people, Victor saw a familiar figure in the red and black uniform of the Kell Hounds. The man stood tall and gave off an aura of strength and power. He wore his salt and pepper hair long enough to reach the shoulders of his red jacket, but kept his white beard closely trimmed. As always, Victor had the strange sensation that death would have to take this man asleep because it could never take

312

him awake.

Victor crossed to where Morgan Kell stood talking with two people from the Free Worlds League and they politely backed away as Davion approached. At the sight of him, Morgan's face lit up.

"Highness," said his mother's cousin and founder of the Kell Hounds, "as always, seeing you is a pleasure without equal."

Taking Morgan's hand, Victor returned the smile. "Without equal? My mother will not be happy to hear that…"

Morgan Kell laughed aloud. "Ah, you've caught me, for your mother has a special place in my heart. Consider my statement amended but no less heartfelt."

"Done."

The mercenary looked Victor up and down, then nodded with satisfaction. "Dan Allard told me good things about you in that action on Twycross. He said you can think on your feet and that you weren't afraid of mixing it up. That's good." His eyes focused distantly. "It got your Uncle Ian killed on Mallory's World, but it's pulled your father and your cousin Morgan Hasek-Davion out of more scrapes than I've got fingers and toes to number."

"If the Hounds hadn't been there and Colonel Allard not been willing to take a chance, things would have turned out much differently."

Morgan's eyes narrowed. "And if you hadn't sent Kai Allard to recon the pass, how would things have turned out?"

Victor looked over to where Kai stood with his mother, father, and twin sisters. "If only he'd allow himself to realize it."

Morgan Kell cupped one hand around the back of Victor's neck. "I think you'll find that warriors like Kai keep a tight rein on themselves because they're afraid of what would happen if they don't. Just be thankful he's on your side. If he ever cuts loose, there's not much in the Inner Sphere that could stop him."

The growing whine of an electric wheelchair precluded any further comment by Victor. He turned to see a man dressed in the uniform of a general in the army of the Free Rasalhague Republic. His silver hair and black-streaked beard were vaguely familiar, but it was the sight of the scar on the left side of the man's face that dredged up a name from Victor's memory. *That's Tor Miraborg. He must be here with Haakon Magnusson, the Silver Fox. Wolf really did get everyone here.*

For a moment, Victor thought the female aerospace pilot following Miraborg might be his daughter, but the nameplate over her left breast pocket read "Janssen."

313

Miraborg fixed Morgan Kell with a savage stare. "You are Morgan Kell?"

The mercenary nodded silently.

"I am Tor Miraborg. Your son murdered my daughter!"

The anger and pain in the crippled man's voice made Victor cringe, but Morgan kept his face impassive. "Explain how my son, dead for a year and a half now, could have murdered your daughter."

Raw hatred washed over Miraborg's face. "Your son came between Tyra and me. His influence drove her away and made her accept a position with the Rasalhague Drakøns. My daughter died fighting the invaders."

Morgan pulled himself up to his full height. "Then your daughter and my son shared one last thing in their too brief lives. I received a holodisk from her not long ago, and she was kind enough to share with me and my wife some remembrances of her times with Phelan..."

Miraborg's shoulders slumped forward and his chin dipped to his chest. "She talked to you?" he asked in a tortured whisper. "She recorded a holodisk for *you*? Why?" Victor recognized the question Miraborg dared not voice. *She never communicated with her father and he doesn't know why...*

"Her disk came in response to one I had sent her," Morgan replied quietly. "I will let you see the message, if you wish."

The Iron Jarl shook himself, and the fire came back into his eyes and voice. "No. I want no part of your message. She stopped being my daughter the day she left Gunzburg." He spun his chair and headed off through the crowd, leaving the slim, blond woman standing alone in his wake.

Anika looked up at Morgan. "Colonel Kell, I'm Anika Janssen. I was Tyra's wingmate. I was also her best friend." She glanced after Miraborg, then shook her head. "Ignore what he said. He's just a bitter old man. I knew your son and was with him and Tyra many times. I was there when they met. You have nothing to be ashamed of in your son. Phelan and Tyra were very good for each other."

The mercenary rested both of his hands on her shoulders. "Thank you, Löjtnant. I'm glad to know Phelan had friends."

Anika swallowed hard. "And, if you wouldn't mind, sir, I'd like to see that holodisk she made. Tyra and I never really had a chance to say good-bye. She took her *Shilone* into the invader flagship, right into the bridge. She did more to stop the invasion than anyone else in the whole Royal Kungsarmé, but the Iron Jarl won't acknowledge her heroism."

"I will have a copy of the disk to you by tomorrow morning."

314

Morgan smiled warmly at her. "And thank you."

As Anika withdrew, a commotion at the door caught Victor's attention. Dressed in a black silk gown with red trim that might have been a parody of the Dragoon uniform, Romano Liao, Chancellor of the Capellan Confederation, was desperately trying to get one of the two Dragoons at the door to announce her. The hapless guards tried to ignore her at first, but when she punched one of them in frustration, the man reacted and drew back his hand to slap her.

A slender, dark-haired man slipped between them, facing Romano. The guard caught himself even as the younger man gently grabbed his mother's wrists. For a moment, Romano's face contorted with rage, but then she kissed her son on the cheek with a look of sheer adoration. Meanwhile, Tsen Shang, her consort, stepped forward to take her arm and lead her away.

Victor shook his head. *No doubt she's as mad as her father was. It looks as though her son, Sun Tzu, can control her, but for how long?* He looked over at Kai, who was watching Sun Tzu Liao trail after his parents. *Both Kai and Sun Tzu are Maximilian Liao's grandsons, each one entitled to press a claim to the throne of the Capellan Confederation. I don't think Kai wants it, but would that stop Sun Tzu from wanting to get rid of a potential rival?*

At the far end of the room, the leader of Wolf's Dragoons mounted a dais. Behind him came another man in a Dragoon uniform, but he stopped as Wolf approached the podium at center stage. The rest of the Dragoon command staff filtered up onto the dais, but remained back along the wall.

Victor frowned. *That's odd. Where's the Black Widow? I hadn't heard that Natasha Kerensky was wounded or killed.*

Jaime Wolf smoothed his thinning gray hair. "Thank you all for responding to the summons that has brought us together here on Outreach. Some of you must have found it strange and yet you have sensed that my reason was not frivolous. Rather, I wish to speak to you about a problem that faces all of us and whose true depth perhaps only the Dragoons can know.

"Before I begin, however, I would like to present my new second in command." With one hand, Wolf indicated the younger man standing a few steps behind him. "Some of you may have known him as Major Darnell Winningham. His real name is MacKenzie Wolf, and he is my son. He will now replace Natasha Kerensky."

Wolf let the whispered reactions to his announcement rise like a wave and then die down again as he continued. "As you all know, the Inner Sphere has been invaded in the last year by an enemy possessing

BattleMechs of extraordinary power. Recently, the forces of the Federated Commonwealth and Draconis Combine have had modest successes against these invaders. After months of trial and error, they finally managed to hand the invaders a defeat. Since then, the invaders, for all intents and purposes, have withdrawn into the shell of the worlds they conquered."

Someone shouted, "It's because we kicked their butts!" Victor couldn't identify the voice, but he found himself caught up in the defiant chorus of assent. *We did hit them hard.*

Wolf shook his head. "Can you really believe that so implacable an enemy is cowed by minor defeats? They withdrew because one Rasalhague pilot sacrificed herself by smashing her *Shilone* into the invader's flagship. At the very least, she killed the invasion leader and devastated the command structure of the enemy forces. If she'd missed ten meters up or down, left or right, the invaders would still be marching inexorably forward.

"If you are so naive as to think that two minor victories and a lucky stroke by a brave pilot could drive these invaders back, our chances for success are poor in our war against them."

"Our war?" It was Romano Liao's voice. "Of course! I knew it all along!" She laughed triumphantly and turned to lord it over the others. "You've just been waiting for our troops to take stock of these invaders. Now Wolf's Dragoons will stalk from their den and into the battle."

She looked up at Jaime Wolf. "Yours are the fiercest mercenaries in the Inner Sphere. With your help, we shall send these rimworld renegades running."

Wolf cut her off with a hard stare. "I'm afraid you have it all wrong, Madam Chancellor. The enemy we face is not composed of either renegades or bandits. The invaders will be back, probably in less than a year. We will have to be ready to meet them with everything we've got because we've seen only a small sample of their strength."

Wolf's voice and expression became grim. "After Radstadt and after the death of their war leader, they'll come at us at full strength. They'll ask no quarter and grant none. Ladies and gentlemen, now begins what could easily be the last days of the Inner Sphere."

Epilogue:

Name of the Beast

Phelan Kell entered the *Dire Wolf*'s small shuttlecraft bay and easily picked out the Precentor Martial from the milling crowd of yellow-robed ComStar Acolytes helping with his baggage. He threaded his way through them and extended his hand to the one-eyed man. "I only just heard you were leaving."

Anastasius Focht shook Phelan's hand warmly. "Yes. Ulric felt it would be for the best. He said I would not be welcome where the Clan is going." The older man released the mercenary's hand, then smiled quizzically at him. "What is going to happen with you? Any news of the inquiry into your behavior during the attack?"

The Kell Hound shook his head slowly. "No. They've kept me virtually incommunicado since the battle at Radstadt, but more pressing matters may have taken precedence over my fate. It's my impression that the Smoke Jaguars wanted to raze Radstadt because survivors from the Rasalhague fleet were likely to take refuge there."

Focht nodded in agreement, then walked Phelan away from the other ComStar personnel. "Ulric said that losing the ilKhan's body to the vacuum of space drove the Jaguars into a frenzy. He was from their Clan, you know. They were upset that you saved Ulric but not the ilKhan."

"If I'd seen him, I'd have done what I could. Don't forget...I pulled Vlad from the bridge, too."

The Precentor Martial nodded. "I know, Phelan."

The young man touched Focht's sleeve. "I realize Ulric may have placed restrictions on the information to be passed on to ComStar. But if there's any way you can get word to my family..."

The Precentor Martial touched his right palm to Phelan's forehead. "The Peace of Blake be with you, Phelan Kell. I don't know what the Primus will approve concerning the Clans. As we are to implement some of the occupation policies for the Clans during their absence, ComStar is in a delicate position. If nothing else, perhaps I can let them know their son made them proud."

The mercenary nodded, then smiled weakly. "Thank you. I feel we've become friends and I'll miss talking with you. And I can't thank you enough for your help during the whole business about Ranna and Vlad. I'm still not fully at ease about that situation, but maybe I've learned from my mistakes."

"Remember," Focht said, almost fondly, "that's why the body forms scars."

Phelan threw the Precentor Martial a salute, then turned and left the bay. Watching from a window in the airlock near the door, he saw Focht board the blocky shuttle and seal the hatch. The viewport frosted over as Launch Control drained the bay of atmosphere and opened the external hatch.

Phelan had no chance to watch the ship depart. Two Elementals in full armor, with red sashes slung across their chests, entered the viewing room. The mottled gray and black camouflage pattern identified them as belonging to the Smoke Jaguar clan. "Phelan Patrick Kell?"

"Yes," Phelan answered, wondering about the seriousness of the man's tone. "I am he."

The one on his right pointed down the corridor. "You will come with us." The first Elemental started off toward the core of the ship and the second followed closely behind, with Phelan sandwiched between.

Full of apprehension, Phelan tugged at the braided cord surrounding his right wrist. *Bondsmen may not be slaves and might get better treatment than bandits and other social misfits, but the word "civil" is not a word that fits the rights or relations between warriors and any other caste in this culture.* Then another sudden thought brought a smile. *Well, at least I know they're a bit leery of me. The Elementals are in armor this time.*

One of the lift doors already stood open, with another Elemental standing there keeping the cage clear. *I've never seen them do that before.* The Elemental behind Phelan nudged him forward into the cage, where the mercenary squeezed back into a corner as the Elemental trio filled the elevator.

Though he could not see the panel showing the deck numbers flashing by, he knew they were headed forward toward the bridge level. When the ride ended somewhat prematurely, Phelan realized they'd stopped on one of the forbidden decks—decks where only warriors were allowed. His mouth went dry, then tasted sour.

The Elementals ushered him along a short corridor, then stopped at a door that bore no identifying icon. One Elemental rapped on the door with a metal fist and it slid noiselessly upward. Suddenly, the Elemental behind Phelan shoved hard, spilling him into the room. The door slid shut again, leaving the mercenary alone in utter darkness.

Blinded, Phelan held his hands out in front of his face, then stepped forward until he felt a wall. Moving to the right, he completed a cautious circuit of the room. *Two meters by two meters, with no furnishings. This is a less hospitable berth than I had when originally captured. The Elementals who brought me here were Smoke Jaguars. Are they going to take revenge upon me for the death of the ilKhan?*

Phelan whirled as a door at his back whisked open. Standing back two meters from the doorway and illuminated by a spotlight from above, a woman beckoned him forward. *Is that you, Ranna?* By her elaborate dress and gestures, he sensed that her silence held special significance.

Dressed in a tight-fitting body suit of white leather that left her arms and legs bare, she might have been an apparition. Silver studded the costume, and long leather thongs hung down like a loincloth. Knee-length MechWarrior boots of polished silver encased her lower legs, and gauntlets of fine steel mesh covered her hands and arms to the elbow. A short cloak of white wolf-fur fell from her shoulders to mid-back. A silver wolf's-head clasp with ruby eyes fastened the cloak at her throat.

Though Phelan thought he recognized her form and stance, he could not be certain because the woman wore a mask. It reminded him of nothing so much as the fierce visage of his *Wolfhound* BattleMech. Worked with the greatest of skill, the white enameled mask took the form of a wolf's-head. The beast's mouth hung open, its lips pulled back in a snarl, but Ranna's blue eyes shining through the mask's eyeslits took away some of the threat.

He took one step forward and she vanished. The light from above winked out, then another light flashed on, and she appeared further on. She invited him forward with a languid gesture, then abruptly shot both her hands up and out above her shoulders. Silver flashed and a metallic ring filled the darkness as her hands stopped twin swords from

321

flashing down.

Phelan rushed forward and passed beneath her right arm. Blackness swept in again as Ranna released the blades and they whistled down to complete their arcs. In the darkness, the Kell Hound felt all his senses come alive and his heart begin pumping. *This must be some strange justice ritual of the Clans. The Smoke Jaguars desire my death, but Ulric has sent a representative of the Wolf Clan to ward me and assist me.*

He felt Ranna move past him, but he concentrated instead on identifying other perceptions. On his left, he heard the dry whisper of boot against deck. Instantly, he dropped to his hands and knees, letting the sword slice air where, a moment or two before, it would have met his spine. He stabbed out with his left foot and hit something. His target did not cry out, but the thump of a body hitting the floor and the clatter of a dropped sword made Phelan smile.

Ahead of him Ranna appeared again within a circle of light. As he trotted toward her, she squatted down, then leaped up. Responding immediately, the Kell Hound dove up and forward. Two swords sparked as they collided, passing centimeters below his belly. Phelan tucked and rolled forward, but as he came up, sensed a motion on his right.

Too late. He twisted away from it, but felt the burning sting as the blade slashed through the flesh on his right thigh. He allowed his pirouette to carry him closer to Ranna, then dropped to one knee and probed the wound with his right hand. Reaching through the cut in his jumpsuit leg, his hand came away warm, wet, and sticky. *That's a good five-centimeter cut, but it seems to be shallow. Hurts like a son of a bitch, but it won't slow me down.*

He reached Ranna's side, fully expecting her to vanish when the light above her died, but it did not. Instead, another spotlight pinned a figure to the black floor. Tall and strong, Ulric stood shrouded in a floor-length cloak of black and gray wolf-fur. The light from above burned brightly from his white hair, but hid his eyes in impenetrable pockets of shadow.

His deep voice filled the void. "Trothkin, seen and unseen, near and far, living and dead, rejoice as the Wolf has brought us a foundling." He let the words echo through the darkness, until silence reigned once more. "It was forty-seven years ago that the Womb of Steel whelped a pup such as this. That birthing is but a thing of legend, but none will deny the rede of it."

From the surrounding dark, Phelan heard a thousand voices whisper as one. "Seyla."

Ulric's voice dropped into a wolfish growl. "I am the Oathmaster! All will be bound by this Conclave, until they are dust and memories, and then beyond that time until the end of all that is."

"Seyla."

The sibilant murmuring raised goosebumps on Phelan's flesh. Tension built in him as his mind struggled frantically to pierce the mysteries of this terrible ceremony. *They try to kill me, then make me the centerpiece of some bizarre ritual. I don't understand half the words or what Ulric is trying to say. I hope like hell I can figure out what's going on, or as sure as this bondcord encircles my wrist, I'm going to be one dead little bondsman.*

Ulric looked around as though his eyes could see those gathered beyond the circle of light. "The Wolf's wisdom is not in doubt, but there are those who believe the Wolf's generosity is too great. Who would deny this pup his life?"

The mercenary saw Ulric's head come up at a rustling sound behind him. Stepping forward into a white circle painted on the deck was a small, slender man of the large-headed body type Phelan had come to associate with Clan aerojocks. His spectacular costume had been cut from green leather and patterned after an aeropilot's flightsuit. Instead of a short cloak of fur, he wore a brilliant gold and malachite pectoral with two stylized wings rising up on either side of his head. His hawk-head mask, also made of gold and malachite, was a master-work of artistry.

As the man removed his mask, Ulric's voice boomed from behind Phelan. "I recognize thee, Cavell Malthus of the Jade Falcons."

"Oathmaster, I ken death from the skies for this pup." Cavell watched the bondsman with huge, hungry brown eyes. "Aye, it is death I see."

Ulric's voice rang out strongly. "Who among the Wolves would deny this vision?"

Moving to eclipse Phelan's view of Cavell, an aerofighter pilot stepped in. His costume paralleled Cavell's in shape, but was made from dark gray leather. Like Ranna's costume, his included a cloak of gray fur settled over his shoulder. As Cavell removed his helmet, the mercenary saw a flash of golden hair.

"I recognize thee, Carew of the Wolves."

"Oathmaster, it is my ken that this pup need fear nothing from the air." As Carew's voice trailed off, both he and Cavell again donned their masks. Neither moved from their places. Beside them, two more spotlights brought illumination to two more circles on the deck.

A titan stepped forward from the darkness. His costume of light gray leather had not been tailored to represent any Clan military garb that Phelan could recognize, but that mattered little. Instead, he marveled at how the material stretched taut to mold itself to the massive, powerfully built man. Though the garment covered him from throat to boot tops, a loincloth of Smoke Jaguar fur had been added to mark his Clan affiliation, as though his savage jaguar-mask could be mistaken for anything else. The Elemental solemnly removed his mask.

"I recognize thee, Lincoln Osis of the Smoke Jaguars."

The black man's voice sounded deeper than Ulric's and was an almost perfect impersonation of a jaguar's hoarse growl. "Oathmaster, I ken death by hand for this pup. Aye, it is death I see."

Again Ulric voiced a request to the assembly hidden in the shadows. "Who among the Wolves would deny this vision?"

Another Wolf moved to stand between Phelan and his challenger. Even if he had not seen the long red braid lying against her spine, he would have known Evantha from the way she stalked out to take her place.

"I recognize thee, Evantha Fetladral of the Wolves."

Phelan sensed the barest hint of challenge and scorn in Evantha's reply. "Oathmaster, it is my ken that this pup need fear nothing from the hand."

As Evantha and Lincoln again donned their masks, the final two circles on the deck blazed to life with reflected light. Almost immediately, a man moved into the challenger's circle. Phelan realized that his costume, like Ranna's, was a version of the abbreviated attire Mech-Warriors wore in their steamy cockpits. A thick cloak of white fur covered the man, fastened at his throat by knotting together the fur around a bear's forward paws. The intermediate paws were similarly tied together at his waist. The bear mask the man wore seemed to be inlaid with opal, which mirrored the shimmering pelt he wore.

"I recognize thee, Garald Winson of the Ghost Bears."

"Oathmaster, I ken death from his equals." His voice dropped to a rime-laden whisper. "Aye, it is death I see."

Phelan heard a change in Ulric's voice as he asked for a Wolf to refute Winson's vision of the future. The mercenary half-expected Ranna to leave his side, but she remained in place as another stepped forward. Obviously a woman, this one's costume matched Ranna's in all but color, yet flattered her figure equally. Where Ranna wore white, this MechWarrior wore black, including the abbreviated cloak of wolf-fur. Red hair cascaded onto her shoulders and Phelan saw a scarlet hourglass symbol on the abdomen of her leather clothing.

324

Phelan's jaw dropped as she removed her mask, and Ulric spoke. "I recognize thee, Natasha Kerensky of the Wolves."

The mercenary stared at her in disbelief, but she shot him a grin before facing her opposition. *Natasha Kerensky! But she's Jaime Wolf's second in command. What is she doing here, and why is she recognized by the Clans?* As quickly as that question formed itself in his head, the answer hit him with frightful clarity. *Oh my God. They're not Wolf's Dragoons, they're the Wolf Dragoons. They've been part of the Clans all along!*

Phelan suddenly realized he was not alone in his shock. Garald Winson had paled visibly. From the darkness enclosing them, the mercenary heard hushed whispers. Still grinning, Natasha seemed to revel in the disturbance she caused.

"Oathmaster," Natasha said contemptuously, "I have known this pup for years. He has nothing to fear from his equals, *or those who would style themselves his betters.*"

"Face me, pup." Ulric's voice brought Phelan around. The Khan regarded him with hollow eyes. "Thrice he has been challenged and three defenders have risen for him. Sponsored by the Wolf, warded by the Clan, all is in order."

From beneath his cloak, Ulric produced a silver dagger with a wolf's-head pommel. He moved forward. "Give me your right hand."

Phelan held up his hand, and Ulric slid the knife down between the mercenary's flesh and the bondcord. "This marked you as a bondsman, but yours is the heart, the mind, and the soul of a warrior. The Wolf has seen it and I, the Oathmaster, proclaim it."

Tugging the knife back toward himself, Ulric sliced the bondcord in half. With an expert flip, he reversed the knife, then pressed its pommel into Phelan's wrist and folded his fingers down over it. Triumphantly, he thrust the Kell Hound's hand into the air. "Let us rejoice and let pride sing out—the Wolves have a new warrior among their number."

A mild burst of respectful applause resounded from the shadows, then quickly died away as Ulric backed away from Phelan to his original position. Phelan lowered his hand, then heard something behind him. He turned slowly and saw another MechWarrior, this one clad in the Wolf clan costume, making his way from the shadows. He stopped in front of Phelan and removed his mask.

The mercenary narrowed his eyes. *What now?* He glanced at the sword in the Wolf's right hand and saw a dark stain on its tip. *Yes. It had to be you, quiaff?*

Vlad removed his mask and nestled it between his right elbow and ribs. Still livid, the scar left from his injury on the bridge ran down from his left eye to his jaw. Phelan shuddered at the sight. *Why do all the MechWarriors who loathe me have Radstadt scars?*

Vlad executed a crisp, formal bow. Coming up again, he locked eyes with Phelan in a stare that left no doubt that Vlad's hatred ran more than, as Griff had said, bone-deep. *That hatred runs soul-deep,* Phelan warned himself. *There may well come a day when you regret having rescued him from the* Dire Wolf's *bridge.*

Vlad swallowed hard before speaking. "Welcome, bloodkin, to the House of Ward." He extended his left hand to Phelan in greeting, but his right hand scraped the bell guard of the sword against the wolf's-head buckle Vlad wore.

Phelan did not miss the gesture. *I'll remember you, Vlad, each and every time I see Tyra's belt buckle on you—just as you'll remember me whenever you look in a mirror. There will come a day when we settle our differences once and for all.* Constrained by the formality of the gathering, Phelan merely met Vlad's grip with one matched in strength.

They broke their handshake and Vlad drifted back into the shadows. Phelan turned to face the Khan once more.

Ulric peered into the room's shadowy depths. "I, Ulric Kerensky, Khan of the Wolves and Oathmaster of this Conclave, do welcome you, Phelan Patrick Kell, to the Clan of the Wolves. According to custom handed down since Aleksandr Kerensky led our forefathers from this place and his son Nicholas saved us from ourselves, you will be known to the Children of Kerensky as Phelan Wolf. All are to abide by the rede given here. Thus shall it stand until we all shall fall."

"Thus shall it stand until we all shall fall," echoed the crowd. The lights illuminating Phelan's challengers and defenders died, leaving visible only Ulric, Ranna, and Phelan. No one spoke, and Phelan interpreted the only sounds he heard as the passage of the assembled Clanspeople from the room.

When complete silence again reigned in the chamber, Ulric stepped forward and offered Phelan his left hand. "You are one of us now, Phelan Wolf. You are a bondsman no more. Through this Conclave, you have become a warrior. You are henceforth accorded all the rights and privileges of your station, as well as all the responsibilities and duty of a Wolf warrior."

Phelan took Ulric's hand and shook it warmly. It was as though, for the first time, he belonged to something outside his family. "I thank you, my Khan, for this honor. But there is so much I don't know or understand. What did the challenges mean? What did Vlad mean in welcoming me to the House of Ward?"

Ulric shook his head. "You are young yet, by our standards. All your questions will be answered in your training. Now, however, is a time for celebration. It has been nearly five decades since the Wolf Warriors adopted someone not born to the caste. You will also be honored and rewarded for your actions on the bridge, though I fear the most suitable reward must wait until our journey's end."

"Journey?" He suddenly remembered the Precentor Martial's fleeting reference to the Clan's "absence." "What is this journey?"

The Khan's eyes narrowed and the light from above made his face into a death's-head. "We will travel to where the Clans—all the Clans —must meet to discuss what we have done. We will elect a new ilKhan and review our successes and our failures. Then, under the leadership of the new ilKhan, we will return to the Inner Sphere and complete the liberation of the Star League from the forces that destroyed it three centuries ago!"

EQUIVALENT RANKS IN INNER SPHERE MILITARIES, 3050

STANDARD MERCENARY	FEDERATED COMMONWEALTH	DRACONIS COMBINE	FREE RASALHAGUE REPUBLIC
OFFICER RANKS:			
	Marshal of the Armies	Tai-shu (Warlord)	Överbefälhavere
	Field Marshal	Tai-sho	General
	Marshal	Sho-sho	Generalmajor
Colonel	Hauptmann General	Tai-sa	Överste-Löjtnant
Lieutenant Colonel	Leftenant General	Chu-sa	Överste
Major	Kommandant	Sho-sa	Major
Captain	Hauptmann	Tai-i	Kapten
Lieutenant	Leftenant	Chu-i	Löjtnant
ENLISTED RANKS:			
Sergeant Major	Sergeant Major	Sho-ko	Fanjunkare
	Kashira		
	Shujin		
Sergeant	Sergeant	Gunso	Sergeant
Corporal	Corporal	Go-cho	Korpral
	Gunjin		
	Private	Heishi	Menig
Private	Hojuhei		

328

Glossary

AUTOCANNON

The autocannon is a rapid-firing autoloading weapon. Light vehicle autocannon range from 30 to 90 mm caliber, while heavy 'Mech autocannon may be 80 to 120 mm or more. The weapon fires high-speed streams of high-explosive, armor-piercing shells. Because of the limitations of 'Mech targeting technology, the autocannon's effective anti-'Mech range is limited to less then 600 meters.

BATTLEMECH

BattleMechs are the most powerful war machines ever built. First developed by Terran scientists and engineers more than 500 years ago, these huge, man-shaped vehicles are faster, more mobile, better armored, and more heavily armed then any 20th-century tank. Ten to twelve meters tall and equipped with particle projection cannons, lasers, rapid-fire autocannon, and missiles, they pack enough firepower to flatten anything but another BattleMech. A small fusion reactor provides virtually unlimited power, and BattleMechs can be adapted to fight in environments ranging from sun-baked deserts to subzero arctic icefields.

COMSTAR

ComStar, the interstellar communications network, was the brainchild of Jerome Blake, formerly Minister of Communications during the latter years of the Star League. After the League's fall, Blake seized Terra and reorganized what was left of the League's communications network into a private organization that sold its services to the five Successor Houses for a profit. Since that time, ComStar has also developed into a powerful, secret society steeped in mysticism and ritual. Initiates to the ComStar Order commit themselves to lifelong service.

JUMPSHIPS AND DROPSHIPS
JumpShip

Interstellar travel is accomplished via JumpShips, first developed in the 22nd century. Named for their ability to "jump" instantaneously from one point to another, the vessels consist of a long, thin drive core and an enormous sail. The sail is constructed from a specially coated polymer that absorbs vast quantities of electromagnetic energy from the nearest star. Energy collected by the sail is slowly transfered to the drive core, which converts it into a space-twisting field. After making its jump, the ship cannot travel again until it has recharged its drive with solar energy at its new location. Safe recharge times range from six to eight days.

JumpShips travel instantaneously across vast interstellar distances by means of the Kearny-Fuchida hyperdrive. The K-F drive generates a field around the JumpShip, then opens a hole into hyperspace. In moments, the JumpShip is transported through to its new destination, across distances of up to 30 light years.

Jump points are the locations within a star system where the system's gravity is next to nothing, the prime prerequisite for operation of the K-F drive. The distance away from the system's star is dependant on that star's mass, and is usually many tens of millions of kilometers away. Every star has two principal jump points, one at the zenith point at the star's north pole, and one at the nadir point at the south pole. An infinite number of other jump points also exist, but they are used only rarely.

JumpShips never land on planets, and only rarely travel into the inner parts of a star system. Interplanetary travel is carried out by DropShips, vessels that attach themselves to the JumpShip until arrival at the jump point. Most of the JumpShips currently in service are already centuries old, because the Successor Lords are unable to construct many new ones each year. For this reason, there is an unspoken agreement among even these bitter enemies to leave one another's JumpShips alone.

DropShip

Because JumpShips generally remain at a considerable distance from a star system's inhabited worlds, DropShips were developed for interplanetary travel. A DropShip attaches to hard points on the JumpShip, and will later be dropped from the parent vessel after entry into a system. DropShips are highly maneuverable, well-armed, and sufficiently aerodynamic to take off from and land on a planetary surface.

LRM

LRM is an abbreviation for "Long-Range Missile," an indirect-fire missile with a high-explosive warhead.

NEW AVALON INSTITUTE OF SCIENCE (NAIS)

In 3015, Prince Hanse Davion decreed the construction of a new university on New Avalon, planetary capitol of the Federated Suns. Known as the New Avalon Institute of Science (NAIS), its purpose is to recover the lost technologies and knowledge of the past. Both House Kurita and House Marik have followed with their own universities, but neither is as well bankrolled or staffed as the NAIS.

PPC

PPC is the abbreviation for "Particle Projection Cannon," a magnetic accelerator firing high-energy proton or ion bolts, causing damage both through impact and high temperature. PPCs are among the most effective weapons available to BattleMechs.

SRM

SRM is the abbreviation for "Short-Range Missiles," direct trajectory missiles with high-explosive or armor-piercing explosive warheads.

STAR LEAGUE

In 2571, the Star League was formed in an attempt to peacefully ally the major star systems inhabited by the human race after it had taken to the stars. The League continued and prospered for almost 200 years, until the Succession Wars broke out in the late 28th century. The League was eventually destroyed when the ruling body known as the High Council disbanded in the midst of a struggle for power. Each of the Council Lords then declared himself First Lord of the Star League, and within months, war had engulfed the Inner Sphere. These centuries of continuous war are now known simply as the Succession Wars, and continue to the present day. As a result, much of the technology that had brought mankind to its highest level of advancement has been destroyed, lost, or forgotten.

SUCCESSOR LORDS

Each of the five Successor States is ruled by a family descended from one of the original Council Lords of the old Star League. All five royal House Lords claim the title of First Lord, and they have been at each other's throats since the beginning of the Succession Wars in the late 28th century. Their battleground is the vast Inner Sphere, which is composed of all the star systems once occupied by the Star League member-states.

About the Author

ComStar ROM Division
Langley, North America, Terra
27 November 3050
Security Alert Advisory

Subject: Michael A. Stackpole

Recap:

On 2 August 3030, Stackpole was the subject of an alert as a result of his escape from our Phoenix Reeducation Center. At the time, the subject claimed to have been born in the 20th century and raised in Vermont, where he took a degree in history from the University of Vermont in 1979. After that he moved to Arizona and began a career as a game designer. While our researches did uncover records of such an individual, and we were able to confirm that he worked for companies such as Flying Buffalo, Inc., FASA Corporation, TSR, Inc., Hero Games, West End Games, Electronic Arts, and Interplay Productions, we cannot accept the conclusion that these two individuals are one in the same. That would make him 1093 years old, though he doesn't look a day over 31. (Our experts deny that a regimen of Szechuan food and indoor soccer would grant that sort of longevity.)

Recent Sighting:

Through the late thirties, we had sightings in the Lyran Commonwealth (mainly on Arc-Royal and Nusaken), but after a confirmed sighting at Archon Katrina Steiner's funeral, the subject vanished. We believe he has resurfaced. We obtained a voiceprint match between his voice and that of a request for recharge clearance on a JumpShip chartered by Wolf's Dragoons. The match came on 25 November and the ship is believed to have been carrying Natasha Kerensky on a mission whose purpose we have not been able to discern.

Conclusion:

Given the subject's past propensity for writing, we suspect he is preparing another multivolume work concerning the history of the Successor States. The Primus found his previous revelations about ComStar vexatious and has not rescinded the 3030 death order. Under no circumstances is he to be allowed to reach the Clans!